Becoming Ted

*Beginning
fed*

Becoming Ted

Matt Cain

JOHN SCOGNAMIGLIO BOOKS
KENSINGTON BOOKS
www.kensingtonbooks.com

JOHN SCOGNAMIGLIO BOOKS are published by

Kensington Publishing Corp.
119 West 40th Street
New York, NY 10018

All Kensington titles, imprints and distributed lines are available at special quantity discounts for bulk purchases for sales promotion, premiums, fund-raising, educational or institutional use.

Special book excerpts or customized printings can also be created to fit specific needs. For details, write or phone the office of the Kensington Special Sales Manager: Kensington Publishing Corp., 119 West 40th Street, New York, NY, 10018. Attn. Special Sales Department. Phone: 1-800-221-2647.

The JS and John Scognamiglio Books logo is a trademark of Kensington Publishing Corp.

ISBN: 978-1-4967-4594-1
First Kensington Hardcover Edition: June 2024

ISBN: 978-1-4967-4596-5 (e-book)

10 9 8 7 6 5 4 3 2 1

Printed in the United States of America

For my first-born nephew, Lucan Dunphy,
who changed everything

PROLOGUE

Ted stands on the stage in complete darkness. Every muscle in his body is clenched. He stretches out his fingers, giving his hands a little shake, and tries to relax his shoulders. But nothing works.

A bolt of panic shoots through him. *Oh God, can I really do this?*

Hanging before him is a thick velvet curtain. From the other side of it comes the muffled sound of an upbeat, cheery pop song playing over the hum of animated chatter rising from the audience and pierced by the occasional clink of glasses.

Ted can almost sense the expectation in the air. His own expectation is twisting his stomach in knots.

He tells himself that when the music fades, if he steps out from behind the curtain, he can achieve his dream. It's a dream he's been chasing for months—months that have led to this moment backstage in Manchester, months during which he's experienced a taste of happiness deeper than any he's ever known.

But am I strong enough to follow it through?

He wonders who's sitting in the audience and pictures all the people who've supported him on his journey—all the plans they've made and the laughs they've had along the way. Then

he remembers that there are other people who've ma~
they *don't* want him to be doing this, people who've trie~
steer him away from his dream or made an effort to put obstacles in his way. *Are they out there too?*

Fear pricks at his insides.

Before he can shake it off, the music starts to fade.

As the chatter from the audience dims, Ted feels his bones
going soft.

He snatches a short breath. *This is it. It's now or never.*

CHAPTER 1

Ted Ainsworth lets out a contented sigh. As he contemplates the scene before him, a grin creeps over his face.

It's Sunday morning, and he and his husband, Giles, are at home in their super king-size bed, Ted propped up on a stack of gunmetal-gray pillows, Giles curled up around the matching duvet. They woke up an hour ago, and Ted browsed ideas for their next holiday destination on his iPad while Giles flicked through messages on his phone. Then Ted went downstairs to make a pot of coffee and came back to find Giles had dozed off. So he crept back into bed, eager to savor every second of what, for him, was the ideal Sunday.

He leans in closer to check if Giles is asleep. "Smiles," he whispers, the pet name he's used since the two of them got together nearly twenty years ago. "Smiles!"

There's no response; he's definitely asleep.

Ted sips his coffee and allows himself a moment to admire his husband. With his dark coloring and designer stubble, Giles has always been good-looking, but Ted thinks his looks may have gotten even better since he entered his forties. It was around this time that he started growing his hair and stepped up his activities in the gym. Two years later, the results of both are clear to see—in the thick, lush locks fanning out on his pillow and the muscular bicep poking out from under the duvet, a bicep Giles recently had decorated with the tattoo of a swallow mid-flight. Ted feels his heart give a little wobble. *Wow. He really is gorgeous.*

Not for the first time, Ted wonders how he managed to bag himself such an amazing husband. Whichever way he looks at it, he and Giles are leagues apart. While Giles is sexy and charismatic, Ted is sweet and shy. While Giles is the manager of a stylish, hip hotel in the center of Manchester, Ted works for his family's ice-cream business, running the shop and café on the high street in Saint Luke's-on-Sea, a sleepy little Lancashire seaside town. And while Giles regularly makes strangers on the street swivel around to get a better look at him, Ted's presence usually goes unnoticed.

But is it any wonder? There isn't anything remotely remarkable about Ted. He's forty-three years old, of average height, with a smattering of freckles on his cheeks and a physique that could best be described as a "dad bod"—if the dad in question broke out in hives at the sight of an exercise bike and every lunchtime was gripped by an irresistible craving for a meat-and-potato pasty. He has pale-gray eyes and hair his mum often says is the color of a perfect batch of coffee ice cream. Except Ted knows from experience that nobody likes coffee ice cream, not even people who like coffee. Besides, that flavor comes out a dull, weak brown, while Giles's hair is the rich, luxurious brown of chocolate, Ainsworth's most popular flavor. It's set off by his equally rich brown eyes and two little moles on his left cheekbone. Not unsightly, unsexy freckles like Ted's; more like those delicious little chocolate drops people love to sprinkle on their ice cream.

God, I'm so lucky. So lucky, so chuffed and so grateful.

Ted wants to snuggle up to his husband, but stretched out between them is their dog, Lily. A brown-and-black short-haired terrier crossbreed, Lily is usually desperate to be taken for a walk first thing in the morning, but today seems happy to snooze. Ted knows he'll have to take her out soon but doesn't want to disturb her, especially when she slides under the crook of Giles's arm. Without opening his eyes, Giles pulls her in closer, and their breathing slowly falls into sync. Ted's heart gives another wobble.

He finishes his coffee and puts his cup on the side, as quietly as he can so he doesn't wake them. It'll be a shame if Giles's coffee goes cold, but he can always go back downstairs and make him a fresh pot. This isn't something he'd admit to his colleagues at work—women who often moan about their inattentive men, many of whom expect to be waited on—but Ted actually *likes* waiting on Giles. *How could I not when he looks like this?*

Ted wants to take a picture, but his phone is on the opposite side of the room, on top of the chest of drawers. Giles's, on the other hand, is resting on the duvet. He grabs it, flicks up the camera, and snaps off a few pics.

He goes into the photo album to see how they've turned out and starts swiping through. They're lovely, so lovely he considers having one of them printed and put in a frame or using one as his screensaver. Then he accidentally swipes too far and stumbles upon a picture he didn't take. *Wait . . . what's this?*

It's a picture of a man he doesn't recognize. He swipes again and the man's clothes disappear.

Shit.

He swipes one more time and is confronted by the sight of the man's genitals.

What the hell?

Just as he's reassuring himself that they're probably pics of some hook-up one of Giles's friends sent him, he swipes onto an image of the same man standing next to Giles. Giles has his arm around the man. Their cheeks are pressed together. And Giles has a big smile on his face.

The sight rips at Ted's heart. He drops the phone onto the bed as if it's on fire.

Shit, what am I supposed to do? Should I say something?

It turns out it isn't his decision to make. He looks up and sees Giles staring directly at him.

"Ted," he says, solemnly, "we need to talk."

"Sorry. I thought you were asleep," Ted stammers. His heart is pounding so violently, he struggles to get his words out.

"No," says Giles. "And I've been meaning to bring this up for a while."

Ted swallows. "I don't understand. Bring what up?"

Giles props himself up on the pillows, revealing the trail of stars he recently had tattooed across his chest muscles. He lifts the phone off the bed and gives a little grimace. "I'm sorry, but I've met someone else."

Ted feels as if he's been shot. "W-w-what do you mean, you've met someone else?"

"It's someone I met through work," Giles continues, his eyes flitting down to the phone. "I wasn't looking for any-thing—I swear. It just sort of happened. And before I knew it, we were seeing each other."

Ted feels woozy, as if he's stood up too quickly. He blinks several times. *This can't be happening.*

Whatever you do, don't let this happen!

Then another voice strikes up. *Oh, it'll blow over. Or maybe you could learn to live with it. Apparently lots of people have open relationships . . .*

But he stops himself. He knows just how much he'd hate sharing Giles with anyone else.

Then again, it would have to be better than losing him com-pletely. *Anything would be better than that.*

"Well, that's not necessarily the end of the world," Ted manages, his voice cracking. "I'm sure we can work through it."

Giles looks up from the phone and into Ted's eyes. "No. I'm in love with him, Ted. I'm leaving you. I want to be with Javier."

Panic tightens Ted's throat. "No!" he bleats, aware of how pathetic he sounds. "Don't say that! *Please* don't say that!"

But Giles doesn't reply.

"We've been together nearly twenty years," Ted continues. "How can you just throw that away? Can't we just slow down and talk about this?"

Giles massages his temples. "I'm sorry, Ted, but I've made up my mind. And Javier's been patient for a long time. I can't keep him waiting anymore."

Oh God, so this isn't a new thing.

Ted falls back onto the pillows. He wonders why he didn't spot something was wrong when Giles started getting those tattoos. Why he wasn't suspicious when Giles became obsessed with the gym and was posting pictures of his physique online. Why he didn't worry when he started coming back from Manchester with bags full of new clothes. *How could I have been so stupid?*

Now that he thinks about it, though, it all makes sense.

At the start of their relationship, Giles worked in junior positions at various hotels in St. Luke's-on-Sea. Eventually, he was offered a job at the Westcliff, the town's most exclusive hotel, and slowly worked his way up until he was appointed manager. But after a few years, he started to feel restless and began looking around for a job in a bigger hotel out of town. Then Covid struck, and he had to shelve his ambitions. He was put on furlough and didn't work at all for months. Neither did Ted during the first lockdown, but after that the shop reopened for takeout orders only. While this wasn't ideal, it at least gave him something to do. Giles, on the other hand, spent all day at home—feeling held back, feeling contained, feeling trapped. *And brooding.*

He became listless and distant. And the affection he showed Ted faded like a photo in sunlight. Ted pretended not to notice, reassuring himself it was just a temporary consequence of the pandemic. If you believed what you heard in the media, plenty of relationships were struggling. Then, gradually, the pandemic started to recede and, one by one, restrictions were lifted. When the hospitality industry finally reawakened, Giles managed to secure a job running a fashionable boutique hotel in Manchester. He became noticeably happier—and Ted thought their unacknowledged little rough patch was over.

But now he's gone and met this Javier.

"So how long has this been going on for?" Ted asks.

"About nine months now," Giles answers. "But the truth is, I already knew something wasn't right between us. In fact, I'm not sure it ever was."

Ted lets out a little breath, as if he's been punched in the stomach.

Well, this had to happen sometime. I couldn't fool him forever. I'm surprised he stuck with me for so long.

Giles inches closer, and Ted can just about make out the scent of his rich, woody aftershave lingering from the day before. "With you and me, it was about . . ." He pauses to search for the right word. "Convenience."

"Convenience?"

"Yeah. It just kind of suited everyone. But now I've met Javier, and I can see that I've just been watching the world through a window. I was never quite *in* it, never really taking part. Do you know what I mean?"

No, I don't know what you mean. I thought we were happy. I thought we were in love.

Ted turns to face him. "But what about *our* world?" he

pleads, repulsed by the note of desperation in his voice. "What about our home? What about Lily?"

Giles rubs his jaw. "I don't know. I don't know about any of that—there's still lots I've got to work out. All I know is, I feel like life's been passing me by while me and you have been stuck in this quiet little seaside town full of old people. Having our takeout and movie nights. Maybe going to a restaurant once a month. And all the time looking forward to our next holiday."

"But we *love* going on holiday," Ted mewls. "We love going off and having adventures."

"Yeah, but that's not enough, Ted. I want an adventure full-time. I want to go off and *live*!"

Ted sits forward and grabs hold of Giles's hands. "I'll change, Smiles. I'll give you as many adventures as you want. All day, every day. I promise I'll make our life more exciting!"

Giles shakes himself free and stands up.

"I'll go to the gym!" Ted squeals. "I'll get myself in shape. Would that help?"

But Giles doesn't respond. He opens his closet and starts pulling out clothes.

"What are you doing?" Ted asks.

"Packing my things."

"What, *now*? You're leaving *now*?"

Giles shrugs. "I might as well. There's no point prolonging it."

Ted rushes to the edge of the bed.

Please don't leave me. Whatever you do, don't leave me!

He considers throwing himself at Giles, clinging to him so tightly that he *can't* leave. But he stops himself.

It isn't pride that holds him back—far from it. It's simply the knowledge that it won't make any difference. *Because I had this coming all along. Giles pretty much said that.*

He feels defeated. He feels broken. He feels ransacked inside. And he has no idea what to do.

Lily jumps off the bed and barks.

"It sounds like she's ready for her walk," Giles says.

Ted nods, his head feeling like a dead weight. This all seems eerily unreal, like he's stepped out of his body and is watching from a distance as somebody else plays his role.

He can't believe that less than half an hour ago, he'd thought he was having the ideal Sunday. He can't believe that just a few minutes ago he was feeling lucky, he was feeling chuffed with his life. Then—just like that—it turns into the worst day ever. And one from which he isn't sure he'll ever recover.

CHAPTER 2

The following morning, when Ted sets off to the beach, his whole body feels laden down with sadness. All he can do is slope along, lugging one foot in front of the other. He tries to quicken his step but can't. If it wasn't for Lily pulling him along, he might even come to a halt.

At the end of his quiet residential street, he turns the corner and emerges onto a wider road that leads down to the seafront. He passes a café with a board in the window advertising pensioner specials, a dealership for mobility scooters with a row of them lined up outside, and a shop selling antiques and bric-a-brac, its window stuffed full of ornaments Ted can't help thinking belong in a skip.

A few paces further on, Lily squats on the pavement for a wee. Ted has to step out of the way as a river of urine flows past him and into the gutter. For a moment, he stands still, mesmerized by it. Then Lily pulls at her lead, and he allows himself to follow.

"Alright, Lil," he says, mournfully. "Let's get to that beach."

Ted and Giles brought Lily to live with them ten years ago, although Ted has no idea how old she is as she was a rescue dog. It took him months to persuade Giles to get a dog, then Giles wanted to buy a French bulldog—until they heard all kinds of horror stories about the operations the dogs needed just to breathe properly. Ted suggested they pop along to the local sanctuary, under the guise of "looking for ideas," where they were introduced to a parade of cute dogs, all of which had been abandoned or mistreated by their owners, each of them pleading for a new home—including, right at the end, the as-yet-unnamed Lily.

She wasn't a cute dog and never has been: her teeth are as yellow as a slab of cheap Cheddar cheese, one of her ears stands up and the other flops over, and she has weapons-grade halitosis. But Ted couldn't help noticing that none of the other visitors were stopping to pet her. He felt a rush of emotion he was convinced was love at first sight but may just have been empathy. He promptly announced that they'd found the dog for them, and Giles didn't argue. Nor did he argue when Ted wanted to name her after his favorite drag queen, Lily Savage. In any case, she soon proved herself to be such an affectionate dog that Giles fell in love with her too. And even though, from the start, Ted was the one to get up early and take her for walks, to feed her and pick up her freshly laid turds, he's always known she prefers Giles.

Giles.

Giles, who's just left me.

Giles, who said things were never quite right between us.

He feels an ache in the core of his gut. He tries to ignore it and plods on.

It's a long road, lined on either side by late Regency terraces painted in a range of pretty pastels and containing small hotels, bed-and-breakfasts or guesthouses. These have columns of bow or curved bay windows, a wrought iron balcony stretching along the first floor, and a short flight of steps leading up from the street to the entrance. The pavements before them are divided by rows of trees and flowerbeds that have recently been replanted with pansies, geraniums, and petunias. Sights like these serve as a reminder that in its day, St. Luke's-on-Sea was considered smart and genteel; the masses of mill and factory workers from the industrial towns around Lancashire preferred to take their holidays in the much more buzzing Blackpool, just up the coast. But that day has long since passed. The paint is peeling off the façade of several of the hotels, some of the awnings bearing their names are ripped or collapsing in on themselves, and Ted has to dodge his way around huge cracks in the pavement.

As though on autopilot, he mentally ticks off his regular sights as he passes.

There are the two hippos standing on either side of the entrance to a guesthouse, both of them painted gold. Ted has no idea of the story behind them but, as ever, is struck by the way they stand out from their surroundings.

Then there's the statue of a minor prince—a younger son of George III—who was instrumental in developing the town. He's dressed in military uniform and holding a sword but is bending his leg in a pose that Ted thinks is delightfully camp, as if he's about to launch into a chorus of some show tune, complete with dance routine.

Finally, at the end of the road there is, of course, the sea—although from this vantage point only a thin strip of it is visible. And standing in front of it on a little traffic island is a huge flagpole, from which flies a Union Jack.

Yes, everything is exactly as it always is. Nothing has changed.

Except, at the same time, everything has changed. Everything's different. Because Giles has left me.

For a moment, Ted misses his husband so badly he can barely draw breath. He comes to a stop in the middle of the pavement and leans on a wall to steady himself. He had no idea it was even possible to feel this sad. He still doesn't think he'll recover. He has no idea how he'll ever regain his capacity to feel any positive emotion.

Before long Lily starts tugging at her lead again. He lumbers on.

Monday is Ted's regular day off work, as he has to supervise the shop every Saturday, which is their busiest day of the week. Although he has mixed feelings about this, today he's thankful as it means he can spend time on his own.

Yesterday, when he returned from his walk, Giles had already left the house. Almost immediately, Ted felt his absence as if it were pressing in on him, as if he could touch it—and he couldn't avoid it.

He was still too shocked to cry, so he spent most of the day replaying the conversation they'd had in his head. When he was sick of that, he did a few household chores, tasks he could complete mechanically. And in the evening, he sat on the sofa and tried to watch TV, but Giles's empty space next to him was too much to bear. So he gave up and did nothing. He just sat there, staring into space. And gradually, the sadness ground its way into his bones.

He drags himself to the end of the road, where stretching out before him is a vast expanse of turquoise sea and a golden, sandy beach. To his left is a row of grand Georgian hotels named after the dukes of Devonshire, Cumberland, and Clarence, each with a glass-fronted lounge in which pensioners are sitting sipping tea. Beyond them is the Victorian wrought iron pier, its thick, rusty legs thrusting up from the sand, an arcade at its entrance and a little funfair at its end. On Ted's right—in the distance—is the old white windmill, the town's most famous landmark, that welcomes visitors arriving from the north. Beyond that, only just about visible, is Blackpool Tower.

He stops at the traffic lights and presses the button to cross the road, Lily's tail whipping out a beat on his legs.

It's a brilliantly sunny spring day, and the sky is one block of bright blue, as though it's been colored in with a felt-tip pen in a children's picture book. The weather strikes Ted as inappropriately cheery, almost as if it's trying to torment him. Overhead, a trio of seagulls squawk, swoop, and soar.

When the lights change, he crosses the road. On the other side, he cuts through a strip of ornamental gardens—stuffed with more bedding plants and some tropical-looking yuccas—and emerges onto the promenade. This is paved with red bricks, scattered with the occasional heap of sand washed over by the sea at high tide, and lined with railings that have been painted cobalt blue. After just a few paces, there's a piece of public art that was commissioned just a few years ago; it's meant to represent a woman emerging from the sea, a woman who embodies the spirit of the town. While it was being created, the inhabitants of St. Luke's were promised their very own Angel of the North, and excitement built. But when the statue was finally unveiled, disappointment was expressed at the figure's stocky frame, her unattractive features, and the sour look on her face. The editor of the local newspaper memorably described her as looking like "a menopausal dinner lady holding in a fart." She's always reminded Ted of his Auntie Brenda when she came out of the hospital after her hysterectomy.

He trudges on in the direction of the pier, passing several benches, some of them with little wooden shelters built around them. He notices that one of them has been dedicated to a man whose name is followed by the inscription, IF I DON'T DO IT, NOBODY ELSE WILL.

I wonder if Giles saw that . . . I wonder if he saw it when he was getting bored of his life with me.

He forces himself to keep walking.

As usual for a Monday morning, the only people Ted sees are fellow dog walkers—some of them jauntily swinging bags of poo—and the occasional jogger or cyclist. But everyone looks happy, and one or two people he recognizes smile at him or wish him good morning. There's the man wearing a baseball cap and Jesus sandals who's walking his Airedale terrier, and the wiry-looking woman who always goes running in the T-shirt of some foreign marathon she's completed and still wears a thick cotton facemask. As he returns their waves, it occurs to Ted that none of them have any idea what he's going through. This only makes him feel worse.

After a few hundred meters, he comes to the steps he usually takes down to the beach. As soon as he reaches the bottom, he lets Lily off her lead. She bounds off to explore, her tail wagging. Ted watches her leap over the dry sand and onto the damp, flat area leading down to the shoreline, at which point her paws create a trail of prints. He follows them toward the sea, towards the calming rhythm of the waves.

And Ted remembers that it was on another beach—on another sunny spring day—that Giles asked him to marry him.

Come on, spit it out!

Ted knew it was coming. *But how long's it going to take?*

It was a glorious spring morning, and he and Giles were on holiday, staying in a farmhouse that had been converted into a hotel in the hills near Lucca, in Tuscany. They'd explored the local area, taking day trips to Pisa, Florence, and Siena, and spent several days relaxing by the hotel's pool. In the evenings they'd enjoyed the local food and wine in friendly, unpretentious *ristoranti*, or al fresco on the hotel's patio, overlooking a lush green valley. Then Giles had suggested they go for a drive to the nearby seaside town of Viareggio.

In itself, this wasn't enough to arouse Ted's suspicions, but he'd accidentally overheard Giles chatting to the woman who ran the hotel about packing a picnic—he'd told her it needed to be special. So Ted had peeped inside the basket and found a bottle of prosecco and two plastic glasses. This had prompted him to rummage further and, slotted in between some pecorino cheese and a packet of Tuscan prosciutto, he'd uncovered a ring box. He'd somehow managed to slot it back in without opening it but ever since had been buzzing with excitement.

When they arrived in Viareggio, they headed straight to the public beach—in between the private beach clubs—and managed to find a quiet spot. It was a weekday in April, so not too busy with tourists or locals. Even so, Ted didn't want Giles to get down on one knee and propose only for some stranger to spoil it by shouting out a homophobic insult. Once he was satisfied they were safe, he spread out their blanket, and they sat down.

"Isn't this ace?" gushed Ted. He gestured to the sapphire-blue Mediterranean and picked up a fistful of white sand, letting it run through his fingers.

A grin split Giles's face. "Yeah, it's beautiful. I'm really glad we came."

Alright, now get on with it. Hit me with that proposal!

Evidently, Giles wanted to take his time. He made Ted sit through the entire meal, then struck up a conversation about what they'd like to do for the remainder of the holiday.

"Shall we check out the Cinque Terre?" he said. "It's supposed to be *the* place to go. Or apparently there are some really cool art galleries in Pietrasanta. Oh, and didn't somebody say that opera composer Puccini lived near here? Apparently his house is a museum."

Stop banging on about opera and ask me to marry you!

Over Giles's shoulder, Ted spotted a group of young men approaching. They were kicking around a football, shoving and shoulder-barging each other, and making low, growling noises. *Oh, please don't let them sit near us. Please don't let them ruin our moment.*

As he willed them to keep going, his heart cannoned in his

chest. Thankfully, they walked past and continued towards the marina.

Right, let's go . . .

"Actually, I'm glad we've got the beach to ourselves," Giles said.

Ted's stomach performed some kind of cartwheel. "Oh yeah? Why's that?"

"There's something I want to ask you." He paused to smooth out his hair and straighten the collar of his shirt.

Trust Giles to want to look perfect for his big moment. Ted didn't know whether to scream with impatience or roll his eyes fondly. He settled on a smile and sat up expectantly.

Giles reached into the picnic basket and pulled out the ring box. He rose up onto one knee and opened it. After another pause—this one for dramatic purposes only—he looked at Ted and his grin crawled into his eyes.

"Ted Ainsworth," he said, "will you marry me?"

Ted felt a tingle like an electric shock run up his spine.

In that moment, he forgot that he and Giles were even on a beach.

In that moment, he felt like they were the only people in the world.

In that moment, he felt a swell of happiness so strong he couldn't imagine it would ever fade.

Back at St. Luke's, Ted stands looking out to sea. As he twists his wedding ring around his finger, the memory of his happiness lodges like a barb in his chest.

How did we get from that to this?

It hadn't helped that they weren't able to travel for two years. Going on holiday was the shared activity they enjoyed most, something for which they saved all their spare money.

But their plans were repeatedly thwarted by the series of COVID lockdowns, then the various travel restrictions, uncertainties, and last-minute changes to border policies. Not to mention the need for Ted to work—a need that was only exacerbated by the pandemic. For the first time in its nearly hundred-year history, Ainsworth's was in crisis. As well as the original ice-cream parlor on the high street and two little kiosks on the seafront, Ted's parents had expanded into a second shop in the Victorian arcade. They'd spent an extortionate amount of money fitting it out, but then, on the week it was due to open, the first lockdown was announced. His parents tried, but failed, to get out of their lease and were left saddled with a massive debt they were still struggling to repay as the shop had to be abandoned. When the tourists and day-trippers eventually started trickling back to St. Luke's, Ted had to stick around and join the effort. "Family first" was his parents' motto. *As if I could ever forget.*

Thankfully, Giles didn't seem too bothered by Ted's long shifts as he was also busy focusing on work—and his new job in Manchester. But it turns out that when they weren't working and their holidays were taken away from them, what was left just wasn't enough for Giles. Their relationship wasn't enough. *Ted* wasn't enough.

I'm never enough for anyone.

He steps back from the shore and continues sloping along the beach in the direction of the windmill. He passes a row of shops, beach cafés, seafood stalls and one of Ainsworth's kiosks, all built into the foundations of the promenade—all of them closed at this time of day. Above them, a little further along, rises the town's showpiece Art Deco bandstand, surrounding it a colonnade of viewing decks that's also built into the promenade. Then, when the promenade comes to an end, an area of sand dunes springs up.

It's at the foot of these that Lily stops to curl out her usual turd. When she's finished, Ted stoops to bag it up and tosses it into a nearby bin. He tries not to remember the first time Giles attempted to pick up her waste but couldn't go through with it. He never tried again and Ted would sometimes complain about it. *Oh, to be able to complain about it now.*

He lets out a ragged sigh. "Oh, Lily, I miss your daddy."

What he doesn't tell her is that he has no idea how he's going to cope without him. He'll miss the rhythm of their life together. Making Giles his coffee and setting it down next to his bed every morning. Texting him to ask what he's had for lunch so he doesn't make the same thing for tea. Spending hours making his favorite meals then seeing his face light up as he sits down and tucks in.

He'll also miss the banter that filled so much of their time together. Offering to drive whenever they set out on a journey, only for Giles to joke that he wants to arrive in one piece. Opening the window before they go to bed at night, complaining that he's suffocating, only for Giles to shut it again, protesting that he's freezing.

And he'll miss the repartee the two of them perform for the benefit of others, the way they tell a story a few times until it settles into something like a script. Of course, Ted's the straight man in this double act, while Giles gets all the laughs. But Ted has always been happy with that arrangement; he's always been happy watching Giles shine.

Without him, Ted can't see his life being anything other than dull. *He's the gravy to my chips. The burger to my bun. The bangers to my mash.*

Tears prick the backs of his eyes. They break through and start running down his cheeks. An older couple who are walking their golden retriever stray into his vicinity, but he doesn't want them to see him so he retreats into the dunes. He climbs to the top of a hill and slumps down. And there, facing the sea, he allows the tears to run. They run and run. They take hold of his body, giving it little convulsions. And he cries himself raw.

After a while, Lily trots up to sit next to him. Her paws are damp from paddling in the sea and are coated with sand. She snuggles up to Ted and licks his face. Her mouth smells like an open sewer, but he doesn't mind. He puts an arm around her and pulls her close.

"I know, Lily," he says between sobs. "I know you miss him too."

When the dog starts to whimper, he realizes she's tired. He gives a big sniff, knuckles the tears out of his eyes, and dries his face on his sleeve. He drags himself to his feet and starts to trudge home.

Just as he's putting Lily on her lead, his phone vibrates to tell him he has a text message. Desperate to see if it's from Giles, he whips the phone out so quickly he almost sends it flying into the air. But it's from his best friend, Denise.

Denise is a few years older than Ted and works at the makeup counter in the town's only department store. Though it doesn't sound like she's enjoying work today.

"This new girl I'm training up is hopeless," reads her text message. **"She's as much use as an ashtray on a motorbike. Roll on Friday night!"**

Every Friday night, Ted goes to Denise's flat to drink prosecco and watch the latest episode of *RuPaul's Drag Race*. Whatever's happening in his life, watching the queens express themselves through drag, letting loose their outrageous alter egos, never fails to raise his spirits. But this week he doesn't think he'll be able to face it. He'll text her later to explain.

As he shuts down his phone, he catches sight of the photo of him and Giles that's set as his screensaver. He supposes he'll have to remove it at some point. But he can't bring himself to do it yet. *What if there's a chance he'll come back?*

He stuffs the phone back into his pocket. *As if.*

When he reaches the flagpole, Ted crosses the road and plods back toward home. On the corner of his street is Memory House, a care home for the elderly, at the front of which is a row of self-contained flats with their own terraces. Standing on one of them is an elderly man with dazzling white hair, wearing a smart and immaculately pressed lilac shirt and a purple cravat and sipping tea out of a delicate-looking antique china cup and saucer. Ted knows some of the residents by sight and often gives them a wave—but he's never seen this one before.

"Good morning!" the man calls out to him.

Ted arranges his features into his best approximation of a smile. It actually hurts to pretend he's happy. "Morning," he mumbles.

Before the man can reply, Ted has crossed the street and is pressing on. There's only so much human interaction he can handle.

He's dreading facing his colleagues at work tomorrow. He's dreading having to tell them what's happened. But most of all he's dreading telling his parents. Because he knows they'll be disappointed. *Yet again they'll be disappointed in me.*

But there are still twenty-four hours until then. Twenty-four hours in which he's going to hide away from the world and wallow.

CHAPTER 3

As Ted steps off the high street and into Ainsworth's ice-cream shop, he braces himself. His plan is to avoid being drawn into chats with his colleagues and to lose himself in work. *It's the only way I'll be able to make it through the day.*

"Hiya!" calls out a chorus of female voices.

"Morning," replies Ted, closing the door behind him. He looks at his watch, hoping to give the impression that he needs to crack on.

Come on, you can do this.

Next to the entrance to the shop stands a huge plastic model of ice cream in a cone, with a flake sticking out of the top. It's been there for as long as Ted can remember and has recently become something of a social media icon, with customers posing next to it for pictures. Beyond it, along the left-hand wall of the shop, runs a counter, its bottom half studded with pink leatherette, its top half glass-fronted and displaying ice creams and sorbets in a dazzling range of colors, plus every conceivable topping, from caramel sauce to hundreds and thousands. Behind this is a board detailing all the available flavors, from the classics to the weekly specials, plus the popular Lancashire Legends collection—including Eccles cake, parkin, and Manchester tart. There are machines for making tea, coffee, waffles, and pancakes, as well as dishes and floats for serving sundaes and banana splits, and jars and trays full of biscuits, shortbread, and cupcakes. Above everything hangs a big sign emblazoned with Ainsworth's distinctive purple logo.

As ever, the shop is bursting with light thanks to the full-length windows that run along the front and a ceiling that's tiled with mirrored squares. In the main seating area, pink wicker-backed chairs are arranged around black circular tables, on a floor mosaicked with triangles of pink and white marble. Along the right-hand wall runs a row of booths, with benches upholstered in the same studded pink leatherette as the counter. And along the back wall is a display cabinet stuffed with all the awards Ainsworth's has won, and next to it a series of black-and-white photos of the shop and its owners over four generations, culminating in a color picture of Ted, his mum, dad, and sister, Jemima, standing in front of the counter. Above this runs another sign carrying the words AINSWORTH'S: THE STORY SO FAR. As ever, Ted's attention snags on the last two words: "so far."

Those two little words that put me under so much pressure.

As the shop doesn't open till ten o'clock, there aren't any customers, just the two young women who work on the counter. Like Ted, they're dressed in purple polo shirts featuring Ainsworth's logo, with a name badge pinned to their opposite breast. Now they've finished setting up, they're leaning on the counter, sipping coffee, and chatting. Once they've greeted Ted, they go back to whatever it is they're discussing. *Which is fine by me—in fact, it's a relief.*

But then, striding toward him from the back of the shop, comes the production manager, Dorothy.

"Ted," she calls out, "can I have a word?"

Dorothy Potts is in her late fifties, a capable yet slightly bossy woman, and—as Ted's mum is fond of saying—"not as good as she thinks she is." She wears glasses that take up most of her face, has fair hair cut in a wedge, and is slim bordering on skinny, with a neck that's starting to look scrawny and which she often clutches during conversation.

Ted gestures to one of the tables. "What can I do for you?"

"It's our Janine," Dorothy begins once they're sitting down. "You know her wedding's coming up?"

Ted's hand darts to his forehead. *Do we really have to talk about weddings?*

"Urm, yeah," he manages. "I did know that."

"Well, we need to decide on the table decorations . . ."

As she lists the various options, Ted zones out and fiddles with a pot holding sachets of sugar and wooden stirrers. When Dorothy leans in closer, he gets a whiff of her perfume. He remembers Giles once joking that it smells like his wee after he's eaten asparagus.

Giles.

His insides give a lurch.

I need to stop thinking about him. I need to get him out of my head.

"Honestly, it's a nightmare," Dorothy goes on, clutching at her neck. "I just want everything to be perfect. I mean, she's my little girl and it's her wedding day; I want it to be the happiest day of her life!"

Ted accidentally rips open a sachet of sugar and spills it onto the table. "Absolutely," he splutters, sweeping it up with his hand.

"Anyway, I was hoping you could do me a favor," Dorothy adds. "I've got a meeting at the venue at six o'clock, but one of our deliveries is coming late. I don't suppose you could stay and deal with it for me?"

Ted writhes in his seat. "Oh, I don't know. I wanted to get off early myself."

Come to think of it, this is the third time you've asked this month.

"Please, Ted," she wheedles. "It's our Janine's special day, her one day to feel like a princess."

"Oh alright," he concedes. "Email me the details, and I'll sort it out."

But before he can finish, Dorothy's whipped out her phone and is firing off a text. "Thanks, Ted," she says, without even looking up. "I knew I could rely on you."

Knew you could rely on me? Or knew you could take me for a mug?

Ted checks in with the girls on the counter, then does his best to keep busy. At least he doesn't have to avoid his mum and dad; they're on their way to Manchester for a meeting about restructuring their debt. Which reminds him: he promised to call in to the factory first thing. Once he's set up the till, he goes through.

Behind the shop, across a tarmacked lane, is a modern building with several forklift trucks lined up outside the entrance. Its interior couldn't be more different from that of the shop; this is a domain of stainless steel machines, of tanks and pipes, of temperature gauges and control pads, of industrial sinks and power hoses. This is where milk from a local farm is turned into Ainsworth's real-dairy homemade ice cream—or, as Ted's dad likes to say, "This is where the magic happens." And, as the company's marketing material is proud to boast, it happens according to a recipe handed down through generations—and is kept a strict secret.

The staff in the factory—who are mainly men—are dressed in white overalls and matching aprons, with nets over their hair and Wellington boots on their feet. They're loading in the morning delivery from the dairy—bags and bags of the basic preblended mix of sugar, whole and skimmed milk, and cream, which has already been pasteurized and homogenized. This will later be loaded into the gleaming steel vats of the ice-cream makers, before the ingredients to create the flavors are added. The results are pumped out into big white tubs and stored in a huge walk-in freezer.

Ted knows that a lot of people would be fascinated to find out how the ice-cream-making process works—and that many of them would say he has a dream job. The problem is, it isn't *his* dream. But his sister, Jemima, has never shown any interest in joining Ainsworth's. For the last twenty years, she's lived in London, where she works as a model. When they were children, Jem was always the loud extroverted one, and had great success competing in local beauty pageants, so no one ever doubted she'd leave St. Luke's-on-Sea to pursue her dream—which meant Ted had to stay and work for the firm. It wouldn't have occurred to him to mount any kind of challenge. It would have just felt wrong. And he couldn't have done that to his parents.

The irony is, Ted doesn't actually like ice cream—and didn't even like it as a child. But he didn't dare tell anyone. Who ever heard of a child who doesn't like ice cream? Especially not the child of the local ice-cream makers. The very idea was preposterous. For nearly one hundred years, ice cream has formed a key part of who the Ainsworth family are. It's what everyone knows about them; it's their identity. So Ted just played along. *And all these years later, I'm still playing along.*

He clears his throat. "Morning everyone."

A group of men nod and raise their hands in greeting.

" 'Ere, Ted," says one. "Cole's just been on his first date."

Ted feels the sadness kick back in. *Do we seriously have to talk about dating now? It's like the universe is trying to kick me when I'm down.*

The man gestures to Cole Egerton, a quiet, lanky, mixed-race boy in his late teens who looks like he bitterly regrets saying anything about going on a date. "Yeah, but it wasn't a big deal," he mumbles.

"Go on," coaxes another young man. "How did it go?"

Oh, please don't tell us. I really don't want to hear about it.

"She was nice," Cole answers, reluctantly. "I liked her."

"So did you get with her?" asks one of the men.

"Did you go back to hers?" prods another.

"Did 'e 'eck!" says a third. "This one couldn't pull a hamstring!"

Everyone laughs until an older man steps in. Derek Slack is the factory supervisor, a portly man with thumb-thick eyebrows and a completely bald head who often turns up in the morning with shaving foam in his ear—as he has today.

" 'Ey, pack it in, lads," he says. "And you ignore 'em teasing, Cole. Enjoy your freedom while you can, before you get tied down by a ball and chain. I'n't that right, Ted?"

God, do we have to do this?

"Urm, yeah," he mutters. "Something like that."

Derek mimes a look of embarrassment. "Oh, sorry, Ted. I forgot you're still loved up."

Ted realizes he needs to change the subject—and fast. "Anyway, how's everything in here? Are you all set for the day?"

"Actually, I were wondering if you could help me out," says Derek, beckoning him to one side. "It's just that we've run out of raspberries, and I'm really up against it. I don't suppose you could nip to the cash-and-carry for us, could you?"

Wait a minute, how's that my job as manager of the shop?

But Ted doesn't voice his objection. *In any case, I was just thinking I want to keep busy.*

"OK, go on, then."

"Thanks," says Derek. "You're a good lad."

Ted pretends not to notice him winking at his friends.

God, I really am a mug.

As he retreats to the shop, Ted spots the girls from the counter standing in the lane, vaping. He looks at his watch; there are just a few minutes to go until the shop opens to the public. But from the looks on their faces, one of them has just received some bad news.

"What's the matter?" he asks. "Is everything alright?"

"No, everything's not alright," seethes Jinger Braithwaite. Jinger is a pretty redhead who's had so much Botox that Giles often jokes she looks like a dummy in search of a ventriloquist. Ted shakes the memory away.

"I've just been dumped," announces the other woman, Bella Winstanley, a California blonde who wears foundation that's almost a perfect match for Ainsworth's mango sorbet. "The worst thing is, he did it by text!"

Ted shifts his weight from one foot to the other. *I really don't want to have this conversation.*

"I'm sorry about that," he manages, flatly.

"He says he doesn't want to be tied down," Bella elaborates, breathing out a cloud of smoke that smells of pineapple. "Well, he wasn't saying that this morning when he wanted to shag me."

"What a bastard," says Jinger. "I can't believe he'd do that to you, babe."

Bella sniffs. "But I love him, Jinge. We've been together a whole *year!*"

A year? Me and Giles were together for twenty.

Ted scrambles around for something comforting to say. "Well, maybe if he's that kind of guy, then he isn't right for you. Maybe you've had a lucky escape."

Bella shoots him a curled look. "But I'm twenty-eight, Ted!" Her face freezes as if registering the full horror of the situation. "God, I can't believe I'm going to be single at *twenty-eight!*"

You do realize I'm forty-three?

But before Ted can say anything, she bursts into loud, theatrical tears.

Jinger looks at Ted and draws in her mouth tightly. "Look at the state she's in, Ted. I don't think she should be at work. Just think of her mental health."

Ted lets out a sigh he hopes doesn't sound exasperated. "OK, let me just nip to the cash-and-carry, then I'll cover for her. It'll be alright; we shouldn't be too busy, and I can work over my lunch."

Bella takes another drag of her e-cigarette, and the tears stop abruptly. "Actually, I might need the whole week off."

Ted blows out his cheeks. He's used to people taking advantage of him, but this is something else.

Well, if I'm going to keep busy, I might as well be dead *busy.*

CHAPTER 4

Further up the high street, Oskar Kozlowski is steeling himself to speak. But he doesn't think his comment will be welcomed.

It's his first week on a job refitting and redecorating an old-fashioned café—what the English call a "greasy spoon"—that's being converted into an organic, gluten-free, vegan restaurant. After a few days of stripping out the fixtures and fittings, Oskar and his workmates have paused to listen to the interior designer present her vision. Misty Playfair is a thin-lipped thirtysomething with a bony décolletage—a word Oskar learned recently and is delighted to bring to mind. Her design combines two color palettes, both inspired by the local area; while the lower floor is to be painted and upholstered in warm, cheery yellows and oranges, inspired by the town's beach, the upper floor will be decorated in much cooler shades of blue, inspired by the sea. But Oskar has spotted a flaw in Misty's plan—in the shape of the wooden banister that runs along the staircase and links one floor to the other. This is to be painted turquoise, to complement the colors upstairs, but he thinks it will look terrible in such a prominent position downstairs. *But as a lowly painter and decorator, dare I point it out?*

He reminds himself that Misty usually looks down her nose

at him, making it clear that, as a Polish immigrant, she sees him as unrefined, uncultured, and uncouth. *Yeah, but you're not, Oskar. And you need to believe in yourself.*

He cautiously raises a hand.

Misty quirks an eyebrow. "Yes?"

"I was just thinking, are you sure you want the banister to be turquoise? It's just so much of it will be downstairs, and it won't really fit the color palette."

Misty looks at him as if his skin has just broken out in angry, pus-oozing boils. "Sorry," she says. "I can't tell what you're saying."

Oskar knows this isn't true; his accent is much softer than it was when he arrived in the UK, and his workmates have complimented him on it several times. And although his English isn't perfect and he still tries to learn a new word every day, it's certainly better than any of the other Polish people he knows. Not that he spends much time mixing with Polish people. The truth is, he does everything he can to shake off any association with his home country. *But unfortunately, people like Misty insist on reminding me of it at every opportunity.*

He lets out a breath, then repeats his point, slowly. "We could always paint it in a more neutral gray or off-white. Maybe like the color of seashells?"

Misty looks unsure how to respond before saying, "Funnily enough, I was thinking of doing something with seashells— you've just reminded me. We could also hang some real seashells from the banister." She pauses, clearly struggling to get the next word out. "Thanks."

A smile plays at the corners of Oskar's mouth. But he's worried he's only going to have annoyed her.

As soon as the presentation is over, he throws himself back into his work. Earlier in the day, he'd added filler to the various holes in the walls and, now that it's dried, he goes from spot to spot with sandpaper, smoothing down the bumps and uneven surfaces. As he focuses on this simple task, everything else fades into the background. He wonders if this is an example of his latest word of the day: mindfulness. Concluding that it probably is makes him feel a little bit better. *And a little bit better about myself.*

Oskar moved to the UK ten years ago, which is when he started working as a painter and decorator. But his dream has always been to be an interior designer, like Misty. After saving up enough money, he recently completed an online course—for which he was awarded a distinction. Since then, he's been bursting with ideas and can no longer walk into a room without wanting to reinvent it. But he doesn't have the confidence to pursue his dream in any professional capacity. He's learned through bitter experience that lots of people in this country view Polish immigrants as laborers or tradesmen, not artists, and he doesn't think anyone would respect him as a designer, let alone hire him. *I'd only fall flat on my face.*

He's distracted from his thoughts by an unusual tapping sound. He looks up to see it's coming from Misty, her acrylic nails skittering across the screen of her iPad. She catches him looking and unleashes a corrosive smile. "This is an iPad, darling. Don't you have them in Romania?"

"Actually," he says, "I'm from Poland, not Romania."

She shrugs. "Is there a difference?"

Don't let her get to you, Oskar. Don't rise to the bait.

He contorts his face into a smile. "Yes, they are two very different countries, Misty. For example, Frédéric Chopin was from Poland, while the most famous person from Romania was Count Dracula."

She examines a chip in one of her nails. "Fascinating."

"Having said that," he adds, "I'm pretty sure you can buy iPads in both countries. Maybe you don't realize but they're actually quite basic."

Across the room, he hears a few of his workmates snigger-
ing. Misty scoffs and goes back to tapping at her screen.

Yes, I shut her up, but why do comments like hers still hurt me?

Oskar returns to his work, eager to focus on sanding once
again and hoping all thoughts of Misty will fade from his mind.

He snatches a quick look at his watch.

Just one hour to go.

One hour and I'll be out of here.

Oskar says goodbye to his workmates and ducks out of the
shop while Misty has her back turned.

He lives in Eastcliff, the mobile home park just outside
town, next to the wind farm that greets visitors as they arrive
on the A-road from inland. He can walk home in half an hour,
which will give him just enough time to go out for a short bike
ride and clear his head before his evening meal.

He sets off down the high street, which is flanked on either
side by a row of tall, grand Victorian buildings. Most of these
are made of redbrick or sandstone, although one has a mock
Tudor frontage and another a mosaic of blue ceramic tiles lining the façade. The buildings are linked by a succession of
wrought iron awnings that form a covered walkway over the
wide, stone pavement. Oskar strides under it, passing three
charity shops, a shop selling trinkets inspired by the seaside,
and another that appears to sell nothing but a range of garishly
colored crystal ornaments in the shape of animals. As he passes
the entrance to the Victorian shopping arcade, he glances inside, but most of its mahogany-framed units are empty. Oskar
has to stop himself imagining how he could update and redesign it.

When he comes to the end of the block, he presses the button to cross the road. While he's waiting, his eyes are drawn to
a huge Egyptian obelisk that rises from an island in the center

of the junction. He can't help wondering how on earth something like that ended up in this little Lancashire seaside town. *Mind you, you could say the same about me . . .*

It suddenly strikes Oskar how strange it is that he's put down roots here—and not just that but that he feels so content and settled. When he was growing up in a small town on the north coast of Poland, he'd never heard of St. Luke's-on-Sea. He'd never even heard of Lancashire. *How funny that it's become my home.*

When the green man flashes, he treads on. He passes Glasstone's, the old family-run department store—and in the window catches sight of his reflection. He looks younger than his thirty-three years, with fair, medium-length messy hair and a natural, unmanicured beard. Apart from a black enamel stud in his left earlobe, he's currently displaying no hint of his personal style; he's dressed for work, in utilitarian shorts with lots of pockets, sturdy boots, and an old T-shirt that is covered in oil and paint stains. Nothing about him stands out from his surroundings or looks like it doesn't belong. He wonders if any of the people passing have the slightest idea he grew up in a completely different world.

He continues down the high street, and the smell of vinegar on steaming hot chips draws his attention to the town's most popular fish-and-chip restaurant. On the tables outside are gathered groups of day-trippers, many of them parents with toddlers or people who've brought disabled relatives to the seaside. A boy in a wheelchair gives him a wave, and Oskar returns it with a smile.

In the next block, the star attraction is without doubt the town's biggest ice-cream shop, Ainsworth's. Oskar knows this is famous all over Lancashire because whenever he tells anyone he lives in St. Luke's, one of the first things they mention is Ainsworth's ice cream. Although, funnily enough, he's never tried it. For the first time, he finds himself drawn to the shop.

He pauses at the window to look at the menu. But his eyes

drift inside and to the décor. It's a strange mix of what he judges to be original features, giving off an almost cool, retro vibe, and ill-judged updates and additions, such as an abundance of 1950s fuchsia leatherette and a mirrored ceiling that would look more at home in a 1980s nightclub. *But it has so much potential . . .*

He stops and gives his feet a little stomp. *Come on, don't torture yourself.*

Even with its unattractive décor, Ainsworth's is packed with customers—which makes Oskar assume the ice cream must be excellent. He looks again at the menu and spots all the usual flavors. Chocolate, strawberry, mint choc chip—and Vimto. *What's Vimto?*

He considers going inside and ordering one, but he's feeling fragile after all the hostility from Misty and just wants to get home. Besides, he doesn't want to spoil his bike ride by giving himself a stitch. So he turns and walks away. And he resolves that as soon as he gets home, he's going to look up the word *Vimto.*

Who knows? Maybe today I'll learn two words.

CHAPTER 5

On Friday night, for the first time since the final Covid lock-down, Ted doesn't see his friend Denise. She's the only person he's told about his split with Giles, but he doesn't feel up to their usual date with *RuPaul's Drag Race*—and still doesn't feel like talking. Instead, he waits until everyone has left work and sneaks into the factory. He wants to do something in secret.

I want to win back Giles.

All week, Ted has stuck to his strategy of burying himself in work, doing his best to look cheerful around his colleagues, al-though at times it's been like trying to light a fire with wet wood. Thankfully, none of them has noticed anything's wrong—but they don't generally show much interest in his life anyway. It would be much more difficult to keep up the pretense around his parents, so Ted has avoided them as much as possible. But no matter how busy he's kept himself, nothing has stopped him thinking about Giles.

He's even ended up texting him a few times. He didn't want to make Giles feel uncomfortable, so just asked how he was. He wanted to somehow let him know that if he changed his mind, he could come back and Ted would forgive and (pre-tend to) forget. But Giles didn't reply to his first text, and after the second Ted received a terse message suggesting it would be a good idea if they avoided all contact for a while.

But Ted still feels lost without Giles. He feels frightened of the life opening up before him and robbed of the future they planned together. *I'm actually not sure I can live without him.*

It was this that inspired him to start plotting ways to win Giles back. Over several evenings, he worked through all his memories of their happy times together—or what he'd *thought* were their happy times together. And, after much reflection, the thing that stood out most was the ice cream he used to make from Giles's favorite chai flavor. It was something he first did in the early days of their relationship, when a branch of Starbucks opened in St. Luke's-on-Sea, and Giles started drinking the then-fashionable chai tea latte. After a few years, Ted fell out of the habit of making it, but he's decided to resurrect it and have a batch delivered to the hotel where Giles works. At the very least he hopes this will persuade him to re-establish contact. *Even if it's just out of pity.*

The only problem is, Ted hasn't made the ice cream for so long, he can't remember the correct proportions of the ingredients. He scatters what he thinks might be the right amount of powder into the top of the machine and switches it on. It clunks into action, spinning and whirring.

As he listens to the ice cream churning, Ted's mind wanders.

Ted whipped out a bowl of ice cream and spooned some into Giles's mouth. He'd been trying to get the proportions right for days and, now he had, he couldn't wait to find out what Giles thought of it.

"Well?" he asked, brightly. "Can you tell what it is?"

A grin lifted Giles's face. "Chai tea latte!"

"Do you like it?"

"I love it!" He took hold of Ted's hands and looked deep into his eyes. "And I love *you*, Ted."

He leaned in to kiss him. But after a few seconds, Ted pulled away.

"Smiles, you've got it all over my mouth!"

"Oh, sorry. It just tastes so good." Giles took hold of the bowl. "If you don't mind, I'm going to have some more." He put a big spoonful into his mouth, then kissed Ted again and smeared it all over his lips and chin.

Ted pushed him away, gurgling with laughter. "Now you've got it everywhere!" He grabbed the spoon and dabbed some onto Giles's nose. Then he dabbed a dollop onto each cheek. By this time they were both gurgling with laughter.

Suddenly, Giles's giggles morphed into something like a low growl. The air between them crackled. Before Ted knew it, they were kissing passionately. And no sooner did he feel a stirring in his trousers than the two of them were pulling their clothes off and throwing them on the floor. Giles pinned Ted up against the ice-cream machine, turned him around and began kissing the back of his neck.

Ted was sure they were breaching the factory's hygiene regulations—and he didn't dare think what would happen if anyone caught them. But he didn't care.

If this is what happens when I make Giles's favorite ice cream, I'm going to do it more often.

Ted looks at the timer and sees the machine has been running for long enough. He switches it off and pumps the ice cream into a plastic tub. Trying to block out the memory of that first tasting, he puts a spoonful into his mouth. It's so sweet it makes him wince.

Shit.

You've messed up, Ted.

Just like you mess everything up.

He slumps against the machine and falls to the floor. He can feel the tears welling in his eyes and blots them away with his cuffs.

Come on, you can have another go.

But then another voice cuts in. *Oh, what's the use? It's not going to work. As if Giles is ever going to want you back.*

The tears begin to leak from his eyes

Then, out of nowhere, a voice shouts, *"Stop right there!"*

The shock of it makes Ted jump and bang the back of his head on the machine. Rubbing his skull, he looks up to see who it is.

Standing over him is his dad, brandishing a cricket bat. "Ted! What are *you* doing here?"

Cowering behind him is Ted's mum, the sharp tip of her umbrella jabbing into the air. "And more to the point, why are you skriking?"

Ted's stomach falls away. *I guess I can't avoid Mum and Dad any longer . . .*

Once Ted's head has stopped hurting and his mum and dad have got over their shock, they explain that they were on their way to a restaurant when Trevor remembered he'd left some documents in the office that he needed to read over the weekend. As they drove down the lane, they saw a light on in the factory and thought they were being burgled. So Trevor picked up a cricket bat from the boot and Hilary grabbed the only weapon she could find—her leopard-print umbrella.

They lay both of these down on a table and take off their coats. Ted can see they're smartly dressed and must have been on their way to somewhere special. *Now I've messed that up too.*

His parents are both in their early sixties but look younger; while Trevor has sparkling eyes, a spring in his step and a full head of hair that has the color and sheen of a newly shelled conker, Hilary has a trim figure that's the envy of her friends, and fair highlighted hair that's cut in a stylish A-line bob. As the three of them sit down around the table, she quickly calls the restaurant to cancel their booking. When she's put her phone down, she looks at Ted, expectantly.

"I'm sorry I spoiled your night," he says.

"Oh, forget about that, love," she says in her strong Lancashire accent, evidence of her humble beginnings as Hilary Taylor. "But we do want to know what's going on."

"Don't think we haven't noticed you've been avoiding us all week," adds Trevor.

"Yeah, sorry about that."

Ted gives a brief summary of what's happened with Giles, then explains what he's doing in the factory. As he speaks, his Adam's apple feels like it keeps getting lodged in his throat. It's as if it causes him physical pain to force the words out of his mouth. When he reaches the end of his explanation, his parents look flabbergasted.

"But I don't understand," Trevor splutters. "I thought you two were so happy together."

Ted frowns. "So did I. But Giles clearly didn't."

From the look on both Trevor and Hilary's faces, they're not only flabbergasted but devastated too. They've always loved Giles, and it was Hilary who first introduced him to Ted. She and his mum used to sit on the committee of a local group for women in business, and, after some networking event that descended into a late-night drinking session in the hotel bar where Giles was working, the two women hatched a vodka-fueled plan to fix up their gay sons. Perhaps surprisingly for two men living in such a small town, Ted and Giles had never met—although Giles went to the local private school, while Ted was educated at the comprehensive. When they eventually did meet, they got on even better than their mums had hoped and were soon saying they felt like they'd known each other forever. A few weeks later, they became each other's first boyfriend.

"So did he give a reason for ending it?" asks Trevor. He arches an eyebrow. "He hasn't met someone else, has he?"

Ted's mouth dries up. *God, how humiliating.*

"He has, I'm afraid," he croaks. "It's someone he works with. Someone called Javier."

Hilary tightens her lips. "*Javier?* What a tacky name!"

Trevor picks up his cricket bat. "I've a good mind to pay him a visit."

"He sounds like a scrote!" hisses Hilary.

"Mum, Dad," Ted protests, "you don't know anything about him. He could be perfectly nice."

A crease of anger scratches across Hilary's face. "He's a homewrecker, love. He can't possibly be *nice.*"

"No, well, I think it's too easy to blame Javier," Ted parries. He swallows before attempting the next sentence. "I'm sure Giles was a willing participant."

From what he said, he was desperate to get away from me.

Hilary gives a huff. "I bet he were, the little toerag. Well, he certainly pulled t' wool over our eyes. To think we welcomed him into our family with open arms! Although now we're on t' subject, I could never stand his mum."

"Mum, that's not true."

"Yes, it is. That stuck-up cow has always looked down on me, like I'm a shit on a white rug."

Ted holds up his hands and says that he doesn't want to talk about this anymore. "There's no point. There's nothing I can do about it. Giles doesn't even want to speak to me at the moment."

"Well, in that case," snaps Hilary, "you're not sending him any of our ice cream."

"Over my dead body!" booms Trevor.

Ted tries to argue, but they won't have any of it.

"No son of mine is making a fool of himself," thunders Trevor.

Oh, maybe they're right. Maybe my whole plan is just desperate and undignified.

His memory of the first time he made Giles chai-flavored ice cream briefly flickers back to life. Then it's gone.

"Now come on," says Trevor. "Let's clean out this machine."

CHAPTER 6

Ted's parents insist he takes a week off work, and he goes straight back to wallowing.

On Monday, he digs out an old shirt Giles left behind that's still imprinted with his scent—or at least the scent of his after-shave. Even though it's a tight fit, Ted puts it on, leaving it untucked so he can twiddle with the material at the bottom, as if it's a comfort blanket. He lies on the sofa, and Lily snuggles up to him. The two of them spend hours watching daytime TV, from *Bargain Hunt* to *Loose Women,* to endless programs on Channel 4 about couples selling their homes and moving to a new life on the coast, in the country, or basically anywhere it's sunny. Although Ted soon finds that other couples' hopes and excitement only make him feel even more miserable. *And I wasn't sure that was possible.*

On Tuesday, he wakes up to find it's raining, and he lies in bed just listening to the pitter-patter on the roof, the trickle down the window pane, and the drip from a leaking gutter onto the windowsill. For a long time, the sound has him caught in a kind of trance. When he needs to eat, he finally snaps himself out of it and slopes downstairs to the kitchen. He stands at the window, forcing cornflakes into his mouth, staring at the rain splashing onto the patio paving. He remembers when he was little and the rain kept him indoors, his mum used to say those splashes were made by fairies dancing. That always used to cheer him up—now it can't even raise a smile.

On Wednesday, he takes his first shower of the week, but afterwards wraps himself in a towel and sits on the side of the bath for so long he starts shivering. He gets dressed and forces himself to do some housework but is so incapable of concentration he puts detergent capsules into the tumble dryer and gets the wire from his phone charger tangled up in the hoover. When he takes the rubbish out, he notices a FOR SALE sign has been put up outside the house next door. For a moment he forgets Giles has left him and takes out his phone to text him the news. Then he remembers—and the shock hits him all over again, swiftly followed by another thump of sadness.

Ted drags himself back into the house and sinks down onto the bottom step of the staircase. Until a few weeks ago, he would never have imagined it was possible to miss someone so much. And the worst thing is, now Giles has said he wants to cease contact, Ted can't even text him. It's as if he's stopped existing, as if he's died.

Now that he thinks about it, Ted does feel like he's grieving. But the strange thing is, it's a process he doesn't want to end. At least grief is a continuation of his love in some form. At least it's a sign of his love clinging on.

Ted wishes he could shut himself off from the world and give himself over to his grief completely—but he finds this impossible. After a stream of unanswered calls and texts from Denise, culminating in GIFs of some of their favorite moments from *RuPaul's Drag Race*, Ted replies saying he can't face talking. But Denise isn't one to give up easily, so Ted just stops answering her messages. His sister, Jemima, calls him on Face-Time, but he only accepts the call with his camera switched off and explains he doesn't feel well enough to speak. Thankfully, she responds with sensitivity, gives him her love, then lets him go.

As if they've set up a rota, one of his parents comes round to check on Ted every day. On Wednesday evening, his dad suggests they go to the pub, but Ted refuses. He just isn't feeling sociable and can't face people's sympathy or looks of pity. What he doesn't say is he knows everyone in the pub will be thrilled to see Trevor, hanging on to his every word, enraptured by his anecdotes and roaring with laughter at anything he says that even remotely resembles a joke—and this will only make Ted feel worse about himself.

Instead, the two men settle on the sofa and watch Doris Day in *Calamity Jane*, a film they often watch together as it catches a rare overlap of Trevor's love of Westerns and Ted's love of song and dance (the only others being *Annie Get Your Gun, Oklahoma!,* and *Seven Brides for Seven Brothers*, but Ted had to rule that last one out when he saw it as an adult and was struck by its rampant misogyny). Father and son assume their usual positions—Ted stretching out so his feet are on Trevor's lap, and Trevor gently massaging Ted's toes, in between sipping his craft ale and tapping out a beat to "The Deadwood Stage (Whip-Crack-Away!)."

On Thursday, Hilary calls in to see Ted on her way home from work.

"Hiya, love!" she shouts from the hallway, in a voice so positive Ted feels like he's being physically assaulted.

She swishes into the living room dressed in faux-leather leggings and an azure blue top that's cinched at the waist with a thick orange belt. She flashes Ted a smile so bright he has to shield his eyes.

"Hi, Mum," he mumbles.

Hilary drops her handbag onto the coffee table. "And how are you feeling?"

He shrugs. "Oh, you know, the same."

She folds her arms. "Right, we need to do summat about that."

Hilary announces that Ted needs to exercise, that getting his body moving will help improve his state of mind and lift his spirits. "You've always liked dancing, so I've enrolled you in a dance class."

Ted sits up, dislodging Lily from under his arm. "What?"

"Actually, it's a dance *exercise* class." Hilary explains it's run by Shelly Topper, a former dancer from St. Luke's who spent several years performing in musicals before returning to the town as something of a local celebrity.

But halfway through her explanation, Ted has stopped listening. In his head, he's somewhere else . . .

Ted checked his watch; Giles wasn't due home for more than an hour. This easily gave him enough time to complete his workout. He and Giles had only just moved in together, so Ted didn't want him to find out how he kept fit. *Not after what happened in Dublin . . .*

Ted pushed back the coffee table and slid a battered old cassette into the VHS player. It was Cher's *Hot Dance* workout, in which the famous singer and actress appeared dressed in a sheer, skintight mesh costume with cutouts and rhinestones, her only nod to workout wear a pair of black legwarmers, and bounced through a gloriously camp exercise routine with immaculate hair and makeup, barely breaking sweat. As a teenager in the 1990s, Ted used to sit, mesmerized, watching his mum copy Cher's every move. As an adult, he struggled with exercise; the only form he could bear was dance. The problem was, Giles didn't like going out to clubs, so the two of them rarely went anywhere with a dance floor. So this had become Ted's secret way of indulging his passion.

He turned up the sound to full blast and, after mouthing along to Cher's introduction, threw himself into the routine, much of which he also knew by heart. As the adrenaline pumped around him, he felt awash with joy. He imagined himself, like Cher, performing on stage to an audience of thousands, and was soon transported far away from his living room in St. Luke's. He even let out a whoop when Cher did his favorite move, "the pony."

"I pony, you pony, we all love the pony!" he joined in.

As he stomped, stretched, and shimmied through every move, he felt ablaze with confidence. But, just as Cher and her instructor were guiding viewers through the "traveling pony"— which was basically the same as "the pony" but on a diagonal— he was distracted by the sound of coughing coming from behind him.

He swiveled around to see Giles leaning on the doorframe. His breath failed. *Fuck! Where did he come from?*

In a flash, Ted felt acutely aware of what he must look like. His eyes flitted down to what he was wearing: a pair of navy mid-length shorts and a matching nylon shirt, which weren't in the slightest bit flamboyant, except he'd rounded off the look with a pair of bright ultramarine legwarmers. As the full horror of what Giles must be thinking sunk in, his neck and hands tingled with embarrassment. He scurried over to the VHS player and hit Stop.

"Hi," he squeaked, as nonchalantly as he could. "How long have you been there?"

There was the hint of a smile on Giles's face, but Ted couldn't read it.

"Oh, only a few minutes," he replied.

Ted reached for a towel and wiped his forehead. He wasn't sweating that much but felt overcome by the urge to hide his face. "I thought you were working late?"

"Yeah, I was supposed to, but there was a change of plan. Anyway, don't stop, I was enjoying your little floorshow!"

Something about Giles's tone of voice made Ted shudder with shame. He desperately cast around for some humor. "Don't tell me, I look like a drunken goat."

Giles gave a little snigger. "I wouldn't say that. More like a tipsy chicken."

Ted whipped him with his towel. "Smiles!" He plonked himself down on the sofa and pushed out a breath. "Oh, I wish you hadn't seen that! I'm dead embarrassed now."

"Don't be daft," said Giles. "I love you, Ted. You don't have to worry what I think."

A wave of gratitude washed through Ted. "Really? Thanks, Smiles."

God knows how he puts up with me. I don't deserve him.

Giles cleared his throat. "But next time you want to put your legwarmers on and dance around to Cher, you might want to close the curtains. You don't want the neighbors to see you."

"Do you think so?"

Giles laid a hand on his shoulder. "I just don't want anyone to laugh at you, that's all. I'd hate anyone to take the piss."

Another twist of shame stabbed through Ted. He stood up, purposefully. "Actually, there won't be a next time. This really isn't my thing."

"You looked like you were enjoying it."

"Oh, I was only having a laugh," Ted insisted. "I don't even like Cher. And that costume she wears makes her look like some low-rent stripper who collects tips in a pint glass."

Giles chuckled. "Alright. If you're sure."

Ted strode over to the VHS player and pressed Eject. "Now I don't know about you," he said, forcing a smile onto his face, "but I'm starving. Shall I make our tea?"

Ted looks out of the window at a pair of tourists trying to eat fish and chips, hiding from the wind in a bus shelter and fending off two particularly bold—and hungry—seagulls. *Welcome to the seaside,* he wants to shout at them.

He's sitting in the passenger seat of his mum's car, outside the old lifeboat station—which is now a community center—at the southern end of the promenade. The sky is the color of old Tupperware, and it's one of those blustery days familiar to anyone who lives in St. Luke's. On the beach, a few brave men are flying kites that snap and swerve in all directions. A group of litter pickers are undertaking their regular collection of the rubbish that's been washed up by the sea but are having to chase after it as it skitters over the sand. And across the promenade, a shopkeeper is running after a bucket and spade that the wind is carrying off down the road.

Ted doesn't want to get out of the car. "Oh, Mum, I'm not sure I'm up to this."

She waves away his objection. "What a load of claptrap—you'll love it."

"But I haven't danced for ages."

"And that's exactly why I think you should."

Ted sighs. "But what if I can't do it anymore?"

"I already checked, love—they take all levels. If you're a bit rusty, you can go in as a beginner."

Ted falls silent. He can't come up with any more excuses.

"Go on, then. Off you go," pipes Hilary, shooing him away. "I'll pick you up in an hour."

Realizing he has no escape, Ted opens the door. The wind blows it shut as soon as he lets go.

As Hilary drives off, she beeps her horn twice—presumably in encouragement. The tourists in the bus shelter look up from their fish and chips, but Ted avoids their gaze. He turns and faces the building.

Come on, you can get through this—you've just got to grin

and bear it. Besides, you can always walk through the moves. You don't have to give it your all.

He shuffles inside, entering a vast hall with walls that have recently been painted white, a gleaming hardwood floor, and a pitched roof that's held up by steel rafters. At the back is a row of stacked chairs and folded-up tables onto which have been thrown several coats. The hall is teeming with people, but Ted quickly scans around and realizes he's the only man. His heart sinks. *Oh, this is going to be embarrassing. It's exactly like Giles said—everyone will laugh at me.*

His stomach contracts. *What am I going to do without Giles to rein me in? How am I going to cope?*

He finds a space at the back and drops his bag onto the floor. He's wearing training shoes that were designed for comfort rather than exercise and the only workout shorts and T-shirt he could find, which are so old he wouldn't be surprised if they were the ones he was wearing when Giles caught him dancing to Cher more than fifteen years ago. At least this time around he isn't wearing legwarmers. He wonders what happened to his favorite ultramarine pair and remembers throwing them away, thrusting them to the bottom of the bin bag to be sure the bin men wouldn't see them. He sniffs the memory back.

He looks around at the women stretching, some of them swigging from bottles of water or energy drinks. He's relieved to find that none of them pay him any attention, let alone laugh at him. He also notices that none of them are wearing particularly fashionable workout clothes and the majority of them are middle-aged and tubby, some of them looking tired and drawn. *Thank God for that—at least that's one way I fit in.*

He recognizes a handful of the women—and in his head hears some of the comments Giles used to make about them. One he said has a figure like a Megabus and another he joked has a bull neck fleshy enough to feed a family of four. Ted sighs. At least now he doesn't have to tell Giles off when he's un-kind about people. *Oh, stop thinking about Giles, you sad loser!*

As Ted lowers himself onto the floor and stretches out his calves, he thinks back over all the events he's attended in this room. The first, shortly after the building was converted into a community center, was a course run by Slimming World, which was where he met Denise. Just before he turned thirty, Ted found himself consumed by another bout of insecurity about his looks. Frightened that Giles was going to lose inter-est, he decided to lose some weight. Ted has always been prone to overeating, but in his late twenties he noticed a roll of fat de-veloping around his waist—what people were starting to call a muffin top—and his upper thighs began rubbing against each other as he walked. When he made Giles's favorite lasagna and whisked the sauce, he was horrified to feel the flab on his arms flapping. Determined to do something about it, he told Giles he had to work late and sneaked into his first session of Slim-ming World. The woman in the seat next to him turned out to be Denise and the two of them became instant friends, spend-ing most of the twelve-week course trying—but failing—to suppress their giggles. Ted can't even remember how much weight he lost, but he can remember that after a few weeks, he and Denise started slipping off to the pub as soon as the ses-sion was over. When the course came to an end, they carried on going to the pub—and their friendship developed from there. *God, I really must call her. I need to stop being so rude.*

He's distracted from his thoughts by the teacher, who's clap-ping her hands to get everyone's attention.

"Good evening!" she calls out from the front of the class.

Ted has never met Shelly Topper but, when she moved back to St. Luke's, he read an interview she did with the local paper. So he knows that she grew up on the same council estate as his mum, won a scholarship to drama school in London, then went on to play the Hungarian jailbird in the West End pro-duction of *Chicago*, a prostitute in *Les Misérables*, and a Pink

Lady in a touring version of *Grease*. Giles used to be sniffy about Shelly's career—pointing out that she only played leads once or twice as an understudy—but Ted has always found her story inspirational. *She followed her dream and gave it her best shot—what's not to admire?*

He can't work out how old she is but knows she must be a few years older than him. Still, she has an incredible body that's shown off by figure-hugging workout wear, striking red hair that's pulled back in a ponytail to reveal a·face almost entirely free of wrinkles, and cheekbones so sharp Ted wouldn't be surprised if they could cut glass. But Shelly isn't remotely intimidating; on the contrary, she radiates a warmth and positivity that has all the women in the class leaning towards her, like sunflowers straining to reach the sun.

"Now it looks like we've got a few newbies today, so say hello, everyone!" Shelly chirps.

The entire class revolves to look at Ted and two women standing in the row in front of him. "Hello!"

Ted coughs into a closed fist. *Oh God, what have I let myself in for?*

When Shelly encourages the newcomers to introduce themselves, he mumbles his name and just about manages a watery smile.

"Now, what's the only rule we need to tell them?" Shelly asks.

"This is a judgment-free space!" chorus the women.

Shelly gives a firm nod. "That's right, we don't want anyone feeling self-conscious."

To Ted's horror, she turns her attention to him. "Now, Ted, I usually address the class as girls. As you're the only boy, do you mind if I continue?"

He feels his face flush with color. "No, urm, that's fine," he stammers.

"Sensational." Shelly gives a little leap in the air and shakes out her arms. "Now come on, let's get this show on the road!"

She releases her hair from the ponytail, puts on a headset mic, and turns around to fiddle with the sound system. Straightaway, Ted recognizes the introduction to Kylie Minogue's "Spinning Around." The woman next to him gives a little squeal.

"OK, girls, we've all seen the video," announces Shelly. "But I want you to picture yourselves wearing Kylie's gold hot pants! And remember, you are strong, seductive, *sensual* women!"

Out of nowhere, Ted feels a surge of excitement so intense it busts the breath right out of him.

"You are goddesses!" Shelly goes on. "Shining down from on high! Now let me see you *slay*!"

For a few moments, Ted stands still as, all around him, the women throw themselves into moves Shelly calls body rolls, hip swizzles, kitty cat crawls, and the bend and snap made famous in *Legally Blonde.*

"Keep those bums tooted in the air, girls!" she calls out.

"Whip that hair around like you're a wild animal!"

"Run your hands down your body as if you can't believe your own gorgeousness!"

Within seconds, all of the women are transformed; not a single one of them looks tired or tubby. They tilt their pelvises, arch their backs, and ripple their bodies with so much sass Ted can't help letting out a little gasp. And their utter lack of inhibition ignites something within him.

Yes, please, I'll be having some of this!

"Now repeat after me!" commands Shelly. "I love myself! I love my body! I am a strong, seductive, *sensual* woman!"

As the women echo her words, Ted can feel his excitement taking control. He forgets all about walking through the moves and throws himself into Shelly's routine with a passion and commitment he didn't know he possessed—or at least had forgotten he possessed. Within just a few moves, he feels exactly like he used to when he did Cher's *Hot Dance* workout at home. Except this is even better because it's happening in public.

Once the adrenaline is pumping around him, he feels as if he's vibrating on a higher frequency. Not for a single moment does it occur to him to worry about anyone laughing at him. Though there is one worry that flashes through his mind: that straight after class he'll bump back down to earth with a thud. But he's determined not to let that spoil it.

For now—even if it's only for an hour—I am a goddess! And I'm going to enjoy every minute of it!

CHAPTER 7

Denise Love is worried about Ted. A few weeks ago, her best friend sent her a text message to say he and his husband Giles had broken up—news that came as such a surprise, it left Denise quite breathless. And ever since then, he's deflected all her attempts to make contact. He even pulled out of their usual Friday night in, which they haven't missed since the last lockdown—and the following week did the same. *Well, I'm not giving up that easily . . .*

She texts him again. **"I know you're struggling, honey, but remember I'm here if you want me. And I've got *loads* of experience with breakups! You don't have to do this on your own!"** She attaches several kisses and—knowing her spelling is terrible—scans the message for mistakes.

Just as she's hitting Send, she catches sight of her boss doing her usual patrols and quickly slides her phone under the counter. The staff in Glasstone's department store are banned from using their mobiles on the shop floor and she's already been told off for it several times.

Denise is a supervisor on the makeup counter of Glasstone's, one of the few department stores left in the country that's independent and family-run. She imagines it only survives because it has such an old customer base; they seem to love the familiarity of its thick brown carpets and Formica-paneled walls and ceilings, not to mention its gentle sound-track of background music, usually piano arrangements of themes from well-known films. She often hears tourists walking in for the first time and commenting that it reminds them of the store in *Are You Being Served?* Sometimes, she wonders what they must think of her. When she first started work here—thirty years ago—she used to compare herself to the sit-com's young, sexy Miss Brahms. Now she's in her late forties, she sometimes worries that she's more like the feisty—but occasionally embarrassing—old lady, Mrs. Slocombe.

She rubs her neck and turns to the new girl. "How's everything going, honey?"

"Yeah, really well, thanks."

Lauria Grimshaw is eighteen years old, with raven hair and caramel skin, a cute little gap between her teeth, and eyelashes so long they could probably create a breeze. A few hours ago, Denise asked her to clean the display stock, taking the testers out and putting them back again, and chopping the tops off all the lipsticks. She hopes it really *is* going well because, so far, Lauria has struggled to complete even the most basic tasks.

Denise wonders if she was equally hopeless when she started at Glasstone's. She casts her mind back, picturing her eigh-teen-year-old self, fresh out of college, having recently gradu-ated with a BTEC in Beauty. Denise has always loved makeup and couldn't believe her luck when she beat off stiff competi-tion to land a job in the town's only department store, which at the time was still considered glamorous. She remembers being keen and eager to please, just as Lauria is now, but also feeling overwhelmed by her first experience of work in such an adult world. She resolves to make more of an effort with Lauria, and to encourage and guide her as much as she can.

"Now don't forget to make sure you put the lipsticks back

in the right place," she chirps. "The customers don't half get annoyed if the colors get mixed up."

Lauria nods. "Don't worry, I'm all over it."

The music changes and Denise gives a wistful smile. "Oh, listen to this; it's that Celine Dion song from *Titanic*. I love that film."

"You sound just like my mum," says Lauria. "It's one of her favorites too."

Your mum? Denise tries not to wince.

"I've actually never seen *Titanic*," Lauria goes on. "It came out before I was born."

Denise's face falls. She wishes Lauria wouldn't constantly remind her of how old she is. On her first day, the trainee gave Denise what she thought was a compliment, saying she had good legs "for her age"—three little words that left Denise smarting. And yesterday, Lauria referred to the thirtysomething floor manager as "ancient," only to realize she'd unwittingly insulted Denise in the process. She'd tried to backtrack, which only made things worse.

Denise picks up a hand mirror and examines her reflection. Her hair is in great condition, despite everything she puts it through to dye it blond. As ever, she's done a great job with her makeup, softening the heavy foundation and strong pinks mandated by her employer to better complement her coloring. Given the choice, she'd like smaller boobs, but she consoles herself that they can still look reasonable in a good bra. And, as the kind of woman who's often referred to as "big-boned," she's perfectly happy with her current weight—and is slimmer than she's been for years. *Yeah, you're looking good, Denise. Mrs. Slocombe's got a few years on you yet!*

She looks up and catches Lauria gazing at her.

"You know, your face is still quite pretty," she says.

Denise lets out something between a gasp and a laugh. "What do you mean, 'still'?"

"Sorry, I just meant . . ."

Denise remembers her vow to encourage and guide her young colleague, and tells herself that she has nothing to feel insecure about. She tries to remember the list she made for her counselor of all the things she loves about herself.

I treat people well.

I'm good at my job.

I survived.

She stops and seizes a breath. *And if I can survive that, I can survive anything . . .*

She turns back to Lauria and smiles. "It's fine, honey, don't worry about it. Now, are you done with that cleaning?"

"Yep, all done!"

But when Denise checks over Lauria's work, she finds she's forgotten to restock the boxes of tissues and cotton buds. And when she pulls a few lipsticks out of the display, she discovers she's put them back in the wrong places. "You've got your pinks mixed up, honey. They don't match the colors on the guide."

Lauria looks crestfallen. "Fuck!"

"I *beg* your pardon!" Staring at them open-mouthed is one of the counter's regular customers, a haughty old lady with a permanently disapproving look. "You never used to hear language like that in Glasstone's. This place must be going downhill."

"Sorry, Mrs. Barclay," Denise simpers. "Our new girl is still getting used to customer service. I promise that won't happen again."

"I should hope not," says Mrs. Barclay, her features pinched. "Now I'd like my usual compact powder, please."

Denise turns to her trainee. "Lauria, why don't you pop into the back and wash the makeup brushes?"

Lauria scuttles off, leaving Denise to focus on placating the angry Mrs. Barclay. After a good deal of flattery—and several free samples—the customer eventually leaves looking happier than when she arrived.

I'm a good diplomat. Denise makes a mental note to add that to her list.

Once she's made sure there are no customers waiting to be served, she checks the floor manager isn't around and slides her phone out from under the counter.

To her dismay, she still hasn't heard back from Ted. That isn't like him at all. In all the years she's known him—and it must be coming up to fifteen—he's never ignored her texts. Increasingly concerned, she wonders if she should just turn up at his house for an impromptu visit that evening. *What if he's struggling to cope? What if he needs me?*

Ted has always been there when Denise has needed him, much more so than her girlfriends from school, pretty much all of whom are married with children and therefore pulled in different directions. Ted, on the other hand, has helped her through several break-ups, including a particularly bad one three years ago with a long-term partner who he insisted—and Denise came to accept—was psychologically abusive. After that, she made a big show of telling all her friends that she was putting up the shutters and giving up on love. She even joked to her colleagues after a few drinks on one of their regular nights out that she might change her name from Denise Love to Denise Doesn't-Do-Love. But behind the wisecracks she was feeling fragile—and three years later still is. As one of the few people she confides in, Ted knows this. And he's always been her fiercest supporter. *Well, now I want to return the favor.*

I'm a good friend. That was another thing she'd written on her list. *Well, I want to be a good friend now . . .*

Just as Denise is preparing to text Ted again, her phone buzzes to let her know she's received a reply.

"Don't worry," it reads, **"am alright, just getting through it.**

But looking forward to seeing you on Friday. That is, if you're still up for it?"

Denise feels her whole body slacken with relief.

"Of course I'm up for it!" she texts back. **"See you at the usual time! I'll stock up on seccy! xx"**

She leans on the counter and releases a long breath. *Thank God for that!*

Now all I have to do is make sure Ted has a good time—and I'm just the friend he needs.

CHAPTER 8

"Now let's see," says Ted. "Oh, I know! I can eat what I want for my tea and don't have to pretend to like sushi or kale. And I can listen to Kylie and Lady Gaga without Giles subjecting me to his cool but dead boring electronic music."

A smile creeps over Denise's face. "There you go; that's not a bad start!"

The two of them are sitting in her living room, which is decorated in calming shades of lilac, has a painting of little fluffy clouds hanging on the wall, is lit in soft tones, and is scented by several candles. Denise has asked Ted if he can find a silver lining to his life without Giles. Although at first he claimed this was impossible, he's starting to warm to the idea. *Although that may be down to the fact I've downed three glasses of prosecco.*

"Oh, and I've been sleeping much better without him," he adds. "I don't have to listen to his heavy breathing. And for the first time I can sleep with the window open without him moaning about being cold."

"You see, that's brilliant!" pipes Denise. "I think we should drink to that!" She notices their glasses are empty. "Hold on, let me get another bottle of seccy."

It's Friday night and, after weeks of burying himself in work or wallowing at home, Ted has finally crawled out of his pit—

or at least he's let Denise heave him out of it. He was a little nervous about coming to her place and having to pick over all the details of the breakup, but as she reappears with another bottle and fills up their glasses, he's glad he has. *She's such an ace friend—I should have come sooner.*

"Now you're feeling a bit more upbeat," she says, steepling her fingers under her chin, "shall we discuss Giles's social media?"

Dread crashes into Ted. "What about his social media?"

"Well, he's been flaunting that skank Javier all over it."

He edges forward on the sofa. "Shit, really?"

"Yeah, have you not seen?"

"No, I didn't think about it. You know I'm not big on social media." Although Ted has accounts on Facebook and Instagram, he hardly ever uses them and certainly never posts. *I always thought I had everything I wanted in Giles.* He curses his stupidity and smothers it with another swig of his drink.

He logs on, finds Giles's profile and straightaway is bombarded by pictures of Giles and Javier; there's one of them strolling hand in hand through a field of lavender, another of them throwing their heads back with laughter over a meal in a swish restaurant, and another of them unwinding in what looks like a hotel hot tub. All the pictures are captioned with #newlove. Ted's heart dives to his stomach.

"I have to say, I was shocked," breathes Denise. "It's so unsubtle."

"More to the point," says Ted, his voice catching in his throat, "it's humiliating for me. What must everyone think?"

Actually, he can imagine what everyone thinks. Most of his and Giles's mutual friends—whether straight couples who live in St. Luke's or gay couples living slightly further afield—are in thrall to Giles, some of them even a little bit in love with him. They're probably laughing at Ted or, even worse, feeling sorry for him. *It's no wonder not a single one of them has been in touch. Not that I'm complaining—I wouldn't want to speak to them anyway.*

He scans through the pictures again. Javier is obviously younger and more attractive than Ted, with a much better body. It looks like he's much wilder and more fun too. *He's obviously giving Giles that nonstop adventure he wanted.*

"Well, I think Giles is being completely insensitive," brays Denise. "But then again, he never was very good at thinking about you."

"What do you mean?"

She takes a swig of her drink. "Just that everything always revolved around him. What you wanted was only ever an afterthought. You know, in some ways I think he held you back."

Ted blinks in shock. "Seriously, Den? Where's this come from all of a sudden?"

"I've always thought it, I just never said anything because you wouldn't have wanted to hear it. But when you and Giles went out or did anything together, you always retreated into the background. You were relegated to being his sidekick."

Ted twiddles the stem of his glass. "But maybe that's what naturally felt right for me. Not everyone can be the front man, you know."

"Teddy, you're not like that with me. What about that time we won that karaoke competition with 'Don't Go Breaking My Heart'?"

"I still think we should have done Brandy and Monica."

She gives him a wry smile. "Or that time we went to London for my fortieth, and you got up on stage and danced on that pole?"

"I was wasted, Den. The next day I was so hungover, I thought I was having a stroke."

"We both were—I woke up with a chicken wing in my hair!"

The two of them bellow with laughter. Ted's surprised at how good it feels. *That's the first time I've laughed in weeks.*

"Alright, well how about that time we went for a shopping day to the Trafford Centre?" Denise goes on. "You got up in front of all the customers and did an impression of Beyoncé, dancing around that wind machine. You weren't wasted then."

"No, but it blew out one of my contact lenses!"

"Yeah, let's gloss over that. The point is, you let yourself go. And when you're away from Giles, you're funny and a bit filthy. I don't know, I just think you're somehow more *you* when you're not around him. When you're out of his shadow."

"Really? I'm not so sure . . ." Ted trails off, distracted by his thoughts. *Did Giles somehow force me into retreating into his shadow? Or maybe just encourage me? Or is that where I genuinely wanted to be?*

"Look, you always thought Giles was so perfect he shat vanilla," Denise continues, "but he wasn't, Teddy. Far from it. And in some ways I think he stopped you really blossoming."

Ted feels the unease shift in his chest. This is a lot to take in and he's not sure he can deal with it. He looks at his phone and scrolls further down his timeline. Underneath Giles's post there's one from his sister, Jemima; she's attending some awards show, posing on a red carpet in a slinky black dress with a split thigh. *Look at her,* she's *never let anyone hold her back.* She's *never let anyone stop her from blossoming.*

He continues scrolling but pretty much everyone on his timeline seems to be doing exciting things. He remembers what Giles said about feeling like life was passing him by. All of a sudden, it strikes Ted that he's the one it's passing by. He expresses this to Denise.

She winches an eyebrow. "Well, you've just been given the chance to make some changes, honey. Maybe you should see this as a time for renewal. An opportunity!"

He lets out a shaky sigh. "Yeah, but I don't want to be some embarrassing cliché and fall into a full-blown midlife crisis."

Denise pushes away a few empty packets of Maltesers,

which are the only thing she lets them eat on a Friday night, insisting they're so low in calories they "don't count." "Who said anything about a midlife crisis? I was thinking more of a midpoint pivot. And after a lifetime of putting your family and your husband first, I think it's time for you to start putting yourself first."

She tips back some prosecco then stops to let out a squeal. "I just thought—it's time to start putting *Ted first*! Do you get it?"

Ted can feel his face breaking into a grin. "It does have a nice ring to it."

"Get on it, then! This is exciting, this is your time, Teddy! If you've got any unfulfilled dreams, now's your chance to make them happen!"

He drains his glass and claps his hands together. "Alright, enough of the life coaching. Top me up and let's watch some RuPaul."

Denise refills their glasses, sets up the TV and hits Play. But, as the title music kicks in, Ted's mind is racing. And one thought in particular keeps trying to break through. It's a thought that first lodged in his head more than thirty years ago, when he was just nine.

Ted and his family were on holiday in Nerja, on Spain's Costa del Sol—and were having a brilliant time. They spent their days on the beach, where Ted and Jemima would play games or jump over the waves with their dad, while their mum lay on a sun lounger, slathered in tanning oil and engrossed in a book by Jackie Collins, Shirley Conran, or Danielle Steel. In the evening, Ted and Jemima would run riot around the hotel gardens, their golden hair bouncing in the final rays of the day and their skin glistening with lotion, while Trevor and Hilary sat at the bar drinking gin and tonic, with each first sip Hilary spluttering, "By 'eck, Trev, these Spanish measures are strong!"

Later, the family would stroll along the narrow streets of the old town, choosing a restaurant in which they'd devour dishes with exotic names like *paella*, *patatas bravas*, and *albondigas*, afterwards heading down to the Balcón de Europa, a palm tree–lined promenade leading to a marble-tiled balcony built into the rock face and offering spectacular views of the Mediterranean. They'd peruse the local ice-cream shops and Trevor would joke about "checking out the competition" or "picking up some tips." Ted would lick his ice cream as he looked out to sea and tried to imagine that same sea connecting him to St. Luke's—but home seemed like a million miles away.

On several evenings, Ted had seen a thickset woman his mum described as "larger than life" swanning around the streets, chatting to people. This woman would invariably be dripping in sequins and sparkling jewelry wearing an extravagant canary-blond wig, and painted in heavy, cartoonish makeup, including fire engine–red lips and thick slashes of silver eyeshadow. Once, Ted overheard someone saying her name was Crystal Ball, which he thought was the most ace name ever. He was spellbound.

One night, Crystal approached the table at which Ted and his family were eating. She struck up a conversation with Trevor and Hilary, who both seemed delighted to be graced with her company. As Crystal chatted about Nerja and recommended things for them to see and do, Ted noticed she had a surprisingly deep voice.

"That woman's so beautiful," he said, once she'd flitted on to the next table, "but how come she talks like a man?"

Hilary gave him a smile. "Because she is a man, love."

"What do you mean?"

"She's a bloke," clarified Trevor. "A man dressed up as a woman."

Ted's parents explained that some men liked dressing up as
women to put on a show—and they were called drag queens.
But when they went home, they took off their disguises and
went back to being men.

Ted remembered the pantomimes his parents took him to
see every Christmas. "So it's like the wicked queen in *Snow
White*? Or the ugly sisters in *Cinderella*?"

"Exactly!" said Trevor, the force of his breath blowing out
the candle on their table.

Hilary leaned back to snatch the candle from a recently va-
cated table behind them. "Well, not quite," she pointed out.
"They're pantomime dames rather than drag queens. But yeah,
it's pretty much t' same thing."

Ted watched as Crystal glided away to the restaurant next
door, grabbed hold of a diamante-encrusted microphone, and
began chatting to the audience. She joked about the differ-
ences between Nerja and her hometown of Middlesborough—
and everyone barked with laughter. Then a backing track began
playing and she launched into ABBA's "Dancing Queen,"
which was greeted with a hoot of approval from Hilary. Trevor
began clapping along.

Ted's mind raced. At home, he occasionally overheard his
mum and dad saying unkind things about men who acted like
women—men they saw on TV, like Larry Grayson, John In-
man, or Kenny Everett. Men they described as "camp" or "effeminate." The kids at school went much further, saying
horrible things about these men, things that deep down Ted
was starting to worry were true about him—things he desperately hoped would stop being true. In the playground, insults
like *queer*, *sissy*, and *Nancy boy* were directed at anyone who
didn't like traditionally boyish sports or games or preferred to
play with the girls. It was like there was a strict rule that a boy
couldn't act like a girl. But the strange thing was, standing here

now was a man who was actually pretending to be a woman—
and everyone loved him.

Ted didn't divert his eyes as Crystal sang Gloria Gaynor's "I
Will Survive," then the Weather Girls' "It's Raining Men," and
everyone sitting outside the line of restaurants sang along.
Even people walking down the street stopped to watch and
join in.

After a while, a young, sunburnt man Hilary said looked
"bladdered" started hassling two women who were quietly
watching the show. A few people tried to intervene, but the
man just brushed them off and carried on. Eventually, Crystal
stepped in and told him to back off. When the man fronted up
to her, she slung him what Trevor called "a blinding right
hook." The entire street cheered.

"Never mess with a drag queen!" Crystal called out after the
man, as he staggered away, defeated.

Ted was awestruck.

He didn't understand everything he'd just witnessed—what
it said about being a man or a woman, or how any of it might
apply to him—but he did understand one thing . . .

When I grow up, I want to be just like Crystal.

As Denise switches off the TV, Ted sits up.

"Den." He pauses to make sure he has her full attention. "I
want to be a drag queen."

As he hears the words come out of his mouth, Ted feels the
world give a little wobble.

There, I've said it.

Denise almost chokes on her prosecco. "Sorry, what?"

"That's my dream," he stresses. "It's always been my dream.
Or at least it has since I saw my first drag queen when I was
nine."

She shakes her head in confusion. "Just a minute, how do I not know this?"

"Well, you kind of do. You know I love RuPaul, and I'm always talking about what I'd do differently to the contestants. You know I named my dog after my favorite drag queen. You know my favorite films are *Priscilla* and *To Wong Foo*. So it's kind of obvious. I just haven't said it out loud."

"But *why* haven't you said it out loud?"

"Because every time I did, people told me it was stupid. Or they laughed at me."

Denise's eyes narrow to slits. "Who said that, honey? Who laughed at you?"

Painful memories—and one in particular of an incident in Dublin—come rushing back, but Ted won't let them take hold. "Oh, it doesn't matter," he says, picking at a stray thread on his trousers. "Anyway, I never got to do anything about it because I had to work in the shop."

Denise holds her hand up for him to stop. "There you go, that's a perfect example of you putting other people first. You need to stop doing that, Teddy. You need to stop doing what other people expect of you."

"Maybe I'm ready to do that," cheeps Ted, inching closer to her. "Maybe that's what this is about. As RuPaul says, drag's about overturning expectations. It's about ripping up the rule-book and shaking the system. That's one of the things I love about it!"

Denise raises her eyebrows. "Look at you, honey. Now you've let this out, your eyes are sparkling! It's like you've really come alive!"

Ted pictures himself on stage, in full drag, entertaining an enraptured audience. He sees himself cracking a risqué joke and everyone roaring with laughter. He sees himself dancing like a Pussycat Doll, hair-whipping with abandon. An electric pulse runs through him.

"But what would my parents say?" he throws in. "They'd be

devastated if they knew I didn't want to work for the business."

Denise shakes her head. "Teddy, what are you on about? Nobody's talking about you suddenly giving up your job. But that doesn't mean you can't explore the idea of being a drag queen."

Ted dashes his hand over his eyes. "It's not as simple as that, Den. My parents don't just want me to work for the business, they want me to *enjoy* doing it. They love it, so they want me to love it too."

"But you *don't* love it, honey! And you can't *make* yourself love something just to keep other people happy. God knows you've tried!"

Ted exhales. "I know, I know. But I just can't bear to let them down. So I pretend I love it."

Denise looks at him, determination burning in her eyes. "Teddy, I'm not going to have you back out of this now. I'm not going to sit by while you go on pretending—maybe even for the rest of your life—just so you don't hurt your mum and dad's feelings. I'm not going to let you miss out on doing what *you* want to do."

Ted crinkles his nose. "You're very persuasive . . ."

Denise stands up and starts pacing the room. "Just think about it, me and you could go to a few drag clubs and see if you get some inspiration. We could go to that drag shop in Blackpool and see what kind of things you'd like to wear. And I'd love to experiment with your makeup. We could have a play around and work out your look."

"I have to say, it does sound very tempting."

She makes for the door. "Let me get my diary! We need to block out some dates!"

Ted suddenly feels his conviction waver. "Hold on a minute, Den. I'm forty-three. Aren't I too old? Haven't I left it too late?"

She puts her hands on her hips. "Oh, stop talking crap! You're never too old, Teddy! It's never too late!"

"Are you sure? I mean, some of the queens on *RuPaul's Drag Race* are young enough to be my daughter—without even making me a gymslip mother. I've got jars of jam in my fridge that are older than some of them."

Denise pushes out a breath. "Alright, so you've got a choice. Either you start your engine a bit later than most queens or you don't start it at all. What's it going to be?"

Ted bites his lip. "But how do I know I'm not just getting excited about this because I've drunk too much prosecco?"

Denise sits down again. "Well, why don't you wait till the morning and see how you feel when you're sober?"

"Alright, that's a good idea."

She cocks her head. "Actually, give it a few days—you don't want to make the decision on a hangover."

A mischievous glint enters her eye.

"Because prepare yourself—I'm opening another bottle!"

CHAPTER 9

By Ted's second week back at work, the diplomatic silences and supportive smiles that first greeted the news of his split with Giles have morphed into expressions of support and sympathy. *And I don't want to be ungrateful, but it feels like an onslaught.*

"Are you sure you're alright, love?"

"Do you fancy a nice cuppa?"

"You know, when you're ready to start dating again, I've got a lovely nephew who's gay."

While Ted appreciates the sentiment behind each comment—and makes sure to respond to each of them politely—they make him feel exposed and uncomfortable. After the excitement of his evening with Denise, they remind him that he's failed. And he doesn't want to feel like a failure; he wants to feel good about himself. *Well, if I am going to start prioritizing what I want, if I am going to start putting myself first, I should try to stop listening to them.*

When it's time for lunch, he checks the back office. As usual, Dorothy has taken one of her extended lunch breaks. He pops to the bakery next door and buys himself his favorite meat-and-potato pasty. Then, as he reaches the exit, he goes back to the counter and buys himself another. Once he's safely in his office, he closes the door behind him and shuts the blinds. *That's it; I'm just going to shut everyone out. I'm going to shut out everyone's sympathy.*

He sits down at the stained and scratched oak desk that's been there for decades and leans back in the much more modern yet creaky chair. He flicks through a news website on his phone and devours his first pasty in three bites. When he comes to an article about people emerging from the pandemic with a renewed determination to pursue their dreams, he stops to read it—and his mind returns to his own dream of becoming a drag queen. But he's distracted by something in his peripheral vision.

What's that?

Sitting at the top of the post tray is an envelope with his name on it. While this isn't anything remotely out of the ordinary, this particular envelope looks different from all the others, which are usually branded with the logos of suppliers or utility companies. He wipes his fingers on a napkin and picks it up.

The address of the shop and his name have been printed in block capitals on a white label that's stuck to the front of a plain white envelope. He rips it open, pulls out the letter and begins to read.

TED,
WATCH OUT. YOUR FAMILY ISN'T AS PERFECT AS YOU THINK IT IS. I KNOW A SECRET THAT WOULD CHANGE EVERYTHING.

His breath stops in his chest.

He can't believe it. It's like something out of *Midsomer Murders* or *Murder She Wrote.*

He snatches a breath and reads the letter again.

The few lines of text are printed on a regular sheet of white

A4 paper in a standard font, probably Times New Roman. It could have come out of any printer in pretty much any office. There's no signature and no information about who sent it at all.

Who could it be? And why would somebody want to send me something like this?

He stands up and goes over to the little kitchen area. He fills the kettle from the tap and flicks it on.

Actually, it's probably some kind of prank. Or someone trying to cause trouble. I bet they'll be asking for money next.

But the adrenaline is coursing through him, and he can't quell his curiosity.

Once he's made a cup of tea, he goes back to his seat and picks up the envelope again. He notices that it's been stamped with a local postmark. *So whoever sent it must live nearby . . .*

He corrugates his brow. *Actually, they don't have to; they could have just driven to the area to make it* look *like they do.*

He searches for some other lead but can't come up with anything. *Then again, sending anonymous letters seems so old-fashioned; it must have come from an older person . . .*

He tugs a hand through his hair. *Unless it's a young person trying to make me* think *it's from an old person.*

A coil of anxiety tightens in his stomach. He examines the letter again. He has no idea what secret the sender is referring to, but it makes him feel very uneasy.

He considers showing the letter to his parents, but he wouldn't want to cause them any worry, especially not with all the financial stress they're under. *And how devastated they are about me splitting up with Giles.*

He decides to try and block it out of his mind, just like he's trying to block out everyone's sympathy. He'll just have to make a massive effort not to think about it—or to give in to any of the thoughts it prompts.

He tucks the letter away in his pocket.

But, as he tucks into his second pasty, already his resolve is giving way.

Ted looked at his mum, lying in bed surrounded by her family.

"You know what," she said, making sure she had everyone's attention. "I've got t' best family in t' world."

Hilary had just been admitted to St. Luke's General Hospital, where she was on a ward waiting to go into the operating room. The previous week—after a routine mammogram—she'd been diagnosed with stage-four breast cancer. The news had come as a complete shock to the whole family, though they didn't really have time to process it; as Hilary was still relatively young—just 51—the doctors wanted to operate as soon as possible. Jemima had traveled up from London and she, Trevor and Ted had brought Hilary into hospital. Now they were waiting to see her off. *And trying to fill her with as much hope as possible.*

"Never mind that," said Ted. "We've got the best mum in the world."

"Absolutely," said Jemima.

"And I've got the best wife in the world," added Trevor.

Hilary opened her mouth to speak, but her emotions got the better of her. She drew in a shaky breath, then slowly released it.

When Hilary had received her diagnosis, it had knocked the wind out of her—usually very perky—sails. As if someone had flicked a switch, her characteristic sense of fun had vanished. And it was only now that it was gone that Ted could appreciate the full force of her strength. It was only now it was gone that he could appreciate how important she was in holding the family together—and not just the family but the business too. When Trevor had announced the news to the workforce, it had instantly changed the atmosphere throughout Ainsworth's. It was clear that all the company's employees were frightened of losing Hilary.

Away from work, Ted was struggling to cope with the diagnosis. This was his first experience of any kind of serious illness and, from the minute he found out, he couldn't think about anything else. He spent various evenings crying on Giles's shoulder and various nights lying awake, worrying about what would happen to his mum. Torturing himself thinking about how much pain she'd be in. Telling himself that he needed to be strong for her. *Imagining what would happen if we lost her.*

Hilary's illness must have had a similar effect on Trevor and Jemima, as it had prompted the entire family to have a series of long, heartfelt conversations. The words "I love you" made their first appearance since Ted and Jemima were children. And, as the date of Hilary's surgery approached, these appearances became increasingly frequent.

"We love you, Mum," Ted reiterated.

"Totally," chipped in Jemima. "We couldn't possibly love you any more."

Hilary tugged in another breath and smoothed out the sheets. "Ta, kids. That's lovely to hear."

"And you just remember," said Trevor, "we're all right here with you. And we're not going anywhere; we'll be right here when you come round."

"We'll get through this together," added Ted.

He was encouraged to see his mum manage a smile. Ever since her diagnosis, Hilary had looked pale and drained—but, even though she was wearing no makeup and a hospital gown she complained made her look washed out, Ted was sure he could see a hint of her vim and verve returning.

"Actually, I can do this," she announced, sitting up against her stack of pillows. "If you three are with me, I know I can do it."

She held out her hands and Ted and Jemima inched forward

on their plastic chairs to take hold of one each. Sitting on the bed between them, Trevor clasped onto each of his children— so all four of them were connected. As they gave one another's hands a squeeze, Hilary's smile grew brighter. And Ted knew that she was right: she *could* do this.

He didn't think the four of them had ever been closer. And he didn't think he'd ever been given such a powerful message about the importance of family.

CHAPTER 10

As Ted walks Lily back from the promenade—they couldn't go down to the beach today because the tide was high—he replays in his head his conversation with Denise. For what feels like the millionth time, he repeats her advice about putting himself first. And he tries to convince himself to go ahead and explore the idea of becoming a drag queen.

Could I really do it? Quiet, unassuming, inconspicuous Ted, who's spent his entire adult life working in his mum and dad's ice-cream shop?

He passes the statue of the prince and once again notices the camp bend in his leg—but this time it feels like it's urging him on, urging him to follow his dream.

When he comes to the gold-painted hippos, as ever he's struck by how much they stand out from their surroundings—but this time it makes him think. *Now, do I want to be like them, or do I want to carry on trying to fit in?*

Lily gives a little bark.

"What do you reckon, Lil?"

She barks again, but he can tell she just wants to go home. She hasn't been herself for the last few weeks; he thinks she must be missing Giles.

You and me both, Lil.

He looks up at the slate-gray sky that's been threatening rain all morning. "Come on," he says. "Let's get you home."

He quickens his step and passes the little row of shops, then turns off the main road and onto his street.

"Would you vada the eek on that?"

He turns around to see the elderly man with dazzling white hair he'd first noticed a few weeks ago. He's standing in the doorway of one of the retirement flats, sipping tea from the same antique china cup and saucer, but today he's wearing a pastel pink shirt with a floral necktie that's pinned at the collar with a diamante brooch in the shape of a flamingo.

"Sorry?" says Ted.

The man tilts his head, as if he's appraising a cute kitten. "Well, aren't you a dolly feely-omi?"

Ted creases his forehead. "I've literally no idea what you're talking about."

The man comes closer and leans on the fence. Ted notices that his cheeks are dabbed with blusher and his nails are painted pink. All of a sudden, he feels dowdy in his faded jeans, scuffed trainers, and gray waterproof. *Oh, who am I kidding? As if I could be a drag queen!*

"I'm speaking Polari," the man says, with a flamboyant twist of his wrist. "It's from the nineteenth century. It's the secret language of queers."

Ted breaks into a smile. "Oh, I've heard of that."

"Fantabulosa!" trills the man. "So I was right!"

"You what?"

The man rests his cup and saucer on the fence post. "Just that I've seen you walking past here a few times and had an inkling you were a fruit. Or at least that's what I was hoping." He holds out his hand. "Stanley Openshaw. Charmed to meet you."

Ted isn't sure whether to shake his hand or kiss it. As it's facing down, he opts for a kiss. "Ted, Ted Ainsworth."

"Oooh, like the ice cream?"

"Yeah, that's my family's business."

Stanley's eyes glitter. "Oh, how splendid. I love Ainsworth's!"

Ted has come to expect reactions like this and follows it up with his usual, "What's your favorite flavor?"

"Raspberry pavlova," Stanley replies without hesitation, "closely followed by peaches and cream. I used to love that as a boy."

"Oh, so you grew up here?"

"Yes, dolly. I'm a true Sandgrownun, born and brought up in St. Luke's—my dad used to be a shrimper in Lytham. But I had to leave the area when I was a teenager."

Ted spots a memory dart behind Stanley's eyes, but it doesn't make it to his lips.

"I spent most of my adult life in Manchester," Stanley moves on, swiftly. "I worked in a gentlemen's tailor's and outfitter's. The owner and most of the staff were fruits. It was—as we say in Polari—fantabulosa."

He explains that, although homosexuality was still illegal in the 1950s, when he moved to Manchester, he and his friends used to frequent a little network of underground bars. Later, he became involved with the Campaign for Homosexual Equality and then the Manchester Gay Alliance—later still, attending the city's first ever Pride. But as he grew older, his pace slowed, and he started to feel disconnected from all the youthful energy that was fueling the boom in nightlife on and around Canal Street. When he hit eighty, he reluctantly retired from work and, as one by one his friends fell ill, lost their faculties, or died, he became bored and lonely. And when he hit ninety, he was surprised to find himself drawn back to his hometown to spend his final years by the sea—and that was how he ended up renting his flat in Memory House.

"But there's one big problem," he says, tartly.

"Oh yeah, what's that?"

"Several of the other residents are homophobic. They're always making snide remarks about my clothes or makeup. The other day, one of the gentlemen even made fun of my limp wrist. I said to him, 'Is that the best you can do? I haven't heard that one for years!'"

"Oh, I'm sorry," says Ted. "That must be awful, especially after you've spent so long fighting to gain people's respect."

"Well, yes, to be quite frank, it is." Stanley pauses and his eyes twinkle. "But it's also *galvanizing*!"

"How do you mean?"

"Well, I'm not just going to stand around and take it—I'm going to do something about it . . . I just have to work out what."

Ted gives his head a little shake. "Oh. Right. That's brilliant."

"Why are you looking at me like that? Just because I'm an old lady doesn't mean I've lost my fight. I'll *never* lose that. And I'll never give up!"

Before Ted can express his admiration, the first drops of rain fall on his face. He quickly fastens his waterproof and pulls his hood up. "Sorry, Stanley, we're going to have to continue our chat some other time. You get inside before you're soaked!"

Stanley gives him a little wave. "Alright. Ta-ta, dolly."

"Bye!"

As Ted jogs towards his house, he keeps his head down. But he's surprised not to feel disheartened by the weather. On the contrary, he feels upbeat and positive.

Stanley's in his nineties, but he still isn't going to let life pass him by. He's determined to make the most of it.

He feels a rush of hope. And he realizes that Denise is right—the breakup of his marriage has given him an opportunity to make some changes. This really is his chance to live a life that doesn't revolve around other people. And he isn't going to suppress his dream any longer.

His heart hammers with excitement.

Yes, I'm going to do it. I'm going to put myself first. I'm going to become a drag queen.

CHAPTER 11

It's Sunday morning and Oskar takes his bike out of the steel storage unit at the side of his caravan and wheels it down the pathway. He's dressed all in black, in fleece-lined cycling shorts; a stretch-mesh jersey; and his favorite ventilated, molded helmet. It's a bright, clear day but, as it's only mid-April, the weather can change, so he's taking a lightweight waterproof gilet that he's rolled up and stuffed in his back pocket. At the thought of the day ahead, his body thrums with excitement. But just as he's about to lift himself onto the seat, he's stopped by his neighbor.

"Hi, toots, how are you?"

Marina Buckland lives in the caravan next door to Oskar and is a slim woman in her early fifties, with a skin tone he thinks might be Latin and jet-black hair that's now streaked with gray—to which she's added a streak of blue at the front. She tends to wear patterned, floaty dresses or baggy harem pants, together with an abundance of ethnic jewelry made from jasper, amethyst, and moonstone. Oskar tries to keep himself to himself so doesn't know much about her but, when she moved in the previous summer, she knocked on his door to introduce herself. He remembers feeling like she was invading his personal space and noticing that she smelled like a scented candle, although a very nice one. He also remembers that she was very chatty, telling him she ran Alternativa, the New-Age shop situated down an alleyway off the high street that sells everything from meditation cushions, incense, and oil burners, to zodiac-inspired art and books about astrology and spiritual improvement.

"Every seaside town has one," she said, rolling her eyes in amusement.

"Does it?" said Oskar. *Not in Poland.*

"I guess you could say I'm the town hippie," Marina went on. "But I'm fine with that. I'm what you might call a free spirit!"

A few weeks later, Oskar was taking out the rubbish one night when he noticed Marina struggling to get her key into the door—and, he soon realized, struggling to even stand up. He rushed over and offered to help and, between hiccups, she explained she'd been out for dinner with her friends but had bumped into the wife of a married man she'd been seeing. She then bombarded Oskar with intimate details of their affair and all the devastation and anger she'd felt when the man had ended it. Oskar suddenly felt desperate to get away. It wasn't that he was prudish or disapproved of the affair, but alcohol had erased the last of Marina's—already very indistinct— boundaries. He quickly helped her into her caravan and bolted.

The next morning, Marina appeared on his doorstep, ashen-faced, complaining of a terrible hangover and thanking him for his help. Then she broke down in tears and began telling Oskar that she was lonely and worried she'd never find love. He had to invite her inside and comfort her, even at one point putting an arm around her so she could literally cry on his shoulder. The memory of it makes him squirm.

He manages to twist out a smile. "Yeah, I'm fine, thanks, Marina. I'm just off on a bike ride."

Please don't try and talk to me . . .

"How lovely!" Marina steps back from loading up her car boot. "So you're not doing anything for Easter?"

Oskar had forgotten it was Easter Sunday. "Oh, no . . . No . . . Easter's not really my thing."

Marina mistakes his discomfort for offense. "Sorry, I'm *so* sorry! You know, I'm not remotely religious; I try to steer clear of structured and repressive forms of spirituality. Although I do think some of the Christian festivals can be a nice prompt for us to get together with friends." She gestures to her car boot and a wicker basket full of food, wine, and Easter eggs. "That's my excuse, anyway!"

Oskar isn't sure what to say. He just wants to end the conversation so he can set off on his bike. "Well, have a nice time," he attempts.

But Marina clearly isn't finished. She closes the boot and leans against it. "You know what, Oskar? I've lived next door to you for nearly a year now, and I still know hardly anything about you."

Oskar presses down on the grips of his handlebars. "Oh, there's not much to tell."

"Well, you're not religious, we've established that much. And I know you live on your own. But is there anyone special in your life?"

He tries not to flinch. "No, just my bike." He gives the handlebars a couple of taps he hopes come across as jolly. "But that's enough for me!"

He lifts himself onto the seat and slides his feet into the pedals. *Come on, Marina, take the hint . . .*

She pushes herself off the car. "Alright, well, I'll let you go. Have a good bike ride!"

Thank God for that!

"Thanks," he manages.

Marina opens the car door, then stops. "And however you choose to interpret it, have a good Easter!"

Oskar gives her a wave over his shoulder. "You too!"

But, as he cycles through the caravan park towards the exit, he resolves not to give the significance of the day any more thought. *If I have my way, this'll be just like any other Sunday* . . .

Oskar cycles along the seafront, passing the piece of art that's supposed to represent the spirit of the town—but which he can't see without remembering one critic's description of it as looking like "a butch prison warder curling out a stubborn dump." He smiles and gives the statue a wave.

Once he's sped past the Art Deco bandstand, the hotels gradually thin out and the promenade comes to an end. As he's traveling in a northerly direction, his view to the left is dominated by the beach, with the sand dunes bobbing up before it, sometimes spilling over onto the pavement, at some points even creeping onto the road. To his right is the town's biggest car park, and behind that the pretty boating lake that's home to the West Lancashire Yacht Club and on which a few lone men are paddling canoes or kayaks.

He pedals on.

Once he's passed the old white windmill, he comes to a stretch of gloriously clear coastline. He marvels at the color palette opening up before him: the perfect teal of the glittering Irish Sea, the coral blue of the infinite expanse of sky, and—to the east—the luscious greens of the Lancashire countryside, enhanced by rays from the cornflower-yellow sun. As the wind buffets his face, he lets out a whoop of joy.

Going out on his bike is something Oskar has always enjoyed. When he was young, cycling along the north coast of Poland was his favorite activity—and something he did with his favorite companion. He imagines one of the reasons he still loves it is because it brings back happy memories. *If only those memories weren't outnumbered by all the unhappy ones. If only they weren't spoiled by one particularly unhappy memory.*

He reassures himself that he doesn't have to revisit any of that now. *That's why you left Poland, to put it all behind you.*

He sometimes feels guilty about putting so much distance

between himself and his home country—and especially his family. Occasionally, when he speaks to his mum on the phone or over FaceTime, she'll subtly accuse him of shirking his duty. His sister, on the other hand, isn't remotely subtle about it. She lives just down the road from his mum so is the first to be called on in case of illness or emergency—and never lets Oskar forget it. Whenever she stokes his guilt, his only way of easing it is to send home more money. But this never erases it completely.

He passes a church with a full car park and the sound of organ music coming from inside. Its exterior is constructed of plain limestone, the windows are transparent rather than stained glass, and the sole decoration is a rudimentary iron cross rising from the steeple. Oskar has noticed that the churches in England tend to be much less ornamental than they are in Catholic Poland, where they're adorned with an abundance of statues and religious iconography. In fact, it isn't unusual in his home country to see lovingly maintained shrines to Our Lady at the side of country roads, such as the ones along the coast where he grew up. His mum even has a shrine of her own in the family home. Oskar remembers the sound of her whispering her prayers as she worked her way along the rosary, the beads gently rattling against each other. His gut twists with more guilt.

He tries to dispel it by telling himself that he doesn't have to revisit memories of religion either. *Not when it caused me so much heartache.*

Here in this little corner of England, he feels much freer. And never is this feeling more pronounced than when he's cycling by the sea. It's as if the wealth of openness unshackles his spirit and allows it to take flight and soar.

He shifts gear to climb a bridge over the railway line, then dips again to enter a little village with its own stretch of beach. He slows down to avoid a huddle of pedestrians walking along the narrow pavement, some of them stepping into the road. He tries not to notice as two teenage girls point at his muscular calves, elbowing each other and sharing a giggle. And he can't stop his attention snagging on a couple who are sitting on a bench with their backs to him, gazing out to sea, arm in arm.

If only I had someone to share my life with.

For a long time, Oskar has felt lonely. For a long time he's yearned to share his life with another person—another man. But despite the strength of his feeling, he still isn't comfortable expressing this side of himself. Or, perhaps more accurately, he's comfortable in theory, but when it comes down to it, he can't help but give in to his fears.

If he's being really honest with himself, Oskar is so full of fear that he struggles to open up to anyone. *Look at what just happened with Marina. She only asked if there was anyone special in my life, and I pedaled off as if she'd told me she was radioactive.*

This same fear has stopped him from establishing friendships with his colleagues from work. Whenever any of them ask him anything vaguely personal, he retreats into himself. On the rare occasion one of them asks him a direct question about his love life, he fobs them off with vague excuses about a run of bad luck, being careful to avoid all mention of anything gender-specific. He doesn't want to lie, nor can he bring himself to tell the truth.

He leaves the village, crosses another bridge over the railway line, and emerges on a section of coastline that juts out to sea. Now all that stands before him is the shimmering endlessness of teal, interrupted only by a few buoys near the shore, a smattering of sailing boats a little further out, a sole ship that's so big he can't tell if it's actually moving, and, in the distance, an indistinct blur that could be an oil rig—although he can't be sure. As he gazes out at the horizon, it strikes him just how big the world is. *And here I am, all alone.*

Something stirs within him.

Well, I don't have to be.

The idea of finding a relationship may be daunting, but he could at least try to open up to the people around him, could at least try to make some friends.

He tells himself that he'll start with Marina. There's no reason for him to avoid her all the time. She may be eccentric and a bit of a hippie, but he, too, has felt that he doesn't fit into the mainstream. She may pride herself on taking a stand against organized religion, but he, too, is mistrustful of a faith that's only been a negative force in his life. Also, she's told him that she's lonely and wants to be loved—and he's just admitted the same thing to himself. Now that he thinks about it, he and Marina might even have a lot in common. *I shouldn't be so . . . What's that really good word I learnt the other day? Standoffish.*

He decides that the next time he sees Marina, he'll speak to her. He'll start with just a short, casual chat—the kind of chat she attempted to initiate with him earlier—but it'll be a step in the right direction. *And I can always assess how I feel after that.*

He presses down on the pedals and picks up speed, the wind roaring around him. And he feels a surge of confidence.

Yes, I'm going to chat to Marina. And it's going to be fine.

CHAPTER 12

Without telling anyone, the following Saturday Ted and Denise slip away from St. Luke's-on-Sea. They catch a taxi to Blackpool, where they're about to take the first step on Ted's journey to becoming a drag queen: they're going for a night out on the gay scene.

To make this possible, Ted has had to evade his parents. They're hosting a dinner party for their friends, the Underhills, whose daughters Ted has known since he was a boy. As one of these daughters has just split up with her husband, Hilary and Trevor wanted Ted to join them, convinced he'd enjoy the company. But he pretended he was going to the anniversary party of a couple of gay friends who live on the outskirts of Manchester, despite the fact that neither one of them has bothered to even text him since Giles left. Then he felt guilty for lying. *But it's one of those white lies that don't really count, because this is important. It's part of my plan to put myself first.*

Into his head pops the anonymous letter he received—and its claim that his family isn't as perfect as he thinks. *If that's true, then maybe I shouldn't be feeling guilty at all . . .* Then he feels guilty for thinking that.

He reminds himself that he's trying to ignore the letter. *Right, I'm not going to think about it anymore.*

When they arrive in Blackpool, he and Denise step out of the taxi and head straight into a place called The Fairy's Tail—although it strikes Ted that it's more like a public toilet with a bar than a pub. They're the only ones who aren't dressed in leather or don't have a neck covered in tattoos or a prominent—and painful-looking—face piercing. More to the point, Denise is the only woman. Before long, several of the men are arrowing murderous looks at her.

"This is awful," she mouths. "I feel about as welcome as a wasp in a lift."

They drink up and move on.

"Sorry about that," says Ted, once they're outside. "I'm a bit out of practice when it comes to the gay scene. I promise this next place will be better."

They head across the road to Queen of Clubs, a cabaret lounge that stages regular drag shows that Ted has read about online. When he agreed to Denise's suggestion of visiting a drag club to find inspiration, this was the first place that occurred to him. But now he's standing outside, he feels a clutch of fear.

God, can I really do this?

"Come on," says Denise, as if reading his mind. "You're not backing out now."

Before Ted can argue, she pays their entrance fee to a woman who for no discernible reason is dressed as a milkmaid. Once their transaction has gone through, the woman throws open the doors.

Bursting into life before them is a colorful chaos of nonconformity. The club has been decorated according to a home-made aesthetic, with plastic ivy and fake flowers pinned around the fringes of the ceiling, shimmering strips of silver foil stuck to the back of the stage, walls covered in murals that could easily have been painted by five-year-olds, and rickety tables and chairs that look like they've been thrown out of offices, classrooms and even a church. It's packed with a crowd of men of all ages and a decent number of women, plus several people Ted imagines identify as falling somewhere in between—or possibly encompassing both. Dancing to a high-energy track by 1980s band Dead or Alive is a woman dressed from head to toe in camouflage and a thickset man with a beard like an overgrown bush, who's wearing a Japanese kimono and has a gold crown perched on top of his head.

Ted feels intoxicated and exhilarated by the unpretentious, nonjudgmental, more than a little louche atmosphere. He's glad that earlier in the week, he'd felt brave enough to give in to his longstanding urge to update his look, an urge he'd suppressed when Giles discouraged it. So he's ditched his usual short-back-and-sides haircut in favor of a more edgy undercut with a fade and has swapped his typical understated wardrobe of unpatterned, muted colors bought from the same safe selection of high street stores for a recent flurry of more adventurous online purchases: a pair of slim, cropped blue-denim jeans; a white fitted shirt that looks like it's been splattered with blue and red paint; and a pair of vintage suede trainers in color-blocked navy and turquoise. *Although I get the impression that nobody would mind if I'd turned up wearing a bin bag with a frying pan on top of my head.*

"Isn't this ace?" he says to Denise.

"There's certainly a lot to take in," she replies. "But yeah, I love it."

"You know, I've always wanted to come here, but Giles never would. He always said going out on the gay scene was a cliché."

Denise doesn't miss a beat. "See, honey, he was holding you back. I told you, he stopped you from blossoming."

Ted tucks his hands under his armpits but says nothing.

"Anyway, this place isn't clichéd at all," Denise goes on. "I've never seen anything like it!"

Ted frowns. "Come on, let's get a drink."

They weave their way through the throng, narrowly avoiding a collision with a man wearing ripped black jeans and an Iron Maiden T-shirt and a person of indeterminable gender who's wearing a scarlet lace-trimmed facemask that looks like a pair of knickers. As Ted orders two margaritas, he spots a pair of drag queens standing further along the bar. According to the club's social media posts, the stars of tonight's show are two queens called Peg Legge and Pussy Squat.

"They must be the girls who are on tonight," he tells Denise, nodding towards them as he hands over her drink. "Which one do you think is which?"

They examine the performers, one of whom is a middle-aged, dumpy, roll-necked queen, dressed from head to toe in pink, while the other is a statuesque black girl in fishnet tights and a purple body suit, her makeup dominated by two thick streaks of metallic gold eyeshadow that are lined with glitter.

"The older one's got to be Peg Legge," Denise says. "I can't imagine her doing a pussy squat."

Ted furrows his brow. "What's a pussy squat?"

"Teddy!" Denise looks at him as if a palm tree has just sprouted from his head. "It's another name for a slut drop!"

"Oh yeah, of course!" Ted turns back to the older queen and tries to picture her doing a slut drop. He lets out a loud honk of a laugh.

"What are you laughing at?" The older queen comes stalking towards them, trailed by her friend.

Shit, you asked for that. Ted tips back half his margarita.

"Oh nothing," he burbles. "We were just saying how much we're looking forward to your show."

Their faces are smoothed by smiles.

"Well, I hope you enjoy it," says the black girl, towering over Ted in a pair of heels. "We'll be asking for a full review later."

"I'm Peg Legge," says the older queen. "This is my sister, Pussy Squat."

So Denise was right.

"Pleased to meet you," says Ted.

The queens compliment Denise on her mint-green halter-neck jumpsuit, her winged eyeliner, and nude lip.

"Thanks," she says, clearly flattered. "You two look gorge."

Peg pulls a face. "I don't know. I'm a bit worried about my dress. Do you think it makes me look like a tub of taramosalata?"

Ted hears a voice say, "More like a bottle of Pepto-Bismol—except one that *gives* you indigestion." Then he realizes it was his.

Shit, why did I say that?

There's a long pause, and Ted worries he's offended Peg. Then she gives a laugh that rolls like a barrel.

"That's a good one. You don't mind if I use it, do you?"

Ted breaks into a grin. "I'd be honored."

"Come on, girl," says Pussy, tugging on Peg's arm. "We need to make a move. We're on in ten minutes!"

Ted and Denise wish the queens good luck.

Once they've gone, Denise grabs Ted's elbow. "Come on, we've just got time for a dance."

Ted stiffens. "Oh, I don't know . . ."

Into his head thumps Giles's joke about him dancing like a tipsy chicken.

"I *do* know," Denise insists. "And I know you're going to enjoy it."

Ted doesn't argue.

They leave their empty glasses on the bar and nudge their way through the crowd and into the center of the dance floor. A 1970s disco classic is playing—"Born to Be Alive" by Patrick Hernandez—and Ted can't help but feel uplifted by its energy. He's now been to four sessions of his dance exercise class and has loved expressing himself through movement, but he still hasn't done this outside of the community center—and at first it feels a little awkward. But, as he and Denise wiggle, shake, and shimmy, he starts to relax. Soon he's experiencing that familiar feeling of being awash with joy.

When the song gives way to Baccara's "Yes Sir, I Can Boogie," the person in the lace-trimmed facemask and a man dressed exclusively in tartan jiggle their way towards Ted and Denise and start prancing around them. Perhaps it's the comic, tongue-in-cheek lyrics, but straight away, all four of them are smiling. And, as they twist and twirl to the beat, once again Ted feels ablaze with confidence.

Out of the corner of his eye, he spots a technician swing up onto the stage and start assembling a microphone stand.

"Come on," Denise shouts into his ear. "Let's get to the bar before the show starts."

Once they've said goodbye to their new friends and bought themselves another margarita, they squeeze into a spot on a slightly raised area next to the cloakroom, from where they have a good view of the stage.

"Here we go, honey," says Denise. "It's show time!"

The performance begins with a comedy duet, a reworked, naughty version of "I Know Him So Well," which pits the two queens against each other, fighting over a man. Then Peg does a stand-up set that showcases her outrageous sense of humor—and does indeed include Ted's line about Pepto-Bismol and indigestion, which he's pleased to see gets one of the biggest laughs of the night. Then Pussy takes over, singing and dancing to a medley of numbers by 00s girl groups. She's an athletic, acrobatic dancer, and Ted's delighted to see her perform the most incredible slut drops he's ever seen. Finally, Peg reappears and the two queens round off the show with another duet—a sexually explicit version of "Anything You Can Do, I Can Do Better."

Throughout the show, Ted is transfixed. He can't help

thinking of the kind of performance he'd like to give and the drag persona he'd like to adopt. As he does, he becomes aware of just how much his spirit has been suppressed and shackled. He's aware of it struggling to break free.

"You're right, Den," he tells her as soon as the applause has ended. "I think Giles has held me back."

She narrows her eyes. "Why do you suddenly say that? Were you wishing it was you up there?"

"I was, yeah. I couldn't stop thinking about it."

"Really? Tell me more."

But before he can reply, they're interrupted by Peg and Pussy.

"So what did you think?" Pussy asks. "Did you like my cunt dips?"

Ted spits a mouthful of his margarita back into the glass. "Sorry, yeah," he manages. "You were dead good. Ace."

"And how about my stand-up?" asks Peg.

"Hilarious," says Ted. "I loved every minute of it."

"Ted's going to be a drag queen," Denise suddenly announces, without the slightest preamble.

They both turn to look at him.

In an instant, all possible responses desert Ted. "Well, yeah, I, urm . . ."

"Just a minute," says Peg, arching an eyebrow. "Are you going to be a drag queen or aren't you?"

Ted snatches a quick breath and pushes it out. "Yes. Yes, I am."

"Well, that's great news!" gushes Pussy.

"Girl, we'd better watch out!" says Peg. "This bitch is coming to get us!"

They tell Ted that Queen of Clubs hosts regular open-mic nights, at which aspiring performers are invited to book a slot and get up on stage.

"You've just missed one," says Peg, "but we're having another in three months. Why don't you enter? You'll have plenty of time to get yourself ready."

Ted feels a stab of nerves and tries to quell it with another swig of margarita. For some reason, his mind jumps to his mum and dad—and he wonders if they're enjoying their evening. *An evening I lied to get out of.*

Wait a minute, do I want to carry on lying to them?

"Thanks," he mumbles. "I'll think about it."

Just as Pussy is wagging her finger and looking like she's about to tell him off, the queens are accosted by a group of admirers.

"No excuses, girl!" warbles Pussy, as they pull her away.

"See you in a few months!" shouts Peg, over her shoulder.

Once they're on their own again, Denise tries to convince Ted to sign up.

He wrinkles his nose. "I don't know, Den. It just seems like a lot. I mean, yeah, I am desperate to get up on stage. But could I really do what they've just done?"

Denise's mouth stiffens. "Is this your parents talking again? Is this you worrying about what they'd think?"

"No, no," Ted insists, cursing himself for telling another lie. "I'm just not sure I'd be any good at it, that's all."

"Teddy, you'd be *brilliant*! There's no way I'd let you go on stage unless I was absolutely sure of it. I tell you what. How about I come up with some ideas for your makeup and we try them out one night—just me and you? And I'll see if I can find some heels in your size, and you can try walking in them."

She's so enthusiastic that Ted can't see any way out of it.

"Alright," he says. "But I'm not committing to the open-mic night. Let's see how this goes first."

Denise's eyes glisten. "Fine. Challenge accepted!"

CHAPTER 13

A week later, Ted parks his car with a crunch on the gravel driveway of his mum and dad's house. He checks his phone and sees that Denise has sent him a link to some size 10 stiletto heels she's found online. They're black patent leather, sturdy, and not particularly stylish, but she assures him they'll do nicely as a pair of "training heels."

"Ace," he texts back. **"I'll order them tonight!"**

Ever since their night out in Blackpool, Ted's imagination has been firing—and in his head, his drag persona is starting to take shape. But he still isn't sure he wants to commit to the open-mic night.

The problem is, every time he sees his parents—which is pretty much every day—he ends up feeling guilty. He knows how passionate they are about the business. He knows how much they'd like to see him share their passion and fully engage in their plans for the future. And he knows how disappointed they'd be if he told them the truth.

He imagines sitting facing them in their office, opening his mouth, and just coming out with it. *"Mum, Dad, I want to be a drag queen. And while I'm on the subject, I don't even like ice cream!"*

He imagines their faces falling. He imagines being confronted by their devastation. And another surge of guilt sluices through him.

It doesn't help that the business is going through a rough patch. Should he discard all distractions and focus on his responsibilities? He remembers his parents' motto of "Family first." *But for once in my life, I'm supposed to be putting Ted first . . .*

All this is going through his head as he takes out his key and lets himself into the house. It's Saturday evening, and his parents have invited him for tea. They still live in the house they designed and built on a plot of land in a pretty little village on the outskirts of town when Ted and Jemima were children. It's a redbrick, five-bedroom detached house surrounded by high walls, a triple driveway, and a thick wooden gate. Despite its scale, it isn't particularly grand or flashy; Ted prefers to think of it as a handsome house. And he's always thought of it as a happy home. *I still think of it as a happy home, despite that stupid letter.*

He recalls his parents' excitement as they looked over the plans for the house—and their elation on the day the family finally moved in. Thirty years later, he steps into the hall. It's dominated by a big central staircase that branches off to the left and right at a little landing, over which hangs a painting of Trevor, Hilary, Ted, and Jemima that was commissioned from a local artist just after they moved in. *Yes, we were happy.*

He hangs his coat up on a hook next to a sideboard, on top of which stands a series of family photos. There's Trevor playing cricket, sailing his boat at the Yacht Club, and posing with fellow members of St. Luke's Rotary Club. There's Hilary flanked by the committees of a few local charities and on holiday with a group of friends she still insists on calling "the girls," despite the fact they're all over sixty and most of them are grandmothers. There's a young Jemima winning several beauty pageants, then in her twenties modeling for a beer commercial and a fashion feature in *Glamour* magazine. And there's Ted and Giles on their wedding day, at a ceremony that took place in a Georgian manor house just outside St. Luke's. Suddenly, he doesn't want to be given any more reminders of his family's happiness. He wishes his parents would take that photo down and stash it away somewhere. *Mind you, I haven't taken mine down yet—or changed my screensaver.*

He hopes at least that his parents won't insist on talking about Giles. *Or at least they won't talk about him too much . . .*

"Evening!" he calls out.

He goes through to the kitchen, which has been painted artichoke green and fitted with custom-made oak units and a central island at which the family sit for informal meals. He greets his parents with a hug, and Hilary tells him she's cooked his favorite mince and bacon pie, which she's serving with chips and carrots.

"So, how are things?" she asks, once they've sat down and she's dished out the food. "How are you feeling about Giles?"

That didn't take long!

Ted stabs at his pastry. "Oh, you know, I still miss him."

But he doesn't go into detail. He doesn't tell them that he struggles eating alone, sitting at the table opposite Giles's empty chair, so has to have his meals on a tray in front of the TV. Or that he struggles when he wakes up in the morning and turns over to see an empty space next to him. Or that this week a customer came into the shop wearing Giles's aftershave, and he had to sneak off into the toilet to have a little cry.

He finishes chewing. "Then again, if he doesn't want to be with me, there's nothing I can do about it. I'm not going to sit around moping."

Hilary takes a sip of her wine. "You know, I were looking at his social media t' other day. This Javier's obviously just a passing fling."

Trevor nods. "Yeah, it won't last."

Ted swirls his wine around the glass. "Thanks, but I'm not sure that's helpful. I can't just put my life on hold, waiting for him to come back."

"But what if he's having a midlife crisis?" argues Trevor. "What if he gets over it and *does* want to come back? What if he says he's made a mistake?"

"Don't you think I've asked myself that? But I still don't think there's much chance." Ted feels the sadness bloat inside him. *This is exactly what I was worried about.*

"Yeah, but not much chance isn't the same as no chance," persists Trevor. "And isn't that worth holding on to?"

Ted tries not to bristle. "Dad, the last time we spoke about this, you said you wanted to go and see him with your cricket bat."

Hilary smiles, thinly. "He were talking about Javier, love."

"Mum, *you* called Giles a toerag! And you said I wasn't allowed to send him any ice cream!"

"Yeah, well, that were probably just the shock. You know me and your dad have always thought t' world of Giles."

How could I forget?

"And you two have always been fab together," she adds.

Have we? Have we really? Because I'm starting to doubt it . . .

But Ted keeps his thoughts inside. "Actually, would you mind if we changed the subject?"

He helps himself to more chips and smothers them in gravy. "This is ace. Thanks, Mum."

"You're welcome, love."

He notices again that Hilary holds her fork with the prongs pointing up, using it as a scoop for her food. She once told him that when she and Trevor first got together, his parents criticized her for holding her fork "the wrong way"—citing this as yet more evidence that she was "common." Hilary grew up on the only council estate in St. Luke's, in a family that didn't have much money, with a pair of brothers who both turned to petty crime. Ted knows that her worst fear has always been losing everything and falling back into a similar situation—a fear he hopes hasn't been reignited by the family's financial problems.

"How's everything going at work?" he asks.

Hilary takes a swig of her wine. "Well, we had another meeting with t' bank this week."

"Oh yeah? And do you reckon you can sort things out?" Ted makes a point of using the pronoun "you" rather than "we"—then regrets it and hopes his parents didn't notice.

"God knows, it's a right nightmare." Hilary tugs at her sleeve, covering the tattoo of a rose she had done as a teenager—a cheap, ugly tattoo in angry green ink that she's tried to remove with laser surgery but still persists as a faint outline that she hides with makeup whenever she goes anywhere special.

"The worst thing is, the other day someone asked me what we're doing for our centenary," Trevor adds. "You know it's only a few years off. We should be planning the celebrations, not worrying if we're going to be around."

Ted swallows. "Shit, are things really that bad?"

Trevor rests his knife and fork on the plate and looks Ted in the eye. "Yeah, things really are that bad. Do you want us to talk you through it? You know we'd love you to get more involved, son."

Hilary nods, hopefully. "It'd be a big support to me and your dad."

Ted first.

Ted first.

Then he remembers that line from the anonymous letter: *"Your family isn't as perfect as you think it is."*

"Actually, sorry, I'm not sure I've got anything to contribute," he says.

Then he feels a rush of guilt. *What are you doing, paying attention to some bonkers letter?*

"I just don't think finance is my forte," he adds. "Giles always looked after that side of things."

At the mention of Giles, Ted's heart takes another dip.

"While we're on the subject," pipes Hilary, "has Giles said owt to you about money? You know, dividing everything up and that?"

"No," says Ted, somberly. "We haven't spoken for weeks." *He doesn't want to speak to me.*

Hilary's face lights up. "Well, that's a good sign, i'n't it?"

"How do you mean?"

"He obviously i'n't thinking about divorce."

"Yeah, maybe . . ." Ted needs to change the subject again. "Anyway, how's Jem? She's been very quiet on the WhatsApp group. Have you heard from her?"

Hilary gives a broad grin. "Oh yeah, she went to a film premiere t' other night. Summat to do with a brand of hand cream she used to work for. Apparently it were a fab do. She said there were that much champagne they could have filled a swimming pool."

Ted feels a flare of resentment. *Why's she allowed to do that kind of thing and I'm not?*

"Ace," he manages, unconvincingly.

"You know what your sister's like," Hilary gushes on. "It's all glamour, glamour, glamour!"

Trevor smiles fondly. "I don't know, the life of a supermodel."

"Dad, I'm not sure Jem qualifies as a supermodel." Ted's alarmed by the note of bitterness in his voice.

"What are you on about, love?" froths Hilary. "She's living t' dream!"

From somewhere deep inside Ted escapes the line, "Well, at least one of us is."

Hilary puts her knife and fork down and places her hand on his. "Oh, love, I can see you're upset. We know Giles were your dream. We know he meant t' world to you."

"Hang on in there, son," says Trevor, rubbing his shoulder. "This is bound to be a tough time. Don't give up yet."

Ted feels rotten. He feels like a failure as a husband, a failure as a son, and a failure as a human being.

For a moment, he wishes he hadn't found those photos of Giles and Javier on his phone—then the two of them could have just carried on and pretended to be happy, even if this would have been a delusion. *At least then my parents wouldn't be sitting here feeling sorry for me. At least they'd still be happy.*

Hilary bounces out of her seat and starts clearing away the plates. "You stay there, love—I know just the thing!"

Hilary came back from the kitchen carrying a tray holding four bowls. "Look what I've got 'ere."

Ted was lying on the sofa under a duvet, his feet resting on the footstool. It was Saturday evening, and he'd been off school all week, suffering from a heavy cold and a chest infection. In all his ten years, he wasn't sure he'd ever been as poorly. And, after a week of being fed canned tomato soup and beans on toast by his mum, he still didn't feel much better. In solidarity—and as a special treat—the other three members of his family had joined him: his mum and sister on the armchairs and his dad on the sofa alongside him, sharing the duvet. They'd demolished a stack of takeaway pizzas as they watched TV.

The Ainsworths' Saturday night viewing had begun with the brand-new American series, *Baywatch*. Although Ted loved the show, sitting through it with his family could be a tense experience. He really fancied the lifeguards in their red shorts, jumping out of helicopters, swimming through waves, or running along the beach clutching their little rescue buoys, their muscles rippling in the California sunshine. Tonight, as he watched, he could feel his face staining the same red as the lifeguards' shorts. He hoped his mum and dad wouldn't notice. *What would they say if they knew I fancied boys, not girls? Would they stop loving me?*

"When I grow up," six-year-old Jemima announced brightly, "I'm going to marry Mitch."

Me too, thought Ted. *Me too.*

"I hate to disappoint you, love," breathed Hilary, "but we don't get lifeguards like that in St. Luke's. More's the pity."

You're telling me.

"Well, I'm going to move away," Jemima went on. "I'm going to move to California and find him!"

"Good luck, love," said Hilary. "If you find Bruce Willis while you're there, chuck him my way."

Into Ted's head burst an image of the muscle-bound, hairy-chested Bruce Willis in his muddied, blood-stained vest in *Die Hard*. His insides billowed.

"Budge up, Ted," broke in Trevor, squeezing his slippers onto the footstool. "You're hogging the pouf."

As usual, Ted flinched at the sound of that word. Heat flooded his face.

"Here, give me those feet," Trevor said.

Ted slid his feet onto his dad's lap, taking up the position in which the two of them usually watched TV. Trevor began to gently massage Ted's toes.

This time, though, Ted couldn't relax. He was so on edge, his hands were sweating. *If Dad knew the truth about me, would he want me out of his family?* While no one was looking, he wiped his hands on the duvet.

Once *Baywatch* was over, Ted felt an enormous relief.

That was when his mum popped into the kitchen—during

the advert break before *Blind Date*—and came back carrying a tray. Ted knew exactly what was on it.

As the title sequence played, Hilary handed out four bowls of ice cream. Each member of the family had their own favorite: while Trevor preferred dandelion and burdock, Hilary opted for rum and raisin, Jemima liked Blackpool rock (including bits of actual crushed rock!), and Ted plumped for plain old vanilla. Every time one of them was ill or feeling down about something—or if one of them had something to celebrate—Hilary would bring out the ice cream. And every time, Ted would pretend he loved it.

"There you go, love," said Hilary, handing him his bowl. "Get that down you."

"Thanks, Mum," said Ted, sitting up.

As he spooned some into his mouth, on the TV Cilla Black introduced the show's first contestants. They were three handsome men, one of whom—Darren from Doncaster—had blond hair in curtains and looked like Jason Donovan. Ted imagined what it would be like to run his fingers through that hair. He imagined what it would be like to kiss him. He could feel himself blushing to the tips of his ears.

This is horrible. I don't want to be like this. I just want to be normal. I just want to be the same as the rest of my family.

He crammed more ice cream into his mouth. "Mum," he chirped, "I think I feel better already."

"There you are," she breathed—and Ted knew what was coming next—"there's nowt that can't be fixed with ice cream."

"You're right there," said Trevor.

Ted made a big show of how much he was enjoying his. And he forced himself to stop imagining kissing Darren from Doncaster.

No, I'm not going to be different. I'm going to be the same as everyone else.

And he snuggled up to his dad under the duvet.

"There's nowt that can't be fixed with ice cream," says Hilary, as she returns to the table with three bowls, "and that includes a broken heart!"

Ted smiles weakly. He doesn't want to throw her good intentions back in her face. He doesn't want to be ungrateful for the support of either of his parents. He feels a judder of self-loathing. *What's wrong with me that I can't appreciate what I've got? Why can't I just be satisfied and enjoy life?*

He picks up his spoon and gouges into the ice cream. "Thanks, Mum."

Between mouthfuls, he updates them on his week in the shop, telling them about the activities of their regular customers and the antics among the staff. They smile and nod along to his—at best banal—anecdotes. But Ted wants more. *I want to see them really happy.*

"You know what," he says, forcing out a grin, "I can feel that broken heart mending already."

Hilary gives a little yelp and waves her spoon in the air. "That's the spirit!"

"Good lad!" chips in Trevor, beaming.

Although Ted's relieved, at the same time—and for the *first* time—his lie tastes sour on his tongue. Because he also understands that he's letting himself down. And he feels hollow in the pit of his stomach.

This is so confusing!

As soon as he can, he makes his excuses, telling his parents he wants an early night. He hugs them goodbye and pulls the front door shut behind him. He leans back against it and lets out a long sigh. Then it hits him.

Actually, this isn't confusing at all.

He may be frustrated at himself for not being satisfied with his lot, but he can't deny his feelings. His first duty is to himself, to be true to himself.

He isn't going to back out of being a drag queen. *Even if the business is going through a rough patch. Even if it will disappoint my parents.*

He grits his teeth.

No, I've got to do this for myself.

CHAPTER 14

It's another hot spring day, so at lunchtime Oskar decides to go and buy an ice cream. He feels emboldened by the chat he struck up the previous weekend with his neighbor Marina. He'd caught sight of her hanging out her washing when he was setting off to do his shopping, and rather than keeping his head down, he decided to stop and engage her in conversation. They only talked about the vegan restaurant in which he was working and how business in her shop was finally picking up after the pandemic—and he did have to hold her off from segueing into an intimate discussion about how her mental health had suffered under Covid-19—but afterwards he felt good. He felt like he'd achieved a small but significant success. *And now I'm ready to follow it up . . .*

As he reaches Ainsworth's and joins the queue stretching outside, he remembers a Polish expression: "Once among the crows, caw as they do." He's pretty sure the English equivalent goes something like, "When in Rome, do as the Romans do." *That's all I'm doing. And I've lived in St. Luke's for ten years— it's about time I tried Ainsworth's ice cream.*

On entering the shop, Oskar draws up alongside a huge— and, he thinks, hideous—model of an ice cream, with a choco- late flake sticking out of the top. But he's not going to torture himself with futile dreams about reworking the décor. Instead, he scans the café area and is struck by the sight and sounds of so many people enjoying their ice cream, slowly drawing out every mouthful, narrowing their eyes and nodding their heads in appreciation, moaning and smacking their lips with pleasure. *It's about time I experienced some of that for myself.*

He looks over to the counter to decide what to order and sees that serving customers is a man in his early forties. This man is of average height and build and, if Oskar was to locate his hair color on the paint chart they use at work, it would fit somewhere between Cedar and Brown Sugar. His eyes, on the other hand, are an almost perfect match for Pearl Gray. The man is handsome in a quiet, understated way—although something about the way he carries himself makes Oskar think he probably has no awareness of this. Something else strikes Oskar: although the man is smiling, he seems a little sad, as if at odds with the cheery atmosphere of his surroundings. And he seems distant, as if his mind is elsewhere.

When the man leans over to hand a batch of ice creams to some tired-looking grandparents and their over-excited grandchildren, Oskar catches sight of his name badge.

Ted.

He tells himself not to stare, and peers into the display cabinet to peruse the ice cream. *Cookies and cream, banana smoothie, old English toffee . . .*

When Ted reaches down to plunge his scoop into the pistachio, Oskar looks up and catches his eye. Ted's gaze lingers for a couple of seconds longer than it should.

Oskar feels ever so slightly faint, like when he stood up too quickly after his Covid booster jab. *Where did that come from?*

You know perfectly well where it came from. You're attracted to Ted. You fancy him.

Oskar takes a deep breath to steady himself but it's too late—his heart rate is already soaring.

All of a sudden, fear slams into him. He considers whipping out his phone, pretending he has to take a call—and bolting.

Yet at the same time, he doesn't want to go anywhere. He feels strongly drawn to Ted and can't resist the pull.

Come on, Oskar. You've got to see this through.

As he tries to focus on the menu, he tells himself that there's nothing to be afraid of; all he's doing is ordering an ice cream, just like everyone else in here. And he doesn't even know if Ted's gay. He finds himself trying to pick up clues as he watches him serve a mother and her boisterous children, lining up their cones in a stand. There's certainly a softness to him, a fluidity to his movements, and he seems to have no need—or desire—to aggressively swing his weight around. But Oskar has no way of telling for sure.

When Ted reaches along the counter for the chocolate sauce, once again the two men catch each other's eye. A flush works its way up Oskar's body. *Is it me or is it hot in here?*

And once again, Ted's gaze hovers a little too long.

OK, I think he probably is gay.

Come on, Oskar, hold your nerve . . .

He reaches the front of the queue just as Ted's handing his customer the card reader.

"I'll be with you in a minute," he says to Oskar, looking away as she enters her PIN. He has a warm voice, with just a hint of a Lancashire accent.

Oskar can't think of any response, so just nods. He suddenly feels self-conscious and looks behind him to see if anyone's listening. But next in the queue are two old ladies wearing floral-print facemasks, engrossed in what sounds like some particularly salacious gossip.

"The cheeky mare, she should have kept her trap shut!"

Oskar turns back, just as Ted is handing the customer her ice cream.

"OK," he says, looking at Oskar. "What can I get you?"

Ted has a smile that's so gentle and charming, it momentarily flummoxes Oskar. "I don't know," he garbles. "I mean, what would you recommend? Sorry, I don't usually eat ice cream."

Oh, Oskar, why did you say that? He works in an ice-cream shop!

But Ted's smile doesn't waver. He seems intrigued. "Really?"

"Don't get me wrong, I do like it," Oskar adds, hastily. "I just haven't been here before. But it's such a sunny day, I thought I'd give it a go."

Oskar, you're blathering! "Blathering"—that's another word he learned recently.

Ted looks unfazed. "Well, chocolate's our biggest seller," he says, leaning on the counter. "Or there's the Lancashire Legends collection, which always goes down well."

Oskar consults the menu to see what this includes. "Oh, Vimto! Yes, I'd like a Vimto, please!"

Ted gives a wry smile. "It sounds like that's tickled your fancy."

"Sorry, yes, I discovered the word a few weeks ago. I try to learn a new word every day. Apparently, Vimto's a type of fruit cordial."

God, Oskar, now you really are blathering. Get a grip—as if Ted could care less!

But Ted continues smiling. "It is indeed. And would you like that in a cone or a tub?"

"A cone please."

"How many scoops?"

"Two."

Although their exchange is simple and functional, a tension fizzes between them. And Oskar's heart continues to pound.

"So I take it English isn't your first language?" Ted asks.

"No, I am from Poland. Originally."

"Ah, you'd never tell," says Ted. "Your English is perfect."

Oskar feels something warm bloom in his chest. "Thanks, I try my best."

Ted drops his scoop into a jar of water. "Would you like any toppings on that? Hundreds and thousands? Marshmallows? Raspberry sauce?"

Oskar doesn't fancy anything, but at the same time, he doesn't want their conversation to be over. "I'll have some raspberry sauce please."

Ted squeezes it on. "And what do you do for a living?"

Oskar's spirit gives a little sag. "I'm a painter and decorator. I'm working on the new vegan café at the other end of the high street."

"Oh yeah, I know the one."

"But that's not all there is to me," Oskar quickly adds.

"Good to hear it. I may work in an ice-cream shop but that's not all there is to me either."

Once again, the two men look into each other's eyes. Oskar is convinced there's a spark between them. *Yeah, I'm pretty sure he's gay.*

He suddenly feels emboldened. "My name's Oskar," he blurts out. "Oskar with a *K*."

"Pleased to meet you, Oskar with a *K*. I'm Ted. With a *T*."

"Oh, get on with it!" bursts in one of the old ladies behind him. "Some of us are desperate for a ninety-niner!"

"Yeah, sorry, just give me a minute," parries Ted.

Oskar can feel the heat prickling his face. He hopes the women weren't listening to their conversation. He hopes they can't tell what he's thinking. He feels another rush of self-consciousness, as if the whole shop is watching him. He reaches into his pocket and tugs out his wallet. "How much is that?"

Ted tells him, and he fumbles through the payment, grabs his ice cream, and says a clumsy goodbye. He's disappointed that their chat has to end so abruptly, but as he walks out of the shop, licking up his raspberry sauce, he gives himself a mental pat on the back. *You did well not to panic. You did well to see that through.*

"Bye!" Ted calls out after him.

He turns around, and they exchange one last smile.

Oskar licks down to his first taste of Vimto and finds he quite likes the flavor. And there's no question: this is the best ice cream he's ever had.

CHAPTER 15

"Even though I've worked here for years," Ted said, "I'm still struck by just how much people love our ice cream. For lots of our customers, coming here is the highlight of their week."

Ted was sitting on the sofa next to Giles, watching himself on the local TV news. His interview formed part of a prerecorded report about the latest investment program undertaken by St. Luke's council—including a complete renovation of the Victorian Winter Gardens and ballroom, a new development of pastel-colored beach huts to the south of the pier, and a show-piece indoor waterpark on the site of a soon-to-be-demolished 1960s car park—that was aiming to attract more tourists to the town. As this coincided with the eighty-fifth anniversary of Ainsworth's, the company's flagship ice cream parlor had been invited to feature in a sequence that had been shot earlier that week. The TV crew had hung around for hours, filming endless shots of the staff scooping ice cream out of tubs and onto cones, slow-motion sequences of the toppings and sauces being sprinkled onto it, and then close-up after close-up of the customers sliding it into their mouths, luxuriating in the texture and flavors, and licking their lips in ecstasy. The crew had also wanted to interview a representative of the family—and Ted's parents had insisted he take part, arguing it would be more appropriate to have a younger member of the family representing the brand in a report that not only celebrated the town's past but also looked forward to the future.

"The other day," Ted watched himself say, a cheeky smile appearing on his face, "one customer told me she'd rather come in here for an ice cream than have a night of passion with Russell Crowe."

Ted laughed at his own joke. What he'd said wasn't strictly true; in fact, it wasn't true at all. He'd simply made up the anecdote, based on his observations of the sensual—occasionally bordering on indecent—pleasure some people took from Ainsworth's ice cream. He hadn't even wanted to do the interview but, once the crew hit Record, he'd found himself standing with his back a little straighter, his mouth a little wider, and his eyes carrying a little more sparkle. In short, it had reawakened his long-dormant inner performer—and he couldn't stop himself from playing up to the camera.

For some reason, though, Giles didn't seem impressed. He gave a little snort.

Oh no, what have I done?

As the reporter signed off, Ted picked up the remote control and pressed Pause. "Well, I wasn't expecting to, but I quite enjoyed that," he said, forcing out a smile. "And the crew said I did well. The cameraman said I was a natural."

Giles looked like he'd just been insulted. "Ted," he snapped, "you've got about as much charisma as a removal van."

Ted felt a twist in his heart. "What? Smiles? Why—"

"Sorry," Giles cut in. "I was only joking. I didn't mean that. I just wasn't sure you came across well, that's all. I don't know what it is, but something weird happens when you speak. I'm not sure your mouth is quite symmetrical."

Ted stood up and went over to the mirror. "Really?" He began mouthing words to himself but couldn't see any problem.

"It's not a big thing," Giles went on. "I probably only noticed because I know you so well. But it did spoil it for me a bit. And I have to say, that comment about Russell Crowe was just tacky."

Ted turned to face him. "Did you think so?"

Giles screwed up his nose and nodded. "Yeah, I'm afraid so."

Ted felt his heart drop. *What was I thinking? Why did I ever think I'd come across well on TV?*

"Don't be upset," Giles said, standing up and putting his arms around him. "Not everyone can be a front man, you know."

Ted nestled into his embrace. He was thankful Giles was able to be so honest with him. He was thankful he could step in and give him the criticism he needed so he wouldn't make a fool of himself in the future. *What would I do without him?*

A few months later, Giles himself would appear on camera, in an internal training video commissioned by the owner of the Westcliff Hotel. Although only a handful of people would view it, Giles spent weeks fretting about what to wear, whether he should get his hair cut, and what he should do with his hands while speaking. He and Ted rehearsed his interview several times, shooting it on their new camera phones and watching it back analytically. And, whatever he thought, Ted was sure to bolster Giles's confidence and give him all the cheerleading he needed.

"You're so charismatic, Smiles," he cooed as they watched the finished video, in which Giles looked stiff and self-conscious, with none of his real-life charisma translating onto the screen. "You should do this kind of thing more often."

By this stage Ted had learned not to mention his own little appearance on the TV news. He'd learned to turn down any more chances to appear in the local media. And he'd learned to deny even to himself how much he'd enjoyed it.

As he works his way around the shop floor clearing tables, Ted wonders why the memory of an incident he hasn't thought about for years suddenly popped into his head. Obviously, he doesn't need much prompting to think about Giles; it's still less than two months since they split up. *But am I starting to question our relationship? Am I starting to question how good it was for me?*

If this is the case, he wonders if it might have anything to do with that Polish man who came into the shop at lunchtime. His name was Oskar, and he was gorgeous, with his messy hair and beard, and dazzling blue eyes. He smelled vaguely of paint, but that didn't bother Ted. On the contrary, it made a change from Giles's strong, achingly fashionable aftershave—and he found it enticingly, excitingly, almost thrillingly *real*.

Ted was surprised to find himself feeling a spike of attraction towards Oskar—and, if he wasn't mistaken, to detect some kind of spark igniting between them. He was also surprised to find himself covering up his wedding ring; for the length of their conversation he'd made sure to keep his hand behind his back or beneath the counter, however difficult this may have made it to serve ice cream. It wasn't something he'd planned or even intended, it just kind of happened.

He stops and rests his tray on a table. *That's what's going on! A handsome man has come into the shop, and I'm looking for justification to fancy him. God, I'm so fickle!*

He resolves to stop questioning his relationship with Giles and to hold on to the happy memories. Anyway, it's too soon after his breakup to start thinking about other men—and it's certainly too soon to consider dating again. In any case, Ted doesn't have the slightest idea if Oskar's even gay. *Not that it matters; if he is, he probably wouldn't fancy me.*

He tells himself that he must have imagined the spark between them. It was probably all in his head. And if he needs
any proof, all he has to do is remember Giles's latest social
media post showing him and Javier picking up matching
leather overnight bags from some swanky shop in Manchester,
their initials embossed at the base of the handles. Ted inter-
prets this as evidence that they're planning their first holiday
or mini-break together. He's reminded of all the holidays he
and Giles went on together. And his conclusion is that he isn't
good enough.

*I told Giles everything about myself, I let him know me better
than anybody, and in the end he didn't want me. So why would
Oskar?*

He casts all thoughts of Oskar out of his mind.

He takes his tray to the dishwasher, checks the clock, and
switches the sign on the door to CLOSED. He hopes his last customers of the day will take the hint. They're a well-dressed
couple in their twenties whose baby is sleeping in a pram behind them. But they seem engrossed in their ice creams, almost
in thrall to them, determined to savor every mouthful. *What is
it with everyone and ice cream? Just what am I missing?*

Ted hovers around them, loudly stacking the last of the banana split boats and sundae dishes. When the couple still fail
to take the hint, he goes back to the counter and makes a big
show of closing up the till.

Just as he's lifting out the cash tray, Jinger accosts him. "Ted,
do you mind if I shoot off early? I said I'd meet my boyfriend."

"Actually," says Bella, nudging her way between them, "can
I go too? I need to get ready for a date."

Ted is just about to say yes when he notices that Bella's
winged eyeliner is a little wonky. *If that were me, I'd do it
again . . .*

Actually, very soon that is going to be me . . .

The thought of his dream prompts a flicker of excitement. And it also reminds him of his resolution to put himself first.

"Sorry, no," he says, firmly. "I need to get off on time tonight." He doesn't tell them he's going to dance class. He doesn't tell them he's been going to dance class for a month now—and that he looks forward to it all week.

"I'm afraid you're going to have to clear up yourselves," he says, as briskly as he can manage. "Anyway, it *is* part of your job."

Before the girls can argue, Ted strides through the shop and into the office. As he shuts the door behind him and lowers the tray of cash onto his desk, his head is spinning with adrenaline. He doesn't know why, but taking this little stand seems significant. It feels like the start of something important.

Well done, Ted. Well done for sticking to your guns.

He lets out a long, uneven breath.

Then he spots something sitting on top of the post tray.

Wait a minute . . .

It's another plain white envelope that looks exactly the same as the one in which the anonymous letter arrived a few weeks ago. And on it is stuck the same white address label.

Don't tell me it's another one . . .

Ted snatches it up and tears it open.

TED,
BEWARE OF YOUR DAD. HE ISN'T WHO YOU THINK HE IS. HE IS NOT A GOOD MAN.

Ted's heart slams into his throat.

What's going on?

Who's sending me these letters?

And why are they trying to turn me against Dad?

Once again, he wishes he could ignore it. But once again, it sets all kinds of memories pinballing around his head. And one in particular comes bursting to the fore.

Ted sat up in bed and blinked himself awake. Downstairs, his mum and dad were shouting, although he had no idea why. The last thing he remembered, his dad was kissing him goodnight before he went out with some friends, and his mum was putting him to bed. As Ted was only five and still scared of the dark, his mum always left his door ajar and the landing light on. He slid along his bed and crept towards the open door.

"You can't seriously expect me to take this," Hilary hissed.

"Come on, Hil," said Trevor. "Try and see it from my point of view."

She gave an exaggerated huff. "Alright, enlighten me, Trevor; what exactly *is* your point of view?"

"I'm still young."

"You're t' same age as me."

"Yeah, but this is hard for me."

"*What* is?"

Trevor lowered his voice. "Just, you know, having kids. Not getting any sleep. Having no excitement in life."

"I'm very sorry, Trevor," snapped Hilary, "but in case you haven't noticed, it's hard for me too. In case you haven't noticed, *I'm* the one stuck at home with t' kids. I'm the one who actually changes t' baby's nappy and has to get up when she's skrikin'!"

"Yeah, but, you know . . ."

"What? What, Trevor?"

"Nothing."

"No, go on. You've got summat to say and I want to hear it."

Trevor let out a long sigh. "*You* wanted this, Hilary. *I* didn't. I didn't want to have kids so soon. I wanted us to enjoy ourselves."

Hilary gasped. "Trevor, you know full well I didn't *choose* to get up the duff. Well, not wi' Ted, any road. We—*both of us*—had an accident. I just chose not to back out of our responsibilities. I chose to do t' decent thing."

Ted didn't quite understand what he was hearing. *What are they saying about me? What do they mean?*

"Yeah, but when you made that choice," boomed Trevor, "you took away mine."

"Only because I knew you wouldn't regret it!" shrieked Hilary. "One of us had to be the grown-up. And you've told me countless times you don't!"

"Yeah, but sometimes I just find it difficult to deal with. Sometimes I just struggle with the reality of the situation."

"Right, so that's your excuse, is it? That's your excuse for carrying on like this. And you expect me to find out and say nowt?"

In the bedroom next to Ted's, Jemima started crying. It was her usual high-pitched wail, which carried all around the house and was impossible to ignore.

"Great, now you've woken up t' baby!" barked Hilary. "And let me guess—you want *me* to see to her!"

But Ted didn't hear his dad's reply because his mum came thundering up the stairs. He quickly slid back along his bed and dived under the covers.

I don't understand what just happened. As he replayed the conversation in his head, he could feel tears springing from his eyes.

He felt terrible. He felt even worse than when his dad took him out sailing, or tried to teach him how to play cricket, and Ted's lack of interest and ability only made his dad look deflated and disappointed. *But now it sounds like he doesn't just want me to be a different kind of boy; it sounds like he doesn't want me at all.*

Whatever was going on, it was obviously Ted's fault. He'd failed in some way. He was a bad son.

His tears came faster, dampening his pillow. He pulled the duvet over his head so nobody would hear him. He didn't want his dad to think he was being soft. He didn't want him to come in and tell him to stop crying.

Ted tried his hardest to fall back to sleep. But one thought kept revolving around his head: *How can I make Dad love me?*

CHAPTER 16

"What's that still doing up?" Denise points at a photo of Ted and Giles that's hanging on the wall.

Ted screws up his face. "I haven't got round to taking it down yet. Sorry."

Denise raises her eyebrows. "Don't apologize to me, honey, apologize to yourself." She hopes she doesn't sound too harsh. *I need to tread gently.*

But Ted doesn't seem remotely bothered. "Alright, alright," he singsongs. "Sorry, *Ted*!"

"That's better. Now come and give me a hug."

Once Denise has hugged Ted, she gives Lily a tickle behind the ears, then Ted helps to carry her bags through to the living room.

From the outside, Ted's three-bedroom 1970s semidetached house looks no different than the others on the street. But inside, it's more like a super stylish, swanky hotel than a residential house. During the third coronavirus lockdown, Giles had spearheaded a major redecoration project that involved stripping out the carpets and sanding down the floorboards, painting the walls a range of cool grays—from lead to charcoal to slate—then adding splashes of velvety purple, inky blue, or serene sage in the furniture, woodwork, and soft furnishings.

As Ted was busy trying to steer the shop through the pandemic, he was happy to let Giles take the lead. He even confided in Denise that he hoped the project would take the edge off Giles's professional frustrations and ease his listlessness. But now that Giles has gone, Ted's left with a house that isn't the slightest bit cozy or homey—and doesn't reflect his personality in any way. *Well, we need to do something about that . . .*

Denise drops her bags onto an armchair and points to the piece of art hanging over the fireplace. "And what about that?"

It's an abstract work Giles bought from a gallery near the hotel in Manchester. It consists of a piece of gray fabric that has been smudged and stained with splotches of green and yellow paint. Denise knows Ted has always hated it but didn't want to pour cold water on Giles's enthusiasm.

"What is it you used to say about it?" she asks.

He smirks. "It looks like someone's blown their nose on an old tea towel."

She chuckles. "Well, I've got news for you, Teddy—you don't have to put up with it anymore. You can get rid of it. In fact, let's have a bonfire with all the crap Giles left."

"Are you serious?"

"Absolutely. I'll light the match."

Ted roofs his eyes. "Steady on, Den! But point taken, I'll get on it."

Denise wags her finger at him. "Don't think I won't be checking up on you!"

Ted swats her on the arm. "Alright, alright, get off my back. Anyway, tonight's supposed to be about drag, remember?"

"I know, and Mama is ready to start your engine!"

As an excitable Lily sniffs around her, Denise unpacks three bags of dresses, blouses, and skirts she's borrowed from work. They're the biggest-sized clothes she could find, and she was only allowed to take them on the proviso she'd have them back before the start of the next working day. She's also brought a few wigs she's borrowed from an old school friend who works part-time in a fancy dress shop. The plan is to play around with ideas and settle on a look before Ted spends money creating the real thing. But Denise is worried that he isn't fully committed and that she's going to have to motivate and inspire him. *Which is all well and good, but if this is going to work it needs to come from him, not me.*

She blinks. *And I really, really want this to work . . .*

Ted begins to rummage around in the bag of wigs. He pulls out a curly, platinum blond one and plonks it on his head. "It's a bit Vera Duckworth," he says. He cocks it at an angle and tugs out the curls. "Or should I say Vera Duckworth when she's just had a fight outside the chippy?"

Lily barks loudly.

Ted puts the wig back and tries on a shorter one that's jet-black. "Now this is more like it. Category is: Alexis Colby realness."

Denise laughs. "Don't you mean Alexis Carrington Colby Dexter?"

Ted ices her with a glare. "Bitch, don't forget the Morell!"

They laugh and swig their drinks. One of the first subjects they bonded over was their love of glamorous 80s soap, *Dynasty*. Denise can remember sitting with Ted in the pub after Slimming World, roaring with laughter as he did his impression of Alexis, quoting some of her most iconic lines.

"How about this?" Ted says, picking up another wig, one that's made of longer, shaggier brunette hair.

"I don't know," says Denise, scowling. "It's a bit secondary-school art teacher."

Ted tosses the hair over his shoulder and gives a saucy pout. "How about secondary-school art teacher having a raging affair with the hot young caretaker? Or slipping away after work to lead an outrageous double life as a pole dancer?"

"Now you're talking!"

Ted takes it off and frowns. "Yeah, they're a good starting point, but I'm not sure any of them are quite right."

"No, me neither. But let's not worry about that for now. What we need to do is teach you how to walk in heels. That's the first step to unleashing the woman within."

Ted gives her a conspiratorial grin. "Den, this queen is ready to slay!"

Denise returns his grin. But she worries that once Ted is in heels, suddenly this is all going to seem real—and he might take fright.

She pulls out a bottle of prosecco. "Hold on, before we do anything, let's crack open this seccy!"

Once Ted has poured them a couple of glasses and they've had a few swigs, he produces his black training heels. "Obviously, this isn't the first time I've worn heels," he points out, "but I haven't tried these new ones yet. I wanted to do it properly so I waited for you."

He slides the shoes onto his feet and starts tottering around the living room. But the floor is uneven, and his heels keep getting stuck in the cracks of the floorboards.

"Bloody Giles!" says Denise. "It's like he's trying to spoil this from afar!"

She leads him into the hall and onto the tiled floor, with Lily trotting along behind them, her tail wagging.

"Now the golden rule of walking in heels," she begins, "is to go heel first. Don't lead with your toes. And don't try to put your whole foot down at once."

She steps back so Ted can walk up and down the hallway. *Please let this go well . . .*

"I love that clacking sound they make on the hard floor!" he tweets.

"I know, isn't it camp?"

Ted gives a little stumble and grabs onto the banister.

"Remember, heel to toe," points out Denise, patiently. "That'll stabilize the foot and give you more balance. But don't over-extend yourself. Take small steps. That's it!"

Once Ted's walk has become steadier and he's gaining in confidence, Denise decides to move things up a gear. "Now sissy that walk! Exaggerate the strut. Make sure one foot goes in front of the other. That'll give you a nice, sassy hip sway."

Ted's face splits into a grin. "This is ace! I love it!"

Denise is thrilled—not to mention more than a little re-lieved. "Teddy, I'm impressed. You really are slaying!"

Soon, he's strutting up and down the hallway as if he's on a catwalk, his hips swinging from side to side. He swivels to a stop in front of her and clicks his fingers over his head. "I am on fire, Den! And I feel like a *glamazon*!"

"That's my girl. And the more you practice, the better you'll get!"

He claps his hands. "This is so exciting! Now, what are we doing next?"

Denise drains her glass. "Right, before we start doing your makeup, you need to tell me what kind of queen you want to be."

They move back through to the living room and sit down.

"Have you got any ideas?" she asks.

"I have, yeah. I've been thinking about it a lot."

Now this is encouraging . . .

"So go on, how would you describe her?"

"She couldn't give a shit about fitting in," Ted bursts out. "In fact, what she likes most is standing out."

Denise nods, thoughtfully.

"She doesn't do what people expect of her," Ted goes on, "or what anybody else wants."

Denise narrows her eyes. "Interesting."

Ted gives his feet a wiggle. "And she doesn't take crap from anyone—under any circumstances."

"She sounds like my kind of girl," pipes Denise, the excitement spreading through her. "Now all we need is to come up with a name."

Ted sits forward in his chair. "Actually, I've got one already."

"Amazing!" *Well, well, it looks like he doesn't need any inspiration at all.*

Denise feels another rush of joy. Before she knows it, her mind is racing ahead, picturing Ted on stage in full drag, blazing with confidence and wowing the audience. *Living his best life—setting himself free!*

"I wanted something that makes her sound like a force of nature," he explains, "like she's impossible to hold back, impossible to keep down."

As her heart hammers with excitement, Denise can't help imagining the impact becoming a drag queen could have on Ted's life. Once he's started expressing himself on stage, his confidence could be boosted in all areas of his life. But she tells herself not to get carried away—if she gives off even the slightest suggestion that he's on the brink of some kind of transformation, he might back off.

"Go on, then," she says, trying her best to sound casual. "What did you come up with? What's your queen going to be called?"

Ted pauses before making his announcement. "Gail Force."

Denise lets out a squeal. "Teddy, that's perfect! I love her already! And I can't wait to do her makeup!"

"Brilliant. Just let me top up our glasses and we'll go upstairs."

But, as Ted pours them more prosecco, Denise spots something on his finger. "Ah-ah. Just a minute, what's that you're wearing?"

"It's my wedding ring." He looks as if he's about to say sorry—then stops himself.

"And what would Gail Force do with an old wedding ring like that?"

He gives an exaggerated frown. "I don't know."

OK, it looks like this might be where he needs some inspiration . . .

"Let me make this easier," says Denise. "What would a strong, sassy, fierce queen like Gail Force do with a wedding ring from some posh twat who stopped her from following her dream then dumped her to run off with some basic, tacky *skank*?"

Ted slowly slides off his ring. "She'd take it off. And she'd chuck it on that bonfire with the rest of his stuff."

"Atta girl! Gail Force has arrived!"

CHAPTER 17

Once Denise has left, Ted sits on the edge of his bed, facing the mirror. He's wearing the art teacher wig that Denise combed back and pulled into a high ponytail. His face is fully made up, with scarlet lipstick, gold glitter eyeshadow, and false eyelashes that are so long they tickle his forehead. Denise had to take home the dresses she'd borrowed—which were too old-fashioned and demure for Gail anyway—so he's wrapped in his own fluffy white bathrobe. He pictures himself dressed like this, preparing to go on stage at the open-mic night.

I could be in a few months—if I'm brave enough . . .

At least he's no longer in any doubt that drag is right for him. He's had more fun tonight than he's had in years. *Possibly more fun than I've ever had in my life.*

But this isn't just about fun. Through drag, Ted is discovering that he can access a confidence he didn't know he possessed. Drag makes him feel strong and powerful. He often thinks people overuse the word "empowered," but in this case he considers it entirely appropriate. In fact, he's so empowered he feels invincible.

He beams at his reflection. "Hello, Gail," he says out loud, "it's ace to meet you."

Excitement licks his insides. As Gail, Ted can now fully ex-

press so many of the thoughts he's kept hidden, so much of the
behavior he's wanted to display, and so much of the attitude
he's wanted to project. He doesn't have to follow any rules or
conform to what people expect of him.

"Where've you been all my life?" he asks.

Then he stops himself. Because he realizes he isn't actually
meeting Gail for the first time. Nor is he becoming someone
else. In a way, she's always been a part of him. *And now I'm
letting her loose, I'm becoming the person I was always meant
to be.*

He's waited for this moment for a long time . . .

When Ted was ten years old, his six-year-old sister, Jemima,
was preparing to compete in her first beauty pageant. She was
showing her brother her outfits and routines and, as if it were
the most natural thing in the world, Ted joined in. He soon
found himself rummaging around their mum's wardrobe and
trying on a pair of pink rhinestone-studded heels and a black
sequined dress with shoulder pads. Before he knew it, the two
of them were strutting up and down the thick swirl-patterned
peach carpet of their parents' bedroom, competing in their
own beauty pageant.

This was something Ted had wanted to do ever since he'd
seen Crystal Ball on that holiday in Spain—but was something
he'd always thought he had to keep to himself. Now he was
daring to indulge his passion, he wasn't surprised to find it felt
good; it felt dead good. But somehow it was more than that; it
awakened something within him, something he still didn't
quite understand. But he did know it was linked to his inability
to play sports or do other boyish activities and that it was
somehow connected to his unshakable attraction to other

boys. *But here, playing with Jemima, it doesn't feel wrong; it feels perfectly right.*

They sat at their mum's dressing table and adorned themselves with every bit of jewelry they could find, giggling as they applied her makeup, clumsily smudging it onto their faces until they looked more like clowns than beauty queens. But Ted didn't care; they were having fun. So much fun he'd forgotten his parents were downstairs.

Until they burst in to the room.

"What's going on 'ere?" gasped Hilary.

"What are you two playing at?" panted Trevor.

Ted looked at them and felt something fall through him. *Oh God, what have I done?*

"We're playing beauty queens," squeaked Jemima.

Ted's throat was so dry he couldn't speak. He looked into his parents' eyes and there was a pause that lasted so long he thought he was going to pass out. It was only broken when Trevor and Hilary turned to each other and exchanged a knowing look.

"Well, that looks like a good game," said Trevor.

"And don't you both look fab?" cooed Hilary.

Ted couldn't believe what he was hearing. *What, so you're not going to shout at me? You're not going to say horrible things and make me feel bad?*

"When we grow up," Jemima fizzed, "we're *both* going to be beauty queens! Not just me but Ted too!"

Trevor stepped forward. "The thing is, princess," he said, softly, "there's only room for one showgirl in this family—and that's you."

"Why can't I be a showgirl too?" protested Ted. "I want to be like Crystal Ball!"

Trevor shook his head. "Crystal Ball lives in Spain, son. That's not how we do things in St. Luke's. It's not how we do things in this family."

Hilary ruffled Ted's hair. "Ted, love, beauty pageants aren't for you. You'll be coming to work in t' business with us."

"Won't that be nice?" threw in Trevor, his hope audible. "To be with your mum and dad every day?"

"With as much ice cream as you want?" added Hilary, an almost desperate glint in her eye.

Ted felt so grateful that his parents weren't shouting at him that he couldn't find it in him to say that this wasn't what he wanted.

"Yeah, that'd be ace," he rasped, twisting his mouth into a smile.

"Come on, then," said Hilary, "let's get take these daft clothes off and get you a wash."

Sitting on the edge of his bed more than thirty years later, Ted wonders if, ever since that day, the course of his life has been determined by a sense of gratitude towards his parents. He wonders if this was only compounded when he was eighteen and came out as gay—and both of them accepted him instantly. In what felt like a prepared speech, his mum told him that it didn't matter to her one jot. And his dad added that it didn't change his feelings for him at all. As the three of them came together for a hug, Ted could tell that they meant what they said. *But has my gratitude stopped me from following my dream? Has it stopped me from becoming the person I'm meant to be?*

Then the memory of the anonymous letters comes crashing in.

"Your family isn't as perfect as you think it is."

"Beware of your dad . . . He is not a good man."

Ted still has no idea what to make of any of this—or how it

relates to his life. *But what if things are more complicated than they seem?*

Whatever the answer, he decides that gratitude isn't going to stop him following his dream—not anymore.

Yes, I'm going to do the open-mic night. And I'm going to give it everything I've got.

CHAPTER 18

A few days later, Ted is on his way back from Lily's regular morning walk when he spots Stanley on his balcony, sipping his usual cup of tea. Today, he's wearing a shirt Ted judges to be a slightly lighter shade of blue than Ainsworth's bubblegum flavor ice cream, with his nails painted to match and a darker blue paisley scarf tied in a bow around his neck.

"Morning!" Ted calls out. "How are you today?"

Stanley frowns. "Not great, dolly. Not great."

"Oh no, what's happened?"

Ted approaches the fence and Stanley confides that he doesn't want to go to his regular exercise class because of the latest spate of homophobic comments made by the other residents. "And it's not just the men but one or two of the women as well. Honestly, it's outrageous. I feel like an outcast in my own home."

When Ted expresses his shared outrage, Stanley invites him in for a cup of tea. As it's Sunday and he doesn't have to go to work, Ted accepts.

"Come on, Lily," he says, tugging her lead. "We're going on a little detour."

The two of them pass through the gate and follow Stanley into his living room. As Ted would expect of a flat in a care home, the décor is neutral, but Stanley has customized it with a pink suede suite, matching pink-tasseled lampshades, a gloriously over-the-top chandelier hanging from the central light fitting, and—tucked away in a corner—a vintage brass hostess trolley, which has been repurposed as a minibar. Propped up against a mahogany coat stand is an antique ebony walking stick with a silver-tipped grip, and perched on one of the hooks above it is a fedora, onto which is pinned a wonderfully flamboyant peacock feather. There's an old record player with a stack of albums by Judy Garland and Barbra Streisand leaning against it, and an antique Singer sewing machine that must still be in use because there's a spool of thread standing on the pin. Scattered around the room are photos of a younger Stanley posing with friends, many of these in black and white.

Once Lily has had a sniff around, she slumps down onto a pink sheepskin rug.

"She looks tired," says Stanley. "Can I give her a biscuit?"

Ted hesitates; she's still missing Giles and he's been overcompensating lately by giving her treats, as evidenced by her rapidly expanding belly. "Go on," he concedes. "I suppose she has had a long walk."

Stanley feeds the dog a few custard creams, which she gobbles up, licking the crumbs off his hand. "So she's called Lily—is that after Lily Savage?"

"Got it in one."

"What a marvelous choice."

Ted gives an impish grin. "I'm glad you approve."

Stanley pours him a cup of tea from a pot he says has just brewed. "It's Lady Grey. I hope that's strong enough for you."

"I'm sure it'll be fine." Ted helps himself to milk from a jug on the side. As he does, he spots the front page of an old edition of the *Manchester Evening News*, which has been mounted in a frame. It features a photo of several men—including a young Stanley—leading the march in Manchester's first ever

Gay Pride, as it was then known. He picks up the frame to have a closer look.

"You know, I can't believe you were part of this," he breathes. "I can't believe you were so brave."

Stanley scatters some custard creams onto a plate, then places it on the coffee table. "I suppose I was, yes. But we didn't have much choice at the time. You either fought for your rights or you hid away, festering in your own shame. Which, as I'm sure you can imagine, wasn't an option for me."

Ted replaces the frame on the sideboard. He wonders which of the two options he would have taken. *I like to think it's the former. I like to think I'd have fought and been proud.*

"Anyway, look at me now," Stanley continues. "All these years later and it hasn't got me anywhere. You know, I want to take on the other residents, I want to stand up to them, but I still haven't worked out how."

"I'm so sorry," says Ted. "I wish there was something I could do."

"It's my own stupid fault," says Stanley, combing his hand through his white hair. "Moving back here was a mistake. I feel like I've regressed, like I'm a child again, back at school, with all the other kids picking on me."

As Ted helps himself to a biscuit, his mind rewinds to his own experience of childhood. And suddenly, something he hasn't considered before strikes him very clearly.

Ted couldn't throw the cricket ball. It wasn't just that he couldn't aim it at the wicket, he couldn't even extend his arm properly; it just didn't seem to rotate above his head in the way it did when the other boys bowled. *What's wrong with me?*

When he started to become self-conscious, this only made his technique worse. Some of the other boys on the field sniggered. One or two of them laughed loudly. In his peripheral vision, Ted caught sight of his dad, standing on the boundary alongside some of the other dads. But unlike the others, Trevor was hanging his head and rubbing his eyes. *God, this is awful.*

"OK, forget about bowling overarm," the coach shouted. "From now on, just do it underarm."

The man muttered something under his breath but Ted didn't catch it. He did, however, catch one of the boys saying, "Like a girl."

Laughter spread around the field.

As Ted lowered his arm below his waist and threw the ball upwards, shame pricked at his insides. *This is like some kind of ritual humiliation. God, I wish I wasn't here.*

But he was here because of his dad. Despite the fact he was eleven years old, despite the fact he'd never shown any talent or interest in cricket, Trevor still hadn't given up on his dream of transferring his passion to his son. When he'd heard the local junior team was short on numbers, he'd called in a favor from a fellow committee member and smuggled Ted into the squad. Trevor had then bought his son a gleaming new set of cricket whites and taken him out to practice several times. During these private sessions, Ted hadn't played that badly—and his dad had been a much more patient teacher than usual, almost as if he understood this was his last chance to get it right. But, now that Ted was out on the field, now that he was being watched and judged by the other boys and their dads, everything Trevor had taught him vanished. The shame swept through him.

It was bad enough in the school playground, where some of the other boys would occasionally seize on the fact that Ted's speech and mannerisms stood out as more feminine than theirs—and call him "poof" or "queer." But, for some reason, this had never got too out of hand; it was as if there was something holding the boys back. Ted could only assume their aggression was tempered by the presence of the girls. *But here on the cricket field, there are no girls . . .*

Once he came to the end of his stint as bowler, Ted switched back to fielding. But just a few overs later, he missed a key catch. After the break, when it was his turn to bat, he saw the hard ball hurtling towards him and flinched. He was bowled out without any runs.

"And he's out for a duck!" shouted Tony Bracewell, a boy who was constantly picking his nose and often plagued with cold sores. "Now off you go and play netball wi' t' girls."

Ted felt sick with shame. He imagined everyone in his eye-line must be appalled by his failure—not just to play cricket but to be a proper boy. His failure to be the boy everyone wanted. His failure to be the boy his dad wanted.

After the game, Ted found a quiet corner of the dressing room, away from the other boys. But, as he was tugging off his whites, Tony came swaggering over.

A flush of fear worked its way up Ted's body.

"You were crap, Ted," boomed Tony. "We lost t' game because of you. You threw like a girl and were frightened of t' ball."

Ted's mouth dried out. "I wasn't frightened," he lied, the words sticking in his throat, like a peanut he hadn't chewed properly.

"Yes, you were," Tony bellowed. "You pathetic little queer!"

He pulled back his arm to throw a punch, and Ted shielded his face. But the blow never came.

"Tony! What are you doing?"

Tony's cousin Mark—who had one eye higher up his face than the other, which gave him a menacing look—rushed over.

"What are you playing at?" he hissed. "You can't hit Ted. His dad's Trevor Ainsworth. We get their ice cream!"

Tony examined his fist as he considered what his cousin was saying.

"Your sister's birthday party's coming up," Mark went on. "Ainsworth's are doing t' ice cream. If they don't, your mum and dad'll go berserk. You'll be in serious shit."

Tony covered his fist with his palm. "I didn't think of that."

He dropped his hands to his sides and slowly backed away.

Then he took a step forward and tilted his head. "Ted, you won't say owt, will you? You know, to your dad?"

"No, no," Ted almost squealed. "I won't say anything, I promise!"

He was disgusted by the ring of desperation in his own voice. He bent down to stuff his jumper into his bag and kept his head lowered as he waited for his insides to settle. Once he could just about make out Tony sitting on the bench next to his clothes, he let out a long breath.

God, that was lucky.

As Ted swallows his custard cream, he's struck by the special status his family business gave him as a child. *But what I hadn't realized till now is how grateful I've been to Mum and Dad for that too.*

Just as he's opening his mouth to share the memory with Stanley, there's a knock on the door and a nurse comes barreling into the room.

"Morning, Stanley!" she chirrups. "Time for your medication, my love!"

The nurse notices Ted sitting in the armchair. "I didn't know you had company."

Ted stands up and introduces himself, and the nurse tells him her name is Alison. She's a sturdy woman in her thirties with short, curly hair and a wide smile revealing a narrow gap between her front teeth. After recognizing Ted's surname and finding out where he works, she tells him her favorite flavor of ice cream is lemon meringue.

"I was just telling Ted about the trouble I've been having with the other residents," Stanley comments.

Alison looks at Ted and purses her lips. "I want to go to management about it, but he won't let me. He says it'll only make things worse. But it's bullying—and nobody should be subjected to that."

"Trust me," says Stanley. "When one of them says anything, I give as good as I get."

Ted smirks. "I'm sure you do."

"I just don't want to antagonize them. This place is different to the real world—and if I turn the other residents against me, the group activities won't be any fun. Nor will mealtimes. I'll be stuck in this room for the rest of my life. And my final chapter will be dismal and dull, rather than the dazzling dénouement I'd imagined."

"If you want the slightest chance of being dazzling," quips Alison, "you need to get these down you." She hands him three different-sized pills on an outstretched palm that's much paler than the brown skin on her arms and face.

Stanley puts them in his mouth and washes them down with a swig of tea. "Anyway, I'm not going to let them win," he declares. "I've just got to approach things carefully. I've got to be strategic."

"Right, I'll leave you to strategize. I'm afraid I've got beds to make." Alison says goodbye to Ted and tells Stanley she'll see him later.

"She's my only supporter in here," Stanley says, once she's closed the door. "She's my only friend."

Sadness plucks at Ted's heart. "Don't say that. I'm your friend. Or at least I'd like to be."

"That's sweet of you, dolly," says Stanley. "I'd like that very much."

Ted bobs up in his seat. "In that case, consider it done."

Stanley smiles, but it's a smile tinged with sorrow. "I wish I had someone to share my life with, though. I used to think the word 'partner' was so dry, so worthy. I much preferred 'lover,' which was the word my friends used too. But now I wish I had a partner in the truest sense of the word—in *every* sense of the word."

Ted wants to hug Stanley but is mindful he's from a different generation, and doesn't want to cross any boundaries. "Did you ever have a partner?" he asks.

"No, but I had several lovers. I'm afraid it was always me who stopped things developing any further." Stanley pauses and presses his hand to his heart. "You see, when I was young, I had a terrible experience that left me very frightened. Frightened of opening myself up or wanting to start a relationship."

Ted's intrigued. "What happened?"

Stanley picks up the plate of biscuits and thrusts it towards him. "Let's not talk about that now. Have another custard cream!"

Reluctantly, Ted picks one and bites into it.

"Anyway, let my life be a lesson to you," Stanley blusters. "Whatever you do, don't end up on your own."

Suddenly, Ted's floored by how much he misses Giles. "Actually, I am on my own," he confesses. "I've just been through a breakup—a really bad one."

Stanley dismisses his objection with a wave. "Well, you're still young. Or at least you are compared to me. Get over it and get back out there."

"Funnily enough, I did meet someone the other day," Ted finds himself saying. "A Polish guy who came into the shop."

He has no idea why he's sharing this information—he hasn't even told Denise. Though he has thought about Oskar a lot.

"Well, that sounds promising," says Stanley.

"I don't know; maybe it's silly," Ted goes on. "I only spoke to him for, like, five minutes."

"Well, every relationship starts with five minutes," says Stanley. "But what harm can it do to build on that the next time and stretch it to ten?"

Ted scrunches up his nose. "I don't know if there'll be a next time. I don't even have his number." Then a thought occurs to him—and he's surprised to find himself expressing it. "Actually, I do know where he works."

Ted, why are you blabbing about this?

Then another voice pops into his head. *Maybe it's because you want Stanley to persuade you to see Oskar . . .*

As if on cue, Stanley says, "In that case, you've no excuses, dolly. Totter on down there and 'bump into him.' What's the worst that can happen?"

CHAPTER 19

Oskar is at work—although at this stage, there isn't much work involved. The job's nearly finished, so it's mainly just cleaning up, wiping down, and snagging. But as the restaurant's owner is currently on site, there's a lot of tension in the air—he's already asked for one or two alterations. To give himself a breather, Oskar has volunteered to clear away some rubbish. He starts by dragging a piece of leftover plasterboard out of the restaurant and over to the skip.

Just as he's approaching it, emerging from the other side comes Ted. The two men almost collide with each other.

"Sorry, I didn't see you there," says Oskar, snapping back.

"Yes, sorry," blurts out Ted. "I've just been running an errand. I'm on my way back to the shop." He gestures to his purple polo shirt, as if submitting it as evidence.

Oskar feels a flash of fear and holds the plasterboard in front of him. *Shit, I'm not ready for this . . .*

Come on, Oskar, don't blow it!

"This is the restaurant I was telling you about," he says. "Although it's pretty much finished now."

He tells himself not to stand in such a defensive position and tosses the plasterboard into the skip.

"What's with the kneepads?" Ted points at the padding around Oskar's knees. "Or shouldn't I ask?"

Oskar feels a trickle of sweat run down his back. *Is he flirting with me?*

"It's just for when I need to get down on the floor," he manages, "for when I'm touching up skirting boards and things."

"Oh, right."

The silence curdles between them. Once again, Oskar wants to run away—but at the same time, he's compelled to stay.

Ted clears his throat. "So what's it like then, this restaurant? Is it looking good?"

Oskar hopes he isn't angling for a tour; all his colleagues are inside, plus the stressed-out owner and that patronizing designer Misty, who's spent all day pretending she thinks he's from Bulgaria. "Well, it's not exactly what *I* would have done with it," he answers. "But you'll be able to see for yourself soon. It opens next week."

"Ace. I'll make sure I pop down and sample their Quorn sausages."

At the mention of the word "sausages," Ted blushes. Then he looks embarrassed to be blushing.

But, rather than making Oskar feel awkward, this makes him feel relieved. "According to the owner, they're the best in Lancashire," he chirps. "But apparently they're not as good as the stuffed aubergine."

At the mention of the word "aubergine," Oskar's eyes land on Ted's crotch—and it's his turn to blush. *God, does he think I'm making some sort of crude joke?*

They hit another bump of silence.

"So do you know what you're working on next?" Ted ventures.

"Yes, the foreign language school," says Oskar, "the one next to the mini golf course."

"I love that golf course! We used to go there when I was a kid."

Oskar frowns. "I'm afraid I've never been."

"You've never *been*?"

Maybe you could take me there, Oskar wants to say. Then he's surprised to find that he has said it. He desperately hopes none of his colleagues are watching but doesn't dare turn round to check.

Ted responds with a smile. "OK, yeah, that'd be fun."

Oskar finds himself feeling a rush of excitement. *He just said yes! He wants to go out with me!*

Then fear slices through him. *Can I actually do this?*

He tells himself to be brave. Ted seems like just the kind of man he should get to know better. He should keep himself open to possibilities; there's no point moving to a country where he can live freely if he doesn't act on it and enjoy the benefits.

"So, shall I give you my number?" he says.

The two of them take out their phones, and Ted inputs Oskar's number. When they lean into each other, Oskar catches a faint smell of chocolate overlaid with something he thinks might be raspberries. He hopes he doesn't whiff of paint—or, even worse, turps.

He wants to keep talking, but now he's handed over his number, he senses the conversation is coming to a natural end.

"OK, well, I'd better get back to work," he says.

Ted looks at his watch and his eyes widen. "Is that the time? Me too!"

They say their goodbyes, and Oskar watches Ted walk away. *Come on, don't stare at him. Don't make it obvious!*

As he turns back to the restaurant, he spots his colleague Mick wiping down the front window. Oskar hopes he hasn't been watching the whole time. Thankfully, he doesn't bat an eyelid. Oskar smiles. "Not batting an eyelid" is one of the first expressions he learned when he moved to the UK, so he always enjoys using it.

He hopes that if any of his other workmates were watching, they don't suspect he and Ted are anything other than two acquaintances who casually bumped into each other. *Now walk back in and act naturally, as if that's all it was.*

Wait a minute, what if that is *all it was? What if I've misread the whole thing?*

Oskar tells himself not to be daft—there was definitely a spark. *And then there were those innuendos about sausages and aubergines . . .*

He bends down to gather up some strips of wallpaper. *But how can I be sure?*

That evening, Oskar goes on a short bike ride, during which he analyzes his conversation with Ted over and over again and tries, but fails, to work out if they've arranged to go on a date or just meet up as friends. As he cycles back through the caravan park, he looks out to the horizon and sees that the sun is starting to slip down the sky, scattering rays of pink and purple. *It's the color of Vimto. It's a Vimto sunset!*

He remembers how he felt when Ted served him Vimto-flavored ice cream—as if something inside him was melting. Then he blinks and shakes his head. *What's happening to you, Oskar? You've only met Ted twice, and you're turning into a soppy, lovesick teenager!*

It occurs to him that he never had the chance to be soppy or lovesick when he actually was a teenager—and feels a pang of sadness. Sadness for the boy he used to be and everything he went through. Sadness for all the years he's spent alone.

He swallows it down.

Just as he's approaching his caravan, Oskar spots Marina doing yoga on her lawn.

"Hi, toots!" she says, coming out of a position he thinks might be the Tree.

"Hi, Marina." He swings himself off his bike. "Don't mind me. I don't want to disturb you."

"It's OK, I was just finishing." Marina pads over the grass towards him. "How are you doing? Good day?"

Where do I start? Then it occurs to Oskar that if he were to tell Marina what's on his mind, she might have some good advice. *The problem is, I wouldn't want to reveal too much.*

He rests his bike against the storage unit. "Yeah, you know, alright. How about you?"

"Great, thanks. I got a text from a man I met online. We had our first date at the weekend, and I really like him but I wasn't sure how he felt. Anyway, he's just asked me out again, so it turns out he is interested!"

Oskar spots an opportunity and, before he can change his mind, grabs it. "How do you know?" he asks. "How do you know if someone's interested?"

Marina tugs on the waistband of her Aztec print leggings. "I'm not sure, toots. Sometimes I get it wrong. Sometimes I get it disastrously wrong. Once I went on three dates with this Scandinavian physiotherapist. He was so gorgeous, I thought he was out of my league, but he seemed really keen. Then I made the lunge, and he pulled back and said he just wanted to be friends. Oh my goddess, it was so humiliating."

"I'm sorry."

"The worst thing was, about a year later, I went to a wedding and he was sitting on my table—with his new girlfriend. She was about ten years younger than me and much prettier. It would have been funny if I hadn't been dying inside."

Sympathy rushes into Oskar. Then another thought enters his head. *What if something similar happens to me? Can I really put myself through that?*

Marina wraps her towel around her shoulders. "Why do you ask, anyway? Are you seeing someone?"

Shit, what am I doing? It hits Oskar that he can't talk about this in any detail without coming out as gay. *And I can't do that, I just can't.*

"Oh no," he says, massaging the back of his ear, "I'm just curious, I suppose."

Marina tilts her head as if examining him. "You know what, why don't you come over later? Why don't we both have a shower, grab something to eat, then meet up for a bottle of wine?"

Oskar is seized by panic. "I'm sorry," he blurts out. "I can't."

To signal that the conversation is over, he turns, opens up the storage unit, and lifts his bike inside.

"Alright, then," says Marina. "Another time?"

"Yeah," he replies, "that'd be nice."

It occurs to Oskar that all he's doing is deferring the problem; Marina will only pick up the subject the next time they speak. And, if he really is going to open up to her, at some point he'll have to tell her he's gay.

But now isn't the time. What he needs to do is stop obsessing about Ted—and whether or not they're going on a date.

He says goodbye to Marina and, as he unlocks the caravan, decides he isn't going to text Ted. *If I rush in and go too fast, I'll only get scared and back out.*

Instead, he'll let Ted take the lead. *And if he does, I'll have to make sure I move slowly and cautiously.*

Fear washes through him.

As he pushes open the door, he tells himself there's nothing to be afraid of. *He probably won't even text.*

CHAPTER 20

Ted loads the tubs of ice cream he's taken out of the freezer onto a trolley. He pretends to check off the flavors against a list fixed to a clipboard—but in reality he's trying to observe his dad. *Although what I'm looking for, I've no idea.*

Trevor is deep in conversation with the factory supervisor Derek Slack, the two of them concocting the recipe for next week's special flavor: rhubarb and custard. Once they've pumped their first attempt out of the machine, they stir it several times, analyzing the texture to make sure it's right. They each pull out a spoonful and hold it up as if it's an object worthy of admiration. Then they pop the spoons into their mouths. There's a long pause as both men nod in concentration.

"Yeah, it's al'reet, that," says Derek, which is what he always says.

"Nah, there's not enough rhubarb," judges Trevor, "and it's a bit heavy on the custard." He scans the room, presumably scouting out another opinion.

Ted puts his head down and goes back to his list. *Ginger and honey . . . fudge . . . white chocolate honeycomb . . .*

Except his mind isn't on ice cream. In his trouser pocket is another anonymous letter that arrived that morning. It's in the same style as the last two and stamped with the same local postmark. Ted doesn't need to take it out to remember what it says.

TED,
YOUR DAD IS A BAD MAN. DO NOT LET HIM FOOL YOU. DO NOT TRUST HIM.

Ted still has no idea who's sending the letters—or what their motivation might be. *Is it a disgruntled business rival trying to cause trouble? Trying to turn our family against each other?*

Nor does he have any idea what to do about it. He can't take the letters to the police. What would he even say? No crime has been committed, and he wouldn't want to be accused of wasting their time. He can't take them to his dad either—not since the sender started singling him out for criticism. And it wouldn't be fair to involve his mum; she'd only be upset and scared and might do something drastic. He wouldn't want anything to threaten the stability of his family. *Not when it's always been so important to us . . .*

But despite all this, ever since Ted received the third letter, its message has been going round and round his head. And he's desperate to know what his dad's supposed to have done. *Just what is the sender getting at? Has he stolen some money? Fiddled the figures?*

But there's something about the letter's tone that makes him think his dad's supposed transgression isn't professional but personal. Whoever he's offended seems angry—and very passionate.

He touches the back of his neck. *Oh God, could I really have got Dad wrong? Could he really be a bad man?*

Ted skipped into the house, a tired Jemima trailing after him. The siblings had just attended their first Halloween party in the home of Kimberley and Andrea Underhill, two sisters whose mum Hilary knew from her work on the committee of a local charity. Mr. Underhill was a car salesman who worked in the big Ford showroom on the A-road that led into St. Luke's and, according to Trevor, something of a "flash Harry" who liked to flaunt his money. Last October half-term, he'd taken his family on holiday to Florida, and they'd come back raving about Halloween, a tradition that was only just taking hold in the UK but was already a major event in the States. This October, Mrs. Underhill was hosting St. Luke's first Halloween-themed party. And judging from the amount of effort she'd put in, she wanted to make a big impression.

The ground floor of the Underhill home was decorated with carved pumpkins lit up by tealights, fluffy cobwebs, plastic bats hanging from the window frames, and so many orange and black balloons that children kept falling over and popping them—although some of the boys were doing it on purpose. There were games that involved tossing rings onto witches' hats, pinning spiders onto webs, and eating apples that bobbed in cauldrons full of water. There was a whole buffet of sweets and cakes, a chocolate fountain—with marshmallows to dip in—and, of course, a mountain of Ainsworth's ice cream. But what really made this party stand out from all the others was that every single child was dressed in a Halloween-themed costume.

Kimberley and Andrea Underhill were dressed as wicked witches and Jemima was a black cat, complete with whiskers fashioned from pipe cleaners, a tail made out of a wool sock stuffed with old newspaper, and ears Hilary had constructed by cutting up an egg carton, painting two of the cups black, then gluing them onto an Alice band. Ted was a ghost, and his costume had taken Hilary hours to create; it consisted of a long silver, synthetic wig; a face full of white makeup, with black

lips and shadows around the eyes; a simple white sheet covering his body (with a hole cut in it for his head); a pair of white
plimsolls—that everyone in Lancashire called pumps—and, on
his legs, a pair of opaque white tights.

Ted had loved having his makeup done and asked his mum
if he could take the lipstick to the party, where he sneaked into
the bathroom to reapply it so often that, by the time the party
was over, all that was left was an uneven, slightly mushy stump.
He also loved wearing the wig, stroking the ends of his long
hair, flicking it over his shoulders and gently tossing it from
side to side. Most of all, though, he loved wearing the tights.
He loved the way they felt on his skin. They were so silky and
soft, it was like every inch of his legs was being hugged, or
lightly tickled, or "caressed"—a word he'd heard Alexis use on
Dynasty and had decided to incorporate into his vocabulary.
He'd never realized any part of his body could be so sensitive.

"Right, come on, let's get them costumes off," commanded
Hilary, as she closed the door behind them.

She began pulling, tugging, and wiping at eight-year-old
Jemima, who was so tired she could hardly stand up straight.
After stuffing her face with cola bottles, she'd stormed around
the party like she'd been turbocharged, until she'd succumbed
to a major energy slump on the back seat of the car home.

Ted, however, was the opposite of tired; he wanted the party
to continue. "Oh, Mum, do I have to take my costume off?"

"It's late, son," said Trevor, coming into the hall to greet them.
"You need to get into your pajamas. But if you're good, we can
watch a bit of telly and have some ice cream before bed."

"But Dad, I don't want to take my costume off!" railed Ted.
"I want to watch telly like this!"

Before Trevor could argue, Ted tossed his fake hair over his
shoulder, skipped through to the lounge, and slid onto the
leather sofa. As his tights made contact with the smooth surface, they felt even slinkier—and his skin even more sensitive.

Ted couldn't help running his hands up and down his legs and whinnying with pleasure. *Oh, I love it!*

Trevor was watching from the doorway. "I'm not sure about that," he said, with a crease of concern.

Not sure about what?

Jemima loped in, wearing nothing but her knickers and sucking her thumb, which was what she did whenever she was feeling sleepy. As Hilary trotted in behind her, Trevor muttered something in her ear. Ted didn't catch it but the look on his face told him exactly how his dad was feeling, exactly what he thought about his son wearing tights, a wig, and makeup. Ted's stomach plunged.

The next day, Trevor took Ted into Ainsworth's, where he showed him around the machines in the factory and taught him the process of making ice cream. He announced that, now Ted had reached the age of twelve, he was old enough to be let in on the family secret—and revealed the ingredients of their famously classified recipe. He demonstrated this by making a batch of the vanilla flavor Ted pretended was his favorite. As he pumped it out of the machine, Trevor churned it around the tub, lifting it up to the light as if it was the most beautiful, valuable, precious thing in the world.

"Look at that," he said. "It's like poetry. I mean, have you ever seen anything finer?"

Not wanting to disappoint his dad, Ted replied, "No. No, I haven't, Dad."

"Ice cream is life, son. That's something my dad told me when I was about your age. I've never forgotten it, and I don't want you to forget it either."

"Ice cream is life," Ted repeated, obediently.

"That's my boy," said Trevor.

All these years later, Ted can still remember the way his dad looked at him. *But was it just the look of a proud dad? Or the look of a man used to getting his own way?*

Ted watches Trevor scouring the factory floor for a taster and feels a surge of resentment towards him. *Does he just swing his weight around so everyone will do what he wants? Is he some kind of low-level bully?*

"Oi, Cole," shouts Trevor to his young trainee, "come here and taste this for us."

Cole Egerton steps away from his machine and lollops over to his bosses.

"By 'eck, have you not stopped growing yet?" Trevor asks, looking him up and down.

"He's like a bloody giraffe," says Derek.

"We're going to have to get you a new apron soon," says Trevor. "That one's starting to look like a miniskirt."

As the older men laugh, Ted spots a wince in Cole's eyes.

"If you get any taller, you'll have to start watching your head on that ceiling fan," Trevor goes on.

"Yeah, you don't want it to get chopped off," tosses in Derek. "Can you imagine explaining that to Health and Safety?"

As the two men roar with laughter, Cole squirms.

Ted wonders if his dad is trying to give the factory junior a gentle ribbing or purposefully tormenting him. He wonders if this qualifies as bullying. The anonymous letters are making him question so many things he hasn't considered before. *Maybe I do look up to Dad too much. Maybe I have wasted too much time trying to keep him happy.*

Without understanding why, his thoughts switch to Oskar. He hopes it wasn't too obvious when he pretended to bump into him last week. Initially, he thought he'd got away with it, until he became nervous and made that tacky joke about Oskar's kneepads. Then—unintentionally—that cheap innuendo about sausages. *With all the dignity of a secretary down-*

ing a bottle of white wine at the Christmas do and throwing herself on the nearest pole.

He tries not to cringe. In any case, there's no point worrying about it now. He takes out his phone and smiles at his new screensaver: a picture of Lily sitting on the beach, her damp paws coated in sand. He opens up his contacts and finds Oskar's number. So far, he's held back from texting him to arrange their date at the golf course. *If it even is a date . . .*

But he can't help wondering if this is because he doesn't want to let his parents down, because he doesn't want to rub their noses in the fact that he and Giles have split up.

I've got to stop worrying about that kind of thing.

And what if the letters are true . . . ?

"Hello, this is Ted." he texts. **"It was good to bump into you the other day. Do you fancy that game of mini golf?"**

He pauses.

He looks at his dad, who's handing Cole a spoonful of ice cream.

He runs his hand over the letter in his pocket.

And he presses Send.

CHAPTER 21

As Oskar and Ted collect their clubs at the entrance to the mini golf course, Oskar feels a rush of nerves. But at the same time, excitement live-wires through him. And he feels a little glow of pride in himself for going through with the meeting—which is what he's calling this until he knows if it's a date. *Mind you, I'm not sure I could have resisted.*

Unfortunately, the weather is miserable. The sky is gunmetal gray and pocked with damson-dark clouds, there's a brisk—although not savage—wind, and the sea is an ugly sludge-like shade of brown, its fierce waves leaping over the railings to lash the promenade. The high tide has brought in the seagulls, several of which honk loudly overhead. But Oskar is determined to look on the positive side; at least this means he and Ted are the only people on the golf course. *Which means I don't have to worry about anyone seeing us.*

As this is the first time Ted has seen him out of his work clothes, Oskar has selected his outfit carefully; he's wearing his favorite oversized black cargo pants with a loose green hoodie, a gray multipocket gilet, some low-top trainers with chunky soles, and a beanie hat—finished off with his usual black enamel ear stud. He's washed his hair and beard so they don't smell of work and has made sure to get rid of every last fleck of paint from underneath his fingernails and in the grooves of his hands.

In order to calm his nerves, he's made a list of subjects to talk about and saved it on his phone. If his mind goes blank, his plan is to pretend he's received an important text message and quickly consult it. But to be on the safe side, he's memorized the first few topics.

Topic one—Ted's job.

"So how long have you worked for Ainsworth's?" he asks, as he takes his opening shot on the first hole. But he misjudges his swing, and the ball doesn't make it to the other side of a little hill, rolling back down to settle at his feet.

"My whole life," says Ted, effortlessly potting the ball in one. "Well, since I left school at eighteen. But to be honest, I didn't have much choice in the matter."

"You don't sound very happy about it," says Oskar, hitting the ball again and this time managing to clear the hill.

"It's a long story." Something like a sigh escapes Ted. "I don't know, working with your family can be a bit full-on. A bit intense."

"I can imagine," says Oskar. *Although I'm not sure I'd like to.*

He pots his ball on the third shot, they write their scores on a sheet and move on to the second hole. This is dotted with garishly colored toadstools through which they need to hit the ball—but Oskar whacks his straight into the trunk of the first.

"Anyway, I'm not sure it's natural for a forty-three-year-old to spend the entire working week with his parents," comments Ted. "I think it's probably healthier to fly the nest and make your own way in life."

"Well, at least you do one of those jobs where people are happy to see you," Oskar chirps, "not like an undertaker or a dentist. You know, when I came into your shop, all the customers were in a good mood. Ice cream makes people happy."

Ted looks like he's about to say something but blinks it away. "I suppose so, yeah."

After several more collisions with toadstools, Oskar pots his ball on the fifth attempt. "Sorry, I'm rubbish at this."

"No, you're not," insists Ted. "I just have an unfair advantage. Honestly, I've played this game thousands of times."

At the next hole, they have to hit the ball into the mouth of a dinosaur and wait for it to reemerge from the end of its tail. But, once again, Oskar misses his target. "Maybe I should have come here during the week for a sneaky practice," he jokes, trying to cover his frustration. He hopes Ted doesn't think he's as useless as he feels. It's definitely not the impression he wanted to give.

"I still can't believe you've never been before," says Ted. "How long have you lived in St. Luke's?"

"Ten years. And somehow I've managed to resist the lure of the mini-golf course."

Ted pots his ball in one. "And now here you are—on a date."

Aha! So this is *a date!* Oskar feels a strange mix of delight and anxiety. Although he noticed that Ted raised his voice at the end of the statement, as if he intended it as a question.

Go on, give him an answer . . . You might be nervous but you want this to be a date.

"And now here I am on a date," he confirms. He hits his ball into the mouth of the dinosaur.

"See, look at that!" says Ted. "You're not rubbish at all!"

Oskar smiles, but now he's confirmed his intentions, the knot of anxiety tightens in his stomach. He pretends to be absorbed in the game, glad of the focus on something else.

He moves the conversation on. *Topic two—the town.*

"So presumably you've always lived in St. Luke's?" he asks Ted.

"Yep, I sure have," Ted replies. "I know it's quiet and not

the most exciting place in the world, but I like it. I don't know, maybe deep down at heart I'm just an old biddy."

" 'Old biddy.' What's that?"

"Sorry. An old lady."

Oskar sends him a beaming smile. "Don't apologize; you've just given me another new word for the day."

"In that case, I'm glad to be of service." Ted hits his ball onto a seesaw, which tips over, sending it rolling down the other side. But he doesn't seem remotely proud of his success; if anything, he looks embarrassed. This puts Oskar at ease.

"How about you?" asks Ted. "Do you like St. Luke's?"

He sounds genuinely interested, which Oskar appreciates. "Yeah, it's sweet, it's pretty. Life moves at a gentle pace." He gestures to all the flowers. "And it's colorful. This may seem like a funny thing to say, but I love color."

Ted angles his head as if considering this for the first time. "Yeah, me too."

Oskar focuses on the seesaw and swings his club, sending his ball up and onto it. But when it rolls down the other side, a gust of wind blows it off course and onto the pathway. He lets out a laugh. "Oh my God, that's so unfair!"

"You were cheated!" says Ted, gasping in mock outrage.

Oskar puts a hand on his hip and makes a show of waiting for the wind to die down. Across the road, a group of young boys are running along the promenade with their coats held up behind their heads, playing superheroes. He can remember doing the same when he was a boy.

I wonder what that boy would think if he could see me now . . .

"Right, let's give this another go," he says, once the wind is calmer. He repositions his ball and aims at the seesaw.

As he watches, Ted folds his arms. "My favorite thing about St. Luke's is the beach. I've got a dog and I take her for a walk there every morning." His eyes flit towards the sea. "That is, when the tide's not in."

Aha! That brings us onto topic three—hobbies.

Oskar asks about his dog, and Ted describes a brown-and-black mongrel called Lily. As he tells Oskar that her favorite treat is sausages and her favorite place to sleep is the bottom of his bed—sometimes keeping him awake with her snoring—there's something about the affection in his voice that makes Oskar's heart give a little flutter. *Come on, pull yourself together!*

Oskar concentrates on potting the ball—finally managing on his eighth attempt.

"My favorite thing about St. Luke's is the sea," he says, picking up his ball. "I like to go for bike rides along the coast. I grew up by the sea, so have always loved it."

"Really?" Ted says. "And why did you leave Poland?"

Oskar pulls a face. Now they're veering off his list of prepared topics. *Do I really want to go there?*

"That's another long story," he mumbles.

"Sorry," says Ted, "you don't have to answer if you don't want to."

Come on, Oskar, you can do this. Get over your anxiety.

"No, it's OK," he reassures Ted. "The short version is that Poland is a very religious country. It's very Catholic. And my family is very Catholic."

"So how do they feel about you being gay?"

Oskar's shocked to hear those words spoken out loud—and fear catches in his throat. Overhead, a seagull gives a particularly loud honk.

It's alright, there's no need to be scared.

"Actually, they don't know," he answers.

Ted looks stunned. "They don't *know*? So you're not out?"

"No, not to them. But we're not close."

Ted's features soften. "So has it always been like that?"

Oskar senses that Ted isn't trying to judge him but wants to understand. He feels encouraged to go on. "Not when I was little. But when I was twelve, something bad happened, and I realized my family would never accept me if they knew I was gay. So as soon as I could, I left home. But I didn't come here straightaway; first I went to Warsaw."

As they work their way around the course—conquering obstacles in the shape of a rocket, a turtle, and a replica of the town's famous windmill with rotating sails that Oskar jokes must have been designed with the exact purpose of intercepting his ball—Oskar explains that he spent a few years living in the Polish capital but found it bleak and joyless. He missed the natural beauty of the coast and kept expecting to see the sea popping up in the gaps between the streets or over the brow of the next hill. On top of that, he felt depressed by the city's pollution and the stark presence of so many gray concrete housing blocks—and intimidated by all the aggressively macho statues glorifying workers and soldiers. "Also, I moved to Warsaw because I thought I'd be freer, but I soon found out this wouldn't be possible."

"So is there no gay scene there?" asks Ted.

Again, Oskar is surprised by the directness of the question, but he tells himself to relax. *And you've started now—there's no point holding back.*

"Not like there is here," he answers. "Or at least there wasn't when I lived there. There were just a couple of underground bars."

Oskar tells Ted that he only ventured to a gay bar once—after he'd been for dinner with some friends and felt emboldened by drink. It was a place he'd read about online that was hidden away in a basement at the end of a back street. But he didn't find it very welcoming and was greeted by sneers from several hard-faced men who looked angry to be spotted, and glances of suspicion from the smattering of sallow-faced rent boys who were trying to attract one of the handful of more adventurous or just plain drunk foreigners. After less than an hour, he decided to leave, only to be told by a bouncer that a gang of thugs had gathered outside and were abusing customers as they left—adding that several customers had been followed home recently and violently assaulted. Oskar retreated downstairs and sat cowering in a corner, hoping more alcohol would obliterate his fear, until the police arrived to escort everyone out.

"But when we got outside," he says, his voice cracking, "the thugs were still there. They shoved and insulted us and one of them even spat at us. Worst of all, the police just stood there, smiling. They smiled and sniggered as if we deserved it."

I can't believe I'm telling him all this. But the more he gets to know Ted, the more Oskar feels he can. And he's surprised to find that it feels good to be opening up—in some ways, it's like an unburdening. *Maybe I shouldn't have kept all this buried for so long.*

Ted is clearly horrified by the story. "My God, that's awful," he says. "I'm so sorry you had to go through that."

Oskar shrugs. "In my country it's normal. I think it is in many countries around the world."

Ted shakes his head in dismay. "So is that why you moved to the UK?"

"Yeah, I came here when I was twenty-three. But I didn't move to St. Luke's straightaway—first I went to Manchester."

Oskar is about to tell him the reason he went to Manchester but stops himself. *No, it's too early.*

"Well, we all know about the gay scene in Manchester," pipes Ted. "I imagine Canal Street must have been quite a culture shock for you."

Oskar makes several attempts to hit his ball through the loop of a rollercoaster but it keeps falling off. "Yeah, it was. I went out in the Gay Village a few times, but it was too much. Everything revolved around getting drunk and having sex with strangers. I didn't have a problem with that, but it wasn't for me. And I felt uncomfortable around people that were so . . . sorry, I don't know how to say it . . ."

"Loud and proud?"

"Yes! Loud and proud."

Ted shows him exactly where to aim his ball to get it through the loop. "That must have been difficult when you'd had to hide that side of yourself away for so long."

"Exactly. I just felt too exposed. I couldn't relax at all."

"And how about apps? Have you ever tried those?"

Oskar has another go at potting his ball but once again misses the loop. "I experimented but people don't really want to meet you when you don't put your photo or any personal details online."

Ted's eyes narrow. "And why won't you post your details?"

"I wouldn't want anyone I know to see them, especially anyone back home in Poland." A chill runs down Oskar's spine. The very idea of it is terrifying.

Ted frowns. "OK, yeah, of course."

"That's why, when I was offered a job in St. Luke's, I grabbed the opportunity. I knew it would be much quieter here, and I'd be near the sea again. I'd tried living in cities, but it hadn't worked, so I wanted to make a fresh start." Finally, Oskar manages to hit his ball through the loop, and it slides down the rollercoaster and into the hole.

Ted gives him a round of applause. "And you don't feel like too much of an outsider here? I can't imagine St. Luke's has many Polish gays. In fact, I'd guess you're the only one."

Oskar tightens his grip on his club. There's only one way to respond to this comment—and the thought of it makes him prickle with dread. But he doesn't want to mislead Ted.

He blows out his cheeks. "I'm not really out here."

Ted's eyebrows shoot up to his hairline. "What? So you're not out at all?"

Oskar looks down and concentrates on driving his ball up one of the legs of a bright-green octopus. "Not really. Don't get me wrong, I'm not in the closet either. I mean, I don't lie to anyone. But people don't usually ask a Polish painter and decorator if he's gay. Most people don't ask about my personal life at all. And if they do, I just dodge their questions and change the subject. I'm sorry if that seems cowardly, but I find it hard."

Ted shakes his head, clearly anxious that he's offended Oskar. "No, no, I totally get it. Sorry, I didn't mean to make you feel bad."

Oskar smiles. "That's OK; you didn't."

Once he's hit his ball up into the octopus and it's dropped out of its belly, it takes Oskar a few attempts to drive it round a corner and into the hole. "Finally! That one was the worst!"

"Never trust an octopus," Ted jokes. "Too many tentacles."

As they laugh, Oskar's relieved that the spark between them hasn't diminished.

"And what about your family?" Ted asks. "Do you have any contact with them now?"

Oskar nods. "Yeah, we speak most weeks. And I visit them once a year, usually at Christmas. Although the last time I went back was before Covid."

As they move on to the final hole—which involves hitting the ball over a moat and through the drawbridge of a castle— Oskar tells Ted that the last time he returned to his hometown in Poland, he witnessed an anti-gay protest. Thousands of members of the public took to the streets, waving placards and chanting slogans about gay people, calling them an affront to family values and a danger to children. Then some far-right politicians mounted the steps of the town hall and declared the region the latest in a series of LGBT-free zones. As the people cheered, Oskar was struck by the hatred in their eyes. "It was like they were wild with it. And I was terrified just imagining what they'd do if they knew I was gay—what my family would do if they knew."

"My God, that sounds horrific," says Ted.

"That's why I haven't been back since. To be honest, Covid and then the various travel restrictions gave me a convenient excuse. And things are only getting worse in my country, so I'm better off here. I may not tell everyone I'm gay, but at least I don't feel unsafe."

Ted leans on his club. "I'm glad to hear that."

"You know, I can't believe I'm telling you all this," Oskar confesses. "I don't think I've ever been so open with anyone."

"Well, I'm flattered." Ted picks up his club and stamps it on the grass. "It's also interesting for me because it reminds me of how lucky I am. I mean, me and my parents had a few issues when I was growing up, but they soon got used to me being different, and they were great when I came out. And they always loved my husband."

Devastation cuts through Oskar. *Husband? So you're married?*

"Sorry, *ex*-husband. I'm separated." Ted imparts this information as if it isn't particularly significant—or as if he wants Oskar to *think* it isn't significant. He pots the ball and steps back to let Oskar finish.

"So how long ago did you split up?" asks Oskar.

"Two and a half months now."

Is that all?

As Oskar hits shot after shot, he's aware that he's drawing back into himself. *If Ted's only just split up with his husband, he's not going to be ready to start a new relationship.*

All of a sudden, he feels awash with dread—and a voice in his head predicts that if he goes on with this, then he'll only end up getting hurt. He'll go backwards, or even end up in a worse position than when he started.

Hold on a minute, since when am I looking to launch into a relationship? I've already said I need to take things slowly.

Then another voice pulls him in a different direction. *Am I just looking for an excuse to back off? Is that's what's going on here? Is it my fear talking?*

Finally, he pots the ball and the game's over. Neither of the men bothers to tot up the scores as it's obvious Ted has won—by some margin.

"Well done," Oskar says, making a show of giving him an over-pumped handshake. "As you Brits say, the best man won!"

Ted shrugs off the praise. "Not at all. It wasn't exactly a fair contest."

"Well, I enjoyed it. It was fun."

Ted looks at his watch. "Listen, it's only early. Do you fancy going for a drink?"

Oskar has no idea how to respond. He wants to go for a drink, but he's also worried that if he does, it will end badly. That he'll regret it.

"No, I'd better get home," he blurts out, before he can change his mind. "I've got things to do."

Why did you say that? You've got nothing to do!

Ted looks dejected. "OK, no probs. But would you like to go out again?"

Oskar knows the answer. *Of course I would.*

But can I say it?

He nods, slowly. "Yeah, I would like to go out again."

As he watches the happiness spread across Ted's face, the emotion is mirrored in him.

"But no more mini golf," Ted quips. "Next time, you pick the activity."

And, as Ted's eyes twinkle at him, Oskar is already looking forward to it.

CHAPTER 22

Ted is at home, in the hallway, taking down photos of him and Giles. He picks one up that was taken shortly after they got engaged; it shows them sitting outside their hotel in Tuscany, holding up glasses of red wine, bursting with excitement about the future. As Ted adds it to his stack, he can't help but feel a flicker of sadness at the loss of that future. *Then again, that was the future Giles wanted. Hopefully the one I'm building now is going to be much better . . .*

He isn't sure what to do with the photos. It seems ruthless to throw them away, not to mention wasteful. He decides to pack them into a box and work out what to do with them later. *You never know when I might want to reuse the frames . . .*

His motivation for the clear-out was his date with Oskar, which went better than he'd expected. He was embarrassed to give him such a thrashing at mini golf, but he did try to hit the ball badly a few times, without making it obvious. Thankfully, Oskar didn't seem to be in the slightest bit competitive—unlike Giles, who Ted would always have to make sure won at every game they played. Ted lifts up another photo—of the two of them on holiday in Norway—and remembers a spectacularly scenic train journey through the fjords from Oslo to Bergen, a journey that was ruined by Giles's foul mood when, despite Ted's best efforts, he somehow ended up beating Giles at a game of cards. As he stashes the photo in the box, Ted can't help thinking that if things work out between him and Oskar, it'll be great not to have to try and lose all the time.

Now come on, don't get ahead of yourself.

In any case, the game of mini golf was incidental to his date. Most importantly, he's established that he and Oskar definitely have a connection—and there's no question that Ted finds him physically attractive. He looked so cute in his skater-boy clothes, with those stunning blue eyes and that sexy beard, that when Ted first saw him, he struggled to catch his breath. Ted didn't know he could feel like that about someone other than Giles. The realization sent excitement shooting through him.

One slight concern is that Oskar seemed a little awkward around him—and at the end of the date refused his invitation to go on for a drink. Plus, the fact he isn't out of the closet is a major worry. That's the golden rule of gay relationships, the advice every gay man reads in every magazine or on every web-site: never fall for someone who isn't out. If he isn't comfortable with himself, how can he possibly be comfortable with you? But Ted tells himself that to dismiss Oskar on these grounds wouldn't be fair. It isn't his fault he had such a terrible experience in Poland. And hearing just a few of the details of that experience was truly heartbreaking.

He reminds himself of one of Denise's favorite sayings: it isn't whether you have baggage that's important; it's how you carry it that counts. *I'll just have to find out how Oskar's carrying his. Maybe I could even help him carry it . . .*

But whatever happens, Ted knows he'll have to tread carefully and take things slowly. *Mind you, that's fine for me too; I'm still recovering from my breakup. I don't want to move too fast, then panic and pull back.*

He takes down the last photo of Giles, of the two of them on a dream holiday to New York, walking along the High Line with the Meatpacking District in the background. Ted drops it into his box and leaves the hallway.

When he enters the living room, straightaway he's confronted by that awful piece of art Giles hung over the mantelpiece. Just as he's toying with whether to take it down now or leave it up until he's found a replacement—something *he'd* like to see in his living room—his phone starts to vibrate. He picks it up to see that Jemima's calling him on FaceTime video. He's surprised, as she doesn't usually show much interest in his life, and has only called him once since Giles left. *Is she just going to brag about being invited to yet another celebrity party? Am I just going to end up feeling down and bad about myself?*

He decides to give her the benefit of the doubt and answers. "Hi, Jem."

"Hi, darling!" she trills. She's sitting on her powder-blue suede curved sofa, surrounded by fluffy white cushions. With her high cheekbones, flawless skin, and full-bodied brunette hair, she looks as gorgeous as ever—even though she's only wearing a dressing gown and has no makeup on.

At the sight of her, Ted feels that familiar flare of resentment—that she was able to go off and follow her dream while he had to stay at home. He smothers it with a smile. "How's it going?"

Jemima attaches her phone to a tripod and leans back against the cushions. "Just having a quiet night in. I've had a hot bath, done a clay facemask, then I thought I'd call my favorite brother."

Ted rolls his eyes. "Your *only* brother."

"A minor detail."

"So you're not going out to some glamorous awards ceremony?" he asks, propping his phone up against an empty mug on the coffee table.

"No. To be honest, I go out a lot less these days."

"Really? But the other day I saw you on social media at some posh do."

She twiddles the ends of her hair. "I know, I can put on a good show for my socials. But it's not much fun mixing with all the hot young things when your career's going down the pan."

Ted feels the corners of his mouth lifting into a smile. *Ted, what's the matter with you?*

He forces back the smile. "Oh no. So work's not going well, then?"

"That's an understatement, darling. In case you've forgotten, I've just turned thirty-nine—and that's ancient for a model. Unless you're a supermodel. But, let's be honest, I've never scaled anything like those dizzy heights, whatever Mum and Dad might think."

Ted feels disarmed by her honesty. *I wonder what's behind it.*

"Anyway, my bookings dropped off during the pandemic," Jemima goes on, "and they still haven't picked up. I don't think there's much chance they will now."

Ted feels a stab of guilt for wanting to smile at her misfortune. He resolves to be more sympathetic and supportive. "So what's your plan? Do you have any idea what else you could do?"

"Well, that's kind of why I called." She sits up and readjusts her tripod. "I wanted to run something by you . . ."

"Oh yeah?" Ted leans in and most of his face disappears from view.

"Darling, all I can see is your chin!"

Ted reframes the shot. "Sorry."

Jemima draws in a breath. "So, I've had a great time in London, but it feels like this chapter in my life is closing. I'm thinking of coming home."

Ted gives a little start; he wasn't expecting this at all. "Seriously?"

"Yeah, I'm thinking of coming back for good. Why, is that a bad idea?"

Ted has mixed feelings. He's always felt like he's been in Jemima's shadow and has always suspected his sister is their parents' favorite—something that wasn't helped by the realization that she was planned but he wasn't. *Will I just feel inferior if she comes home? Will I be relegated to playing a bit part in* The Jemima Show?

On the other hand, the two of them have always got on well and Jemima's fun to be around. *And from a selfish point of view, if she does come home, it might take some of the pressure off me. She might even turn out to be an ally, just like she was when we were kids.*

Then another thought occurs to him. *Maybe I could tell her about the anonymous letters. Maybe if she was here, we could deal with them together?*

He sends her an encouraging smile. "No, I think it's an ace idea."

She gives a squeak. "Oh good! Anyway, don't get excited as it isn't definite yet. Besides, it's not a decision I can make on my own."

"How do you mean?"

She runs her palms down her thighs. "That brings me onto the other thing I wanted to talk to you about. I've got a new man."

"Aha! Now I know why you've been so quiet on Whats-App! So come on, who is he? What's he like?"

"I don't want to say too much. But his name's Raj, he's from Birmingham, he's a few years older than me, and he works in finance. It's weird; he's not my usual type at all."

Ted raises an eyebrow. "What, you mean he doesn't have biceps thicker than my neck and a brain smaller than my fingernail?"

Jemima rolls her eyes. "Alright, steady on, Ted. But yeah, he is actually intelligent, although I'll have you know the bod's more than satisfactory. Anyway, I really like him. He's exactly the kind of man I didn't realize I've been looking for my whole life."

"Well, that's ace news, Jem. I'm dead chuffed for you."

"Thanks, darling. I'm really excited about it. And let's be honest, it can't come a moment too soon. If I'm lucky, I might be able to jump on that last train just as it pulls out of the station."

Ted laughs. "Don't say that, you're four years younger than me! That means I've missed the train!"

"No, darling, you just caught the wrong one."

Oh God, don't tell me she thought Giles was bad for me too.

But before Ted can follow up on her comment, Jemima interjects with: "Anyway, you've still got plenty of time. I'm sure I don't need to remind you that it's different for men. You can mature and people say you're like a fine wine or an expensive cheese. It's not the same for women. We just rot."

Ted does his best to convince her that not everyone thinks that. "And seriously, you're looking fantastic at the moment. Whatever was in that facemask is clearly working!"

She pretends to bask in a warm glow. "Thanks, darling. And I hope I do come back. It'll be nice for me and you to hang out more. You know, like we used to."

"Yeah, it will. I hope you can convince Raj."

"Well, don't say anything to Mum and Dad just yet. I don't want to tell them about Raj—we haven't been together long, and I don't want to jinx things." Jemima lifts up a cushion and picks at the fluff. "Anyway, enough about me—how are things with you? What have you been up to?"

There's a pause. Even though Jemima has been open with him, Ted doesn't want to tell her about becoming a drag queen. He doesn't want to tell her he's just had his second makeup tutorial with Denise, or that they're about to go shopping for outfits. He certainly doesn't want to tell her he's been watching videos on YouTube to learn how to do the famous drag queen tuck. *Not because I'm ashamed of it—but because I want to keep it to myself. I want it to be my secret, something nobody can spoil. At least for the time being.*

He sighs. "You know, same as ever. Everything's ticking over in the shop." He notices some glitter on the arm of the sofa and brushes it onto the carpet, making a mental note to hoover it up later. *Honestly, that stuff gets everywhere!*

"And how about the love life?"

"Love life?" Does she know about Oskar?

"Don't look so scared," she says. "I'm not asking if you've been on Grindr. I just want to know if you're getting over Giles. Are you starting to face your future without him?"

"Funnily enough, I was just clearing away some of his stuff. You know, old photos and things."

"Well, that's great, darling."

"Yeah, it feels like the right thing to do. And the right time. I mean, the whole thing is still quite nerve-wracking, but yeah, I think I'm ready."

She congratulates him, then says she'll leave him to get on with his clear-out. They say goodbye, promising to speak again soon.

As Ted lifts the phone to end the call, his mind starts racing. *If Jemima comes home, it'll change the family dynamic. It could change everything . . .*

He reminds himself of his resolution to put himself first. *I mustn't forget that. Whatever happens, I mustn't lose sight of it.*

He stands up and yanks the snotty tea towel off the wall.

CHAPTER 23

On Friday afternoon, Ted sneaks away from work, and he and Denise drive to Blackpool. Their destination is Off the Peg, a shop that specializes in drag clothes and accessories and is owned by Peg Legge. But when they arrive, they find that Peg isn't in drag—and is serving customers as plain old Sid Clugston. Ted can't get over the transformation. *He looks like some out-of-shape divorced dad who goes to salsa classes in the upstairs room of a tapas bar.*

He notices Sid's belly, straining at the buttons of his shirt. *And maybe stops off for a kebab on the way home.*

But rather than feeling disappointed, Ted decides to see this as a reminder of the magic of drag. The excitement catches in his chest. *If it can turn Sid into Peg, what can it do to me?*

"So I take it you've decided to do the open-mic night?" Sid asks, leaning over a counter strewn with jewelry made out of fake crystals, rubies, and sapphires.

Ted grins. "Yeah, I'm bang up for it."

"Well, that's beltin' news!"

"At the same time, I'm dead nervous."

Sid shakes his head. "Don't be. Drag's like armor. Once you've strapped it on, nothing can get to you. Nothing can touch you."

"That's why we're here," Denise jumps in. "We need to find his suit of armor!"

Ted tells Sid about Gail Force and the kind of queen he wants her to be. "I'd describe her as rebellious, sparky, and a little bit naughty."

"She sounds like hell on heels," quips Sid. "And what kind of aesthetic are you thinking? Well-crafted and old school, or unpolished and East London?"

Ted creases his forehead. "I couldn't pull off that cool East London thing. I'm definitely thinking old school."

"Condragulations, you've come to the right place!"

Sid steps out from behind the counter and leads them through the shop, past posters advertising shows by Peg Legge and celebrating classic queens like Danny La Rue and Divine, over to walls studded with wigs, breast plates, padding, and tucking tape, racks of boots and shoes with scary-high heels, and rail after rail of clothes in every conceivable shade, shape, size, and style, although an inordinate number of them are shimmering with sequins. Along the way, Sid pulls out a few items he thinks might work for Gail and hands them to Ted. Then he has to step away to take a quick phone call.

"Don't worry," he trills. "I'll be back in two shakes of a donkey's dick."

Ted and Denise carry on rummaging through the rails.

"How about this?" says Ted, pulling out an emerald PVC cat suit.

"Oh, I don't know," muses Denise. "It's a bit . . . green."

Ted hangs it up again. "Yeah, I don't want to look like a bottle of Fairy liquid."

Denise pulls out a lace-trimmed bustier and holds it up against herself. "What do you think of this? For me, I mean. Would it make me look like a sexy saloon girl?"

Ted screws up his nose. "More like an aging madam in a one-horse town."

Denise gasps and gives him a playful slap. "Teddy, you are getting sassier by the minute!"

"I guess that's the magic of drag! It must be kicking in already."

Denise slots the bustier back onto the rack. "Anyway, today's about Gail, not me. Let's grab everything that looks vaguely promising and take it into the changing room."

As they carry through their first bundles, Denise questions Ted about his date with Oskar. He revealed the news that he's met someone on their journey over to Blackpool. Since he's texted Oskar to ask about a second date—and Oskar's agreed and said he'll come up with a plan—it felt right to tell her. But Ted only had time to give Denise a basic outline of their trip to the golf course, so she's keen for him to fill in the gaps.

"Well, I think he sounds lovely," she declares. "And what did he say about you doing drag?"

Ted clenches his jaw. "I didn't tell him. I didn't want to risk spoiling it."

Denise balances her dresses on the back of a chair. "'Spoiling it'? Why should it spoil it?"

Ted and Giles were in Dublin, in a bar called Euphoria, or Elysium. *Or maybe it's Electric?* Ted was so drunk, he had no idea.

They'd only been together for a year, and this was their first weekend away. On the plane, Ted had been eager for the holiday to begin but also apprehensive. How would they get on for a whole weekend with only each other for company? He wondered if Giles might also be nervous. *I wonder if that's why we've both ended up getting so wasted.*

As soon as they'd arrived in Dublin, they'd gone for what was supposed to have been a quick drink in a bar next to the hotel—and several pubs later had staggered into a gay bar that was advertising a drag show. The queen performing was called Fanny Spank—that much Ted could remember. She had a gloriously trashy look, with ripped fishnets, hooker-red lips, a nicotine-blond wig, and an uproariously crude sense of humor that had both him and Giles whooping and hollering at every joke. Fanny had singled them out as the most enthusiastic members of her audience and hauled Giles onto the stage to help her perform an X-rated version of "Let's Hear It for the Boy" by Deniece Williams. Ted had been surprised at how eager Giles was to take part, letting her wriggle and writhe around him, at one point even joining in with a few moves of his own. The two of them had ended up enjoying the show so much that once it was over, they felt compelled to approach Fanny and tell her. The next thing Ted knew, she was inviting them into her dressing room, where she said she could smoke a sneaky cigarette. Then, when Giles popped to the bar to buy them drinks, Ted confessed he'd always wanted to try drag, and Fanny suggested dragging him up to surprise Giles.

"Come on, you're clean shaven and your eyebrows aren't too thick." She gave him a conspiratorial grin. "I think you'd make a great queen."

Ted felt a shiver of excitement run up his spine. But Fanny's red lipstick suddenly signaled danger. He'd never told Giles he wanted to be a drag queen. He wasn't sure what Giles would make of it—and he didn't want to risk putting him off so early in the relationship.

He told himself to relax. *Giles loved Fanny's show, so you've obviously nothing to worry about.*

"Yeah, that'd be ace," he fizzed. "But have we got enough time?"

"There's a massive queue," said Fanny. "He'll be away for at least fifteen minutes. I'll only do quick drag, just a wig and basic makeup, and you can chuck my fur coat over what you've got on."

"Alright, let's do it!"

Fanny began darting around Ted's face as she dabbed, brushed, blotted, painted, and powdered. She pulled a copper-colored wig over his head then swept her coat around his shoulders. "Ta-da!" she said, stepping to one side so he could see himself in the mirror.

Ted was stunned. His complexion had been smoothed out with foundation, he had contoured cheekbones, taupe eyeshadow with black wings, lashes coated with thick mascara, and—best of all—his lips painted the same hot red as Fanny's. In just a few minutes the dull, unremarkable, barely noticeable Ted Ainsworth had blossomed into a glamorous, fierce-looking, powerful queen. The adrenaline spiked through him. "Oh, Fanny, I love it!"

Her eyes twinkled. "Well, it didn't take much. Honestly, you're a natural."

"I can't wait for Giles to see it!"

Just then, the door to the bar opened, letting in a blast of the latest single by Girls Aloud.

"Quick, get behind that!" hissed Fanny.

Ted ducked behind a screen as he heard Giles's footsteps approaching down the corridor. Then the door creaked open.

"Here we are," Giles bellowed. "Just a minute, where's Ted?"

"Do you want to come out?" shouted Fanny.

Ted slid out from behind the screen and gave Giles what he hoped was a sultry look. "Well, hello, stranger. You're so sexy I could climb you like a tree."

Giles almost dropped his tray of drinks. "Ted, what are you doing?"

"Fanny's put me in drag. We thought we'd surprise you. What do you think?"

Giles's face thickened with disgust. "You look a right state. I've never seen anything more embarrassing in my life."

Ted's heart plummeted to his toes. "I was hoping you'd like it."

"Well, I don't. You look like some ugly old boiler." Giles turned to Fanny. "Was this your idea?"

"Chill out, fella. We were only having a laugh."

"But I thought you enjoyed the show," Ted protested. "I thought you liked watching Fanny."

"Yeah, I did," said Giles, "but that doesn't mean I want my boyfriend to make a spectacle of himself. You know I'm not into camp. How am I supposed to fancy you like that?"

Ted looked at himself in the mirror. All his earlier enthusiasm had morphed into a sickening feeling of shame. *What was I thinking? I look horrendous.*

Over his shoulder, he caught sight of Giles, the disgust still etched on his face. Suddenly, he felt disgusted in himself too.

"Well, I'm not going out there with you like that," Giles thundered. "I'd die of humiliation. Get that shit off your face now."

Fanny opened her mouth to object but, Ted silenced her. "It's alright, Fanny. It was only an experiment. There's no harm done."

Fanny winched an eyebrow. "Are you sure about that, sweetheart?"

No, but I can't do this. I can't do anything to upset Giles. I can't risk losing him. The very thought of it made Ted's throat tighten with fear. His heart was thumping as heavily as the bass line coming through from the bar.

He moved over to the dressing table and snatched up some wet wipes. He began rubbing off his makeup so vigorously that he staggered and had to grab hold of the table.

Thank God I'm pissed. And thank God Giles is too. With any luck, he won't remember this. Or at the very least I can pass it off as a drunken mistake.

He shook the fur coat from his shoulders and tugged off his wig.

One thing's for sure—I'm never doing drag again. If Giles doesn't like it, I'll just have to forget about it.

From now on, I'm not even going to mention it again.

"The thing is," says Ted, as he pulls off his T-shirt, "if Oskar's still uncomfortable with his sexuality, I'm worried he won't like drag. You know, it's such an extreme expression of gayness, I just think you've got to be really comfortable in yourself to be happy around it. And I don't think he's there yet."

Denise nods. "From what you've said, it's no wonder."

"Yeah, and I just want to be sensitive with him. Drag can be a bit in-your-face."

"I know what you mean," says Denise.

Ted gives her a smirk. "And let's be honest, Gail Force is hardly going to be shy or modest."

"I should hope not. In fact, I'm banking on it." Denise lets out a sigh. "But this isn't just about Oskar, honey. It's also about you. And you've decided to put yourself first—in all areas of your life."

Ted unzips his jeans and tugs them off. "Yeah, you're right, Den. And that hasn't changed."

She averts her eyes. "You know, if a relationship's based on secrets, it's not going to be a great one."

"Absolutely not." Ted pulls the curtain shut with a rattle.

"And one thing I've learned," Denise calls out, "is you can only really be in love with someone when you're not afraid to be your true self around them."

"Yeah, yeah, alright!" shouts Ted, tugging off his socks so he's wearing nothing but his underpants. "I get the message!"

"So basically, you've got to tell Oskar." Denise gives the curtain a shake, as if to drive home her point.

Ted stands still and looks at himself in the mirror. For a moment he's back in the dressing room in Dublin, seeing himself in drag for the first time. He feels a swelling of fear but forces it back. "I will, I will," he concedes. "I just have to pick my moment."

"Alright, but promise me you'll pick it soon."

"I promise!"

"Great." Denise thrusts a slinky silver metallic dress through the curtain. "Now try this on!"

CHAPTER 24

After leaving Off the Peg with a clearer idea of Ted's vision for Gail Force's style, Denise and Ted move on to Queen of Clubs. It has the same thrown-together décor Denise remembers from their last visit—the same plastic ivy, strips of silver foil, and rickety furniture—but none of the wild, chaotic energy it had when it was packed with customers. As it's only just opened and the drag show doesn't start for a few hours, it's still very quiet. But that suits Denise. *It means me and Ted can have a nice, relaxed drink and talk things through.*

"Well, I think we've made a really good start today," she cheeps.

"Yeah, so do I," says Ted. "I just need to keep practicing my makeup. And I need to keep walking in heels. I've been wearing my training heels around the house, but I need to do the same thing with the ones we've just bought."

Denise takes a sip of her margarita. "And what about material, honey? Have you decided what you're going to talk about in your set?"

Ted spreads his hands on the table. "I was thinking I could use my own story and talk about being dumped by my husband and suddenly finding myself on my own in my forties. I was going to try and come up with some funny observations about it."

"I think that's a great idea! As a fellow single forty-something, I'd love to hear that."

"Ace." Ted swills his ice around the glass; as he's driving them back later, he's only drinking a Diet Coke. "And now we're on the subject, when do you think *you're* going to get yourself back out there?"

Denise's shoulders stiffen. "I'm over that, Teddy. You know I haven't thought about dating since Karl."

Three years ago, Denise split up with Karl, her boyfriend of more than half a decade. He was gorgeous, funny, and charming—and most people loved him. But what most people didn't know—because Karl was careful not to show them—was that he was constantly simmering with anger—anger at a world he thought had cheated him out of a career as a professional footballer, when he'd contracted glandular fever (according to him, from some girl he'd kissed at the school disco) just before his trial for the youth team of the local lower-league club. This anger would erupt if ever a waiter, shop assistant, or taxi driver made the slightest mistake—but most often it erupted when he was on his own with Denise. He'd criticize her cooking, housework, friends, appearance, how long she took to get ready for a night out, how slowly she walked in heels, and on one occasion even how much toilet roll she used. Of course, he made sure to offset this with sporadic expressions of remorse and tantalizing flashes of affection—just enough to keep her hanging, to keep her hopeful that one day he might change. But he didn't change. *If anything, he got worse.*

Whenever Denise would come home late from a night out with Ted or her girlfriends, Karl would accuse her of cheating on him, and if she ever so much as smiled at another man when they were out together, as soon as they were on their way home, he'd attack her for flirting. In the early days, part of her quite liked this; she thought it was a sign of how passionately he cared about her and felt lucky that she was able to attract a man capable of such intense emotions—especially when so many of her colleagues at work moaned about neglectful husbands and boyfriends who hardly noticed them. But she soon grew to loathe it and to feel ashamed of her part in encouraging or at least excusing it. She also grew to fear Karl's anger and was soon living in a constant state of high alert, in expectation of the next outburst. But if she ever tried to initiate a discussion about it—under the guise of wanting to improve their relationship or make life calmer for Karl—he'd insist he didn't have a problem, that it was all in her head, that she was imagining it, that she was a "nutjob" or a "psycho." Then, finally, that awful thing happened, that awful thing that brought their relationship to its messy, dramatic, painful end. *That awful thing that made Ted insist I get out.*

Denise shakes the memory from her head. "I don't know," she says. "Relationships have always been trouble for me, you know that."

Ted leans towards her. "Yeah, but you've dealt with that now. You've worked out why that kept happening."

Several sessions with a counselor helped Denise trace the roots of her unhappy love life back to her childhood. The conclusion they reached was that she was attracted to the wrong kind of men—men who didn't treat her well or were untrustworthy—because she'd spent years witnessing her parents' unhappy relationship. Years seeing her dad failing to come home at night and making no effort to hide his infidelity, once shouting at her mum that if she were a better wife and his home life weren't so dull, he wouldn't have to stray. Years lying in bed listening to her mum tipping back bottles of cheap white wine at the kitchen table and sobbing, sometimes trying to smother her tears under sorrowful music by the Carpenters. According to the counselor, this explained why the adult Denise would put up with boyfriends telling her she was fat or ugly or cheating on her—discovering one affair when she found a woman's underwear in the glove compartment of her boyfriend's car and being hit with another when a different boyfriend gave her chlamydia. But none of that compared to Karl or what he did at the end of their relationship. The memory of it makes her shudder. *But all that's behind me now. It can't hurt me anymore.*

And I want to keep it that way.

Denise straightens her back and draws in a long, fortifying breath. "Yeah, I do feel much stronger now, but that's only because I stay away from men."

"I know, but you can't stay away forever."

"*Can't* I? *Why* can't I?"

Ted stabs at the ice in his glass. "Sorry, you *can* stay away from men. Of course you can. You've proved you can be completely independent and perfectly happy on your own. But I know you. And I don't think you *want* to be on your own. I think that deep down, you'd like to find the right man. I don't buy all that bravado about giving up on love. I think you still want to be loved."

Denise feels short of breath. Until Ted said that, she hadn't realized just how much she *does* still want to be loved. *I've been trying to deny it, even to myself.*

But the thought of looking for it terrifies her. *What if I open up all that pain and heartache again? What if I slip back into my old habits?*

She smiles, vaguely. "Yeah, maybe . . ."

"I sense there's a 'but' coming."

"But why would I risk it, Teddy? After spending all this time concentrating on self-care and building self-love, why would I do anything to jeopardize that?"

"Because you deserve it, Den. Yes, you've got an ace life on your own, but you deserve the cherry on the cake. The flake in the ice cream. The lime in the margarita."

Denise takes the wedge of lime from the rim of her glass and squeezes it into her drink. "Yeah, I know I do, honey. But is now really the right time for me to get back out there? Aren't I a bit past it?"

Ted gives her a withering look. "No! Stop making excuses!"

"It's not about excuses. It's . . ." She trails off.

"Sorry, I get it," Ted says. "It's about trying to protect yourself. I also get that it's much tougher for women than it is for men. But there's no way you're past it, Den. And, as you said yourself, it's never too late. Look at me, starting out as a drag queen in my forties. I'm an old bag compared to some of the kids out there. But you told me not to worry about that, remember?"

"Yeah, I did."

"So listen to your own advice. And please start dating again. Just dip your toe into the water. I promise I'll be there if anything goes wrong."

She drains her glass, leaving the wedge of lime lying at the bottom. "OK, I'll think about it."

It doesn't look like she has much choice. Now Ted's put the idea in her head, now she's admitted to herself that she does still want to be loved, Denise knows she won't be able to *stop* herself thinking about it. Terror creeps up her spine, but she swallows it back and smiles.

"Ace," says Ted. "Same again?"

CHAPTER 25

Ted walks through the restaurant and finds Oskar reading a menu at a table tucked around a corner. It strikes him as the worst possible spot for them to sit, cut off from all the other diners, shielded from view by a hip-high partition on top of which sits a row of plants. They might as well be in a private room. *Then again, I wonder if that's the point.*

He feels a rumble of dread.

Then Oskar looks up and their eyes meet. And Oskar unleashes a smile that takes Ted's breath away.

Well, if he is uncomfortable being seen with another man, I'm not going to dwell on it.

They're meeting in Urchins, a restaurant on the seafront that specializes in fish sourced from nearby Fleetwood. Although the food has a fantastic reputation, the venue's décor follows a tired old nautical theme: the walls are papered white and stamped with navy-blue anchors, fishermen's nets stuffed with plastic seaweed and lobsters are hanging from the ceiling, and ring-shaped lifebuoys are nailed to the toilet doors. Ted has eaten here several times and knows the restaurant serves Ainsworth's ice cream, but thankfully he doesn't have any contact with the company's business clients and so doesn't know the owner. *And Oskar booked the table under his name, so we shouldn't be disturbed.*

Once they've greeted each other—with a bungled hug but one that's warm and tingles with promise—they begin perusing their menus.

"You know, I came here for the first time just after I moved to St. Luke's," comments Oskar. "Practically as soon as I landed in England, my family back in Poland started asking if I'd had fish and chips. When I got to the seaside, I figured I should finally try it."

"And I'm assuming you liked it?" asks Ted.

"Yeah, I love it—and I reckon this place is the best in St. Luke's. But the first time I came, I didn't understand the menu. I'd never heard of a chip barm or rag pudding. And I was baffled by pea wet."

Ted chuckles. "That doesn't surprise me. Pea wet's a very Lancashire thing. Do you know what it is now?"

Oskar beams. "Yeah, it's the liquid that's left over from boiling mushy peas."

"Very good! Full marks!"

Sidling up to their table comes a young man with a shaved head and a pierced eyebrow who's dressed in the restaurant's uniform of traditional sailor trousers and a navy-and-white-striped top. "What can I get you gentlemen?" he asks.

They order a bottle of white wine, and Ted goes for the haddock and chips while Oskar opts for the cod.

"Can I get mine with gravy and mushy peas?" adds Ted.

"I'll have mine with some pea wet," says Oskar, grinning wryly.

"Wow, you really have gone native," quips Ted.

"There's nowt better than a bit of pea wet," Oskar jokes in a Lancashire accent.

They laugh as the waiter leaves.

"That's another thing I didn't understand when I first came to England," says Oskar, "the difference between lunch, dinner, and tea."

"Yeah, I bet that's dead confusing," Ted agrees. "Basically, people in different parts of the country say different things. And I'm pretty sure social class comes into it too."

"I've got a workmate from London who calls his evening meal 'supper,'" says Oskar.

Ted gasps in mock outrage. "Supper? That's a piece of toast and a Horlicks before you go to bed!"

Oskar smirks mischievously. "In that case, isn't 'tea' a cup of tea and some cake in the afternoon?"

"Oskar! Wash your mouth out immediately!"

They give another burst of laughter. *Well, what do you know? This is going brilliantly!*

When the wine arrives, Ted sloshes a generous amount into their glasses.

"And pants and underpants," Oskar goes on. "Why do some people call underwear 'pants'? Surely pants are trousers and underpants go *under* them?"

"Now that's more like it! That's what we say around here anyway. Or in America or Australia or pretty much anywhere else they speak English. It's only people from the south of England who call underpants 'pants.'"

"And what about kecks?" Oskar says. "Are they pants or underpants?"

Ted burbles with laughter. "Pants—*trousers*! But that's another Lancashire thing, I don't think anyone else in the UK would understand that."

They're interrupted by the sound of Ted's phone vibrating against the laminated table top. "Sorry, let me switch that off."

When he picks it up, he catches sight of a text from Denise on his home screen. **"Good luck, Teddy! Make sure he knows you're looking for romance and not just to get layed xx"**

God, her spelling's terrible.

Then he panics. *Shit, I don't want Oskar to think I've been talking about him to all my friends. I don't want to scare him off.*

He quickly switches the phone onto airplane mode, making sure to angle it away from Oskar.

"So I'm assuming you already spoke English when you came to the UK?" he asks, brightly.

Oskar takes a sip of his wine. "Yeah, I learned at school. But it wasn't just the local vocabulary I had to get used to. It took me a while to adjust to the northern accent. Particularly those flat vowels."

The waiter reappears with their food.

"Ta," Ted says to him. He turns back to Oskar. "I'm assuming you're familiar with that Lancashire word?"

Oskar smiles. "Ta? Yeah, it's short for thanks. Funnily enough, I was thinking about that the other day. I saw it written on the whiteboard in the language school where I'm working. Along with 'ta-ra,' which means bye."

"It does." Ted squeezes some lemon over his fish. "And how's that going, working in the language school?"

"Fine, thanks. Or fine, ta." Oskar merrily skewers a chip. "They want us finished by the start of the school holidays, but they're not asking for anything too adventurous."

Ted dashes some vinegar onto his chips. "You don't sound very enthusiastic about it."

Oskar sighs. "This job is a living, but it isn't my dream." He cuts into his fish and the steam rises.

"And what *is* your dream?"

Oskar pauses, a forkful of fish hovering in the air. "My dream is to be an interior designer."

Ted smiles out of the corner of his mouth. He knew there was something going on beneath the surface. He knew Oskar was hiding some kind of passion. *I wonder if that's one of the reasons I was first attracted to him.*

Wanting to know more, he questions Oskar about his taste, so Oskar runs him through what he'd do with the restaurant they're in. He details ideas not just to switch the old-fashioned wallpaper for clean white Metro tiles, and to replace the fishermen's nets with low-hanging plants and brushed chrome pendant lights, but to rip out partition walls, relocate the entrance, and open up the kitchen. Ted has to admit, the new layout would make better sense, and Oskar's décor would give the place a much fresher look. *He's obviously very talented—and that only makes him even more attractive.*

Oskar flashes him a rakish smile. "Do you want to know what I'd do with *your* shop?"

"Yeah, go on, then."

Without any preamble, Oskar launches into his detailed vision for a radical redesign of Ainsworth's flagship ice-cream parlor, retaining the original vintage elements but accentuating the period feel by stripping out recent additions and throwing in more retro touches—such as neon lighting and chrome diner-style stools. He'd line the walls with white tiles textured with swirls to evoke the whipped surface of ice cream and intersperse these with pastel greens and blues to represent the sprinkles on top. As he speaks, his passion transforms his voice, the way he holds himself, the way he inhabits who he is. Ted can't help smiling. *I know just how he feels.*

"And I'd get rid of that awful fuchsia you've got everywhere," Oskar adds, "and replace it with a much softer, candyfloss pink. So the whole place has the feel of an enormous ice-cream sundae."

"That's ace; I love it," gushes Ted. "Your ideas are really impressive. And it's obvious you're passionate about design." He pushes away his plate.

Is now the right time to tell him about my *dream?*

He remembers Denise's advice: *If a relationship's based on secrets, it's not going to be a great one.*

He reaches out and takes hold of Oskar's hand. His fingers are a little stiff, but Ted is encouraged to find he doesn't resist.

"Can I take your plates?"

Ted swivels around to see the waiter standing over them.

Oskar drops Ted's hand as if it's scalding him. "Urm, yes," he garbles. "Thanks."

"And is there anything else I can get you?" the waiter asks. "Would you like to see the dessert menu?"

"No, thanks," splutters Oskar. "Just the bill."

Disappointment thumps into Ted. *What just happened? Did I move too fast and frighten him?* He sags back in his chair.

Actually, I won't let this date have a downbeat ending.

As soon as the waiter leaves, Ted takes control of the situation.

"You know what, let's get out of here. Let's go somewhere we can be on our own. We could go for a walk on the beach."

"What, at this time?"

Ted looks out of the window. "Yeah, the sun sets really late in June. If we're lucky, we might even catch it."

Oskar pauses. A smile traces itself over his face. "OK, I'd like that."

CHAPTER 26

Oskar and Ted make it to the beach just as the sun is setting. To the sound of the sea stroking the shore, they stroll under a sky that's salmon pink and strewn with light, fluffy clouds that glow a pumpkin orange. *Not quite a Vimto sunset, but it's beautiful all the same.*

Oskar tells himself to give in to romance. *Go on, hold Ted's hand.*

He opens his palm and Ted takes it.

"I'm sorry I was so jumpy in there," Oskar says.

"It's fine," breezes Ted. "I totally get it."

A lone jogger bounds towards them, and Oskar tells himself not to panic—it doesn't matter who sees them. She springs past without so much as giving them a second glance. *See, you've nothing to worry about.*

Oskar allows himself to smile.

"So you weren't hoping for a dessert?" he teases. "You didn't fancy some ice cream?"

Ted grins. "Honestly, I spend my entire life surrounded by ice cream. I couldn't care less if I never saw it again."

Oskar snickers. "Is that a case of too much of a good thing?"

Ted draws in a long breath, then lets it out. Oskar senses he's about to say something significant.

"No," he states, "I just don't like ice cream. I never have."

"Seriously?"

"Yeah, I'd rather have a bag of crisps. Give me a bag of prawn cocktail any day. And I go *wild* for smoky bacon!"

Oskar laughs but senses Ted is using humor as a diversion. "It can't be much fun working in an ice-cream shop if you don't like ice cream."

Thick lines appear on Ted's forehead. "Not really, no. But the business has been in the family for nearly a hundred years now. And my mum and dad have always made it clear it's my duty to keep it going."

Oskar feels his stomach dip with guilt. "In that case, you're a better man than I am. I just dodge my family duty—as my sister never fails to remind me."

"Yeah, I'm not sure that makes me a better man than you—possibly even the opposite. That's something I'm trying to get my head round at the moment."

They come to the sand dunes, and Ted trots up a little hill and sits down. Oskar settles next to him.

"You and me both," Oskar says. "I just wish I could stop feeling so guilty. But I can't shake it off."

"Guilt can be a powerful thing."

"It can."

Oskar runs his hand over his beard. *Dare I tell him?*

"I should probably tell you what happened when I was twelve." He can't believe the words are coming out of his mouth; he almost looks around to see if someone else has said them.

"You don't need to if it's too painful," offers Ted.

No, I've started now. I'm not going to stop. And once again, something about Ted tells Oskar that it won't be painful. He feels safe.

"It's OK," he persists. "I want to."

As he looks out to sea, Oskar tells Ted that when he was twelve, just as he was starting to realize that he was attracted to boys, his dad was caught having sex with another man. "It was in a well-known cruising ground in some woods not far from our house. Being gay wasn't actually illegal by that time, so he wasn't arrested or anything, but it caused a huge scandal and brought great shame on the family."

Ted stares at him, saucer-eyed. "God, that's terrible."

"You know, in some ways I can remember what happened really clearly," Oskar goes on, "but in others it's all a bit of a blur. My parents kept as much as they could from me and my sister. But I remember lots of men coming over to the house, standing outside, shouting insults, and throwing stones at the windows. And I remember lying in bed and listening to my mum yelling at my dad, telling him he was a pervert who made her sick. The next morning, I woke up and he was gone."

"And have you seen him since?"

"No, never."

Oskar picks up a stone and turns it around in his hands. He explains that for a year or so after his dad left, he tried to make contact with Oskar and his sister, but his mum blocked it, saying his dad couldn't be trusted around children and would only try to corrupt them. "I didn't have the confidence to argue as I was frightened of her realizing I was gay as well. To be honest, I was frightened of it myself."

Ted mops a hand through his hair. "I'm not surprised when you'd seen what had happened to your dad. You must have been terrified."

"I was, yeah. I was terrified the whole time. At first, the kids at school said horrible things about Dad, but then they started saying I must be a pervert like him. So I learned to do everything I could to cover it up. If I spotted myself displaying the slightest mannerism they might think was feminine, I'd change it. I studied old-fashioned macho men and taught myself to act like them. I'd try out little gestures in my bedroom mirror and practice for hours."

"God, that must have been exhausting," says Ted. "Keeping it up all the time."

"It was, but after a while it became a habit—to the extent that I lost sight of what my natural behavior was. It was buried under so many layers of pretending." Oskar throws his stone out towards the sea. "Then, when I got older, I made sure I had girlfriends. Again, I was trying to hide who I really was and pretending to be someone else. But I think I was also hoping they'd somehow *make* me straight, that they could *correct* me. Or that I could somehow force myself to find them attractive."

Ted takes his hand again and weaves his fingers through Oskar's.

Oskar likes it. It's soothing.

"While all that was going on," he continues, "my mum became even more religious. I mean, I understand none of it was her fault and it must have been hard for her, but after my dad left, she'd just sit there praying with her rosary beads and saying nasty things about everyone. And not just gay people but any women who had affairs or sex before marriage—anything that wasn't in the Bible, basically. She was so judgmental. And totally obsessed. When I was sixteen, she dragged me and my sister to Lourdes."

"How was that?"

"I just remember going to the grotto and praying to Our Lady to make me straight."

Ted looks concerned. "You don't *still* want to be straight, do you?"

"No, no." Oskar pulls at a tuft of grass. "Well, if I'm honest, a tiny part of me still does—just because it would make everything much easier. But deep down I know there'd be no point as that would make me a completely different person. I wouldn't be me if I were straight."

"And have you ever had any kind of relationship with a man?"

"No, I haven't."

Suddenly, Oskar becomes aware of how that must sound; *thirty-three and I've never had a relationship?* Ted doesn't seem perturbed, but Oskar wants to give him an explanation. He steels himself to open up even more.

"For a long time, whenever I tried to get close to a man," Oskar says, "a voice in my head told me I was a pervert, just like my dad. And I couldn't escape the feeling that if I gave in and accepted being gay, it would only end badly, like it did with him. So for years I just tried to be nothing. I shut that side of my life down completely."

Ted gives his hand a squeeze. "But it's impossible to live like that, Oskar. Sooner or later, your emotions will come bursting out."

Oskar smiles. "I guess that's how I ended up here with you."

"I'm glad you did. And you know I'll do everything I can to help."

Oskar shakes his head. "Thanks, but this isn't your problem. It's mine. It's my responsibility. And I'll deal with it."

Ted kisses his hand. "Do you think seeing your dad again might help? Have you ever thought about trying to find him?"

"I have, yeah. And I did try once. But I didn't get anywhere, so I gave up."

Ted turns to face him and wraps both his hands around Oskar's. "Well, maybe it's time to try again. Maybe finding him would be healing for you. Maybe it would help silence that voice in your head—and kill it off for good."

"Yeah, maybe." Oskar lets out a long sigh. He realizes they've been discussing his emotional torment for a long time and wants to lift the mood. "Anyway, let's not talk about it any-more. That's about as much misery as I can handle in one evening."

"OK," says Ted, "let's try and enjoy the moment."

Oskar looks out to sea, to the sun dipping below the hori-zon, its golden rays waltzing over the ripples of water. Over-head, a pair of seagulls dance through the sky. "Isn't this beautiful?"

"Yeah, it's gorgeous."

"You know, I might be messed up," Oskar adds, "but I am happy to be here. And I'm happy to be here with you."

Go on, show him how happy you are.

Oskar leans in and kisses Ted softly on the lips. He almost doesn't recognize the person he's becoming. *Wow, I really am doing this!*

When Ted opens his mouth and reciprocates, Oskar feels a tickle in his chest. As their kissing intensifies, it brings his heart to a canter.

"Just so you know," cuts in Ted, pulling back, "I'm happy to take this slowly. To tell you the truth, I'm a bit nervous about it too."

"Why's that?"

Ted scoops up a handful of sand and lets it run through his fingers. "I know my situation is very different to yours, but I'm still getting over my ex. And I've only ever been with him. I've never so much as kissed another man. So this is a big deal for me too."

Oskar sits back. He's surprised by the revelation, but it makes him feel more comfortable about his own inexperience. Although he wants Ted to feel equally comfortable. "Well, we can stop if you like," he offers.

"No, I don't want to. I want to do this. And I'm trying to stick to a policy of prioritizing what I want."

"That's good. Maybe I should do the same thing. Starting right now."

Ted hoists an eyebrow. "And what do you want right now?"

Oskar smiles. "I want to kiss you again."

And as the last rays of sun disappear beneath the skyline, he does.

CHAPTER 27

"A choir?"

"Yeah, a choir."

Giles feigned bewilderment. "Sorry, you want to join a *gay choir*?"

"Yeah," said Ted. "Why, do you think it's a bad idea?"

Ted and Giles were in the car, with Ted driving and a borderline drunk Giles sprawled out on the passenger seat next to him. They'd been for dinner with their friends Lucas and Hartley, a smart gay couple who worked in marketing and graphic design and lived half an hour away from St. Luke's, on the outskirts of Manchester. Ted and Giles had met them on holiday in Santorini but, since coming back to the UK, Ted hadn't always enjoyed their company, as Hartley would often discuss trips to the theatre to see plays he didn't understand, and Lucas would chat to Giles about fashions he found pretentious. Their sweet spots for conversation were travel, food, and dogs—Lucas and Hartley had a cockapoo called Cleo—but this time, as it was January, the chat had turned to New Year's resolutions. Lucas and Hartley had revealed they'd each decided to take up a hobby they'd enjoyed as children but had since let slide. While Lucas had returned to playing his oboe, Hartley was rediscovering his love of cross-country running.

To help revive their passions, they'd joined an orchestra and a running club—both of which were only open to gay men.

"There are gay groups for everything these days," Hartley commented. "Football, rugby, chess. There's even a gay knitting club. And there are *loads* of gay choirs!"

On hearing the word "choir," Ted sat up. As a child, he'd always enjoyed singing. Singing in the school choir and annual shows, singing carols at the Rotary Club Christmas party, even just singing around the house as he got ready for school in the morning. As an adult, it was something he missed. Even in his midthirties, he missed the joy it had given him and the feeling of release he'd experienced as he lost himself in a song. *That feeling of really letting my heart out.*

But now Hartley's comment had given him an idea. *If my dream of being a drag queen is out of the question, maybe this could be a way of indulging at least one part of it . . .*

He didn't share this thought with Giles; he didn't dare bring up the subject of drag, not since that disastrous night in Dublin. Besides, Giles was already shaking his head.

"Well, I think it's a terrible idea," he said. "You've got a voice like hell yawning."

As often happened after a long dinner with friends, alcohol had loosened Giles's tongue. And any attempt at diplomacy, tact—or even just softening the blow—had gone out of the window.

But Ted was surprised at the strength of his soon-to-be-husband's disapproval. *Besides, what he says isn't true; everyone used to say I had a good voice.*

The memory of this stoked an urge to stand up for himself. "Smiles, I don't think that's true."

Giles held up a hand. "Sorry, ignore me. You've got a lovely voice, honestly. It's just those gay choirs are always a bit embarrassing. Don't you remember Four Poofs and a Piano on *Friday Night with Jonathan Ross*? We always used to laugh at them."

We *didn't laugh at them*. You *did*. I *used to enjoy them!*

"Can you imagine a whole choir of that?" Giles spluttered on. "Forty fat poofs in matching T-shirts straining at their bellies, bobbing up and down to the beat, moobs jiggling all over the place, as they belt out a barbershop version of 'I Am What I Am'?"

Ted thought that actually sounded quite appealing. *Well, maybe not the moobs*. But he was determined to stand up for what he wanted. *And this could be my last chance . . .*

"And? What's wrong with that?" he attempted, meekly.

"It's just a bit of a cliché. Another gay stereotype. And I thought we didn't do that?"

Don't we? But Ted didn't express his disagreement. He simply let Giles's question hang in the air, along with his own desperate attempt to salvage something from his dream, to give himself some kind of consolation prize for not being able to be a drag queen.

"I suppose if you did it in Manchester, it might not be too bad," Giles conceded. "And we could always keep it secret from people. Just don't expect me to come and watch you!"

Ted felt all his earlier excitement leak out of him. *This is hopeless. What's the point? I might as well just give up on my dream completely.*

"You know what? It's fine," he managed. "Forget I even mentioned it. I don't want to join a choir, really. I probably just got carried away with all that talk about gay clubs and societies."

Giles nodded and took out his phone. As he began reading his messages, Ted put all thoughts of a gay choir out of his head.

On his way to see Stanley, swinging a bag of Ainsworth's ice cream, Ted breaks into a chorus of "I Am What I Am." He gives a little skip.

Yeah, I've got a good voice.

And I'm not going to doubt it again.

In preparation for his slot at the open-mic night, he's already started rehearsing a few numbers. It's the first time he's sung properly in years—decades even—but he's been pleasantly surprised. And, slowly, his confidence as a singer is returning. *Now I can start looking forward to singing on stage.*

Fear catches in his chest. *But can I really do it?*

Come on, you've got to shake off those nerves!

He draws in a series of deep breaths.

When he arrives at Stanley's, he opens his bag and pulls out a tub of raspberry pavlova ice cream. Stanley squeaks with delight and insists Ted join him to eat it, which prompts Ted to confess for the second time that he doesn't actually like ice cream.

On hearing this, Stanley gives an even louder squeak. "How wonderfully rebellious of you! How gloriously disobedient! How magnificently *individual*!"

Ted doesn't have the heart to say that it hardly qualifies as any of those things if he's never dared to tell his parents.

But Gail's rebellious, she's disobedient, she's individual. Maybe one day I could dare to tell them . . .

Stanley disappears into the kitchen and returns with a tin of old-fashioned Pink Wafers, which he hands to Ted. As they sit on the pink suede suite and Ted nibbles on them, Stanley asks him how things are going with Oskar.

Ted talks him through their second date—including everything Oskar told him about his past.

"Now we've opened up to each other, I feel like we've made a breakthrough," he discloses. "And I really want the relationship to work. I really like him, Stanley."

"Well, that's wonderful, dolly. But why are you looking so worried?"

Ted swallows a mouthful of wafer. "There's something I still haven't told him."

A loud thud comes from the bedroom, where Alison is busy changing Stanley's sheets. "Sorry!" she shouts. "Don't mind me!"

"And what's that?" Stanley asks Ted.

"Something I'm worried will freak him out."

Stanley clutches at his jewelry—a marcasite brooch in the shape of a butterfly that's pinned onto his apricot velvet blazer. "Come on, dolly, spit it out."

Alison stops what she's doing and steps through to the lounge. "Sorry, I couldn't help overhearing that."

"It's alright," Ted says. "You're welcome to join us."

"Thanks." She sits next to him on the sofa. "I need to listen to this properly."

"OK." Ted looks from one to the other. "I'm going to be a drag queen."

"Splendid!" tweets Stanley, clasping his hands.

"Amazing!" burbles Alison. "Now spill the deets!"

As Ted serves Alison a bowl of her favorite lemon meringue ice cream, he fills them in on his journey so far. He tells them about all the steps he's taken towards his dream, and about the open-mic night at which he's going to perform in just over a month's time. "I'm dead excited about it, but I still can't shake my nerves."

Stanley gives him a warm smile. "What have you got to be nervous about?"

Ted exhales. "Not being good enough, that's the main thing."

Alison peers at him, curiously. "But why would you think that, my love?"

"I don't know, I always have."

Actually, I do know where it comes from—or at least I'm starting to figure it out. But that's my responsibility, not theirs.

"It's alright," he adds, hastily. "I just need to keep practicing and build up my confidence."

"That's the spirit!" trills Stanley. "If you're doubting yourself, you've only got yourself to prove wrong."

Ted snaps a Pink Wafer in half but pauses before putting it in his mouth. "I tried my costumes on the other day. Either I need to shift some weight or some of them need adjusting."

"I can help you there!" Stanley reveals that his old Singer sewing machine is in full working order and he still enjoys using it.

"That's ace! Thanks, Stanley." Ted pops the wafer into his mouth.

"My pleasure. Any excuse to help a feely-omi."

Ted frowns. "Is that Polari again? I'm afraid you're going to have to translate."

"It means, any excuse to help out a young boy."

Ted gives a little snort. "I'm hardly young."

"You are compared to me. And you are in dog years."

The three of them roar with laughter.

"Can I use that in my set?" Ted asks.

Stanley's eyes glisten. "I'd be delighted."

Ted sits forward. "Actually, that's another thing—my material. I could do with trying it out. I mean, I can always rehearse at home, but I wish I had some low-key way of giving it a go in front of an audience. You know, before appearing in a bar full of drunk, rowdy gays. I don't suppose I could practice on you two, could I?"

Alison finishes her ice cream and puts down her bowl. "I can go one better than that, my love. Every Sunday I organize an entertainer to come into Memory House and put on a little show. We get all the residents together and do it in the common room. Next week we were supposed to have a juggler coming, in but he's just pulled out. Why don't you take his place?"

"Really? But what about all the residents who are homophobic, the ones who've been having a go at Stanley? Won't they heckle me?"

Stanley shrugs. "If they do, it'll be good training. As far as I'm concerned, a drag show without heckling isn't a show."

Ted pinches the bridge of his nose. *Maybe it could be a good idea . . .*

He sighs. *But what if nobody laughs? What if it just ends up denting my confidence?*

Before he can voice his objection, Alison throws in, "And you wouldn't just be testing out your material, you'd be doing Stanley a favor too."

"How do you work that out?"

She twiddles with her short, Afro curls, the ends of which have been highlighted copper. "Well, if you take on the hecklers and slap them down, you'll be showing them their point of view is unacceptable. You'll be showing them the world has moved on. And that might shame them into moving on too."

Ted nods, slowly. "OK, if you think it'll help."

Stanley taps his spoon on the side of the bowl. "You know what, I think it might. And I've always been a fan of direct action and ruffling feathers. Maybe now I'm an old lady, it's time for Ted to step in and ruffle some for me."

Ted grins. "In that case, count me in."

"Marvelous." Stanley licks his spoon and drops it in the bowl. "Now all you have to do is tell Oskar."

Ted waggles his eyebrows. "I don't know about that. I'm still not sure he's ready."

"Why not?" asks Alison. "What's the problem?"

Ted lets out a breath. "It's just that when we were on our date, he told me how much he used to hate being effeminate. He was so terrified of being gay that he did everything he could to change the way he acted."

Alison goes back to twiddling her hair. "I see what you

mean. And that's perfectly understandable after what he went through."

"Absolutely," says Ted. "But after all that, I can't imagine he's going to enjoy seeing me playing up my feminine mannerisms. Seeing me being as camp and extra as possible."

Stanley turns his empty bowl around between his hands. "You never know, he might surprise you. In some ways, he and I have had similar experiences. I had to put up with all those insults at school. I had all the kids doing impressions of me, making fun of the way I spoke and the way I walked—the way I held my wrist. And then I had to get out of my hometown, I had to escape. But that didn't stop me liking drag."

Ted feels a flicker of hope. "Did it not?"

"No! I couldn't get enough of it! And that was decades before it became fashionable. It was a lifetime before RuPaul! So try him. Who knows how he'll react?"

CHAPTER 28

That Sunday—and for the first time since Giles left him—Ted doesn't wake up alone. He wakes up next to Oskar. But, as he gazes at him lying in the space formerly occupied by his husband, not a single part of him wishes he were gazing at Giles. *And if I'm being honest with myself, that's the first time I've lain here and thought that.*

He angles himself towards Oskar and watches him sleep, his body gently rising and falling with his breath. It occurs to him that while Oskar is completely relaxed, all his barriers are down—and he's never been more adorable. He's also struck by the sheer force of his good looks. One of his forearms rests on top of the duvet, the veins standing out against the hard muscle. As Ted's eyes linger on it, he feels slightly dizzy. *I slept with that arm around me . . .*

In his head, Ted goes over the events that led the two of them here. For their third date, he and Oskar went to the local amusement park, where they rode the pirate ship, the big dipper, and the log flume. They got on brilliantly and at one point were laughing so hard Ted's stomach ached. Afterwards, Ted invited Oskar to his place—and it was obvious from Oskar's reaction that he knew what that meant. On the journey back, their carefree laughter gave way to a nervous tension. As Ted contemplated the prospect of his first sexual experience with anyone other than Giles, the anxiety came rushing in. It only increased when they entered the house, sat on the sofa for a coffee, and started kissing. When their kissing gathered pace and Oskar pulled his T-shirt off to reveal a body packed with natural muscle, Ted panicked. But then Oskar unbuttoned Ted's shirt and gently, softly started kissing his neck. Within seconds, Ted forgot all his worries. And within minutes, the two of them were rushing upstairs.

And now here we are, waking up in my bedroom.

A tingle passes through his stomach as he remembers what happened in this bed. And remembering how well it went— much better than he'd dared to hope—gives way to an enormous relief. It also opens the gates to more excitement about the future. *The future I might build with Oskar.*

At Oskar's feet lies Lily, who's sleeping just as soundly. Ted remembers the moment he introduced the two of them. He'd been worried about this as Lily hasn't been herself since Giles left; he'd worried that she might see Oskar as some kind of interloper and take against him. But the second she saw him, she rolled over, flashed her tummy flirtatiously, and Oskar obliged her with a tickle. Lily reveled in the attention, prompting Oskar to give her more. Much later, when she was finally allowed into the bedroom, it was at Oskar's feet that she chose to lie. *Well, it's obvious she's got a new favorite. But I'm fine with that. In fact, I couldn't be happier.*

Oskar and Lily look cute together, and Ted doesn't want to disturb them. But he needs to relieve himself and is keen to brush away his morning breath. So he slips into the bathroom and slides the door shut behind him. Once he's done, he sneaks back in and slips back under the duvet.

Despite his best efforts, Oskar stirs. "Morning," he murmurs, his eyes only half open.

"Morning. Did you sleep alright?"

Oskar blinks himself awake. "Great, thanks."

"So the ghost train didn't give you nightmares then?"

Oskar smirks. "Hardly. But thanks for taking me there, I really enjoyed myself."

"Except when you screamed out loud on the crazy mouse."

Oskar picks up his pillow and throws it at Ted. "I did *not* scream out loud!"

Their giggles rouse Lily from her sleep. Oskar reaches down and tickles her ears. "Alright, how about when you burst out crying in the haunted house?"

Ted shakes his head in mock annoyance. "I told you, I had something in my eye!"

"Yeah, yeah." Oskar roofs his eyes. "Anyway, it was a great night. I enjoyed all of it."

They slip into silence. Something shifts between them; it's as if the air sharpens.

"My favorite part was when we came back here," Oskar says.

"Mine too," says Ted. He leans in to kiss him.

Oskar springs back. "That's not fair, you've brushed your teeth!"

Ted crinkles his nose. "Sorry, I didn't want to risk it."

Oskar leaps out of bed, revealing another flash of his impressive body, covered only by a pair of black briefs, and disappears into the bathroom. To the sound of gargling, Ted takes over the stroking of Lily's ears until Oskar reemerges. Immediately, the dog turns away from him and begins simpering at Oskar.

"I thought you said you lived on your own," he comments, as he slides back into bed.

"I do. Why do you say that?"

Oskar's forehead creases. "There's a lot of makeup next to the sink."

A hook of fear rips into Ted. *Shit, this is it. This is your chance to tell him . . .*

But what's he going to say?

"Oh yeah," he chirps, as casually as he can manage. "That'll be mine."

"Yours?"

Come on, surely after last night it's safe to tell him . . .

Ted swallows. "Yeah. I'm going to be a drag queen."

"A drag queen?"

"A drag queen called Gail Force. Well, I'm only just starting out, so we'll see how it goes."

Stop playing it down. Stop trying to act like this isn't important.

"But I'm loving it so far," he adds, firmly. "And it's something I've always wanted to do, so I'm definitely going to pursue it."

Oskar's expression is unreadable. He gives a smile, but it doesn't make it to his eyes. "Great," he mumbles.

Ted's face tightens. "Is it? You don't seem too sure."

"No, it's not that. It's just, I don't know anything about drag. I mean, I know it's about dressing up as a woman, but that's about it."

"Oskar, it's about much more than that." Ted tells him that drag can be anarchic, that it can disrupt gender stereotypes, that it can mock the limitations of masculinity. As he speaks, a fire burns in the pit of his stomach, and his words come out faster and faster. But then he remembers what Oskar said to him about trying to smooth out his own feminine mannerisms—and he feels his conviction wavering.

Come on, stand up for what you believe in. Fight for your dream!

"Anyway, that's one of the things I love about it," he rounds off, emphatically.

This time, Oskar gives him a more enthusiastic smile. "You sound like me when I talk about interior design. It's obvious you're passionate about it."

"Yeah."

"Well, in that case, you should go for it."

Although his words are encouraging, there's something about his tone of voice that tells Ted he's still wary. Something that stops Ted allowing himself to feel relieved. *Then again, it's a big improvement on Giles.*

He gives Oskar a grin. "Thanks. I will."

Oskar smooths out the duvet between them. "So when can I see you perform?"

Ted considers inviting him to his little show in Memory House but has second thoughts. *What if I fall flat on my face? What if my jokes go down like a shit in a swimming pool?*

He decides to wait until he's absolutely sure he's ready. "Not yet, but soon. I'll let you know."

"OK."

Ted sits up and gives a little pout. "Now I never thought I'd say this, but I'm getting jealous of my dog. Come here and stroke *my* ears."

CHAPTER 29

"Just having a look to see what's out there."

Too casual—they might think I only want sex.

"After taking a break for a few years, am looking for something meaningful."

Too desperate. I need to keep it playful and fun.

"Looking for a reason to delete this profile."

Denise puts her phone down while she considers the line. She's composing the header for her new profile on a dating app. After lots of reflection—and lots of nagging from Ted— she's decided to follow his advice and give dating another go. She still isn't completely sure she's ready but has been inspired by Ted's experience with Oskar. *And, as he says, I'm only dipping my toe in the water. What harm can it do?*

She decides the header is the best she can come up with, gives her profile one last scan for spelling mistakes, and hits Submit.

While she's waiting for it to be approved, she goes to the kitchen to fix herself something to eat, then pops up to her bedroom to remove her makeup and take off her bra. *If I'm doing this, I need to be as comfortable as possible.*

To bolster her confidence, she takes out the list she made with her counselor of all the things she loves about herself.

I treat people well.

I'm good at my job.

I'm a good friend.

She presses it to her heart and takes a deep breath. *Any man would be lucky to have me.*

By the time she's settled back on the sofa—with a mug of tea and a bag of Maltesers—she's received notification that her profile has been approved.

Fear shoots through her stomach.

She reminds herself of Ted's words. *You deserve this. You deserve the cherry on the cake.*

She takes a deep breath and begins swiping through the suggested profiles. Man after man slides across her screen—tall men, short men, black men, white men, fat men, thin men . . . Some of them have successful careers, others haven't worked out what career they want to do yet. Most of them around her age are single dads or at least divorced—but she's fine with that. *After all, it isn't whether you've got baggage that's important, it's how you carry it that counts.*

Some of the men strike her as feasible prospects—and she swipes right to indicate her interest. But she's careful to filter out anyone who displays the warning signs she's learned to look out for. She doesn't want to fall back into old habits.

She comes across a hot blond guy who runs his own gym and has posted several pictures of himself training topless. There's no question Denise is attracted to him physically, but she reads his biography and learns he "doesn't like to feel suffocated" in a relationship. *Yeah, that's code for "can't commit."* She swipes left.

Next up is a sexy mixed-race guy who doesn't appear to have ever held down a job and describes himself as an "entrepreneur," one who's waiting to spot his "next big business idea." *Yeah, that's code for "unemployed and looking for someone to sponge off."* She swipes left.

A few minutes later, she's offered a handsome, suave-looking Italian guy who casually brands his ex-girlfriend a "psycho." *Yeah, I've heard that one before—that's code for "didn't like her expressing her emotions."* She swipes left.

Then, out of the blue, she's confronted by the profile of her ex-boyfriend, Karl.

Fuck.

Where did that come from?

The sight of him knocks the breath out of her. As Karl moved back to his hometown a few months after they broke up, Denise hasn't seen or heard of him for nearly three years. She's so shocked, her vision blurs, and all she can hear is the sound of the blood pounding in her ears. She blinks her way back to focus and scrolls down to read his profile.

"Passionate type who's been dealt a raw deal in life but is hoping his luck will change. Has had enough of drama from high-maintenance women. Is looking for a nice, simple girl, someone who wants to be looked after, someone who'll appreciate what I can offer."

He's looking for a vulnerable victim, more like.

As Denise's heart hammers so fiercely she's worried it might burst out of her chest, she reads Karl's description of himself as "chilled and charming," in possession of "a full head of hair and all my own teeth," and "good with animals and children."

"Good with children?" How dare he?

As the bile leaps into her throat, she's transported back to the awful way their relationship ended.

Just after they'd celebrated their fifth anniversary, Denise had fallen pregnant. It had come as a complete surprise as they'd been using contraception and, as far as she was aware, had been careful. Also, she'd never got caught before, even when she'd been younger and slapdash about these things. Over the years, she'd come to think she might not be particularly fertile, but this hadn't bothered her as she didn't consider herself maternal—and had never been desperate to have kids. But, at the age of forty-five, she realized this would be her last chance to be a mum. She found herself warming to the idea— and, much to her surprise, her maternal feelings began to kick in. But when she told Karl about the pregnancy, he said the baby couldn't possibly be his. When she offered to carry out a DNA test, he switched his story and accused her of sabotaging their contraception in order to trap him. He insisted she have a termination, saying he didn't want kids and, in any case, she'd make a terrible mother. If she didn't, he threatened to leave her.

Denise was desperate and didn't know where to turn. She didn't want to discuss the issue with her girlfriends; as they were all in happy, stable relationships, most of them with perfectly well-behaved children, and she worried about being judged. And she couldn't bear to consult Ted as she knew what he'd say—and she didn't feel strong enough to leave Karl. So she ended up giving in. She let Karl convince her that going through with the pregnancy was a bad idea, and—despite her yearning to be a mum—had an abortion at ten weeks. Almost immediately, she regretted it. She sank into a deep depression, though Karl showed her no sympathy and instead taunted and tormented her. That's when she finally realized that Ted had been right all along when he said the relationship was abusive. That's when she finally let him step in while Karl was out at work, pack up all her belongings and move her out of their shared flat and into one he'd rented for her. That's when she took Ted's advice and started seeing the counselor he'd found in order to understand—and find out how to carry—her emotional baggage,

But now here's Karl, bursting back into my life. And just seeing him makes me feel bad about myself.

She swipes left to clear all trace of him and shuts down the app. She goes into the kitchen, stands on her tiptoes and fishes around on top of the units. She gave up smoking years ago but still keeps a packet of cigarettes for emergencies—and there's no question this constitutes an emergency. She pulls one out, opens the window and lights it. As she draws in the nicotine and slowly blows out the fumes, she thinks back over everything Karl put her through. How worthless and pathetic he made her feel—and how sometimes he even made her doubt her own sanity. A cold anger uncoils inside her.

I missed out on the chance of being a mum because of him.

The idea beats at the walls of her skull.

Across the room—attached to the fridge door—she catches sight of a photo. It's a photo of herself aged five, playing with a Girl's World makeup set she'd received that Christmas, flashing an enormous grin to her mum, who was standing behind the camera. Denise had dug out the photo when her counselor asked her to find one that represented her pure, innocent self, before the low self-esteem set in, before she was made to feel bad about herself. She told her to pin it up somewhere she'd see it every day—to remind herself of what it felt like to be that child.

I was such a sweet, kind, good-natured girl. And I had such simple dreams.

She remembers that one of those dreams was finding love. *Well, that's still possible . . .*

And I'm certainly not going to miss out on it because of Karl!

She screws out her cigarette and stomps back to the sofa. When she reopens the app, she's encouraged to find she already has a handful of matches. *Well, that didn't take long.*

Her first message is from a man who confesses the pictures she liked were taken twenty years ago; he's now in his late sixties and is only looking for "companionship."

I might be knocking on a bit, but I'm not ready to give up on sex yet . . . She hits Delete.

She reads one from a younger guy who says he's only looking for casual sex—what he calls the "pump and dump"—and asks if she's free right now.

OK, that's a little too far in the other direction. Grimacing, she presses Delete.

Just as she thinks she might need to consider adjusting her stipulated age range, she opens a message from a man who doesn't even bother to say hello but asks her for "tit pics" and promises he can follow these up with a shot of his penis, adding that right now "it's as hard as a spanner." She doesn't just press Delete but goes back into his profile and hits Unlike—then does the same with the other two.

So much for finding love. What a disaster!

She feels dirty and putrid inside. *Is this what people really think of me? Am I just kidding myself that I deserve more?*

Sadness grinds its way into her bones, and she can feel the tears building behind her eyes.

What am I doing? This is hopeless.

She eats her last Malteser and looks down into the empty bag. It's labeled a "sharing bag," but she's polished them all off herself. Whatever she tells herself about the chocolates being so low in calories that they don't count, she's pretty sure they do when you eat that many. *Well, it's not as if I've got anyone to share them with. And it doesn't look like I'll be finding anyone either.*

She pictures her five-year-old self in the photo stuck on the fridge and wonders what that girl would make of her now. *She'd probably be horrified. Or would she just feel sorry for me?*

As the loneliness bores through her, she shuts down the app. And the tears start to fall.

CHAPTER 30

"A few months ago, my husband dumped me for a Spaniard," recounts Ted. "In his eyes, this guy was the hottest thing to come out of Spain since chorizo. I wished the pain from Spain had stayed mainly in the plain."

There's a light ripple of laughter.

"Anyway, my husband got himself a Spanish boyfriend," he goes on, "while all I got was the Spanish violin—*el bow*."

There's a barely audible titter.

Oh God, this isn't going well.

Ted's performing his first ever gig as Gail Force in the common room of Memory House. There's no stage, so he's standing on a raised area in front of a windowsill that's lined with potted ivy and spider plants, facing rows of high-backed orange and turquoise wipe-clean vinyl chairs, on which are sitting—or snoozing—men and women with an average age of well over ninety. It's about as far from the dazzlingly glamorous drag debut of Ted's dreams as it's possible to be. A pair of straight-backed, prim-looking women sitting in the front row are staring at him as if he's just suggested they join him for a naked mud wrestle. Thankfully, Denise, Stanley, and Alison have also positioned themselves at the front too—and the three of them send him supportive smiles.

Ted didn't expect an easy ride, but he has no idea why things can be going quite so wrong. He's looking great, in a backless silver mini dress Stanley has adjusted for a more flattering fit, together with a pink fake-fur stole and a brunette bobbed wig with bangs. He spent hours doing his makeup, creating dramatic pink-and-silver spotlight eyes with blended edges and pointed tips that prompted compliments from Denise. But, even though it's a warm day in June, the central heating is turned up so high he's sweating—and he's worried his makeup is going to run. The fact his show is bombing is bringing him out in an added stress sweat. *What am I playing at? How did I possibly think I'd get away with this?*

He considers bolting but remembers he's not just doing this for himself—he's also doing it for Stanley. He straightens his spine and holds his head up high. *Come on, Ted, you can turn this around.*

He takes off his stole and flings it at Denise, who catches it and gives him a nod, urging him on.

"Hey, I've got a joke for you," he manages to chirp. "How many Spaniards does it take to steal a husband?"

His question is met with absolute silence.

"I don't know," cuts in Stanley. "How many Spaniards does it take to steal a husband?"

"Just Juan," says Ted.

His friends laugh but nobody else reacts. *What's the Spanish for a slow, painful death?*

He takes a step back but almost goes over on one of his silver-heeled sandals and wishes he'd worn shoes with more support. He's sure he can hear someone snigger.

Come on, Ted, you're not going down without a fight.

"Well, I feel about as welcome as the words 'Here's a track from my new album' at a Madonna concert," he comments.

There's another dead silence, broken only by Denise, who howls loudly.

Shit, I misjudged that one.

Get it together, Ted, know your audience. Who was famous in their day . . . ?

"Scrap that," he says. "I feel about as welcome as Julie Andrews at an orgy."

There are a couple of laughs.

"As Mae West in a nunnery," he adds.

There's another ripple of laughter, but it's interrupted by a ruddy-faced man with a completely bald scalp and what looks like a full head of hair sprouting from his nostrils. "Get off!" he barks. "You're not funny and you're t' ugliest bird I've ever clapped eyes on."

Come on, Ted, you're not going to stand for that.

"And *you* look like a slug someone's sprinkled salt on," he shoots back at him.

Several people laugh. *Now that's interesting—that man mustn't be popular.* Ted makes a mental note.

"Anyway, I was telling you about my husband," he picks up. "Sorry, my *ex*-husband."

But someone else, one of the prim-looking women on the front row, interjects, "Excuse me, I don't believe in gay marriage."

"Well, nobody's forcing you to have one," Ted tweets, merrily.

He's encouraged when this gets a decent laugh.

"But doesn't the Bible say being gay is a sin?" asks her friend.

"Yes, but it also says it's OK to commit incest and polygamy and keep slaves," Ted breezes, "and that women should be executed if they have sex before marriage. Thankfully, the world's moved on since then."

"And a good job it has too!" quips Stanley.

"But aren't you worried about going to Hell?" asks the first woman.

"If Heaven's full of people who follow the Bible," Ted answers, "show me the way!"

This elicits a laugh that's actually quite loud.

"See you there!" shouts a sprightly, sparrowlike woman in the back row.

"Ace," says Ted, "you and me can have a party!"

Someone else pipes up. "I'm coming too!"

"And me!" squeaks someone in the corner.

OK, this is more promising . . .

Ted goes on to entertain the audience with stories about all the comfort eating he did when Giles dumped him—including, at one point, scoffing three steak and kidney pies and a whole jar of red cabbage that gave him such bad heartburn he took himself to A & E, convinced he was having a coronary. Once he's sure the audience is warming to him, he decides to move things up a gear.

"Right, who's ready for a song?" he asks—and the response is overwhelmingly positive. He launches into "The Man That Got Away" by Judy Garland, which he dedicates to his exhusband. It's a downtempo, sincere number, and he gives his vocal all the emotion he can muster. He's encouraged when several people begin swaying along to the music. One or two of the women turn misty-eyed, and the sparrowlike woman joins in and sings some of the lyrics.

Now we're talking!

When the song is over, Ted tells the audience that he may have been devastated when his man got away, but it's this that inspired him to become a drag queen—so it all worked out for the best. "And I know you might be thinking I'm a bit old to launch a career in showbiz. But I'm only twenty-one in dog years."

This gets the biggest laugh so far. *Thanks, Stanley.*

"In that case I'm only forty!" shouts a woman who's so old

all the color has drained out of her eyes. "And suddenly I feel *fabulous*!"

"Woof, woof!" jokes Ted.

But the cantankerous, ruddy-faced man pipes up again. "Get back to t' kennels, you ugly hound!"

"Says the man who's got a face like a poodle's minge," Ted fires back.

He isn't sure whether he's crossed a line, but the audience laughs so hard one of them falls off her chair and Alison has to help her back onto it. Ted can feel his confidence building. By the time he's belting out the next number—"Que Será, Será" by Doris Day—he's feeling much more self-assured. As the raised area that's standing in for a stage is so small, there's no room for him to dance, but he enjoys focusing on his vocals—and is delighted when the majority of the audience join in with the lyrics, even the prim-looking women on the front row. The only one who doesn't is the bald, ruddy-faced man, who just sits there sulkily with his arms folded. Ted realizes he might not be able to win him round but at least the rest of the audience is sending him a clear message that he's in a minority and his views aren't accepted.

Buoyed up by a wave of applause at the end of the song, he soars through the rest of the show. Every time his eyes land on Denise, Stanley, or Alison, he can read their relief—and their pride. Happiness swells inside him.

Thank God I stuck at it. Thank God I didn't give up.

Then, all too quickly, the show's over. As Ted takes a bow to a final burst of delighted applause—and even a few cheers—the adrenaline vibrates through him.

He can't wait to speak to Stanley. And not just that, but he can't wait to make his debut at the open-mic night in Queen of Clubs. In front of an audience of gay men—and on a proper stage—he won't have to compromise. He can incorporate all kinds of up-tempo numbers into his set, with full dance routines. He's excited at the prospect and no longer feels anything as nervous as he did before. *If I can handle this audience of ninetysomethings, I can handle anything.*

As he clacks out of the room and makes his way to the disabled loo that's doubling as his changing area, he resolves to give his next performance everything he's got. *I've dimmed my light for decades—now it's time to turn it up to the max!*

CHAPTER 31

As soon as Ted steps into the freezer and closes the door behind him, he breaks into one of the songs he's going to perform in his show—"Stronger" by Britney Spears. It's a self-empowerment anthem that he's chosen because it's a perfect fit for his chat about finding himself on his own after a painful split.

He grabs a little stepladder and straddles it like Britney does the silver chair in the video, writhing and leaping around between the shelves of ice cream as he imagines himself on stage, wearing a long wig and hair-whipping wildly. He steps away from the ladder and slithers and sashays his way through body rolls, hip swizzles, and kitty cat crawls, moves he's learned in dance class. And he belts out Britney's lyrics with a heartfelt passion, safe in the knowledge that no one outside can hear him. *And I feel like I'm really letting my heart out, just like I used to.*

Within seconds Ted is sixteen again, the age he was the last time he performed on stage.

Ted lifted up his skirt to reveal a pair of shocking-pink bloomers with bright-green polka dots—and gave his legs a wiggle. The audience howled with laughter.

He was in his first year at sixth-form college and appearing in the drama group's pantomime, *Aladdin*—playing the dame, Widow Twankey. Since discovering drag at the age of nine, this was the closest Ted had come to achieving his dream. But the way he saw it, playing a panto dame was basically drag by another name, drag by stealth, a form of drag that even his parents considered acceptable. Best of all, because of the long tradition of a man playing the panto dame, it didn't involve telling anyone he was gay, which he wasn't ready to do—even if he suspected everyone knew already, not least his parents. Even if his character flirted outrageously with practically every man on stage, asking the emperor if that was a proclamation in his pocket or if he was pleased to see her, and the genie if she could give his lamp a good rub. Playing a dame was like hiding in plain sight. *And I love it!*

Ted loved preparing for the show, carefully putting on his wig, makeup, and his brightly colored washerwoman costume; stuffing his bra with balloons; and pulling on not just a pair of tights but Twankey's real silk polka-dot bloomers. He loved making his entrance on stage and introducing the audience to a character he'd based on what he remembered of Crystal Ball, with a dash of all the gruff northern comedians he'd seen play panto dames as a child. He loved performing his comic scenes in the launderette Twankey ran with her son Wishee Washee—particularly when the humor became smutty, as it did when she taught Wishee how to clean a man's shirt with a technique she called the "squeeze and squirt." Most of all, though, he loved performing the musical numbers.

During the course of the show, Ted took part in several group numbers, but his big solo was a cover of Donna Summer's "Hot Stuff," in which he was flanked by several shirtless male dancers who twisted and twirled him around, at one point lifting him high above their heads. He felt like he was flying.

If Ted had any doubts that he wanted to be a performer, taking part in the panto dispelled them. As he even said in a line of Twankey's, "This isn't a stage I'm going through." *No, this is what I'm meant to be doing. This is who I am. This is me.*

And his performance was a massive hit with audiences. He was invariably given a huge round of applause during the curtain call and, on opening night, his parents were very complimentary.

"That were fab, love," his mum gushed afterwards. "Although I don't know how you managed to sing and dance at t' same time—I were out of breath just watching you!"

"Yeah, it was very impressive," said his dad. "You reminded me of Les Dawson and Roy Barraclough doing Cissie and Ada. Top class!"

But it was over all too quickly. The following week, it was the final show and the cast celebrated afterwards by going out to The Bee's Knees, the only nightclub in St. Luke's that would allow sixteen-year-olds in. The celebrations resulted in Ted's first hangover, which was so severe it turned his skin the color of an olive and made him think he was having a migraine, but only in one eye. While he was suffering, Trevor came into his bedroom and said he wanted to talk. He sat at the bottom of the bed, and Ted just about managed to sit up and face him.

"I think it's time you got a Saturday job," Trevor stated. "I think it's time you started work in the shop."

Ted's face must have fallen.

"There's nothing to worry about," Trevor assured him. "You won't be serving customers at first. You'll start at the bottom, clearing dishes off the tables and stocking up the flavors on the counter. But once you've settled in, you can work your way up."

His words came at Ted as if through a fog. For a moment he questioned if this was really happening.

Just when I thought I'd found a way out. Just when I thought I'd found an answer!

"Once you've finished college," Trevor went on, "you'll be ready to start full-time."

Panic tightened Ted's throat. He coughed and retched at the same time.

"Are you alright, son?"

"Yeah, sorry, I'm just hungover." He stood up and darted to the bathroom.

"You've had your fun, son," Trevor called after him. "Now it's time to knuckle down!"

Determined not to let the memory make him feel down-hearted, Ted injects even more energy into his song and dance routine. He snarls and slides up and down the freezer, giving a performance he's convinced would make Britney jealous. And he reawakens the joy that seized him on stage as a sixteen-year-old. *I've always loved performing. And I'm not going to let anyone stop me again!*

But just as he reaches the middle eight, his muscles start to seize up with the cold—and he becomes worried about damaging his voice. He grabs the tubs of ice cream he needs and dashes to the exit.

Never mind, he thinks, dropping them onto the trolley. *I'll have plenty of time to rehearse at home. And I've got dance class tonight, so I'll be able to perfect my new moves.*

On his way back to the shop, he calls into his office to pick up the iPad that has his stock chart on it. But he's stopped by Dorothy Potts, who's sitting at her desk, engrossed in a Google search for wedding florists.

"Ted, this came for you," she says, holding out a letter, her eyes fixed on the screen.

Ted's about to point out that she shouldn't be organizing her daughter's wedding during work hours when he sees she's holding a plain white envelope with a white address label. *Oh no, not another one.*

He shivers as if he's still in the freezer.

It's been more than a month since the last one—I thought they'd stopped.

He takes the letter from Dorothy's hand, drops off the tubs of ice cream at the counter, then wheels the trolley back to the factory. En route, he stops in the lane. Once he's made sure no one else is around, he rips open the letter.

TED,
YOUR DAD HAS BEEN UNFAITHFUL TO YOUR MUM. I KNOW BECAUSE HE HAD AN AFFAIR WITH ME. HE'S A LIAR AND A CHEAT.

The words hit Ted like a blow to the solar plexus.

No, it can't be true.

His dad's a decent, moral person, and he and his mum may have had the odd row when he was a child, but they've always been a happy couple. *Or have they . . . ?*

"Al'reet, lad?" Derek Slack steps into the lane and lights a cigarette. "What's that? You look like you've seen a ghost."

Ted stuffs the letter back into the envelope. "No, not at all. It's just my gas and leccy bill. I can't believe they've put it up again!"

Derek shakes his head. "It's bang out of order what's going on. This country's going to t' dogs!" He leans on one of the forklift trucks and launches into a long account of how much his energy bills have increased recently.

But Ted isn't listening—all he can think about is his dad and this supposed affair. *I don't believe it. I just don't believe that the same man who'd sit with me to watch* Calamity Jane *could have been lying to us all.*

At what he hopes is an appropriate point, he throws in a half-hearted "Outrageous." Then he adds, "If you'll excuse me, Derek, I've got to get on."

Before Derek can argue, Ted wheels his trolley into the factory. And his mind continues to race.

But what if the sender's telling the truth? What if I really have got Dad wrong? Could he even have cheated on Mum with someone who works for us?

Just as he's parking the trolley, Ted spots his dad washing his hands at one of the sinks—and Dorothy sidling up to him. He isn't close enough to hear what she's saying, but she's clutching at her neck and giggling in a way she must imagine is coquettish. He knows she's divorced and has heard some of the men in the factory teasing Trevor that she has a crush on him. He wonders if that's why she's topped up her perfume, spraying on so much he can smell it from across the factory floor. *But if she is flirting, is Dad flirting back?*

It's difficult to tell and, anyway, if they are having an affair, Ted doesn't think his dad would make it so obvious. He dismisses the idea; cheating on his mum with someone like Dorothy would be far too close to home. *If he is being unfaithful, it's much more likely to be with a customer or client.*

In an instant, his mind is swirling with possibilities. There's the woman who runs the dairy—his dad always insists on dealing with her himself. Or that woman who owns the Westcliff Hotel—he remembers Giles saying something about her marriage being in trouble. Come to think of it, didn't his mum say the manager of Urchins was known as some kind of local femme fatale? *Well, those weren't quite the words she used . . .*

Then again, surely if Trevor is having an affair with a business associate, the family would somehow have found out about it? Surely he'd have left clues or the secret would have slipped out? On reflection, it's probably more likely to be someone he knows through the Rotary or the Yacht or Cricket Club, as Hilary doesn't really get involved with any of those. *Or maybe it's someone he met online . . .*

Ted's so lost in his thoughts that he doesn't notice Cole approaching him.

"Are you alright, mate?" the young man asks.

Ted shakes his head and blinks. "You what?"

"Just, are you feeling alright? You look a million miles away."

Ted pulls himself together. "Sorry, I was, yeah. But I need to get on. See you later, Cole."

As he crosses the lane, it occurs to Ted that he only read the letter ten minutes ago and already he's started to believe what it says. *But what if the sender's just made it all up and is trying to cause trouble? What if she goes further and does something to hurt Mum—or to tear the family apart?*

When he gets back to the shop, Jinger and Bella are leaning on the counter, discussing Bella's latest relationship.

Jinger's mouth falls open. "I am dead!" she says, although her heavily Botoxed forehead doesn't reflect any of her shock. "But what about his wife? Don't you feel guilty?"

Bella tugs at a strand of her hair and wraps it around her finger. "Apparently she's a bitch. And they haven't had sex for years. Anyway, as far as I'm concerned, his wife, his problem."

Once again, suspicion slams into Ted. *Don't tell me Dad's having an affair with Bella . . .*

He knows the age gap might be ridiculous but, at the same time, some people are attracted to older men. *And Dad looks much younger than he is . . .*

He lets out a short breath. *Come on, Ted. Now you're just being daft!*

He snaps back to reality. "Girls, there's a customer waiting!" he barks.

Jinger and Bella turn around. "Sorry, we didn't notice."

"Alright, well, maybe you could pay attention and do some work."

Oops, was that too harsh?

Ted doesn't want them to realize how flustered he is, so he picks up a tray and starts clearing some tables. As he does, he tries to cast all thought of his dad's supposed infidelity out of his mind.

Instead, he looks forward to bolting from the building the second the clock hits six. *And heading to dance class!*

In the main hall of the community center, Ted stretches out his glutes. He's wearing his new workout gear, just practical, sweat-wicking clothes, and cushioned sports trainers so he's in keeping with the girls, but he's permitted himself one flash of flamboyance: a pair of legwarmers. He may have thrown away his original pair, but he's managed to source another identical pair in ultramarine. *And I might be imagining this, but I'm sure they make me dance better.*

It's now three months since he started attending dance class, three months during which he's noticed a big change in himself. Although he's only lost a little weight, his body feels firmer, and his general fitness level is a good deal higher. Most importantly, he's become a much more agile, expressive, accomplished dancer.

As he's grown in confidence, Ted has gradually moved from the back of the class towards the front. Along the way, he's made friends with a handful of the other girls, such as Julie and Kelly, two sisters who joined in the same week as him. Both in their late thirties, with the dark coloring of their Greek Cypriot heritage, the sisters had had babies within a few months of each other and had started coming to dance class to lose the weight they'd gained—and, as they told Ted, to feel sexy again.

"Hey, Teddy Boy!" Julie chirps as she and Kelly take up their places next to him.

He hugs them both. "Are you alright, girls?"

"Yeah, great, thanks," says Julie.

"Actually, I've had a shit day," says Kelly, curling her lip. "I had a massive row with my boss, and I can't stop going over and over it in my head."

"Oh no! Are you OK?"

She lunges forward to stretch her thighs. "Yeah, or at least I will be once we start. Once I get moving!"

Ted thinks of the letter he received that morning and how its message has been plaguing him ever since. *I know just what you mean.*

But when the class does start—with Shelly directing the participants to assume the role of goddess, as usual—Ted's relieved to find that he is able to block out his worries. It's Destiny's Child night and he bops and pops along to "Survivor," "Independent Women Part 1," and "Bootylicious." Within minutes, the adrenaline is pumping, just like it always does.

"Repeat after me!" Shelly booms into her microphone. "I love myself! I love my body! I am a strong, seductive, *sensual* woman!"

As the class chants the words back at her, each of them breaks into an adoring smile—as does Ted. *I think we all might be a little bit in love with her.*

As usual, Ted gives the class his all. But he can't quite master one of tonight's new moves: the double leg swoop. He's able to rotate his hips and slide his heel through the circle, but he can't come out of it correctly; he can't extend his right leg to the front, or at least he can't do it anything as sexily as Shelly.

"Well done, girls! That was sensational." says the teacher, drawing the session to a close.

Before Ted has even caught his breath, he grabs his bag and rushes over to her. He wants to ask what he's doing wrong as he'd love to incorporate the double leg swoop into one of his routines for the upcoming show. *Not that I'm going to divulge that detail.*

He's sure everyone here would be supportive, but he has to remember that he lives in a small town. *And news spreads around St. Luke's faster than syphilis through a swingers' party.*

"Shelly, can I have a word?"

"Hiya, Ted," she says, disentangling her headset from her red hair. "How's it going?"

He drops his bag onto the floor. "Ace, thanks. I just wanted to ask you about the double leg swoop. I can't get the ending right, and it's dead frustrating."

Shelly furrows her brow. "I wonder why that is. You usually pick things up really quickly."

"I don't know," says Ted, shrugging. "Maybe I'm just tired after spending all day on my feet."

"Are you still working in the shop?"

Ted tries not to feel a twinge of irritation. *That's the one thing everyone in this town knows about me.* But he covers it up with a smile. "Yeah, you know me."

Shelly folds her arms and cocks her head to one side. "And how's your dad? I haven't seen him for a long time."

Ted's breath fails. Immediately, suspicion cuts through him. *Oh my God, did Dad have an affair with Shelly? Did he fall a little bit in love with her too?*

He pretends he needs to tie his shoelace so he can bend down. "I had no idea you knew my dad."

As Shelly crouches down to sweep up her water bottle, the abs below her crop top ripple in his eyeline. "What do you mean? *Everyone* knows your dad!"

Ted stands up again and looks her in the eye. He isn't sure what to say, so he scratches his head.

"Everyone *loves* your dad!" Shelly adds.

What does that mean?

Ted snaps himself back to his senses. "He's fine, thanks. Still doing his sailing and his cricket. Although he's too old to play now, even for the vets. The only thing they'll let him do is umpire, and you can imagine how that goes down with his ego."

He manages to push out a weak laugh, but his whole body is ringing with fear. *What if Shelly did have an affair with Dad, and I have to stop coming to dance class?*

Shelly says something, but Ted realizes he's withdrawn from the scene around him. He flaps his eyelids several times. "Sorry, can we just run through that double leg swoop?"

CHAPTER 32

Oskar types the name "Andrzej Kozlowski" into his computer. He seizes a breath and starts sifting through the results.

Come on, Dad, show yourself . . .

His search throws up an academic on Twitter, a minor film-maker on IMDb, and a TV news report about a man who represented Poland in the world championships of something called beer pong—which apparently combines Ping-Pong with a forfeit of drinking beer. But there's no sign of his dad.

He logs onto Facebook and trawls through every profile with the same name, but there's nobody who even remotely resembles the man he's looking for. His heart sinks.

What do I do now?

He goes back to Google and types "Andrzej Kozlowski" into the search bar, plus the words "gay" and "Poland," but all that comes up are pictures of men with their shirts off and links to amateur porn videos made in Eastern Europe.

For God's sake!

He closes his laptop and walks over to the kitchen. When he renovated his home as the principal assignment for his online course in interior design, Oskar refitted the kitchen completely, using Nordic oak and natural slate and stone. These blend in with the color palette he used on the walls of the caravan, which includes various shades of terracotta as well as a creamy off-white, a truffle brown, and a dusky ochre. The furniture in the lounge area is made entirely from natural materials, such as bamboo, rattan, palm, and unfinished wood, and this is complemented by accessories and soft furnishings made from natural fabrics, such as jute, hessian, wool, and even alpaca. Oskar worked hard to eliminate the cramped feel of a typical caravan by adding various devices to increase the storage space—including all kinds of shelves, slabs, slots, and surfaces that fold out, tuck away, slide under, and open up. He's very proud of the result.

He wonders what Ted will make of it—and is excited to show him. Ordinarily, Oskar would worry about what someone he wanted to impress would think of him living in a caravan—especially as Ted has a whole spacious house, albeit one he can't help thinking is decorated more like a coolly stylish hotel than a cozy home. But already he knows Ted well enough to be confident that he won't judge him or be even remotely snobbish.

It's only a couple of months since Oskar stepped into Ainsworth's to buy an ice cream, but already he and Ted have established a strong bond—one that continues to delight and surprise him. Never having shared any level of physical intimacy with anyone before, Oskar is taken aback at how this translates into emotions—emotions that are more intense than any he'd imagined feeling, emotions he'd begun to think were experienced only by other people and were forever closed to him. So many of his thoughts are occupied by Ted and, although this can sometimes trigger a judder of fear, he doesn't want to think about him any less. Because thinking about Ted gives him a lift and makes him feel like his whole body is smiling.

Come on, Oskar, stop daydreaming—you've got an important job to do . . .

He makes himself a hot chocolate and goes back to his computer. But before resuming his search, he slides out one of his hidden storage compartments and removes a photo. It's a picture of his dad, the only one he has. The morning after Andrzej left Poland, Oskar's mum went around the house destroying all the images of his dad, but as soon as Oskar realized what she was doing, he managed to grab one and stash it away. He looks at it and breathes in and out, slowly. It shows his dad sitting on the beach on a folding deckchair, his hands clasped and smiling at the camera, the setting sun casting a reddish glow onto his lightly weather-beaten skin as a breeze lifts the fringe of his fair hair. Oskar loves the photo as it captures his dad's warm smile and kindly eyes. When he first moved into the caravan, he considered putting it up on the wall but decided against it. Because his feelings for his dad are complicated.

When he was growing up, Oskar loved his dad more than he loved anyone. Andrzej was an intelligent and sensitive man, and he understood Oskar better than anyone else. But he made one terrible, catastrophic mistake that plunged the family into so much trouble that for most of his teens, Oskar couldn't help resenting him. Equally, there were times when he needed his dad—times when he was growing up and trying to understand the world, not to mention how he fitted into it as a gay man—and felt abandoned by him. Couldn't he have tried harder to get in touch? Surely he must have expected Oskar's mum to block all contact?

Also, if Oskar is really honest with himself, for a long time, part of him felt disgusted by his dad, just like everyone else in his hometown, except probably more so because Oskar was also disgusted at the same urges—what he saw as the same perversions—in himself. And in some ways, he blamed his dad for making him a pervert. But now he's developing feelings for Ted, he's realizing that these urges *aren't* perverted, that he can be happy as he is. The resentment and disgust are fading—and all that's left for his dad is love.

Ted's right—I've got to find him.

He takes a sip of his hot chocolate and racks his brain for leads. In Poland his dad worked for the local government in some kind of senior administrative role. Oskar was too young to know exactly what this entailed—and there's no guarantee he'd still be doing anything similar anyway. *But it's worth a try . . .*

He types in the name "Andrzej Kozlowski" plus every vaguely relevant job title he can think of. But still there's nothing.

He knows his dad originally moved from Poland to Manchester because his aunt—Andrzej's sister—let this slip when Oskar was still a teenager. That's why Oskar originally chose to move there, so he could look for his dad. He tried everything he could to find him, even trawling the bars of the Gay Village asking complete strangers if they knew him—until eventually he had to accept he'd hit a dead end. And now his aunt has died, so he has no way of asking her for more information.

He types in "Andrzej Kozlowski" plus "Manchester." When a link appears, his pulse trips. But he clicks on it to find an article about the academic who showed up in his first search going to Manchester University to do a guest lecture.

This is hopeless.

No, you've got to keep the faith!

To bolster his conviction, Oskar takes the photo of his dad and holds it up against the wall. The wicker frame in which it's mounted actually matches the colors and materials he's used in the caravan. This only strengthens his belief that what he's doing is the right thing.

"This is where you're meant to be, Dad," he says out loud in Polish. "Here with me."

He finds a nail and hangs the photo on the wall.

"That's a nice picture," Marina says as she sits down.

Oskar has been putting off their chat for weeks but, when he bumped into her that morning, she asked if he was avoiding her—and suddenly, he felt ashamed of himself. He insisted he wasn't and, to prove the point, invited her round that same evening.

When Marina showed up at his caravan wearing dangly crystal earrings and a butterfly-print maxidress, waving a bottle of Sauvignon Blanc in the air, he realized he was genuinely pleased to see her. He showed her around and enjoyed listening to her praise his interior design, particularly her approval of his choice of natural materials. Then she spotted the photograph he'd hung up the day before—which he can now see represents the only personal touch in his entire home. *It's no wonder it draws the eye.*

"I don't need to ask who it is," she comments. "I can tell a mile off it's your dad."

Oskar feels a rumble of fear but doesn't let it take hold. "Yeah, it is."

Marina peers closer. "Oh my goddess, you two are *really* alike."

If only you knew. But Oskar is still feeling disheartened by his inability to track down his dad and would rather not pursue the topic. "We are, yeah," is all he says.

Marina rests her arms on the table. "You know, I never really knew my dad."

Oskar has to stop himself from breaking into a smile; she's managed five minutes of casual chat and is already straining at the leash to launch into a full, emotional heart-to-heart.

"Oh no," he says. "Why's that?"

She tucks her hair behind her ear. "My mum and him were

never really together—not properly. She was a bit of a wild child and got pregnant by some Romany gypsy who didn't stick around. Not that she wanted him to stick around. To be honest, I'm not sure he even knows about me."

"Oh no. How do you feel about that?"

Marina sighs. "It's all I've ever known, really. I have to admit, it wasn't great when I was growing up. In a town like this back in the seventies, I was pretty much the only kid in my school who didn't have a dad. And sticking out isn't very nice when you're that age."

"No, it isn't, is it?"

Oskar looks out the window. It's a dull day, and the sky's the color of unwashed net curtains. Into his head rush some of the insults the other kids at school used to hurl at him.

"Anyway, all that's a long time ago now," Marina adds, breezily. "And I couldn't care less what people think of me anymore. I've learned to embrace what makes me stand out— it makes me who I am."

As he turns back to face her, Oskar realizes just how much he likes her.

"I only wish I knew more about him," Marina goes on. "All I know is I got my coloring from him. Sometimes I think I may have inherited some of his gypsy spirit, whatever that means. Maybe that's why I've always felt most comfortable outside mainstream culture. Sometimes I wonder if that's why I was attracted to living here in this caravan park. But maybe that's me just being romantic."

"Well, there's nothing wrong with a bit of romance." Oskar feels a tingle of surprise. *Did I really just say that?*

"No, there isn't, is there?" Marina runs her hand over the table. "I never asked, how did you get on with that guy?"

Fear sluices through Oskar. "What guy?"

"The one you were seeing? You said something about not being sure if he liked you?"

Fuck, I can't lie now.

Anyway, what's the point? She already knows I'm gay!

"He does like me," he begins, hesitantly. "And I like him. We've been seeing each other for a while now."

A grin illuminates Marina's face. "Brilliant! Now crack open that Sauvie B and tell me all about it!"

Oskar goes to the kitchen to fetch the wine and a couple of glasses. *Oh my God, I've just come out!*

Although, does it count as coming out when I didn't actually decide to? When it just kind of happened?

"And I've got to tell you about *my* man!" Marina bursts out. "We've been seeing each other for six weeks now, and it's going really well!"

Oskar returns to the table and unscrews the wine.

Marina gives a squeak of excitement. "We've got *so* much to talk about!"

Oskar feels the breath catch in his chest.

Come on, don't get scared. You can do this . . .

He sits down opposite Marina and splashes wine into their glasses.

"Thanks, toots," she chirps. "Now you go first—I want to know everything!"

CHAPTER 33

Ted puts on a wig cap, pulling his skin back and tucking it under to give himself a bit of a facelift. He applies a line of glue just below his hairline, then positions the wig over his head, lines up the ear tabs, and tugs it forward so it's sitting on top of the glue. He attaches the little combs inside the wig to his own hair and pulls the adjustable strap to fasten it tight. He then hairsprays the lace front and blasts it with the hairdryer until it melts down.

"Right, so this is what I did last time," he says to Denise, "but when I was rehearsing the Britney routine, it kept coming loose. And I just want to whip my hair around without worrying about it flying off."

Denise nods, seriously. "OK, well I've watched a few YouTube tutorials, and I think the best thing is to try and fix it in place with some Kirby grips." She attaches the first, piercing it through the wig and gripping it onto Ted's own hair.

"Oh yeah, that might work."

The two of them are in his living room, with Ted kneeling on the floor so he can monitor what they're doing in a mirror they've set up on the coffee table. Denise is perched on the edge of the sofa, her thighs pressing against either side of him. On the armchair next to them sits Lily, wearing the diamante collar that Ted—when he was feeling extravagant after his gig in the care home—bought for her online. But her tail's tucked between her legs, and she hasn't been able to relax since she caught sight of the wig.

"Don't worry, Lil. It's not alive!" Ted jokes. He shakes his head to prove it, and she barks at him, loudly.

As he and Denise are laughing, Ted's phone vibrates to let him know he's received a text.

His stomach contracts. It's from Giles.

What does he want?

Ted hasn't heard from his ex-husband for three months—since he received the message suggesting they cease contact. As he opens this new communication, he's surprised to feel dread flood into him.

But all it says is, **"Hi, Ted, how's it going?"**

Is that it? A casual inquiry about how things are going? After everything that's happened?

"What do you make of this, Den?" he asks, handing her his phone.

"Well, it's obvious he's after something," is her immediate assessment. "Do you think it's a divorce? His share of the house?"

"Possibly. But he hasn't made any move on that front. And wouldn't that kind of thing come from a solicitor?"

"Yeah, maybe. Unless a formal letter's on its way, and he's trying to prepare you for it—to soften the blow." She stabs another Kirby grip into his wig. "Then again, maybe he's just missing you."

Ted tilts his head as he considers this. "I didn't think of that."

"You don't seem that bothered," she comments.

He screws up his face. "It's weird, but a few months ago, all I wanted was for Giles to get in touch. And now he has, I don't really feel anything. Except minor irritation. Like when you're cracking eggs into a frying pan and you break one of the yolks."

Denise laughs so hard she drops a Kirby grip. "My God, how the mighty have fallen!"

As she gets down on all fours to search for it, Ted gazes up at the wall, at the painting of the beach at St. Luke's that he's bought to replace Giles's snotty tea towel. "I don't know, maybe I'm just enjoying life without him."

He feels a pang of guilt.

"Don't get me wrong," he adds, quickly. "I do still think about Giles—and I do miss him sometimes. How could I not when we spent nearly twenty years together?"

Denise finds the Kirby grip and straightens herself up again.

"But now I'm seeing Oskar," he goes on. "I've been thinking a lot about my relationship with Giles. And I'm not sure it was as great as I thought."

Ted hung up his coat and shouted for Giles. From his response, it sounded like he was in the kitchen.

Ted strode through and found his husband sitting on a stool, sipping a glass of red wine and flicking through his iPad.

"Hiya, Smiles."

"Hey," said Giles, without looking up.

Ted had been to the hairdresser's, the same hairdresser's he'd been using for years. And he'd come back with the same standard short-back-and-sides cut he always had. *Although I almost didn't . . .*

He kissed Giles on the forehead. "Are you missing something?"

Giles looked up. "What's that?"

"I've been to the hairdresser's." Ted raised an eyebrow in expectation of what was coming.

"Was it closed?"

It was Giles's usual line, and Ted greeted it with his usual laugh. But beneath it, he couldn't help feeling a little down-hearted. *What's the matter with me? Where's that come from?*

Actually, he knew exactly where the feeling had come from. Lately, Giles had been buying a lot of new clothes, as well as spending lots of time in the gym and posting progress pics on social media. This had prompted Ted to have a think about his own appearance—and he'd been considering making some changes and giving it a refresh. *But then I stood in my own way . . .*

"You know, I was thinking of asking for something different this time," he ventured. "I was going to ask for an undercut with a fade. But as soon as I sat in the chair, I got nervous and chickened out."

Giles wrinkled his nose. "Maybe that's just as well."

"Why do you say that?"

"I don't know. I'm just not sure it'd suit you, that's all."

"Oh." Ted pulled out the stool next to him and sat down.

"It's not that you wouldn't look nice or anything," Giles explained. "But it might have been a bit showy for you."

"Showy?"

"Yeah, a bit loud. A bit . . ." Giles paused. "Directional."

"What does that mean?"

"Just fashionable, I suppose. And fashion's not really your thing, is it?"

No, but couldn't it be? Just a bit?

Ted simply frowned. "No, I guess not."

He felt stupid for even considering striking out of his usual style. *As if I could pull off a fade. I'd just look ridiculous.*

"Anyway, what are you up to?" He nodded towards Giles's iPad. "What's that?"

Giles angled the screen so Ted could get a better view. "Tattoos."

"Tattoos?"

"Yeah, I'm thinking of getting one."

Since when is that your *thing?*

But the thought didn't make it out of Ted's head. Instead, he smiled and said, "Ace. Why don't I pour myself a glass of wine and you can tell me all about it?"

"The more I think about Giles," says Ted, his fingers following the line of his undercut around the back of his scalp, "the more I can see how he chipped away at my confidence. And what I always thought of as light-hearted banter was actually his subtle way of putting me down. To boost himself up."

Denise stabs in another Kirkby grip. "I'd say that's a pretty accurate interpretation."

"Don't get me wrong, he wasn't abusive or anything," Ted points out, "at least not in the way Karl was to you."

Denise pulls on his wig to test it's secure and transfers her attention to the other side. "No, but that doesn't mean he didn't treat you badly, honey."

Ted looks again at the painting of the beach. "Yeah, you're right. And I can see now that he didn't just stop me from blossoming in the big ways—like putting me off drag—but in lots of little ways too."

Ted sucks in a breath and lets it out slowly. It feels good to be voicing his thoughts. It's like he's shaking off an encumbrance that he now realizes has been holding him back.

"Yeah, but all that's over now," Denise reassures him.

"Yeah, it is."

Ted pauses. It's at this point he imagines he should feel a twinge of sadness. *But I don't.*

"So what are you going to do about this text?" Denise asks.

"Nothing. I don't think I'm even going to reply. At least not for the time being."

Denise steps back and puts her hands on her hips. "And you're sure you're not doing that just to try and get back at him? For telling you not to get in touch?"

"No. I don't really care enough to do that. Not anymore."

She pretends to stagger back in shock. "Wow, you really are over him."

"Yeah, I guess I am." *And all I can conclude is that this proves the relationship wasn't right in the first place.*

Ted springs to his feet. "Anyway, we've got far more important things to think about. I've got a show coming up—so put some Britney on and let's try out this wig!"

CHAPTER 34

After another wonderful date—and another wonderful night together—Ted kisses Oskar goodbye. But their kiss continues for longer than it should and their breathing quickens. When Ted feels the tickle of Oskar's beard, his kissing becomes hungrier, more urgent—and Oskar's follows suit. Before they get carried away, Ted forces himself to pull back. *I don't want to make Oskar late for work. I don't want to get him into trouble.*

"Go on, then," he booms, dusting his hands and throwing open the door. "Get gone!"

"Ta-ra then!" Oskar says, adopting a broad Lancashire accent.

He gives an exaggeratedly cheery wave, and Ted can't help but snicker. "Ta-ra!"

Oskar mounts his bike but, before he cycles off, he turns around to flash Ted one last smile. Ted feels the joy rush to the tips of his fingers.

As he stands on the doorstep and watches Oskar cycle away, Lily barks in protest.

"I know, Lil," he says, running his hand along her left flank. "I don't want him to go either. But he'll be back soon."

It's lovely to know that—and lovely to say it out loud.

Once Oskar has rounded the corner, Ted takes Lily on her

walk. As he bounces his way to the beach, even though it's a dull, dank day, everything strikes him as beautiful—even the mobility scooters and the tat on display outside the antique shop. Everything seems brighter and more colorful and somehow in much sharper focus than it did just a few weeks ago. He even manages to forget about the anonymous letters, which have been plaguing him ever since he received the latest.

When Ted passes the golden hippos, it's as if they're smiling at him, and he could almost swear the statue of the prince gives him a wink. As he practically skips along the row of hotels and guesthouses, he doesn't notice the peeling paintwork or ripped awnings. He doesn't dodge the cracks in the pavement but dances around them. And, when he comes to the statue that's supposed to represent the spirit of the town, he's convinced she's the most beautiful woman he's ever seen.

He isn't sure what's happening but he's never felt like this. *Is this what it's like to be genuinely happy? Is this what it's like to be in love?*

Whatever's going on, the effect on him is noticeable. Everyone he passes gives him a wide grin and, when he glides into work a few hours later, Dorothy comments that Ted seems much more cheerful these days—and Jinger and Bella agree. Once they've finished setting up the shop, the three of them insist on collaring him for a cup of tea. And they're eager to find out what's behind his transformation.

"It's like you've had a complete makeover," observes Jinger.

"Those new shoes you've got are sick," says Bella.

"And that haircut is sharp," chimes in Jinger.

"What's it all about, Ted?" asks Dorothy.

"Nothing!" Ted protests, but he's unable to stop himself from smiling. "It's nothing!"

"Bollocks!" says Jinger. "I heard you humming Ariana Grande the other day."

"Come on," wheedles Bella. "Have you got a new man?"

Well, funnily enough . . . But Ted doesn't want people to know about Oskar yet—it'll put too much pressure on the relationship.

He gives a loud tut and roofs his eyes. "Not everything's about men, Bella."

"Alright, well you must be taking some kind of health supplement," attempts Dorothy. "Or are you on some new diet or exercise regime?"

"If you are," chips in Jinger, "you need to tell me so I can get on it too."

Ted wonders what they'd say if he told them he was leading a double life as a drag queen. But before he can reply, someone shouts his name.

He turns around to find Cole standing at the back of the shop. "Hilary and Trevor are asking for you in the office," he says.

Ted thanks him and turns back to the women. "Sorry, ladies, but I'll have to leave you guessing," he says, mischievously. And to a chorus of objections, he tips back the rest of his tea and gambols away.

But, as he crosses the lane, walks through the factory, and climbs up the spiral staircase to his parents' office, Ted feels a weight pressing in on him. *What do Mum and Dad want? I hope it's not bad news. I hope they're not going to tell me the company's going bust.*

The weight presses in further. *What if it's to do with the anonymous letters? What if they've been getting them too?*

But when he enters their office, he finds his parents caught up in a flurry of excitement. Trevor's pacing the room and cracking his knuckles, while Hilary's holding up a mirror and tugging at her hair. "I need to get my roots done," she warbles to Trevor. "They're absolutely shocking."

"And I need to get some guest passes for the Yacht Club," Trevor bellows back at her. "Do you reckon he'll be into sailing?"

"Who'll be into sailing?" breaks in Ted. "What's going on? What are you two so worked up about?"

"It's your sister," says Trevor. "She's coming up to see us. In just over three weeks."

"And she's got a new bloke," says Hilary, putting the mirror down and smiling. "She's bringing him to meet us!"

Ted sits down in the sofa area. "I knew about that."

"You *knew* about it?" says Hilary, her hand flying to her chest. "And you didn't tell us?"

Hilary and Trevor step out from behind their enormous mahogany pedestal desks that are topped with battered old computers and piles of bills and brochures. They sit down on the sofa opposite him. Ted apologizes and relays what he knows, which isn't much more than Jemima's just told them. Although it doesn't sound like she's mentioned the idea of moving home permanently, so Ted keeps that to himself.

"Well, this Raj is obviously dead posh," squeaks Hilary. "Apparently his granddad were a maharajah."

Trevor nods, gravely. "We'll have to roll out the red carpet, Hil."

"I wonder if I've got time to give this tattoo another blast with that laser." Hilary clutches her right hand. "Look at t' state of it—it looks like a wilted cabbage."

"You can hardly see it, woman," puffs Trevor. "Just shove a load of makeup on it and he won't notice."

Hilary chews on the inside of her mouth. "What should I make 'em for tea? Should I do my lamb hotpot?"

"Or should we take them out somewhere?" pipes Trevor. "What about the Westcliff?"

Hilary turns to Ted. "What do you think, love? It's pricey, but we've got to do summat special. We haven't seen our Jem since Christmas. We need to make a fuss of her."

OK, so Jemima doesn't make any effort all year, and now she's suddenly decided to come home, we have to drop everything and treat her like a queen? Ted can't help feeling a surge of sourness. *Would everyone do the same for me?*

"What's up, son?" Trevor asks.

"Nothing."

Hilary lets out a sigh. "I know what it is, love. It's the Westcliff, i'n't it? It reminds you of Giles."

"Are you still missing him?" asks Trevor.

Ted imagines their reaction if he tells them he barely thinks about Giles these days—if he tells them that he too has met a new man. *A man I think I might be falling in love with.*

But he tells himself it's too soon. He needs to give them a little longer to get over their disappointment at his split with Giles—and to get used to the fact that they're not going to get back together. *Besides, as soon as they know about Oskar, they'll want to meet him. And I can't inflict that on him yet . . .*

"No, it's not that," he reassures them. "Funnily enough, I was saying to Denise the other day that I feel like I'm over Giles now. I've moved on."

Trevor raises an eyebrow suspiciously. "Where to?"

"What do you mean? No one." Heat floods Ted's face. "Sorry, no*where*."

Hilary inches forward in her seat. "What a load of claptrap. I can tell you're hiding summat. And you've had a massive smile on your face for t' last few weeks. What's going on, love?"

I've met someone new, and I think I'm falling in love, he wants to say.

And not just that, but I'm finally living my dream of being a drag queen.

But his stomach dips with guilt, and he can't bring himself to answer.

Ted and Jemima helped their mum down the path, steering her away from the hospital.

"Come on," said Jemima, "you can do this."

"I parked as close as I could," Ted reassured her, "and there was hardly any traffic, so we'll be home in no time."

As Ted felt her weak grip on his arm, a wave of love washed through him. *Oh, Mum . . .*

The operation to remove Hilary's cancer had been a success, but it had been followed by six months of chemotherapy—and that had been far worse. If the diagnosis had taken the wind out of her sails and the operation had lowered them further, the chemotherapy had left her like a ship battered by a particularly aggressive storm. It had reduced her to a wreck of a woman. But she'd just completed her last session. Somehow she'd made it through.

"I tell you what, kids, I'll be glad to see t' back of that place," she said, as she crumpled herself into the car and took one last look behind her. "I hope I never have to step foot in it again!"

Ted sat in the driver's seat and started the engine. As a combination of problems with staffing and the supply chain had forced Trevor to remain at work, Ted had stepped in to pick up Hilary and drive her home. As usual, Jemima had gone to hospital with her and stayed while she had the chemotherapy. Over the last six months, she'd made regular trips to St. Luke's from London—turning down work and even ending a relationship with a boyfriend who'd proven to be unsupportive. As if intuiting where she was needed most, Jemima had assumed responsibility for Hilary's personal care and emotional wellbeing. Before chemotherapy robbed her mum of her luscious fair hair, Jemima had taken her into the bedroom and shaved it all off, having read that this was a positive, empowered way for a woman and her female relatives to take control of the situation, and much less distressing than seeing her hair gradually fall out in clumps. She'd taken Hilary shopping for wigs and had also bought her a collection of designer head-scarves from Selfridge's and Liberty in London. Ted had to hand it to his sister; she'd exceeded all his expectations and had really come through when she was needed.

As had Giles. Ted's husband had been a huge support to him from the minute Hilary received her diagnosis, and he'd never failed to be there for him. Not just when Ted was feeling emotional but when he'd been working long hours, filling in for his mum as much as he could to keep the business running smoothly. Giles had never once complained about the lack of time they had together, had quietly assumed responsibility for doing the laundry and making their evening meal, and had even booked a holiday to Croatia for the two of them when Hilary's treatment came to an end. Ted knew he'd need it as he was feeling frazzled. *But that's nothing compared to how Mum must be feeling.*

As he and Jemima talked through the details of the final blast of treatment, Ted noticed that Hilary was sitting with her eyes closed.

"Hang on in there, Mum," he coaxed. "We're nearly home."

When Ted pulled into the drive, Trevor was waiting for them outside the front door. He gave Hilary a round of applause, opened the car door, and scooped her up into his arms.

"What are you doing, you daft beggar?" she said, giving him a light slap.

"What does it look like? I'm carrying you over the threshold. I never did it when we got married, and I've always regretted it."

Hilary managed something approaching a smile. "Yeah, well, you might regret it now. I ha'n't lost that much weight, you know."

Trevor gave a loud tut. "Rubbish, woman. You're as light as a feather! And just as gorgeous as the day we met!"

Hilary said nothing but rested her head on his chest.

Once she was safely settled on the sofa, Ted made everyone a cup of tea, and they all sat down around her.

"Well, that's it," he said. "You did it, Mum."

She batted away his comment. "No, love, it were a team effort. I only got through it because we all stuck together."

"Yeah, but you're the one who had to take all the physical pain," he pointed out. "We couldn't help you there."

"Well, I've done it now. It's over. And the consultant is hopeful it'll have worked. He's hopeful I'll have seen t' cancer off."

"You nailed it, Mum!" cheeped Jemima.

"You pissed all over it!" echoed Ted.

Hilary managed a chuckle. "Thanks, kids. And who knows? When t' dust settles and I'm back to my best, maybe this whole episode won't have been completely bad."

Ted wondered if the chemotherapy had drained her so much that she was raving. "Mum, what are you on about?"

She let out a breath. "Just that it's given me and your dad time to talk through some important stuff."

"What important stuff?" asked Jemima, the concern etched on her face.

"Nowt you kids need to worry about," Hilary went on. "But there's nowt like staring death in t' face to make you focus on what you want out of life."

Ted looked to his dad for some kind of clarification, but Trevor diverted his eyes. He began scratching at an imaginary mark on the arm of the sofa. *What's he looking so shifty about?*

"Mum, you're scaring me now," he said. "What do you mean?"

"Nowt, love. I'm just saying that if this cancer has brought the four of us closer together, it may have had a little silver lining." She put her mug down on the side. "Now this brew i'n't cutting it, I'm afraid. Who's going to get me some ice cream?"

All three of them shot to their feet. Then they looked at each other and burst into laughter. Hilary even managed to join in with a little giggle.

It was the first time Ted could remember any of them laughing in months. And it felt good. It felt really good.

No, I can't tell them yet. I can't do that to them.

Ted apologizes to his parents and tells them that a lot has been happening lately but he doesn't feel ready to reveal what it is. Their upset is almost palpable.

"So you're keeping secrets from us now, are you?" says Trevor, folding his arms. "I thought we didn't do that in this family. I thought we stuck together as a team."

"No," Ted protests, "we do. It's just . . ."

"Well, we're obviously not exciting enough for you anymore," jumps in Hilary, her lower lip trembling.

"No, it's not that," Ted parries, "honestly."

"I don't know, maybe you're just bored of us," says Hilary. "Maybe you're planning to stretch your wings and fly off and leave us."

Ted feels another stab of guilt. He remembers what Oskar told him about his parents and the family trauma he experienced in Poland. *I should be grateful I didn't have to go through anything like that.*

"Sorry, I promise it's nothing to worry about," he reassures them. "And I promise I'll tell you everything—just not yet."

Hilary lets out a long breath and brushes some imaginary crumbs from her lap. "Alright, love. Just make sure it's not too long, will you?"

"I will," says Ted.

He stands up and smooths his hands down his trousers. "Now, where shall we go for this meal?"

CHAPTER 35

The following Sunday, Ted has arranged to go with Oskar on one of his regular bike rides, so he is driving to Eastcliff Caravan Park, with Oskar in the passenger seat. By now the two of them are spending most of their time together, but always at Ted's house because it's easier for the dog. Partly out of curiosity—because Ted wants to see Oskar's home—and partly because he knows how important cycling is to him, he's suggested he accompany Oskar on a ride.

"So have you thought about what route you're going to take me on?" Ted asks.

"I always start by heading north," says Oskar, "as it's got the best scenery and the most open views. But then there are various options. It depends how long you want to cycle for. It depends on your stamina."

Although he can tell from his tone that Oskar's teasing him, Ted can't help but feel apprehensive. *What if I'm rubbish? What if I hold him back? What if it puts him off me?*

"Don't worry," Oskar adds. "We don't have to decide now. We can always set off and see how you get on."

Ted is relieved when they pull into the caravan park and he can switch the conversation onto Oskar's home. He's looking forward to seeing what he's done with it—and if he's as talented a designer as he suspects. But just as they're stepping out of the car, a voice calls out.

"Morning, boys!"

It belongs to Oskar's neighbor, who's wearing walking trousers, a sleeveless vest, and boots, and has a little rucksack on her back with a fleece tied around her waist. "I just wanted to say hello," she chirps as she approaches. "I'm Marina. And you must be Ted."

Ted gives her a wide smile. "Dead right. And it's ace to meet you."

Marina returns his smile. "You too. Oskar's told me so much about you."

"Likewise."

They come together for a hug, and Ted notices that she smells like a scented candle.

"Obviously I know who you are," he tells her. He turns to Oskar and gives a little eye roll. "In case you haven't noticed, St. Luke's is a small town."

"It is indeed," chirps Marina. "Funnily enough, I know your dad."

Ted feels suspicion thump into him again. Then he feels annoyed at himself. *Come on, you can't suspect every woman who's ever met your dad of having an affair with him.*

"What a coincidence," says Oskar. "You never mentioned that."

Marina bats away his comment. "It's not a big deal—everyone knows Trevor Ainsworth."

Yeah, but how well *do you know him?* Ted wants to ask. But he beats back his suspicion. Marina's becoming important to Oskar and he wouldn't want to do anything to jeopardize their friendship.

He tells Marina that they're going on a bike ride and are hoping to make an early start.

"I'm off out too," she says, gesturing to her hiking gear. "I'm meeting some friends for a walk."

They wish one another a good day, and Ted and Oskar wave Marina off.

Right, you've got to stop thinking about her now!

Ted skips over to the caravan. "Come on," he says to Oskar. "I'm dying to see this!"

Oskar opens up and gives him a little tour.

Ted's impressed by how spacious and comfortable the caravan is—and he loves Oskar's design. *He's every bit as talented as I expected.*

But his attention is caught by a framed photo of a man that's hanging on the wall. The man has a warm smile and the same fair hair as Oskar—and the family resemblance is striking.

"Is this your dad?" Ted asks.

Oskar smiles. "Yeah, yeah it is."

"He looks lovely."

"Yeah, he is. Or he was."

"Have you not had any luck finding him?"

"Not yet, but I'll tell you about that later." Oskar goes to the bedroom. "Come on, we need to hit the road!"

He disappears from view and reemerges holding helmets and studded shoes, then disappears again to produce a whole range of cycling clothes he says should fit Ted, and again to find two water bottles with clips to attach them to the bikes. It's becoming more and more obvious that Oskar's a serious cyclist—and Ted feels another stab of nerves. Then he remembers something Denise once said to him: *you can only really love someone when you're not afraid to be your true self with them.*

"I'm nervous," Ted blurts out. "I just thought I should say that."

Oskar stops filling the water bottles and switches off the tap. "What do you mean? Why are you nervous?"

"I don't know, it's just you've got all this proper cycling gear so you're obviously dead good at it. I don't want to be crap and let you down."

Oskar steps closer and runs his hand down Ted's cheek. "Ted, it's not the gear that's important—all that does is make things more comfortable. The reason I love cycling is because of the way it makes me *feel.*"

They sit down and Oskar tells Ted that cycling gives him the sense of his spirit being unshackled, that it makes him feel like he's leaving behind his problems and rising above them, that it's the closest he can get to flying—flying free.

Oskar looks him in the eye and Ted feels an understanding pass between them.

"That's kind of why I do drag," Ted says. "To feel like I'm rising above everything and letting my spirit soar."

Oskar nods. "And I'm looking forward to seeing that."

"You will. I'm just still not sure when." *I'm not sure when I'll be brave enough . . .*

Ted springs to his feet. "Anyway, today's all about cycling. And I'm going to pedal through my nerves. Come on, let's do it!"

Once they've put their clothes and shoes on, Oskar leads Ted out to a storage unit at the side of the caravan, opening it up to reveal two bikes. He explains that the older, scuffed, and slightly battered one is the first bike he bought when he moved to St. Luke's, which he now keeps as a spare. He offers to ride it himself, but Ted insists Oskar take the better one. *At least then if I'm rubbish, I won't feel bad.*

There's a little awkwardness when Oskar has to show him how to operate the gears—and Ted becomes flustered.

"It's so confusing," he moans, frustrated at himself more than anything. "I just don't get it."

Oskar dismounts his bike and gestures to the cassette at the back of Ted's. "Look at all these rings; the chain moves up to the big ring when you're traveling on flat roads and want to go fast, and it drops down to the little one when you're going uphill and need a bit of help."

"But how am I supposed to know which ring I'm on when I'm pedaling away? If I twist around and look down, I might crash!"

"Actually, forget about the rings. Just concentrate on the numbers on the handlebars." Oskar walks around to the front of Ted's bike.

"But there are so many of them!" Ted complains. "Why do I need twenty-one?"

"You don't *need* any—they're just meant to make things easier. Just remember that the lower numbers are the low gears and the higher numbers are the high gears."

"The lower numbers are the low gears and the higher numbers are the high gears," Ted repeats.

Oskar rests his hands on Ted's and looks him in the eye. "Ted, don't worry. I can always shout out to you when I think we should change gear. Or we can always just forget the gears completely. We can push a bit harder when we're going uphill or just sit up out of the saddle."

"No, I'm not going to do that. I'm going to do this properly."

Oskar leans forward and kisses him. "Honestly, Ted, it doesn't matter if you don't. And I promise, you'll be much better at this than I'd ever be at drag."

Ted manages to laugh. "Don't say that, you haven't seen me yet."

Oskar laughs along with him, and Ted can feel himself calming down. *This is going to be alright. I'll be safe with Oskar.*

"Come on," he says. "Let's give it a go!"

They set off and cycle out of the caravan park. Although Ted hasn't ridden a bike since he was a child, once they've made it down the steep hill and he's changed gear to glide along the seafront, he's relieved to find that his nervousness is disappearing. With the wind buffeting his face and roaring in his ears, he understands exactly why Oskar loves it—he understands everything he said about how it makes him feel. But, when they come to the end of the promenade, Oskar suddenly pulls over at the side of the road.

"Why are we stopping?" Ted asks.

"I just want to see if you're alright. And to check you want to carry on."

Ted's eyes bulge. "Are you kidding? I *love* it!"

Oskar grins. "OK, great. Let's keep going!"

They pull away and speed up along the road. Once they pass the windmill and enter the stretch of open coastline, the traffic thins out and Oskar falls back so he can ride alongside Ted. Whenever a car appears, he pulls away again so they're riding single file. As he does, Ted admires his confidence and control. He loves riding behind Oskar, watching his thick calf muscles powering the pedals. Equally, he loves riding next to him, savoring the easy silence between them, and enjoying their occasional expressions of exhilaration. These are usually inspired by the stunning views. It's a bright summer's day, but the sun is behind them so doesn't obscure their vision. Instead, its rays make everything before them shimmer and sparkle. Ted isn't sure he's ever appreciated the landscape of his home county quite so much.

He's almost disappointed when it's time to stop for lunch. Oskar pulls up by a stretch of green overlooking the sea, and the two of them skid along the pavement on their studs. They tread across the grass and sit down on a bench facing the horizon. Oskar pulls a packed lunch out of his backpack.

"I hope you're hungry," he says, "because I've brought loads of food."

"My God, I didn't even think about lunch," admits Ted. "I just thought we'd be grabbing something in town."

"Well, you soon cover long distances on a bike."

"So I'm discovering." Ted spreads out his arms to embrace the view. "Anyway, this is gorgeous. And it's the perfect place to eat lunch."

Oskar pulls out a bag of radishes. "Here we go."

"I love radishes!"

"Me too. My dad always used to eat them." Oskar opens the bag and offers him one. "I didn't tell you this earlier, but that's another reason why I love cycling; I used to do it with my dad."

As they nibble away, Oskar tells Ted that when he was young, he and his dad would spend whole days cycling along Poland's north coast, stopping somewhere quiet and scenic for a picnic lunch. "And my dad would always start by pulling out a bag of radishes. So every time I go on a bike ride, I bring some with me."

Although he's sharing happy memories, there's a sadness to Oskar's voice. Ted can tell how much he misses his dad and his heart gives a little lurch.

In that moment, he knows that he *is* in love with Oskar. *But I'm not going to say anything yet. I don't want to make him feel uncomfortable.*

Ted asks for more details on his search for his dad, and Oskar updates him on the various leads he's tried. Ted wishes there was something he could do to help. Then he has an idea.

He remembers a comment his friend Hartley made several years ago. *"There are gay groups for everything these days."*

He inches closer to Oskar. "Have you tried looking for any cycling groups?"

"No. I didn't think of that."

"You know, if your dad was really into it, it's possible he's a member of some club. There's a massive cycling scene in Manchester; the Team GB squad is based there, at the velodrome."

"Of course."

"And there are clubs specifically for gay people who are into all kinds of sports and hobbies. What if Manchester has a gay cycling club?"

Ted whips out his phone, does a quick online search, and discovers that Manchester does indeed have such a club. He shows the website to Oskar. When he clicks on the menu, he finds there's a photo gallery. But he doesn't want to open it himself, so he hands the phone to Oskar.

Within seconds, Oskar lets out a gasp. "Oh my God, that's him!"

He zooms into a photo and shows it to Ted, who recognizes the man from the photo in the caravan. Then Oskar says something in Polish. Ted hasn't heard him speak Polish before, so he assumes he must be overwhelmed with either excitement or some other emotion. He's also rapt, scouring every page on the club's website. When he comes to a list of its members, he scrolls down. Then he stops.

"So *that's* why I couldn't find him!"

"Why? What is it?"

Oskar turns to face him. "My dad's changed his name from the Polish spelling of Andrzej to the English version—Andrew."

Ted narrows his eyes. "Why do you think he'd do that?"

"Possibly to put some distance between himself and his home country. Possibly so he couldn't be found when he first moved. To be fair, it's kind of what I still do; I try not to leave any trace of myself online."

As Oskar turns back to the website, Ted feels a wave of anxiety passing through his gut. He's reminded of how much Oskar's life is still ruled by shame. If the two of them are going to have a future together, Ted needs to encourage Oskar to live more openly. But he doesn't want to do it now. *I don't want to ruin the moment or spoil Oskar's excitement.*

"You know, this actually sounds quite fun," Oskar says, looking up from the website. "They do take part in events at the velodrome and apparently they have monthly socials in the Gay Village."

He shows Ted.

"I like the name," Ted comments. "Riders—whoever came up with that has got exactly my sense of humor."

They laugh.

"Is there a contact address?" Ted asks.

Oskar goes back into the menu. "Yeah. It's only a general info one, but I'm sure someone will check it occasionally. Hopefully, if I send an email, they'll pass it on to my dad."

Ted notices Oskar's jaw tense and runs a hand across his eyes.

"What's the matter?" he asks.

Oskar lets out a long sigh. "It's just my dad is obviously happy living as a gay man; he's got loads of gay friends, and he doesn't seem to be remotely ashamed of who he is. I feel like I'm lagging behind. And that doesn't make me feel great about myself."

Ted spots his chance and seizes it. "Well, maybe it's time for you to start opening up a bit more. Maybe it's time for you to start being a bit more honest about who you are."

Oskar massages his beard as he considers what Ted's saying. "Do you mean coming out?"

"Yeah. You said it went well with Marina, so maybe it's time for you to start coming out to more people. You never know, it might help you feel proud of who you are."

Oskar nods, somberly. "You're right. I think I should do that. And it's what I *want* to do."

Ted leans forward and kisses him. Oskar's lips and tongue have the slightly peppery taste of radishes. *Yeah, there's no question; I am in love with him.*

When they eventually pull away, Oskar says, "OK, I'm going to come out to my workmates. And I'm going to do it soon."

Ted sends him a beam. "That's ace. How do you think they'll react?"

"I've no idea. They're very different to Marina, so I'll probably just do it quickly. Then I don't have the chance to get nervous. I'll probably just do it in the moment, without any planning."

"That sounds like a good strategy. But it's a big step, so don't go through with it unless you're one hundred percent sure."

"Don't worry, I won't."

Ted budges closer to him and rubs his shoulder up and down Oskar's. "And whenever you do it, know that I'm with you all the way."

"Thanks." Oskar smiles and hands Ted his phone. "Now come on, pass me those radishes."

CHAPTER 36

Just as he was hoping, a few days later Oskar spots his chance to come out to his workmates. They're in the language school, where Oskar's applying gloss to the skirting boards along the main staircase, while his colleagues are in the hallway rolling the first coat of emulsion onto the walls and ceiling. It's supposed to be their last day on the job, but they're running a week behind schedule. Oskar's working as fast as he can, but all he can think about is the email he sent to the cycling club to pass on to his dad. It's been four days since he wrote. *I hope I get a response soon . . .*

Just as he's considering what to do if he doesn't, he's distracted by a news item on the radio that's on in the background. The presenters are discussing the breakup of a famous gay actor and his husband, an equally famous singer. Oskar isn't particularly interested in the story but listens out for his colleagues' reactions.

"That's a shame," comments Mick, a middle-aged man with a sturdy frame and a short, graying beard, wearing a bandana in the colors of his home country of Ghana, "I always thought they were good together."

Come on, Oskar. This is the moment you've been waiting for . . .

But he examines the rest of his workmates, some of them wearing football shirts, others with cigarettes tucked behind their ears, the majority of them with muscular, paint-splattered, sometimes heavily-tattooed arms. They're what he's heard British people call "men's men," and their banter often revolves around women—or denigrating each other's ability to attract women. *They're hardly going to be gay-friendly, are they?*

When one of the men squeaks out a long, high-pitched fart, the others growl in protest. A wave of fear licks Oskar's insides. *No, I can't . . .*

"I thought they made a good couple too," says Fletch, a wiry, snaggle-toothed, stubbly man who goes fishing at weekends. "But they're both decent-looking lads, I'm sure they won't have a problem finding someone else."

Maybe I'm wrong . . .

Oskar tries to gather the courage to speak. *Come on, you've got nothing to be afraid of . . .*

"You know, I wish I were gay," booms a man called Will, who has hands the size of paddles and a chest as wide as a windscreen—which have earned him the nickname Will Da Beast. "Women love gays. Or at least they like them more than they do us straight blokes."

"Not *all* women like us," Oskar blurts out.

Did I really just say that?

He freezes. It feels as though his eyes are about to burst out of their sockets but he daren't blink.

There's no backtracking now . . .

"Anyway," he adds, his heartbeat in his ears, "maybe the only reason they do is because we're not trying to have sex with them."

He struggles to fill his lungs. *I've just come out. I've actually just come out.*

But none of the other men—to use one of his favorite expressions—bats an eyelid.

"That's another thing, gay men have way more sex than we do," comments Will, as he rolls paint onto the ceiling, "and it's much easier for them to get it. All they have to do is go online, and it's practically on tap."

His tone is so casual, it's as if he's discussing the weather. Oskar wonders if Will and the rest of his colleagues have misheard him.

"I suppose it is easier for gay men to find sex," Oskar says, his voice cracking, "but not all of us are looking for that."

He does his best to stress the word "us"—and still no one bats an eyelid. *Have they all gone deaf? Or am I going mad and speaking another language?*

Determined to drive his message home, he puts down his paintbrush and says, "Anyway, isn't it easier for you straight guys to find sex these days?"

In an instant Oskar is bombarded with stories—about being treated badly by women who've had terrible experiences with previous boyfriends and expect the worst of every straight man; about feeling afraid to give a woman a compliment in case they're accused of being predatory or sexist; about being reeled in by the occasional manipulative woman who just wants to be bought drinks then lets slip she isn't even single; and a story from Mick about white women viewing him as the means of fulfilling a sexual fantasy but failing to consider him a suitable prospect for a more meaningful, long-term relationship.

"Some of them just want to see what it's like to sleep with a black guy," he says. "Then they can tick it off their list and have a good story to tell on hen nights."

"Thankfully, I don't have to put up with that," comments Fletch, roller in hand. "I find dating hard enough as it is."

"Whatever color you are, it can be hard to be straight these days," reflects Will, leaning on his ladder.

Oskar tries to engage, but the best he can do is ooh and ahh in vague interest. *Just a minute, what about what I just said? Didn't you hear that I'm gay?*

He can't possibly allow the conversation to move on without knowing for sure. "Anyway, I'm off the dating scene now as I've got a boyfriend," he says.

"Great."

"Good for you."

"Get in!"

Oskar is flabbergasted. "Wait a minute, did you guys already *know*?"

Fletch shrugs. "That you're gay? Yeah, of course we did."

Oskar can't believe it. He thought he'd managed to dodge the subject, to evade his colleagues' attempts to lure him into conversation about his personal life. "But I don't understand," he splutters. "*How*?"

"The first time I worked it out was when you were mouthing along to Steps on the radio," reveals Will.

"You always know better than the designer we're working with which colors will look good," says Fletch.

Oskar straightens his back. "Yeah, but hold on, that doesn't necessarily—"

"What about when we were working on that Indian restaurant?" interrupts Will, pulling away a piece of masking tape from around a window frame. "And that fit florist from next door kept flirting with you? You didn't even notice!"

"Or when that guy from Ainsworth's pretended to accidentally bump into you outside the vegan restaurant?" says Mick, dabbing at a stain on the wall with a damp cloth. "And it was really obvious you were flirting with each other?"

Shit, so I didn't pull that off after all.

Oskar slides down a few steps. "That's Ted. That's who I'm seeing."

"That doesn't surprise me," says Mick. "I could tell something was going on between you two."

I think I'm in love with him, Oskar wants to say. But he stops himself. *That might be a step too far.*

"Anyway, does this Ted have any female friends?" asks Mick.

Oskar can't believe how easily this has gone. "Urm, yeah, funnily enough, he does. There's one called Denise who I know is single. I haven't met her yet, but apparently she's great."

Oskar is due to meet Denise at the open-mic night next weekend. Finally, Ted has agreed to let him share in his dream. Oskar's nervous that he won't like drag but knows how important it is to Ted, so he is trying to keep an open mind; he doesn't want to let him down. But he's also nervous about meeting Denise as he wants to make a good impression on her. He's not sure how she'll respond if he tries to fix her up with his workmate the first time they meet. *But Mick seems keen . . .*

"Well, do a little digging for us, will you?" he asks.

"Yeah, I will."

Then, as if it's the most natural thing in the world, the conversation moves on to a discussion of the latest form of the local football team. As Oskar goes back to painting the skirting boards, he's stunned at what's just happened—it was so easy he isn't even sure it *did* happen.

No, it happened. It definitely happened.

He can't suppress a grin.

And I can't wait to tell Ted.

CHAPTER 37

Ted can't believe it. Just as he's completing the day's health and safety checklist, the door to the shop swings open and in sweeps Stanley, closely followed by Alison. Stanley removes his fedora—with the flamboyant peacock feather sticking out of it—and uncovers his dazzling halo of white hair. He looks so superior to everything around him, so elevated from his surroundings, that he puts Ted in mind of the Queen visiting the set of *Coronation Street. With Alison as his lady-in-waiting.*

A few of the other customers glance over at the new arrivals, and it occurs to Ted that they must make an unusual sight: a ninety-year-old man in a sky-blue three-piece suit with a lemon shirt and necktie, his lemon-painted nails standing out against the silver grip of an antique ebony walking stick, and a black woman in her thirties wearing a charcoal-gray dungaree pinafore dress over a navy-blue-and-white-striped Breton shirt with matching navy Doc Martens boots. Ted has only ever seen Alison in her nurse's uniform, and he's surprised by how quirky a dresser she is. He rushes forward to greet them.

"Hiya, Stanley. Hi, Alison. Ace to see you!"

A smile lifts Stanley's face. "Likewise, dolly. And I'm charmed to be here."

Alison explains that when her shift finished, she had a free hour, so offered to take Stanley for a trip out.

"I'm bored by all the repetition in my life," he comments, "all the visits to the doctor, the rigid meal times, and the endless rounds of medication. And I fancied an ice cream. When I was a boy and I was unhappy, coming here was the only thing that would cheer me up."

"Well, I hope the place hasn't lost any of its magic," says Ted.

Stanley looks around, his eyes flitting from the pink leatherette of the counter to the distinctive purple sign bearing Ainsworth's logo, from the huge plastic model of an ice cream to the flavors of real ice cream on display, eventually settling on all the customers enjoying their ice cream, their faces aglow with pleasure as the sound of their spoons hitting the glass dishes creates a symphony of tinkles. His hand rushes to his heart. "It's splendid, dolly. And with you here, I'd say it's more magical than ever."

Ted feels suddenly—and quite unexpectedly—moved.

Oh, what's the matter with you? It's only a simple compliment!

Before his emotions can come tumbling out in full view of the staff, Ted bustles his guests over to his favorite booth that's just become free.

"Here you are," he announces, breezily, "the best seats in the house!"

"And very nice they are too," says Alison. As she slides onto the bench and budges along, she gives a surreptitious glance around the shop. "Is your dad not in today?"

Ted's stomach churns. "Do you know him?"

Alison pulls on one of her copper curls and twiddles with the ends. "Of course! I've known Trevor for years."

Oh God, do I have to suspect her now too?

Ted feels a rush of nausea but plasters on a smile. "Yeah, Dad's here; he's just round the back with Mum. Now, what can I get you?"

"I've no need to look at the menu," trills Alison. "I know just what I want. I'll have a couple of scoops of lemon meringue please—in a bowl, rather than a cone. With a squeeze of rasp-berry sauce on top."

"I'll have a bowl too, please," says Stanley, who's settled on the bench opposite her. "I'll have two scoops of raspberry pavlova, with one scoop of peaches and cream."

"Any toppings?"

"No, thanks," says Stanley.

"He's extra enough as it is," quips Alison.

"Extra?" says Stanley. "Extra what?"

"Extra *everything!*"

They chuckle.

"OK," says Ted, clicking his heels together. "Coming right up!"

He bounces off to prepare their order.

Now don't get carried away imagining Alison had an affair with Dad. You've no evidence at all—and you're only going to spoil their visit.

Once Ted's composed himself, he returns with their ice cream. He's greeted by gasps of delight—and Stanley gives a jig of ex-citement. As soon as they begin spooning the ice cream into their mouths, both Stanley and Alison let out little groans of pleasure.

"This is magnificent!" gushes Stanley.

"It's better than sex!" burbles Alison.

Stanley erupts in laughter. "Well, that depends on the sex you've been having."

She arches an eyebrow. "Who says I've been having any?"

"Exactly!"

All three of them laugh.

Ted slides onto the bench next to Stanley.

"You know, being here takes me back to my time in the gentlemen's outfitters," says Stanley. "The buzz, the excite-ment, the customers' faces when they tried on something new. That place was always so full of joy. And that made *me* joyful."

Alison wags her spoon in agreement. "There's definitely a lot of joy in here."

Ted can't help feeling deflated. "There is, isn't there?"

Stanley swallows his mouthful. "That can't be much fun for you, dolly."

Alison stops eating. "What do you mean?"

Stanley lowers his voice to a stage whisper. "Don't tell anyone, but Ted doesn't like ice cream."

Alison looks shocked. "That's a shame."

Ted's shoulders sag.

"Actually, sorry," she backtracks. "That's not a shame at all. What I mean is, it must make you feel . . ." She pauses and peers at him. "I don't know, how *does* it make you feel?"

For a moment, Ted's thrown. He's never been asked this question before. He's never even asked it of himself.

"It makes me feel wrong, I suppose," he begins, tentatively. "Like I'm different than everyone else. Like I don't work properly. Like there's something defective or faulty with me."

Stanley stabs his spoon into his ice cream. "That doesn't surprise me. You're excluded from the joy. You're not part of it."

Ted nods solemnly. "You know, one of my dad's favorite sayings is 'ice cream is life.' And all you have to do is look around here, and you've got lots of evidence backing him up."

He gestures at the café full of babies, children, adults, and elderly people, all of them reveling in the simple act of eating ice cream, all of them relishing the texture and flavors, all of them emitting words or sounds that express their pleasure.

"Yes, well, ice cream may be life for lots of people," Stanley points out, "but it isn't for you, dolly. You get your life force from somewhere else entirely. And that's what makes you special!"

Ted gives a lopsided smile. "Thanks, Stanley. You're very wise."

Stanley shoos away his praise. "Not at all. I just know what it's like to have tastes, to have desires, to have a reason for living that's out of sync with everyone else. I know what that can do to your soul."

"Yeah, but I'm doing something about that now, aren't I?" counters Ted, lowering his voice. "I'm exploring my tastes and desires. I'm discovering the thing that gives me life. That's why I'm becoming a drag queen."

Stanley notices that his crystal daffodil-shaped brooch is pointing downwards and readjusts it. "Yes, but you still haven't told your parents, have you?"

Ted slumps back in his seat. "No."

"Exactly. So you're still keeping it secret. And that isn't good for the soul either."

Alison finishes her ice cream and pushes away her bowl. "Why haven't you told your parents, my love?"

Ted licks the back of his bottom teeth. "It's complicated. But the short answer is I don't want to disappoint them. They want me to be one kind of person, and I don't want them to know I'm somebody else."

"And what makes you think they don't know already?"

Ted bobs up in his seat. "Why do you say that?"

Alison folds her arms. "Parents often know more about their children than their children like to think. Take it from the one of us who's a parent."

"Sorry," says Ted. "I didn't know you were a mum."

"Yep, I'm a mum—a single mum—to Gabriel, who's just turned ten. And actually, I'm pretty sure he's gay."

"What makes you say that?" Ted asks.

Alison lets out a breath. "I'd like to say it's maternal intuition, but the truth is it's quite easy to spot. I don't want to fall back on stereotypes, but he's a bit camp, a bit girlie, a bit effeminate. I'm not sure of the right word. He's just my Gabriel.

But yeah, he hates sport and is in the school drama group and cheerleading society."

Ted raises an eyebrow. "Cheerleading society? I didn't know schools had cheerleading societies these days. Or that boys could join!"

"I think it's a very recent thing, but Gabe loves it."

Stanley licks his spoon clean. "Well, I think you're right; he's definitely a fruit."

"Stanley!" protests Ted. "You can't say that!"

Stanley drops his spoon into his empty bowl. "Why not? It's a compliment!"

"And I'll take it as one." Alison flashes him a wide smile, revealing the little gap between her front teeth. "Anyway, to go back to what we were saying, I'd love it if Gabe grew up to be a drag queen—if that's what he wanted. Because I want him to have the conviction to be the person he's meant to be, the version of himself that will make him the happiest."

She looks at Ted. "And once they've got used to the idea, I'm sure your parents will feel the same way about you."

But they've seen flashes of my dream before; I've shown them the odd sign—and they've never given me even the slightest hint that they might like it or approve.

Actually, didn't Mum create my costume for that Halloween party? Didn't she sign me up for dance class when Giles dumped me? And what about all those knowing looks she gave Dad whenever they caught me dressing up?

Then again, if she does know I like drag, why hasn't she said anything? Oh God, she must be really against it. And so must Dad.

Ted clenches his thighs. "Yeah, but these are different times," he tells Alison. "You're much younger than they are. Come to think of it, you're much younger than me! Your son's probably young enough to be their grandson."

Alison snatches a look at her watch. "Shit, sorry, speaking

of Gabe, I've got to go. I've got to pick him up from cheer-leading."

Stanley shuffles to the end of the bench. "Well, I enjoyed that—and the ice cream was magnificent. Will you tot up the bill, dolly?"

"Not at all," insists Ted. "It's my treat. Anyway, you guys have been a big help to me. And Stanley, you're making me a dress for my gig in Blackpool."

Ted realizes he said that in a voice loud enough to activate an Alexa on the other side of the street. He looks around to check no one heard him. But behind the counter, Jinger and Bella are—as usual—engrossed in their own conversation. *Thank God for that!*

Reluctantly, Stanley and Alison agree to accept Ted's hospitality.

"But you'll have to let us pay next time," says Stanley, "or we won't be able to come back!"

As he stands up, he clutches at his lower back and gives a little yelp.

"Are you alright?" Ted asks.

"Yes, thanks, I'm just a bit stiff. The old lacoddy took quite a pounding yesterday."

"Are you talking about sex again?" teases Alison.

"If only!" Stanley picks up his cane and faces Ted. "I went to a Zumba class, and my poor old body's been aching ever since."

"What, with the other residents?" Ted asks.

"Yes, dolly. I quite enjoyed it."

Ted grins. "That's ace. So are you getting on better with them?"

"Much better, thanks. It was your show that did it. I mean, I still have to deal with the odd meese fungus—that's Polari for ugly old ratbag—but the general situation has improved splendidly."

"Well, I'm pleased to hear it."

Stanley jabs at him with his stick. "Now we've just got to improve *your* situation."

Ted nods. "I'm working on it, I promise!"

Stanley taps him on the shoulder. "Very good. But work a bit harder."

CHAPTER 38

"Let's pretend I'm a heckler," says Denise. She adopts the voice of a burly, barrel-chested man. "Shut the fuck up, you ugly bitch!"

Ted bursts out laughing. "You sound like an X-rated version of that bloke in Memory House. Can't you come up with something witty?"

"Alright, how's this?" Denise slips back into the deep voice. "If you were performing in my backyard, I'd shut the curtains."

Ted gives her a vinegary smile and assumes the voice of Gail Force. "Please do, spare me the sight of that face, like a moldy turnip dumped on a slagheap."

Denise shrieks in mock outrage. "You cheeky bitch!"

"It's what's known in drag as reading for filth," Ted explains. "I'm trying to get into the swing of it!"

It's the evening of the open-mic night, and Denise, Ted, and Oskar are on their way to Blackpool. Ted's in the driving seat, while Denise has made the decision to sit in the back so that he and Oskar can be next to each other. She doesn't want Oskar to feel like the odd one out, like he's tagging along as some kind of afterthought. *I've known Ted for such a long time—and we've been through so much together—I don't need to feel insecure about our friendship.*

As they pass the windmill and leave St. Luke's, Denise leans forward. "And are you going to do your material about getting old?"

Ted switches back into the voice of Gail. "I've now reached an age when I'm too old to die young. These days, my wildest fantasy is being able to trust a fart."

Oskar chuckles.

"Brilliant!" tweets Denise. "I love it!"

But she can't help feeling a twinge of foreboding. *I really want this to go well . . .*

What worries her is that a bad show will dent Ted's confidence, a really bad one will set him back, and a terrible one might put him off drag forever. *Well, I've got to be as good a friend to him as he's been to me; I've got to do everything I can to fill him with confidence.*

"Teddy, you're going to be amazing," she states, emphatically.

"I agree," asserts Oskar. "As you Brits say, you're going to *smash it.*"

Denise smiles. She likes Oskar. He seems sensitive and kind—and he obviously cares about Ted. And he doesn't seem as shy or awkward as Ted made out. But maybe he's changing; Ted told her that he's just come out to his work colleagues, so that might be helping him relax into his sexuality. *Anyway, he's turned up tonight—so when it comes to drag, he's already a big improvement on Giles.*

As they cross the railway line, she slaps the sides of their seats. "Boys, I've got an announcement to make."

"What's that?" asks Ted.

She adopts a haughty tone. "I am not going to exercise my veto."

Ted corners his eyes. "What do you mean, 'exercise your veto'?"

Denise looks at him as if he's asked a stupid question. "Best friends get a veto over boyfriends, obviously."

Ted sniggers. "Den, I don't remember agreeing to that."

Denise waves away his objection. "Anyway, it doesn't matter because I like Oskar. That's what I'm telling you—I'm giving him my approval."

Oskar beams. "Thanks, Denise."

"Well, that wasn't a very rigorous process," teases Ted. "You've only known him ten minutes. Let's hope he's not a serial killer, or I'll hold you responsible."

"Don't worry," Oskar whispers to Denise. "I'll make sure it looks like an accident."

They laugh as Ted pulls up at some traffic lights just outside Lytham. It's still early, and there are plenty of people who are only just leaving the beach; the lane opposite is packed with cars transporting families away from Blackpool and back to their lives. In the distance stands the iconic Victorian tower, its distinctive red trunk rooted in its sturdy brick base.

Ted turns to Denise. "While we're on the subject of dating, how are you doing on your apps?"

Denise feels her heart sink. Ted's been so encouraging, she can't bear to tell him she's almost given up. She knows how much he wants her to be happy and she doesn't want to disappoint him. *Well, the only way forward is to make light of it.*

"It's a bit uninspiring," she says. "The other day I was chatting to some guy who said his hobbies were 'going out and staying in.'"

"Which basically means living," clarifies Ted, as the lights change.

"And I can't tell you the number of men who describe themselves as having a 'rugby build' when what they mean is—"

"They're overweight," interjects Ted.

"Exactly! And bizarrely, the other day I got liked by some guy whose entire profile was pics of loaded potato skins."

"Now he sounds like a dead cert for a serial killer," says Ted.

"Honestly, I hit Block faster than you can say 'weirdo.'"

They all laugh.

Then Denise remembers that she doesn't just want to make a joke out of her situation. She remembers that photo of the little girl she has stuck up on her fridge and how innocent and hopeful she looks. She remembers her dream about finding love—and how much she still wants to find it. *How much I deserve to find it.*

As they come into St Anne's-on-Sea, she turns to Oskar. "I don't suppose you've got any nice workmates, have you?"

Oskar wriggles around to face her. "Funnily enough, I do."

Denise feels a flicker of fear. *Just a minute, can I really do this?*

"I was only joking," she backtracks. "I'm not really that bothered."

"Ignore her," throws in Ted. "She *is* bothered."

Denise gasps. "Ted, can't you let me get scared and back out?"

"No," he fires back. "I love you too much for that."

Denise can't help smiling.

"Anyway, I've got this colleague called Mick," says Oskar. "He's single and looking to meet the right woman." He gives a brief description and tells her that Mick's divorced with two teenage daughters. "And he must be a good dad because he talks about them all the time—he knows everything about their friends and what they're doing at school. Would you like me to fix you up?"

"Go on," urges Ted. "You're ready for this now. You're strong enough. What can you lose?"

Denise sighs. "I don't know, my dignity."

"Dignity's overrated," quips Ted. "I'm about to go on stage in a dress that's supposed to be the color of a flamingo but makes me look like a gone-off prawn."

"Good point." Denise turns back to Oskar. "How about you show me some pictures, and I'll have a scroll through his socials?"

Oskar nods. "And after that, if you're interested, let me know."

Denise feels another surge of fear. *Hold on, what do I actually think about this? Could I be interested?*

From deep inside, another voice replies, *Yes, you could.*

She pats her thighs. "Alright, that sounds like a plan."

She catches Ted grinning in the mirror. She grins back at him.

They leave St Anne's, passing the housing development on the site of the old Pontin's holiday camp, then Blackpool Airport. As the Big One rollercoaster swings into view, Ted gives a loud tap on the steering wheel. "OK, guys, now can we get back to talking about my show?" He switches into the voice of Gail. "Because I'm on stage in a few hours and I'm so nervous even my fanny's sweating."

CHAPTER 39

Denise puts the final touches to Ted's makeup, which includes thick ombré block eyebrows, double-stacked lashes that are brushed with three types of glitter, and lips that are painted the same pink as his dress, with the middle of the pout highlighted white then blended in. It's taken Denise a long time to create the look, and Ted appreciates her effort. *Mind you, I'm looking forward to getting out of this dressing room.*

<TX>They're deep in the basement of Queen of Clubs, in a dressing room that has damp-stained walls and windows that have been painted shut. Ted imagines it must be a tight squeeze at the best of times, but tonight it's packed with amateur queens who are getting ready to perform, many of them spilling out into the corridor.

"Look at the state of her slagline," shouts one, pointing at a queen whose face is a different color than her neck. "It looks like she's put her makeup on with a ruler!"

"Sis, have you had your leccy cut off?" the queen bellows back at her. "It looks like you put yours on in the dark."

The banter is so loud Ted can't hear the music that's playing, let alone hear himself think. Plus, there's so much clutter strewn across the floor that he can't see an inch of the carpet— if there even is a carpet—and there's so much hairspray in the air, he's convinced it constitutes a choking hazard.

One of the queens gives an attention-demanding cough. "Which of you bitches is spraying Femfresh? I can taste it at the back of my throat!"

"Sis, you're the one who needs to freshen up down there," another shrieks at her. "You've had more loads in you than a knackered old washing machine."

As they cackle so raucously that Ted can't help wincing, another queen totters past him in a pair of skyscraper stilettos she's obviously wearing for the first time, trips over a string of pearls, and only just stops herself from crashing to the floor by grabbing onto a wig stand. *God, this is chaos!*

Thankfully, Peg Legge and Pussy Squat, who are emceeing the show, have made sure Ted has his own dressing table—and just about enough space for Denise to do his makeup. She moves closer to apply more contouring to his cheekbones and touch up a peachy pink, cut-crease eyeshadow that makes his eyes stand out dramatically.

"There, I think that's it."

"Thanks, Den. I don't know what I'd do without you!"

Peg and Pussy have also managed to make space for Oskar, as he didn't want to stand in the bar on his own—although they've insisted he sit behind a rack of costumes till Ted has finished transforming himself into Gail. They're adamant Ted shouldn't expose the secrets of what they call his "feminine mystique" but should unleash the finished Gail in one big reveal. When they first suggested this, Ted was only too happy to comply, but now he isn't sure he's made the right decision. *I should be nervous about the show, but all I can think about is Oskar . . .*

Ted's worried about how he's coping amidst all the chaos, and it doesn't help that the other queens won't leave him alone—and are flirting with him outrageously.

"You're so hot I can't breathe," says Pussy.

"Your smile could melt away my knickers," gushes Peg.

"How do you fancy rearranging my guts?" purrs a queen in blue lipstick.

"Rearrange 'em?" screeches another. "He can flip mine inside out!"

As they laugh so loudly the clothes rail rattles, Ted imagines Oskar squirming. "Thanks," he can just about hear him mumble. "That's very flattering."

God, this is a nightmare! Ted doesn't want to rush his transformation, but as far as he's concerned, it can't be over soon enough.

Once his wig is secured firmly in place and Denise has blended the lace front into his makeup, he squeezes himself into the dress Stanley made for him: a pink bandage dress with a sweetheart neckline, which he's tailored around a breast plate and a generous amount of hip padding. It fits perfectly, accentuating Gail's fake curves.

"There you go," says Denise, beaming. "You don't look like a gone-off prawn; you look like a gorgeous, in-the-prime-of-her-life, hot-as-hell flamingo."

"Girl, I am gagging!" says Pussy.

"You look fierce!" agrees Peg.

"Thanks, ladies," says Ted. "Thanks a lot."

But what he really wants to know is what Oskar makes of it. His heart flinches. *Will he be able to handle the reality of seeing his boyfriend in drag?*

Peg and Pussy step behind the rack and slowly lead Oskar out, their hands covering his eyes. When they've positioned him directly in front of Ted, they lift their hands away.

"Ta-dah!"

Suddenly, Ted is transported back to the dressing room in Dublin. He's stepping out from behind the screen in a fur coat and a copper-colored wig to the delight of Fanny Spank—and the horror of Giles. *Please don't tell me the same thing's going to happen now . . .*

Oskar's eyes run up and down him, absorbing every detail. There's a pause, and he moves in closer to examine Ted's makeup. Then he takes a step back, and his eyes run up and down him again.

Fear creeps up Ted's spine.

"Well, what do you think?" he asks, his mouth dry.

There's a curve to Oskar's lips and, slowly, it grows into a grin. "You look amazing," he says.

Thank God for that! Ted's shoulders slacken with relief.

"And now I understand why it takes so long," Oskar goes on. "There's so much to it. It's like a work of art!"

Ted beams. "Oh, Oskar, I'm so happy you like it!"

"It's funny, but I'm also starting to see how Gail has grown out of Ted," Oskar adds. "Or is part of Ted. Or should I say she's you but she's not you? Oh, I don't know how to express it, but I'm starting to understand where she comes from."

Ted wants to kiss Oskar but doesn't want to ruin his makeup. "It's fine, don't worry. You're saying all the right things."

"And it only makes you hotter," says Pussy, fanning herself with her hand.

"I think I might be pregnant," says Peg, pretending to faint.

Ted shoots her a sassy look. "Bitch, aren't you a bit past that? Surely your eggs dried up a long time ago?"

As Peg gasps and slaps him, Oskar lets out a loud honk of a laugh. "Now I can't wait to see the show. I can't wait to see Gail in full force!"

Ted dusts his hands. "Well, now I know you're happy, I can get ready to let her loose!"

Ted's performance as Gail is a huge success.

He opens his set with a rousing rendition of "Stronger" by

Britney Spears, and even though he's hair-whipping so wildly that he lashes the baseball cap off a man in the front row, his wig stays firmly on his head. He manages to nail all his dance moves, working in several he's learned from Shelly. He's selected these according to his age and agility—and doesn't attempt to do the splits or the famous death drop that's a signature move of so many young queens. He does, however, push his abilities to their outer limits and knows he's never danced better. He can tell from the audience's raised eyebrows—not to mention a few gasps from those towards the front—that they're impressed.

Thank God for that. Now I can relax and let rip!

When the cheers have died down, he introduces himself as Gail Force and asks if the audience like his dress, giving them a twirl. "Pink to make the boys wink," he jokes.

When a handsome man in the front row does indeed give him a wink, Ted pretends to be overcome with desire and slumps to his knees. "Pink to make the queen sink!" he quips.

The man on the front row chortles loudly and wiggles his bum.

"I'm only joking," Ted says. "I'm a classy lady really. Besides, I've only just got over a breakup."

This is his cue to launch into his material about being dumped by his husband, which goes down brilliantly. He follows this up with the lines about finding drag later in life, which land equally well. Then he gives a spirited interpretation of another self-empowerment anthem, "Fighter" by Christina Aguilera. When he reaches the end, he's stunned by the force of the applause—but knows he's already more than halfway through his set. *Oh no, I don't want this to end!*

He asks the audience what they think of the queens who've performed before him—then passes comment on all of them. Although he makes sure to pay each of them plenty of compliments, he also slips in the occasional bitchy criticism. *I'm going to read them for filth!*

"That first queen had gorgeous makeup, but she danced with all the grace of a fly-tipped wardrobe . . ."

"The second one was so convincing as a woman, she even had camel toe . . ."

"And that third was in a dress so tight, I could see what she'd had for her tea."

The audience snorts, splutters, and hoots with laughter. And Ted is relieved to see that, standing next to Denise at the bar, Oskar does too. He feels buoyant with happiness. *This couldn't be going any better. I couldn't have wished for more.*

Before he has time to draw breath, it's time for Gail's final number: "Express Yourself" by Madonna. He gives the performance everything he's got, stomping and strutting around the stage, determined to enjoy every last second and relish the happiness he's worked so hard to feel, determined to luxuriate in the reality of his dream coming true. Then, all too soon, the backing track thunders to a stop, and he ends his routine with a fist held high in the air. There's an eruption of applause.

As Ted takes a bow to cheers, hollers, and cries for more, he's flushed with adrenaline. He's on a high he's convinced has to be more intense than that of any drug.

You did it, Ted! And you did yourself proud!

This has to rank as the happiest moment of his life. At the same time, it feels like the experience has *changed* his life—it's helped him say goodbye to the old Ted and finally become the person he was meant to be. *I suppose that's what happens when you put yourself first.*

He wonders if tonight represents the culmination of his journey, the ultimate expression of "Ted first." But, as he was the last queen to perform, he doesn't have time to reflect on it. Peg and Pussy pop back on stage to deliver their closing gags, then declare the show over.

Eager to find Oskar and Denise, Ted treads down a short flight of stairs and weaves his way through the crowd.

"Girl, you slayed!" yells a button-crooked drunk with garlic breath he's tried to mask with a mint.

"Shantay, you stay!" screams a woman wearing a white vest with clumps of black hair under her arms.

"Thanks," splutters Ted. "Thanks a lot!"

When he finally makes it to the bar, he gives Oskar and Denise a kiss, no longer caring if he smudges his makeup.

"You were fantastic, honey!" oozes Denise.

"You totally smashed it!" burbles Oskar.

But before they can say any more, Peg and Pussy push their way through.

"Well done, girl," says Pussy.

"How was it for you?" asks Peg. "Did you manage to enjoy it?"

Ted's eyes sparkle. "Enjoy it? I *loved* it!"

"Good. Now, what are you doing next Saturday?"

Ted is flummoxed. *I didn't expect this.* "Nothing, I don't think. Why?"

They explain that they're performing a gig at Seraphina's, the most famous drag club in Manchester's Gay Village. They've purposefully left a slot on the bill free, to offer to the queen who gave the strongest performance tonight. "And that's you!"

Ted's so shocked, every possible response exits his head. "Wow, thanks so much. I . . . urm . . ."

"It'll be your first professional gig," tosses in Pussy.

"But we think you're ready," adds Peg, "*more* than ready."

"What do you reckon?"

Ted opens his mouth to speak but nothing comes out.

Get it together, Ted! This is your chance to take your dream to the next level.

"Honey, you've *got* to do it," breaks in Denise.

"It could set up your career!" adds Oskar.

Ted eases his weight from one foot to the other. Just when

he was thinking he'd reached the culmination of his journey, this comes out of nowhere—and offers him the chance to fly even higher. *So why am I hesitating?*

Come on, Ted, this is your chance to feel as amazing as this all the time . . .

Then he remembers the following Saturday is the night his parents are organizing the family meal for Jemima—and his mood deflates like a punctured tire. *Shit, can I really miss that?*

But before he's even finished asking himself the question, he's answering it. *Yes, you can. Jem went off to pursue her dream, now it's time for you to pursue yours. It's time for you to lock it down so you never lose sight of it again.*

He looks from Peg to Pussy and nods enthusiastically. "Yeah, count me in!"

CHAPTER 40

Ted is at work, but all he can think about is his upcoming gig in Manchester. He still hasn't come down from the high he hit when he was on stage in Queen of Clubs. But he tells himself that he needs to focus; he only performed a twenty-minute spot at the open-mic night and needs material for a full forty-minute set in Seraphina's. *And I've only got five more days to come up with it . . .*

As he moves around the café clearing tables, he toys with ideas for a couple of new numbers. They need to fit Gail's persona, but they also need to fit Ted's vocal range. *How about "Shout Out to My Ex" by Little Mix? "Since U Been Gone" by Kelly Clarkson? "Man! I Feel Like a Woman!" by Shania Twain?*

Jinger yanks him out of his thoughts. "Ted, can I go on my break?"

"Alright, I'll jump on the counter," he says, setting down his tray.

As he switches to serving customers, in his head he tries out new lines, imagining how they'd sound coming from Gail. While scooping black cherry ice cream into a tub, he comes up with one about getting over his marriage.

If anyone thinks I'm moving on too quickly, I just want to point out that I'm still in mourning—I'm wearing a black bra.

He imagines Gail smiling wickedly before delivering the next line. *And it's a dead sexy one.*

Just as he's wondering if this is good enough, an irritated voice breaks in. "I said banana smoothie, not black cherry!"

Ted gives his head a shake. "Sorry, I'm miles away. Let me start again."

But however hard he tries, whatever activity he undertakes, Ted can't concentrate on work. And it isn't just that he's thinking about the show; everything about his old life seems wrong now that he's turned his dream of being a drag queen into a reality. On his left ring finger, he spots a smudge of pink nail varnish he mustn't have removed properly. In an instant, it transports him back to being on stage as the fabulous, fiercely rebellious, fantastically independent Gail Force. *What am I doing stuck here in this ice-cream shop?*

In a flash, it hits him that he can't do this for much longer. He doesn't just want drag to be a hobby; he wants it to be his full-time profession. And he's wasted far too many hours, days, weeks, months, years, trapped in this shop, suppressing his sparkle, denying himself happiness. *Well, I need to get out. I need to give it up. I need to set myself free.*

As soon as Jinger comes back from her break, Ted makes the decision to take the rest of the week off work. He's owed plenty of annual leave, so he knows it won't be an issue. *And this way I can concentrate on writing and rehearsing for the show. I might even try out my new material on Stanley.*

Before he goes through to speak to his parents, Ted calls into his own office to clear his desk. He fires off a few emails, sets up his out-of-office, then lifts a pile of mail out of the post tray and sifts through it. Sitting right at the bottom is a familiar plain white envelope he knows must contain another anonymous letter. The shock of it stops his breath.

Oh no, you're not serious?

As he turns the envelope around in his hands, the blood

sings loudly in his ears. He hopes the letter doesn't say anything that might disrupt his plans, anything that might perforate his newfound happiness. He briefly considers locking it in his bottom drawer and not opening it till after the show. But he can't. *I need to know what it says.*

He tears open the envelope and yanks out the letter. But the contents of it barely register. His attention is drawn to just one word. One word that arouses his suspicions. One word that reveals to him who's sent the letter—as well as all the previous ones.

But . . . no . . . it can't be . . .

Except he knows without any doubt that it is.

Almost immediately, a storm is raging in his head. Because the realization slashes open a whole tangled mess of emotions. And with such an important—and hopefully life-changing—week ahead of him, Ted isn't sure he can handle it. He certainly doesn't think he can act on it. But at the same time, it's so significant, he can't just ignore it.

What am I going to do?

CHAPTER 41

Oskar slams a mallet into the wooden unit, and the door caves in. He's at work on a new job, removing the kitchen from what used to be a youth hostel before refitting the downstairs as a kebab shop and converting the upstairs into Airbnb apartments. The property is located at the rougher end of St. Luke's, half a mile up a main road that starts at the southernmost tip of the promenade, just past the old lifeboat station. In this area, there are no vestiges of the town's genteel Victorian past, just cheap, tatty guesthouses, greasy fried chicken shops, and rudimentary, no-frills accommodation that's used in resettlement programs for refugees—plus a launderette, an Indian takeaway, and a whole slew of kebab shops. *And very soon there'll be another.*

Oskar continues smashing up the kitchen, hammering a cupboard until it comes away from the wall and crashes onto the floor. Destroying the fixtures from a property's previous incarnation is something he finds strangely satisfying. *Especially if I'm feeling frustrated.*

As he bashes away, his mind rewinds to being backstage at the open-mic night and having to force himself to be enthusiastic when the drag queens brought him out from behind the clothes rack and revealed Gail Force. In principle, he has no problem with drag and genuinely enjoyed watching the show, during which he found it quite easy to separate Gail from Ted. But when Gail appeared before him, it was another matter— and he instinctively shrank away into himself. He hopes he managed to babble over his discomfort; he wouldn't want Ted to pick up on it, especially not after what he went through with Giles. The last thing Oskar wants to do is hurt him. *What's the matter with me? I thought all this would get easier now I've come out.*

He's distracted by a vibration coming from his phone. He fishes it out of his pocket and sees he's received a new email. When he opens his inbox, the name of the sender flashes up: Andrew Kozlowski.

Oh my God.

Oskar's so shocked he almost drops his phone. All he can hear is the roar of his breathing. He lowers his mallet and leans on the doorframe.

"You alright, mate?" asks Fletch.

"Yeah, yeah, fine, thanks," Oskar croaks.

He leaves the kitchen and stumbles out into the street, his heart beating twice for every step he takes. He removes his safety goggles and slumps onto a wall. When he opens the message, he sees it's written in Polish.

Dear Oskar,
How wonderful to hear from you. I've wanted this to happen for such a long time but didn't dare to keep hoping.
First of all, are you OK? Where are you living? Are you happy? And how is your sister?
I've got so much to tell you I don't know where to start. But, in case you're worried, don't—everything is good with me.
Please can we meet up in person so we can talk properly? I'll drop everything and make myself free whenever suits you. Just tell me where you are, and I'll come and find you.

Thanks so much for getting in touch. Your mum told me you never wanted to hear from me again, but I'm overjoyed to find out this isn't true.
Dad x

Oskar clutches the phone to his chest and breathes in and out, slowly.

Dad. My dad.

He feels a sense of calm descending on him, a sense of a skewed world shifting and righting itself, a sense of a weight he's been carrying turning out to be much heavier than he thought but finally being lifted from his shoulders.

Excitement crashes into him. He imagines how good it will feel to hug his dad, to cling onto him, to breathe him in. He wonders how soon they can meet up, and in his head a reel of potential reunions starts to play. There's the two of them chatting over coffee, laughing at a joke in a bar, cycling along the coast and stopping for a picnic . . .

Then, out of nowhere, Oskar feels a resurgence of his old fears –of being exposed, of being judged, of being rejected. It doesn't surprise him to learn that his mum told his dad Oskar didn't want to hear from him—he can even imagine the words she would have used—but he hopes his dad hasn't spent all these years feeling offended. He hopes he doesn't need to re-build any bridges.

More importantly, Oskar also needs to tell his dad that he too is gay. And he has no idea how he'll react. Obviously, Oskar isn't expecting him to disapprove, but he is worried his dad will feel let down. *After being so brave himself, will he be disappointed by the way I've handled it?*

His mind flashes back to Queen of Clubs and that instinctive feeling of fear when confronted by Gail. *Will I ever be able to get over it? Will I ever be able to be happy with myself?*

He's ripped out of his reflections by another crashing sound coming from inside the building. It reminds him that he needs to return to work. He shuts down his phone and straps on his goggles.

He'll reply to his dad's email later. Right now he just wants to go back to destroying things.

That evening, Oskar decides to ask Marina for her advice. Over the last few weeks, he's been confiding in her more and more and has already told her about his search for his dad. He keeps an eye open for her coming home from work and, as soon as he spots her, knocks on her door clutching a bottle of Sauvignon Blanc.

"Toots!" she squeaks. She gives him a hug and invites him in.

Marina's caravan is decorated with native American wall hangings, African tribal heads, and elaborate Indian tapestries. There are crystal pendants dangling from the light fittings, a crystal suncatcher in the window, and a crystal mobile hanging over the entrance to her bedroom. In the corner rests Marina's rolled-up yoga mat, in the kitchen stands a stack of herbal teas, and on a side table is an oil burner Oskar's pretty sure is giving off the scent of patchouli. He parts a mountain of batik cushions and sits down. As Marina opens the bottle of wine and serves them each a glass, he tells her about the email from his dad.

"That's amazing!" she says, sitting next to him. "But why do you look so scared?"

He lets out a long sigh. "I don't know. I really wanted it, but now it's happening it feels like I've lost control. It's like I'm pedaling my bike, but the chain has come off."

Marina takes a sip of her wine and nods. "That's understandable. I can see how the whole thing must be unsettling."

"You know, when I think about meeting up with him, I see this whole new world opening up before me."

"And you're not sure you're ready for it?"

"Exactly!" Oskar takes a sip of his wine but finds he can't stomach it. He puts his glass down on the side. "It's like, in some ways I still haven't properly moved on from my old life, from the world I grew up in. I mean, I have—I got out of that world—but . . . Oh, I don't know how to express it."

"You've escaped it physically, but that doesn't mean you have in your soul," offers Marina. "That can take much longer."

Oskar breathes a sigh of relief. *So I'm not going mad. Marina knows exactly how I feel.*

He's emboldened to go further. "I just keep thinking, what if my dad's disappointed in me?"

Marina sets her glass down next to Oskar's. "Why should he be disappointed?"

Oskar goes into his phone and opens up the website for the gay cycling club. He shows Marina a picture from the photo gallery of the club's members all gathered together at Manchester Pride. They're dressed in identical T-shirts bearing the club's logo, but some of them have stamped their cheeks with rainbow-colored face paint, others are wearing rainbow-colored feather boas, and one is holding up an enormous rainbow flag in the air behind him—and there's his dad in the center of it all, a rainbow whistle hanging from his neck, and his arms around an enormous, multicolored, extravagantly frocked drag queen.

"Look at him," he says. "Look how happy he is. And here I am, thirty-three and I've never been to a single Gay Pride. Here I am, only just getting my act together."

And here I am, frightened of my boyfriend doing drag! he wants to add. But he's too embarrassed to share that detail. Just like he's too embarrassed to admit he loves Ted but still hasn't been brave enough to tell him. He's wanted to—several times—but every time he opens his mouth, the words just won't come out. *It's like something's stopping me from saying "I love you" to another man.*

And that something is probably me.

"Everyone does things at their own pace, toots," Marina counsels. "No one else's map will work for you."

"Yeah, but . . ."

Oskar picks up a cushion and runs his fingers over the embroidery. He contemplates everything he's been through and compares it to everything his dad has been through. *He's had it so much worse than me. And still he's been able to emerge from it with his pride intact—his pride in himself as a gay man.*

"But what if seeing him is only going to make me feel like a failure?" he asks.

"Oh my goddess, you really have got yourself worked up about this, haven't you?" Marina reaches out and takes his hand. "I think you probably need to pause and have a think. You're doing really well and making great progress, but you don't want to do anything to jeopardize that. You can always message your dad and say you need a bit more time, tell him you don't feel ready."

"But what if he's offended?" *That is, if he isn't already.*

"I think you need to stop worrying about how he feels. A parent has a duty to their child, but your first duty is to yourself. Are you really sure you want to go through with this?"

Oskar lets go of her hand. He isn't sure. He isn't sure at all.

CHAPTER 42

"So your surname's Love," says Mick. "Is that an invitation or an order?"

Denise raises an eyebrow. "Think of it as more of a challenge. A chance to prove you're worthy."

Mick sips his wine. "I like a challenge."

"Me too."

Denise wants to smile but keeps it inside.

She's on a date with Oskar's colleague, Mick. They're in an organic, gluten-free, vegan restaurant he tells her he worked on and has been looking forward to checking out for a while. Denise's colleagues at work have told her the restaurant is a big success, but tonight is a Tuesday, so it's fairly quiet. This suits her; it's her first date in years, her first date since Karl, and she's nervous. Under the table, she clenches her thighs and gives her feet a wiggle. *Just take this slowly and you'll be fine.*

Before leaving the house, Denise spent ages choosing her outfit, eventually settling on a green leaf-print midi dress with a V neckline and long sleeves. She washed off the strong, sweet perfume she has to wear for work and replaced it with a spritz of her favorite scent, Ghost. And she wiped away the heavy makeup of the working day and substituted it with a more subtle nude lip and smoky eye. She's put in a lot of effort, but so far it hasn't been wasted. *Mick seems like a decent bloke. And I'm pretty sure I like him—or at least I want to like him.*

Another voice cuts in. *Be careful, Denise; he could be putting on an act. He could be pretending to be someone he's not. You've been here before, remember?*

Into her head flash the faces of several of her past boyfriends, boyfriends who either disrespected or flat-out insulted her, boyfriends who lied to her or were flagrantly unfaithful. *There's no way I'm going back there.*

At the same time, she knows there's no point being here if she's not going to give Mick a chance. She tries to relax.

"Right, so what do you fancy eating?" she asks, picking up her menu.

"Let's have a look."

At least Denise knows there aren't any issues physically. Mick's very attractive, with a handsome, symmetrical face, dark-brown skin, and a short beard flecked with gray that gives him an air of maturity and authority. And then there's the sheer bulk of him, which seems to somehow dominate the restaurant, and Denise can't help but find arousing. She tries not to gaze at the curve of his biceps as they bulge over the short sleeves of his shirt. *Come on, Denise, hold it together. Don't get carried away until you properly know him . . .*

"I seem to remember the owner saying stuffed aubergine is the specialty," Mick comments. "And no, that isn't an innuendo."

Denise allows herself the faint hint of a smile. "Good to hear it. Otherwise I'd be straight out the door."

"I should hope so." Mick holds her gaze and his eyes sparkle. "A tacky line like that would be an insult to a lady like you."

Denise has to make a real effort to stop her smile from spreading. *This is going to be difficult . . .*

They're approached by a waitress who has long, uncombed

hair and is wearing so much heavy wooden jewelry Denise thinks she must have a backache. "Are you ready to order?"

After some discussion, they decide to start with a sharing platter of edamame, hummus, and artichoke fritters, then Mick orders the red lentil kofte with whipped tahini and a side order of sweet potato fries, while Denise opts for a salad made up of quinoa, goji berries, avocado, and something called cashew cheese.

"Well, this is all very intriguing," she says, as the waitress leaves them. "I've never been to a vegan restaurant before."

"I've actually eaten this kind of food a lot," says Mick. "One of my daughters is vegan."

Denise spreads her napkin on her lap. "Oh yeah? And how old is she?"

"Actually, I've got two. That one's fifteen. She's principled and headstrong and at the moment is focused on environmental activism. The other one's thirteen and the opposite; she's a joker and just wants to have a laugh. She can't concentrate on anything remotely serious. Unfortunately, that includes her schoolwork."

At the discussion of children, Denise feels her muscles tightening. "They sound like quite a handful," she offers, stiffly.

"They are, but in a good way. I love them to bits."

There's a pause, and Denise plugs it with her wine. She made a point of mentioning that she doesn't have children when she and Mick were texting the other day. *Please don't bring it up now. Please don't ask me why.*

With a jolt, she's whipped back to the early stages of her pregnancy, telling Karl she wanted to go through with it and pleading with him to support her. "If you want me to stick around, you'll get rid of it," he hissed. "And anyway, you'd make a terrible mother."

As his words reverberate around her head, Denise tips back the rest of her wine. "Well, you're very lucky," she manages, her voice wobbling. "But it sounds like they are too. I bet they adore you."

"They're a bit old for that now—these days they just find me embarrassing."

Denise tilts her head to one side. "I'm sure they'll grow out of that."

"Let's hope so." Mick swirls his wine around the glass. "I have to admit, I was relieved when you said you were child-free."

Denise arches an eyebrow. She likes the expression "child-free." It's so much better than "child-less." But she doesn't remember using it when they were texting. *How sensitive of him.*

She gives him another hint of a smile. "Why's that?"

"Just, you know, I'd probably find it tough to take on any more kids. And I wouldn't want my two to lose out. If that's not too selfish."

"No, not at all."

To be perfectly frank, it's a massive relief. Denise straightens out her napkin. *Now can I let myself like him? Can I believe he's a nice bloke?*

She steels herself to ask her next question. "And what are your daughters like with your girlfriends?"

Mick shrugs. "I haven't had many, and I've only introduced them to one or two. But yeah, they've been very friendly with them. And they're always trying to fix me up. Between us, I think they're desperate to marry me off. Either that or they just want to be bridesmaids."

"So do you want to get married again?"

"Yeah, I'd love to. But me and my ex weren't actually married. She didn't want any of that."

"Why not?" Denise blurts out. "Sorry. I mean, if that's not too personal a question."

"No, it's fine." Mick runs his finger down a groove in the table. "I don't know why Sadie didn't want to get married.

Sometimes I think she was just a middle-class white girl who saw me as a bit of rough. I'm not sure she ever really loved me; I think she was just trying to rebel against her parents."

Denise feels a lump in her throat. "That can't have been much fun for you. And it can't have made you feel great about yourself."

"It didn't, no. But to be honest, her parents *were* a nightmare. They were really strict when she was growing up, and they were terribly judgmental and snobbish. So I can hardly blame her."

How refreshing—a man who doesn't claim his ex was a bitch or a psycho. Denise realizes she's stopped feeling nervous and has started relaxing.

"My parents weren't the best either," she hears someone say. To her surprise, she realizes it was her.

"In what way?" asks Mick.

She hesitates.

"If that isn't too personal a question," he adds.

Come on, Denise, you've got nothing to be afraid of. If Mick's opening up, so can you.

She lets out a sigh. "Basically, my dad was always out chasing tail, and my mum sat at home drinking through it. I grew up terrified he'd leave us but at the same time not really blaming him if he did—and thinking it was all our fault."

Mick nods, slowly. "I'm sorry to hear that. Wounds like that can take a long time to heal."

"They can, yeah."

He goes back to tracing the groove in the table. "If it's any consolation, my dad was a dead loss too. That's why I've always wanted to do a better job with my girls."

In some disused part of Denise that's buried so deep she's almost forgotten it exists, something like hope begins to stir. She catches a tiny glimpse of a future that might just involve happiness, that might just involve love. Yes, she's coping perfectly well on her own, and yes, she values her independence, and without a doubt she's benefited enormously from three years of focusing on self-care. *But wouldn't it be great to find that slice of lime to finish off my margarita?*

She worries the conversation is becoming too intense and decides to lighten the tone. "Anyway, the worst thing about my mum and dad was this awful surname they lumbered me with," she chirps, picking up the bottle of wine and topping up their glasses. "Honestly, it's like a noose around my neck. Every time I meet someone, they automatically assume I'm like some character out of a rom com and am going to fall in love at the drop of a hat."

Mick unleashes a raffish grin. "Well, I hope that's not true. Or else where would be that challenge you promised?"

Denise flicks her hair, coyly. "You're very confident. But I like that."

"Good. Because I've got one thing to say to you: challenge accepted."

And just like that, Denise feels herself giving in. She lets her mouth bloom into a smile that sweeps across her face.

Yes, I'm going to stop worrying. I'm going to let myself like him. And I'm going to look forward to getting to know him better . . .

CHAPTER 43

Ted parks his car outside Oskar's caravan. It's late and he hasn't told Oskar he's coming, but he's too anxious to stay at home. They were supposed to be meeting up for dinner, but Oskar sent him a brief text to say he couldn't make it. When Ted called to ask why, he was evasive and sounded like there was something on his mind, or something bad had happened— then he ended the call abruptly. After a few hours of worrying alone at home, Ted can't take it anymore so has driven to East-cliff. *But is Oskar going to think I'm intruding?*

Surely we're at the stage where I can turn up unannounced?

Either way, he's about to find out.

He knocks on the door, but when Oskar answers, he doesn't give him a kiss. He doesn't even say hello. He just steps back to let Ted in—and begins shuffling around the room, nervously.

"Oskar, what's going on?" Ted asks. "Is everything alright?"

Oskar hangs his head. "I heard from my dad today."

"But that's ace!" Ted stops himself. "Isn't it?"

Oskar kneads his eyelids. "Yeah, it is. He's fine and well and was really pleased to hear from me. He wants to meet up."

Ted leans back on the kitchen worktop. "So what's the problem? Why are you looking so worried?"

"I don't think I can go through with it."

Ted spots his jaw quiver and understands he's frightened. In a flash, he's overcome with love. Oskar suddenly seems so vulnerable and fragile, he just wants to do everything he can to help him.

Go on, tell him you're here for him. Tell him you love him.

But instead—almost despite himself—Ted somehow ends up grinning manically and unleashing a wildly overenthusiastic, "Don't be daft, you've *got* to go through with it! Why don't you do it this Saturday, when we're in Manchester for my show?"

Oskar shoots him a frigid look. "Stop hassling me, Ted. I can't do that either."

"You what? What do you mean?"

"I can't come and see the show. It's too much. It's all too much."

Ted stands up and moves over to him. "What is? What's too much, Oskar?"

Oskar stops shuffling. "Seeing my dad. Drag. Everything."

"*Drag?* But I thought you said you enjoyed it the other day?"

Oskar sighs. "I did. I did enjoy the show. But I don't like it when it's just me and you. I don't like it when it's just me and you, and you're dressed as a woman. I'm sorry but I've tried, and I can't. There it is, I've said it."

His admission hits Ted like a body blow. *Oh God, here we go again . . .*

He opens his mouth but has no idea what to say.

I knew this was too good to be true. I knew it couldn't last. I knew I didn't deserve to be this happy.

He sits down heavily on the sofa.

"I'm sorry," says Oskar, resuming his shuffling. "But I just don't like it when you're acting all camp and girlie and pretending to be a woman. I want to be with a man."

Ted raises his hand in objection. "But I *am* a man, Oskar. And I'm happy being a man. Drag's about performance; it's an exaggerated way of saying I don't want to be *just one kind* of man."

Oskar slumps back against the door. "I don't know what that means."

Ted draws in a breath and lets it out. "I want to push the boundaries of what we understand by being a man and explore different sides of me. And hopefully, while I'm at it, learn to be a *better* man."

Thick lines appear on Oskar's forehead.

"Among other things, obviously," Ted adds. "I mean, part of it is just about dressing up and having a laugh."

"But why do you want to do that?" Oskar asks. "I like the way you are now, Ted. I like you as you are. I *really* like you."

He looks like he's going to say something else but stops.

Go on, are you going to tell me you love *me . . . ?*

But a stony silence sets in.

God, Ted, you're so deluded. As if Oskar could ever love you.

He feels the choke of sadness. "The thing is, Oskar, if you like me, you should like Gail. Because you said it yourself: although she's a different character, at the same time she came out of me." His tone is plaintive, pleading.

"Yeah, well, I guess what I'm saying is I want her to go back in."

Suddenly, Ted feels defeated. He feels defeated by everything going on in his life—not just in his fight to be a drag queen, but in the urge to please his parents, the need to confront the sender of the letters, his anger at what he's found out about his dad, even his grief at Giles leaving him, which he thought he'd conquered months ago. And the obstacles to establishing a meaningful, long-term relationship with Oskar suddenly seem insurmountable. *I should never have tried.*

Then—almost involuntarily—something stirs within him. To Ted's surprise, it emerges as a desire to keep fighting.

Come on, Ted, it doesn't have to be like this. You've worked hard for your dream. Stand your ground!

He springs to his feet, his hands curled into fists. "I'm sorry, Oskar," he bursts out. "But I won't let you hold me back."

Oskar seems outraged at the suggestion. "I'm not trying to hold you back! You're pushing me. And you're pushing me too far."

In Ted's head, it's as if a whip has been cracked. "No, I'm not! And I won't give up on my dream just because you're struggling to accept who you are. It's not my fault you can't deal with being gay!"

Oskar's face falls. "Ted, I can't believe you just said that. It's not fair."

But now Ted's started, he can't stop himself. "Isn't it? Don't you see? The reason you don't like me dressing up as a woman is because you're repulsed by any signs of femininity in yourself. Because you've been told that anything other than the old-fashioned stereotype of a man is wrong. And you've fallen for it."

As Ted's words slash at him, Oskar looks like he's withering in humiliation—and Ted hates himself for it. But for some reason, this only fires him up more. Red mist clouds his vision, and his entire body pumps with adrenaline.

"Well, that's just homophobic," he yells, his nostrils flaring. "And I won't stand for it."

Oskar pushes himself away from the door and leans towards him. "That's not true," he argues, his voice hardening. "I'm fine with being gay."

"No, you're not. And now you're trying to push all your homophobia onto me. Well, I don't see why I should suffer just because you haven't got your shit together!" Ted doesn't know where this last comment came from; it's as if it said itself.

"Well, that's nice," Oskar booms, a thick vein pulsing on his forehead. "You decide to put yourself first and in the process just disregard everyone else's feelings. You basically become a dick."

"If you think I'm a dick," spits Ted, "then why are you going out with me?"

Oskar pinions Ted with his eyes. "Well, maybe after this I don't *want* to go out with you. Maybe I don't want to be forced into going out with a drag queen."

Ted breaks his gaze. "Fine, well, in that case you don't have to. I'm letting you go, Oskar. If you can't accept Gail, if you can't accept me—*all* of me—then there's no point carrying on."

It's as if his words are reverberating around the caravan. *Did I really just say that?*

Apparently he did. Because Oskar is replying. "OK, then, let's forget it."

"Ace. Fine. Wonderful." Ted turns and stalks out.

But even as he flings the door open, he feels overwhelmed with regret—regret about losing his temper, regret about what he said, regret about making a mess of everything. He wants to slam the door behind him but stumbles on the steps and only manages to close it with a click. *For God's sake, I can't even get that right.*

He stomps over to the car and slams himself into the driving seat. As he presses the button to turn on the engine, his heartbeat seems out of control. By the time he's putting his foot down on the accelerator, he's feeling hot-eyed.

He drives a few meters away from Oskar's caravan and, once he's out of view, parks again. He lets the tears fall.

CHAPTER 44

"Mum? Dad? It's me," calls out Ted.

"We're in t' kitchen!" shouts Hilary.

As Ted crosses the hallway, a wave of anxiety passes through his gut. *I really hope I'm not about to walk into another drama . . .*

If he is, he's not sure he can handle it. He's spent all day stressing about his argument with Oskar—and last night he hardly slept, tormenting himself about what he'd said and wondering if he should apologize, see if they can find some way of working through it. If that isn't enough, he's also panicking about how to confront the sender of the letters, going over and over in his head what he should say. Then his parents asked him to come to their house after work. They said they wanted to talk something over. *But what can it be?*

When he enters the kitchen, he finds his dad sitting at the island, cradling a cup of tea. He hopes Trevor can't sense his anger towards him, an anger that's been raging since he worked out who sent the letters—but an anger he knows he needs to suppress until after he's confronted her. He looks for his mum and finds her cooking.

"Hiya, love," she says, turning down the hob. "Do you want a brew?"

"No, ta," says Ted. "I'm alright."

She nods and sits next to Trevor.

"So come on then, what is it?" Ted asks, lowering himself onto a stool. "What do you want to talk about?"

They give each other a loaded look. Then Trevor speaks. "We're ready to hand over the business."

Oh God, this is all I need.

"Not immediately," cuts in Hilary, "but we want to start planning for our retirement."

"We'll be hitting sixty-five in a couple of years," Trevor continues, "around the same time as Ainsworth's turns one hundred. So it seems like a good time to hand over to the next generation. And that's you, son."

Under the table, Ted starts wringing his hands. *I can't believe this is happening now. The timing couldn't be any worse.*

"You don't need to worry, love," Hilary coos. "We're thinking it'll be a long handover. So you'll have plenty of time to get used to things."

Trevor clears his throat. "But if this isn't something you want, then we're going to have to start thinking about other options."

"Although obviously we're hoping it won't come to that," Hilary adds. She spreads her hands out on the table. "Any road, that's it. So what do you think?"

Ted gives a little wriggle on his stool. Now he's been put on the spot, despite everything that's happened over the last four months, despite all the progress he's made, he can't bring himself to disappoint them—or at least not his mum. "I don't know, I'm not sure what to think. It's a lot to take in."

Trevor takes a swig of his tea. "But surely it isn't coming as a surprise? You must have been expecting it?"

Ted feels a flash of resentment. *Give me a break, Dad! After what I've found out about you, you're not in any position to guilt-trip me!*

He forces his resentment back. "Yeah, but you've been talking about it for so long, I kind of *stopped* expecting it. I mean, why now?"

Hilary rubs her collarbone. "The truth is, love, we're not coping."

Fear slams into Ted. "What do you mean, you're not coping?"

Trevor swirls what's left of his tea around the mug, then tips it back. "The stress of being in so much debt is really getting to us, son. We didn't tell you this because we didn't want you to get worried, but your mum's had to go to the doctor for some pills."

As Hilary gives a thin smile, Ted feels the burn of self-loathing. *God, I'm so selfish. They tell me they want to hand over the business, and all I can think about is me.*

He inches forward on his stool. "Oh, Mum, I'm sorry. I had no idea."

"It's alright, love. Now I'm doing summat about it, it's starting to get better. But it'd be a big help if we knew what were happening wi' t' business."

Ted frowns. "Yeah, I get that."

There's an awkward silence. Hilary goes over to the hob and stirs her pan.

"Now that doesn't mean we want to just offload our problems," Trevor points out. "We'll be around to help and advise, and we wouldn't dump you in it with the bank straight away. We're not trying to shirk our responsibilities."

"Any road, we're hoping things'll get better," Hilary adds. "And they're starting to look more positive—at least takings are up."

Trevor sighs. "But if that isn't enough, the business may have to be cut back. It may be that at a later date it can be built up again. But we feel like it should be someone else who does that, rather than us two old fogeys."

Ted can't bring himself to smile at his dad but manages to

say, "You're not old fogeys. But OK, I get where you're coming from. And I get why you want to do it now."

Hilary returns to the island. "We also have to factor in our Jem and what she wants. And when she's back at t' weekend, we'll have t' chance to have a proper conversation about it, a family conference."

Shit, I need to tell them I won't be there. I need to tell them I've got a drag show in Manchester.

But he can't face it. *Not right now. I can't do it to them—I can't do it to Mum.*

"Yeah, this affects your sister too," chips in Trevor. "Obviously, she's going to own half of the business . . ."

"And she hasn't said owt," Hilary insists, "but the modeling i'n't going to last forever, is it? I get the impression she might be looking for some sort of long-term security. That is, assuming you can get t' business back on its feet."

Ted can't help feeling another spike of resentment. *Heaven forbid Jemima should miss out on having the long-term future she wants. Heaven forbid she should have to put up with the slightest insecurity.*

He forces it back again. *Jem's struggling too, remember? She's had to give up her dream.*

He nods, somberly. "Yeah, OK, I understand."

"Any road, it'd be nice to tell her everything's in safe hands," Hilary says, "and hopefully she's got nowt to worry about."

Ted smiles weakly. The silence grows thick between them.

"You know how important the business is to us, son," Trevor tells Ted.

"Of course, how could I forget?" Ted feels repulsed by the ring of bitterness in his voice. *Stop acting like a spoiled brat!*

"It'd break our hearts if we had to flog it," adds Hilary, driving their message home.

Trevor looks at him, hopefully. "But I'm sure it won't come to that, will it, son? What's our motto?"

"Family first," Ted rasps.

But into his head crashes his own motto: Ted first. *What about that? Am I supposed to just give up on it? Am I supposed to give up on my dream?*

He remembers what Oskar said to him during their argument. *"You decide to put yourself first and in the process just disregard everyone else's feelings."*

Ted wonders if he's right. At the memory of all the hurtful things he said to Oskar, guilt slices through him. Oskar has been through so much and hasn't had an easy life. *And whatever I might think of my dad, my parents have just offered to give me their business. God, I'm so ungrateful!*

All of a sudden, his conviction in putting what he wants first slips away. *What if doing drag really is a stupid idea? What if it means I lose Oskar forever?*

He tugs a hand through his hair. "Mum, Dad, sorry, but it's a lot to think about. Can I go away and get my head around it?"

"Course you can, love."

"But don't take too long, will you?" pipes Trevor. "Remember, Jemima's up this Saturday."

"Yeah, I won't."

Hilary stands up and returns to the hob. "Now, do you not want to stop for your tea? I'm doing my chicken curry, the one with raisins and bananas you used to like as a kid."

Ted smiles. Right now, there's nothing he'd like more than a good dose of comfort food. "Thanks, Mum, but I've got something waiting at home."

He isn't actually sure he does have anything to eat at home, but he needs to get away; he needs to be on his own.

He says his goodbyes and pulls the door shut behind him.

Just as he's crunching along the driveway, he receives a text. It's from Giles.

He freezes. *Giles? What does he want?*

"How's it going?" the message reads. **"Am back in town. Don't suppose I can come round for a chat?"**

And before he can give it a second thought—before he can even work out how he feels—Ted replies, **"Yeah, of course. See you in half an hour?"**

CHAPTER 45

Ted yanks open his fridge door. But other than a few sauce bottles, a carton of spread, and an almost-full jar of pickled onions, there's nothing to eat. He's been so preoccupied, he's forgotten about shopping. He lifts the lid of the bread bin, but all that's in it are a few crumbs. And by now he's really hungry. Just as he's rummaging down the side of the microwave to dig out the takeaway menus, the doorbell rings.

Shit, that'll be Giles.

Doubt thumps into him. *What am I doing? Why did I agree to this?*

He tells himself that he must have been having a moment of weakness. *Well, I can't back out now.*

As he walks to the door, his heart rate soars. *That's interesting—the last time Giles got in touch, I hardly felt anything. In fact, I forgot to reply to his text. So why am I getting so worked up now?*

When he arrives at the door, he stops and seizes a breath. Before he can work himself up any further, he opens it.

There's Giles, standing in front of him.

In that moment Ted realizes why he's so worked up. *It's because I want to see him.*

"Hello, Ted," Giles says.

"Hiya."

After so much time apart, Ted's struck by how good-looking Giles is, by his luscious chocolate-colored hair, his mesmerizing deep-brown eyes, and those cute little moles on his left cheekbone. As he catches a whiff of his aftershave—the aftershave he used to find so sexy—he's surprised to feel a flicker of longing, chased by a pang of grief. But these emotions are quickly swept away by the awkwardness that springs up between them. Ted isn't sure whether to hug or kiss him. Shaking his hand seems too formal but not touching him at all too hostile.

Thankfully, Lily comes to the rescue. She jumps up at Giles, barking so loudly that a passing jogger looks over and asks if everything's alright.

I've no idea, Ted wants to say. But he raises his hand and smiles.

"I've missed you, my girl," says Giles, bending down to greet Lily. "And look at your new collar!"

Ted had forgotten about buying Lily the diamante collar but realizes it's just the kind of thing Giles doesn't like. *I hope he doesn't say anything . . .*

But Giles is too busy managing Lily's barrage of affection to criticize. As he ruffles her fur, wraps his arms around her, and kisses her on the top of the head, her tail wags so forcefully Ted has to step back to avoid getting hurt.

It's nice to see . . . it's nice to see Lily so happy . . .

Once the dog has started to calm down, Giles draws himself up to full height and gives Ted a nod. "It's good to see you, Ted."

"Yeah, it's good to see you too." Part of Ted feels disappointed in himself for saying it, but he can't deny it's true.

"It's been a long time," says Giles.

His voice sounds exactly the same as it used to, but Ted finds the familiarity unsettling. He nods back at him, unsure of how to respond. *What do you say in this situation? What even is this situation?*

He settles on, "It's a bit weird answering the door to you."

Giles rocks backwards on the balls of his feet. "Yeah, well, I've still got a key but didn't want to let myself in."

"No."

Ted closes the door, and suddenly the three of them are on their own. *On our own at home, just like it used to be.*

He feels another pang of grief.

Come on, get a grip.

He gestures to the living room, and they walk through, Lily clinging to Giles's side.

"Do you want something to drink?" Ted offers.

"No, thanks, I'm fine."

On entering the living room, Giles stops. "Oh. You've got a new painting."

Shit, I'd forgotten about that too.

"Yeah, I bought it a few weeks ago," Ted mutters, somewhat sheepishly, "from one of the galleries on the high street."

Please don't criticize it. Please don't make me feel bad about it.

Giles smiles, tightly. "Well, I like it. It's very . . . calming."

Ted breathes out with relief. "Yeah, I thought that. Anyway, I've still got your fabric thing if you want it back."

Giles sits on the sofa and straight away Lily jumps up to sit next to him. "Actually, that's why I'm here. That's what I wanted to talk to you about."

Ted corrugates his brow. "What, the snotty tea towel?"

"No, our stuff in general," Giles says, fondling the dog's ear. "Well, you know, everything."

OK, so he wants a divorce. Ted is surprised to feel a grief so strong it's like it's burning a hole inside him. He sinks down into the armchair.

"Yeah, I suppose we should get ourselves some lawyers," he says. "Start dividing everything up."

"No, I didn't mean that," counters Giles. "In fact, I was hoping we could do the opposite."

"You what?"

Giles stops stroking the dog and looks Ted in the eye. "I was hoping we could give it another go, Ted. You and me."

Ted's so shocked he doubts he heard him correctly. "Sorry, what did you say?"

"I'm hoping we can get back together," Giles repeats.

Fuck.

And then, from somewhere deep inside Ted, comes another reaction: *Ace!*

"I've missed you," says Giles.

"But what about Javier?" Ted splutters.

"We split up. It wasn't working. I was stupid, Ted. I didn't appreciate what I had. And I'm so sorry. I'm sorry for everything. I really hope you can forgive me."

Ted shakes his head in confusion. "Giles, this is a massive shock. It's literally the last thing I was expecting."

Giles runs his hand along the arm of the sofa. "Yeah, I thought it might be. But for me, it's been building up for a while."

"I thought you were happy. You always seemed it on social media." Then Ted realizes he hasn't looked at Giles's social media for a couple of months.

"I might have made it look like that, but I wasn't. Basically, Javier tricked me into thinking there was more to life than what I had with you. But I found out there wasn't. And whenever I tried to picture my future, I couldn't imagine it without you. I can't be happy without you, Ted."

But Ted doesn't listen to his last few sentences; his attention has hooked on what Giles said at the start of his speech, what he said about Javier. *Is he seriously trying to blame him for the whole thing? Is he refusing to accept any responsibility?*

Ted stands up and walks over to the window. "I don't know what to say, Giles."

Behind him, Giles shifts onto the edge of the sofa. "I'm hoping you'll say you'll accept my apology. I'm hoping you'll take me back."

"I don't know. I really don't know."

Giles stands up and moves to his side. Ted catches another whiff of his aftershave. For a moment, the two of them stand in silence, staring out of the window.

"We were happy, weren't we?" Giles asks, quietly.

I don't know, were we?

Ted had thought they were at the time. But he's spent the last few months thinking they weren't. And now he isn't sure at all.

Ted and Giles stood side by side on the stone terrace of a Georgian manor house just outside St. Luke's. Stretching out before them were squares and rectangles of ornamental gardens crisscrossed by stripes of flowers in all the colors of the rainbow. Giles was wearing an electric-blue suit, while Ted was wearing baby blue, with each of them in the opposite tie. Just a few meters away, their wedding party was in full swing, the cheery chatter of guests carrying on the warm summer air.

"So what's going on?" Ted asked. "Why did you want to come out here?"

"It's nothing to worry about," said Giles. "It's just my mum mentioned she got to the end of her wedding day and she'd hardly spoken to my dad. So I thought I'd bring you out here and make sure we got a little moment on our own."

"Oh, right, that's nice." Ted was so touched, his voice trembled—and he was worried he might cry. *God, I'm so lucky. Giles is so thoughtful and romantic. I can't believe he's just married me!*

"Are you having a good time?" Giles asked.

Ted swallowed back his tears. "Yeah, dead good. Although Karl's being a dick—I just heard him telling Denise her dress makes her look fat."

Giles frowned. "Why does that not surprise me? I've no idea why she puts up with him."

"Me neither."

A sparrow landed on the stone balustrade and hopped along.

"And my mum's wasted," added Ted, rolling his eyes in amusement. "As soon as the ceremony was over, she hit the bar like a Labrador out of a Volvo."

Giles chuckled. "So's mine. I just saw her slumped in her chair looking like a melted candle. God knows what state she'll be in later."

The two of them laughed. A second sparrow landed on the balustrade and tweeted at the first—and they flew off together. There was a pause.

Ted and Giles looked into each other's eyes.

"I love you, Smiles," said Ted.

"I love you too," said Giles.

They kissed then rested their foreheads against each other's. The chatter from the guests faded to silence.

Hold on to this moment, Ted. You'll probably never feel happier. Life probably won't get any better.

But after a few minutes, the romantic moment was broken by the sound of a glass smashing then loud cheers coming from a group of men.

"God knows what's going on in there," said Giles, his breath tickling Ted's forehead, "but we should probably head back."

"Yeah," said Ted, stepping away, "but thanks for suggesting we do this. It was lovely."

"Yeah, I'm glad we did it too." Giles straightened his tie. "I tell you what, though, I'm nervous about the speeches."

"Me too! I can't stop changing my opening. But I've decided to go with that story about the first time I made you chai tea latte ice cream."

Giles's face sagged. "I was going to open with that!"

"You're joking?"

"No, I was going to say that's when I knew I wanted to marry you."

Shit, that's exactly what I was going to say.

But Ted kept his thought to himself. "OK, you have it. I can jiggle my speech around and start with something else."

Giles hoisted an eyebrow. "Are you sure?"

"Yeah, of course. Don't worry about it. Anyway, you'll do a much better job of telling it than me."

"I don't know about that but thanks, Ted." Giles smoothed out the fabric of his suit. "Now, come on, let's get back in—before people wonder what we've been up to."

He held out his arm, and Ted took it.

As he stands looking out of the window, Ted suddenly wonders if he's misjudged their relationship. *Did Giles really hold me back, or did I willingly put myself in that position? Was my self-esteem so low I gladly stepped back to let him shine?*

He has no idea. So many feelings are swirling around him, feelings about things that happened a long time ago and things that have happened more recently, some of these in direct conflict with each other. *And I know my relationship with Giles wasn't perfect. But no relationship is, is it? Surely there are always things one partner dislikes about the other? Was I just adapting around things I didn't like in Giles? Isn't that what compromise is? Isn't that what marriage is about?*

With a jolt, he realizes that he misses his old self, the Ted he used to be. At least his old life was familiar and safe and easy—this new one is turning out to be difficult and stressful and emotionally challenging. At least he wasn't plagued with anxiety when he was with Giles. At least he didn't have to live in fear of his entire life coming crashing down. *What if I've aimed too high? What if I've been chasing a dream that's unachievable in reality? What if my relationship with Oskar is just unworkable?*

Then another thought slams into him. *What if what I had with Giles really is the best there is?*

"Come on," says Giles. "Tell me I'm wrong. Tell me we weren't happy."

Ted turns to face him. "Well, I thought we were at the time."

Giles raises his arms and lets them fall to his sides. "There you are. So what's the problem?"

"A lot has happened since then, Giles—and now I'm not sure I was."

"*What's* happened?"

Ted feels too fragile to tell him about becoming a drag queen— he isn't sure he could cope with any more disapproval. *Besides, I'm not even sure I can carry on doing drag, not after what happened with Oskar.*

Nor can he face telling Giles that he's been seeing someone, not when he isn't sure if Oskar is even going to speak to him again. The last thing he said was that he didn't want to go out with a drag queen. *So based on the evidence I've got, is there any difference between Oskar and Giles? Have I just been kidding myself that Oskar's a better man?*

That voice from deep within him resurfaces. *Was Giles really so bad after all?*

"It's complicated," is all he can manage.

"Exactly!" says Giles. "And we were so simple. We just *worked.*"

Ted folds his arms. "Wait a minute, you said we were only together because it was convenient, because it suited everyone."

"Yeah, but I wasn't thinking straight. I wasn't myself. The pandemic really took it out of me, you know that. To be honest, I think I might have been having some kind of breakdown."

Almost out of nowhere, Ted feels a glimmer of hope. *If what happened was only a temporary blip—something caused by forces beyond our control—maybe we could we go back to the way things were . . . Maybe Giles will even behave better now we've had this time apart . . .*

He expels a lungful of air. "Wait a minute. You were restless *before* the pandemic, Giles. You were already getting itchy feet."

"Only professionally," insists Giles. "Not in any other area."

Ted folds his arms a little tighter. "Really? That's not how I remember it."

Through the window, a motorbike roars along the street.

"Well, maybe my breakdown started before I was properly aware of it," argues Giles. "You know, I've never struggled with my mental health before, so maybe I didn't recognize the signs."

Hang on a minute, is he just dodging blame again? "I'm not sure you can blame everything on poor mental health, Giles."

"Sorry. I'm not doing a very good job of explaining myself. I just know that ever since we split up—"

"Ever since *you left me*," Ted corrects him.

"Ever since *I left you* . . . nothing's felt quite right. I just didn't feel like me without you."

But what if being with you meant I couldn't feel like me—or the real me I've just started to discover? What if I made too much of a compromise, and somewhere along the way lost my true self? But Ted doesn't feel strong enough to voice his thoughts. It doesn't help that he hasn't eaten; he's so hungry he feels light-headed.

"Look, you're going to have to give me some time to think about this," he states. "It's come as too much of a shock for me to make any kind of decision now."

Giles frowns. "That's OK. I understand."

They hit a bump of silence.

"Alright, well, I'll leave you to it," says Giles, backing away.

He says goodbye to Lily, and he and Ted exchange a stiff hug.

"I'll speak to you soon," Ted offers.

"Yeah, I'll look forward to it."

Ted stands at the door and watches him walk away. As he disappears around the corner, Ted feels another wave of grief.

You know you don't have to feel like that. If you get back with Giles, you won't feel like that anymore.

He shuts the door.

Almost immediately, Lily starts whining.

"Alright, Lil. I get the point," he says. "You want me and your daddy to give it another go. You're not very subtle!"

He goes into the kitchen and feeds her. Once she's quietened down, he returns to the fridge. *Surely I must have something to eat?*

As he shifts around a bottle of ketchup, the cloudy jar of pickles, and a few eyemasks he's put in there, his mind races with the various options that are opening up to him, each of which could lead to a very different future. Should he consider giving Giles another chance and trying to rebuild what they had together—a *better* version of what they had together? Or should he apologize to Oskar and hope they can resurrect their relationship? And what should he do about the drag show? He considers pulling out of it but doesn't want to cause problems for Peg and Pussy. He then wonders if he should just do this one show and see if he can get drag out of his system. His stomach roars again.

He decides to sleep on it and work out what to do in the

morning. Then he remembers that tomorrow he's confronting the woman who's been sending him the anonymous letters. His spirit wilts. *God, I knew things were complicated, but how did they get so complicated?*

Abandoning all hope of finding anything approaching a meal, he closes the fridge and walks over to the microwave. He'll have to order a takeaway.

CHAPTER 46

Denise sits outside a café, waiting for Ted. It's her lunch break, but he's texted to say he's not hungry so she's just bought them two mugs of tea. They're meeting in Waves, an old-fashioned café with red plastic furniture, laminated menus, squeezy sauce bottles, and wipe-clean gingham tablecloths. It's built into the foundations of the promenade and has a large wooden decking area that stretches out on to the beach. Denise has managed to secure a table with a seat facing away from the sun, but it's a hot day, so she fans herself with the menu. She's intrigued to know why Ted wanted to meet as they don't usually see each other at lunchtime.

She spots him in the distance wearing shorts and a T-shirt, striding towards her at a pace. She can't tell if he's excited or angry as he's directly facing the sun and has dark glasses covering his eyes. But as he approaches, she notices his mouth is fixed in a hard line. *Uh-oh, this looks ominous . . .*

"Hi, Teddy." She throws her arms around him, but it's like hugging a plank of wood.

"Alright?" is all he says.

"Well, I would be if I knew why you've been ignoring my texts," she chirps as they sit down. "I've been dying to tell you about my date. Can you believe we're going out again tomorrow?"

But Ted doesn't reply.

"Honey, is everything OK?" Denise asks.

He pulls a bundle of letters out of his pocket and drops them on the table.

Fuck.

What do I say to that?

Denise can't deny that she sent the letters, but she's no idea how he's worked it out.

As if reading her mind, Ted says, "You're the only person I know who spells 'getting laid' with a 'y.'"

She forces out a laugh that sounds borderline hysterical. "Sorry, yeah, my spelling's crap. But let me explain . . ."

"Explain what?" Ted snaps at her. "Why you sent the letters or why you had an affair with my dad?"

Fuck, I really am in trouble.

She draws in a ragged breath. "OK, yeah, I did have an affair with your dad. But it was twenty years ago, way before I met you."

Denise explains that she and Trevor met when she and some of her work colleagues were taking part in a charity auction run by the Rotary Club. Glasstone's department store had donated a full makeover, and she was the member of staff who had to go on stage to sell the prize. Afterwards, Trevor approached her, bought her a drink and was very flirtatious. Denise felt flattered and appreciated and, even though he was much older than her, found herself attracted to him. Before she knew it, they were texting and arranging to meet—and gradually this developed into a relationship. "And before you ask, yes, I did know he was married. I wasn't proud of myself. But I'd never met his wife—"

"*My mum.*"

She nods and continues, "I'd never met your mum, so she didn't seem real. Or at least it was easy for me to put her out of my mind. To be honest, it's no excuse, but I was lonely. And I know it might sound pathetic, but I was probably looking for some kind of father figure."

"Yeah, it does sound pathetic," states Ted, flatly.

Denise feels his words like a barb in her chest. An elderly woman drives past on a mobility scooter, while at the next table a pair of fiftysomething grandparents are feeding a toddler candyfloss.

"Anyway, Trevor—*your dad*—made me feel good about myself," she presses on. "He used to—"

"I don't want to know, Denise," interrupts Ted, holding up a hand. "You can spare me the details."

But already, the details of her relationship with Trevor are rushing back into Denise's head—their snatched lunchtimes, when they'd meet in her flat and Trevor would seem unable to control his desire, and she'd marvel at the effect she had on him, quite taken aback that a man could feel that way about her; their days out, driving along the coast, when they'd get out of town and settle on a quiet beach, where Denise would hope for romance but Trevor would initiate sex, claiming she was impossible to resist, only flattering her further; and their occasional nights in Manchester, when Trevor would tell Hilary he was away on a sailing trip and the two of them would stay in a hotel, enjoy an intimate dinner, and a stroll around the city arm in arm, Denise indulging her fantasy that one day they could be a real couple and Trevor might care about her enough to properly commit to a relationship. *But that was never going to happen. God, I was so desperate!*

She takes a sip of her tea and is surprised to notice that her hand is trembling, spilling some of the hot liquid on the tablecloth. She wipes it up with a tissue. "All you need to know is that the relationship started off well, but after a while I worked out that I was only going to get hurt. So I ended it. And a few years later, I met you. At first, you were cagey about what you did for a living; you kept saying your job was irrelevant and didn't define you. By the time you told me you worked at Ainsworth's, we were already mates."

She notices Ted wince at the word "mates." *What have I done?*

"Anyway, I didn't want to tell you because I knew you'd be hurt," she rattles on. "And I didn't think it mattered; it was all in the past."

"So what's changed? Why did you suddenly tell me now?" Ted holds up the bundle of letters.

Denise takes another sip of her tea, this time gripping the mug with both hands. A few meters away, a road sweeper parks up his cart, sits on a wall, and lights a cigarette. "You might not believe me, but I was trying to help," she says.

Ted scoffs theatrically. "*Help?*"

"Yeah. You split up with Giles, and suddenly you had this chance to make your dream come true, but there was something still holding you back. I thought you felt guilty about doing anything your parents wouldn't approve of, I thought you were held back by a sense of duty. So I was trying to make you see that you didn't owe them anything."

A sneer twists across Ted's face. "How very thoughtful of you."

"Yeah, alright, I can see now that it wasn't the best way to go about it. But I was only trying to make you happy. I promise."

"That's bullshit, Denise," Ted hisses. "You were trying to cause trouble."

Denise feels a sickness building in the pit of her stomach. "Cause trouble? Why would I do that?"

Ted throws up his hands. "I don't know, because you were angry at my dad? Maybe you wanted to get back with him. Maybe he was the one who dumped you."

The injustice of his accusation takes her breath away. "Ted, that's bollocks. *I* ended it with him! And for ages *he* kept trying to get back with *me*." She wraps her hands around her mug and looks down at her tea. "From what I've heard, I wasn't the only one either."

Ted pushes back his chair. "Denise, that's a lie. You're just saying that out of spite."

"I'm not, Teddy! I promise I haven't felt anything for your dad for years. Look at the dates. I sent you the first letter when you told me you wanted to be a drag queen but wouldn't commit; I sent you the second when we went to Blackpool, but you were too scared to sign up for the open-mic night—"

Ted shakes his head vigorously. "Save your breath, Denise. I don't want to hear it."

"But Teddy, you've *got* to believe me!"

"No, I don't, Denise. I don't even have to *see* you again if I don't want to."

Denise feels the sickness spreading through her. "Honey, please don't say that. I promise I was only thinking of you. But yeah, I fucked up, and I'm sorry. Please forgive me!"

But Ted is already standing up. "No, Denise," he says, pushing his chair back in. "I can't forgive you."

And with that, he turns and leaves.

Nice one, Denise. Once again, you've managed to ruin everything. But this time you've really excelled yourself!

Sitting there all alone—watching Ted walk away—she hates herself just as much as she did in her twenties, just as much as she did when she met Trevor and he made her feel seen, made her feel wanted, made her feel so much better than she had as a young girl. *Oh God, how have I ended up back here? Just when I was thinking I had the chance of putting all that behind me. How could I have got it so wrong?*

She looks at Ted's mug of tea. He hasn't touched it.

CHAPTER 47

On his way back from meeting Denise, Ted calls in to see Stanley. Originally, he'd arranged to see him to test out material for his show, but he hasn't been able to write any. He still hasn't decided if he's going to perform in Manchester. All he can think about is what he's just learned from Denise—and he's so angry with his dad that he's no idea what he's going to say to him. He tries to snap himself out of it. *Come on, you don't want your foul mood to infect Stanley.*

As he waits at the door, he tries on various smiles, eventually settling on one he hopes reads as carefree and cheerful.

"Good morning, dolly!" says Stanley as he opens the door.

"You're looking good!" Ted cheeps as they exchange a hug. "That hairdo is sharp!"

Stanley touches his hair, which he's had treated with a pink rinse. "Do you think so? Me and the girls had it done together."

"'The girls'?"

"Some of the other residents."

Ted's forced smile gives way to a genuine one. "Right, so you really are getting on better!"

"Yes, we're getting on marvelously, thank you." Stanley walks inside and Ted follows. "Anyway, I needed to do something with my hair before your show in Manchester."

Ted's eyebrows shoot up. "My show in Manchester? What, you're coming?"

"Yes, Alison said she'd take me in the car. It'll be such a treat to revisit my old stomping ground."

Ted shifts on the spot. "Right. Yes, well."

"What's the matter?"

"I'm not sure I'm doing it now."

Stanley gives a dramatic gasp. "I *beg* your pardon? I think you'd better sit down. I'll make us a pot of Lady Grey, and you can tell me what on earth's going on."

Where do I start?

Once Stanley has served tea—tea that Ted drinks this time—he starts by working backwards. He tells Stanley everything about the anonymous letters, his confrontation with Denise, and what she revealed about her affair with his dad. Then he tells him about his parents wanting to hand over control of the family business.

"I just don't know what to do," he confesses. "I don't want to let them down, but at the same time I'm so angry with my dad, I don't want to go anywhere near him."

Stanley purses his lips. "I'm not surprised."

Ted can't believe that Denise has confirmed his worst fears—and his dad has turned out to be a serial liar. And he hasn't just lied to Ted's mum but to everyone, to all of them. He feels so betrayed. *All this time I've been beating myself up for not measuring up to his example, but it turns out he's never measured up to it either!*

He breathes in and tries to let out his anger. "Anyway, even without everything Denise just told me, I'm not sure I can take over the business. I don't think I can devote the rest of my life to ice cream."

Stanley twists his wrist to reveal fingers coated in a pink nail varnish that matches his hair. "Well, it's obvious to me you can't do it. You've got to do what *you* want to do."

"Yeah, but I can't just forget about what everyone else wants me to do; no one can disregard duty completely. What about people with kids or parents who get old and need looking after? Nobody can just do what they want regardless of their responsibilities."

"Let me tell you a story about duty, dolly—and what I learned about responsibilities."

From the look on Stanley's face, this is going to be important. Ted finishes his cup of tea and sets it down on the saucer.

Stanley starts by explaining that when he was young and living in St. Luke's, it was still illegal to be gay—and the only way for gay men to meet each other was on a cruising ground that sprung up on the sand dunes after dark. There, when he was in his late teens, he had several liaisons with a man who was in his early thirties called Alan. "Well, that's what I thought he was called. At least, that's the name he gave me. But false names were common in those days. We'd all heard stories about unscrupulous trade blackmailing men they'd been with. Or men who were out cruising, caught by Lilly Law, and forced to hand over the names of everyone they'd been with—in order to avoid being prosecuted themselves."

"God, how awful."

"Yes, it was. But it was all we knew, it was normal to us. Some gay men even believed the disgusting things people said about us and thought we deserved that kind of fate—skulking around in the shadows, always living in fear."

That could so easily have been me. Ted feels another rush of gratitude. "Thank God I wasn't around then. Thank God I was born later."

"If only Alan had been . . ."

Stanley explains that, over time, he developed feelings for Alan and wanted them to have a relationship, to find some way of seeing each other in real life, even if in public they would have had to pretend they were only friends. But Alan rejected every single one of his suggestions. He explained that he felt duty-bound to stay with his wife and children and couldn't bear to do anything that risked disrupting their happiness or bringing shame on the family. So he and Stanley carried on as before; they continued to meet up on the dunes for late-night snatches of sexual activity. "Until one night there was a raid by the Lilly—and both of us were arrested."

Ted sits up. "Shit, I had no idea. What happened to you?"

Stanley gives a high-pitched sigh. "Oh, dolly, it was horrendous. We were thrown in prison cells and interrogated for hours—and I won't repeat some of the things the sharpies said to us. Then we were sent to court."

"And what sentence did you get?"

"I was lucky, I was fined and given a suspended sentence. But I had to undergo a course of electric shock therapy."

"That was *lucky*?"

"Well, no, it was torture, and it left me damaged for a long time—but eventually I came through it. I managed to move on with my life. Poor Alan, on the other hand, had it much worse. So I only mean I was lucky compared to him."

"What happened to him?"

Stanley scrapes his fingernails through his hair. He takes a moment to compose himself before carrying on. "Because he was a good ten years older than me, Alan was considered to have corrupted me—which I don't mind admitting couldn't have been further from the truth. Because he was married and a father, he was also considered to be more of a danger to society. So in order to avoid a lengthy prison sentence, he had to submit to a course of chemical castration with injections of estrogen—to remove all his sexual urges. But that wasn't the worst of it."

Ted shakes his head. "That wasn't the *worst* of it?"

"Our names and addresses were printed in the local paper. That's when I found out Alan's name wasn't Alan at all. It was Tom—Tom Bracewell. But more importantly, everybody else found out what he'd done. The whole of St. Luke's found out he was queer."

"That must have been terrible."

Stanley nods, shakily. "The scandal, the disapproval, the sheer hatred from everyone was astounding. It was bad enough for me, but Alan was fired from his job, his wife filed for divorce, his parents disowned him, and he wasn't allowed to see his children. He was so ashamed he committed suicide."

"Stanley, I'm so sorry."

Stanley stares into the distance—in the direction of the coat stand, but somewhere far beyond. For a while, the two men sit in silence.

As Ted reflects on Stanley's memories, sadness trickles into him. He finds himself thinking about Oskar, growing up amidst similar disapproval in Poland—and his dad being caught in another cruising ground. *Life must have been terrible for Oskar after that. It's no wonder he's still feeling the effects now . . .*

From outside in the corridor comes the sound of a door closing. Ted snaps back to the present.

"So is that when you left St. Luke's?" he asks. "When Alan died?"

"No," says Stanley, "my parents had thrown me out by then, so I was already living in Manchester; I found out what had happened from a female friend who sent me a cutting from the local newspaper. But that's why I wanted to tell you this story—I wanted to tell you about my parents."

"Yeah?"

Stanley strokes a diamante brooch in the shape of a daisy that's pinned to his necktie. "My parents forgot all about their duty to me, but in a way that released me from mine to them. It meant I was free to move away and explore the person I was meant to be, without being held back by guilt. Alan, on the other hand, was crushed by his sense of duty. He was crushed by his failure to live up to the man people wanted him to be. And yes, I agree with you that people with children do have a duty to them, absolutely. But Alan should never have got married and started a family in the first place. He only did that so he wouldn't disappoint his parents. And he ended up being tormented by so much guilt, it killed him. So that's what I'd like you to take from this. That's what I'd like you to remember."

Ted feels embarrassed that Stanley is comparing his experiences to Alan's—or his own, for that matter. He feels embarrassed that he's even shared his troubles with someone who's been through such an ordeal. *Embarrassed, spoilt, and self-indulgent.*

"I don't know if my situation's anything like yours," he proffers. "What I'm talking about is hardly a matter of life or death."

"No, but that doesn't mean it's not important. And you could argue that your generation owes it to ours to be brave enough to explore your true selves, to get out there and grab everything you want from life, to honor the sacrifices we made—so that they were actually worth something."

Ted raises his hands to his mouth. "I didn't think of it like that."

"Well, maybe you should."

Stanley picks up the pot and pours them both another cup. "Now let's have some more tea. While I explain the other reason I wanted to tell you my story."

"What's that?"

"When you came in here, you started talking about your friend, Denise."

"Denise?" says Ted, adding a dash of milk. "What's Denise got to do with anything?"

"I don't think you should be so hard on her." As Stanley stirs sugar into his tea, the spoon clinks against the china.

"Why do you say that?"

"Well, I don't think I'm a bad person, but *I* had an affair with a married man—and I knew exactly what I was doing."

"Yeah, but you had a valid reason," protests Ted. "You had no other way of finding love."

"Even so, but I could have found someone who wasn't married," points out Stanley. "I'm sure Alan's wife and children would have preferred it if I had."

"Yeah, but you were lonely and desperate."

"And who's to say Denise wasn't? I've only met her once, and I don't know her story, but I'd hazard a guess she wasn't feeling great about herself—for whatever reason."

Ted sighs through his nose. "I don't think she was, no."

"Well, once you've stopped being angry with her—which is completely understandable—I'd suggest you try and find it in yourself to forgive her."

Ted turns away and looks at the record player, an album by Bette Midler sitting on the turntable. "I don't know . . ."

"Human beings are complex, dolly. And what you learn by the time you get to my age is that there are all kinds of reasons good people do bad things. But usually, it comes down to just being human."

As Ted finishes his tea, he finds himself repeating these words in his head. Then, as if out of nowhere, he finds himself thinking they might also apply to Giles. *What if he really did make a mistake? What if he really was suffering?*

Shouldn't I give him a chance?

He realizes he still hasn't told Stanley about his conversation with Giles, or his row with Oskar—and both of these ex-

changes complicate his situation even more. *But I can't face
doing it now.*

In any case, it looks like Stanley is drawing this particular
conversation to a close. He rises to his feet and picks up the tea
tray. "Now I'm going to clear this away, and when I come back,
shall we have a chat about that new material?"

CHAPTER 48

The next morning, Ted takes Lily out for her walk. The sunshine of the day before has disappeared, and although it's July, the weather is doing its best impression of January. It's cold, the sky is charcoal-gray—and everyone he passes is wearing a doleful expression. But this strikes Ted as appropriate. *Entirely appropriate.*

He walks along the front, passing the row of benches with wooden shelters built around them, giving a desultory wave to the woman who runs marathons—who today is wearing a face-mask like a balaclava—and the man in Jesus sandals who's walking his Airedale terrier. As he trots down the steps to the beach, he reflects on what Stanley said to him. *"There are all kinds of reasons good people do bad things. But usually, it comes down to just being human."*

Much as it pains him to consider it, might his dad have had a reason for behaving badly too? *Rather than letting out my anger and laying into him, should I hear him out?*

He reaches the bottom of the steps and pauses to look at the sand stretching out before him.

And what about Mum? If I feel let down and betrayed, how's she going to feel? He tells himself that he needs to tread carefully as he's no idea what his mum knows. Though the memory of the row he overheard when he was five years old suggests she may not be completely in the dark.

All of a sudden, he's five again, listening to the argument at his bedroom door. *"You can't seriously expect me to take this?" "That's your excuse for carrying on like this?" "You expect me to find out and say nowt?"*

Lily barks at him, impatient to be let off her lead, and he releases her so she can dart off across the sand. He walks in the direction of the windmill, passing the row of shops and beach cafés on his right that includes Waves and one of Ainsworth's kiosks. The sky is scowling at him, and it looks like it's about to start raining; the clouds have turned the color of blueberry sorbet or the whimberrypie–flavored ice cream Ainsworth's make as a special every autumn. *Stop thinking about ice cream!*

As he walks past the bandstand, it dawns on Ted that while he may feel betrayed by his dad, in some ways—just as Stanley said—he also feels relieved. It's as if he's been liberated from his sense of duty, from the obligation to do what his parents want, or at least what his dad wants.

This realization prompts another: that he no longer has to feel grateful to his parents for their acceptance. In fact, he should never have felt this. Acceptance of a child—whatever their sexuality—should come as part of the unconditional love that everyone agrees is a key component of good parenting. *I shouldn't have to be grateful for their love just because I'm different—just because I'm gay.*

As he approaches the sand dunes, he tries to imagine what it must have been like to come here years ago, after dark, when the area was full of gay men, desperate to feel any kind of connection with others like them. He imagines how terrified they must have been, terrified of being caught, but also terrified of what they no doubt saw as dark impulses and desires—impulses and desires that they couldn't control, that could bring them down or even destroy them.

He feels a rush of outrage at a world that instilled these men with such fear, outrage at a world that persecuted them—some of them, like Alan, to the point of death. But this time, he refuses to feel grateful that he was born in a different world. *People like me should be able to rely on acceptance without question—just like everyone else does.*

I shouldn't feel grateful to anyone for anything.

He enters the dunes, trots up a hill and sits down. He's pretty sure it's the same hill where he sat with Oskar after their second date, the same hill where they shared their first kiss. As he relives the memory, it strikes him just how brave Oskar has been, moving to another country, coming out as gay, and starting a relationship with another man. All of a sudden, he feels a rush of warmth towards him. And he realizes that it's Oskar he wants to be with, not Giles.

Of course it is! I only thought otherwise because I was feeling low.

Oskar's the one I love. There's no doubt about that.

Then—with a thud—he remembers their argument in the caravan. *But if I apologize, will he take me back?*

He feels the first drops of rain land on his cagoule. He treads down the hill, waits for Lily to go to the toilet, cleans up her mess, then pulls up his hood.

"Come on," he says to the dog. "It's time to go home."

As the rain starts to fall harder, splattering his cagoule, Ted jogs along the beach and back up the steps.

When he reaches the promenade, his phone vibrates with a text from Denise. He ducks under a nearby shelter to open it.

"Ted, I just want to say again how sorry I am," the message reads. **"I really hope we can work this out."**

Ted sits down on the bench while he decides how to reply. Lily settles at his feet. "What do you think, Lil?"

A second message arrives. **"In the spirit of being open and honest,"** it reads, **"I've just seen on social media that Javier**

has dumped Giles. It happened about a month ago apparently."

Ted remembers that when Giles left him, he asked Denise to check on Javier's profile so he wouldn't have to—and to pass on any important updates. He also remembers that it's been about a month since Giles broke his silence and sent him that first text. *So it was Javier who ended the relationship, not Giles.* That's *why he wants to get back with me . . .*

"There's no need to reply," reads a third message from Denise, **"but please know that I love you xxx"**

In an instant, Ted realizes how much he wants to reply—and what exactly he wants to say. But before he can type anything, his mind zips off in another direction.

Giles lied to me . . .

Of course he did!

To his surprise, Ted finds that he can't be angry with him. *That doesn't necessarily mean he's a bad person. If he was in love with Javier, he was probably hurting; he was probably lonely. After all, he's only human.*

While he's on the subject, Ted can't be angry with Giles for leaving him either. Their life together *was* dull and boring—that's why ever since it ended, he's been trying to create a very different one for himself. And he wouldn't have wanted Giles to stay with him out of a sense of duty. *If I'm going to resist doing what other people want of me, I have to understand that he wanted to do the same.*

The rain is now pelting down so hard it sets off someone's car alarm. Ted stands up and examines the sky. It doesn't look like it's going to stop soon, so he'll have to jog home through it. "What do you think, Lil? Shall we make a move?"

Although he's about to get soaked, Ted can feel a smile creeping up his face. Because it was Oskar towards whom his feelings were directing him—and the news from Denise has only confirmed that he's made the right decision.

And Ted can see now that there *is* a difference between Oskar and Giles, even if neither of them likes him doing drag. To be the person he wanted to be, Giles suppressed Ted's spirit; for Oskar to be the person he wants to be, he only has to conquer himself. *And after what he's lived through, I'll just have to cut him some slack . . .*

But first of all, I have to convince him to give me another chance. I have to convince him that what we've got is worth fighting for.

He tugs on Lily's lead. "Come on, let's go."

But the dog doesn't budge. As Ted turns to plead with her, he catches sight of the inscription on the bench.

"If I don't do it, nobody else will," he reads aloud.

He stops and stares at the words. And he lets them inspire him.

He screws his eyes shut and thinks of Stanley—and not just Stanley, but Alan too. He remembers what Stanley said about honoring the sacrifices his generation made.

I'm not giving up on my dream.

He snaps his eyes open.

Stand by, Manchester—Gail Force is coming to get you!

CHAPTER 49

Ted faces his mum and dad.

It's the end of the working day, and they're sitting in the empty shop, in the last leatherette booth at the back. Next to them stands the display cabinet full of all the awards won by Ainsworth's, and next to that the series of photos of the business and its four generations of owners, ending with the one of Trevor, Hilary, Ted, and Jemima. Ted looks at it then reads the sign above it: AINSWORTH'S: THE STORY SO FAR. As ever, his attention sticks on the words "So Far."

Come on, you're not bottling it now . . .

He tugs in a long breath. "Dad, did you have an affair with Denise?"

Ted's almost shocked to hear the words coming out of his mouth. He can hardly bear to watch his dad's reaction.

But Trevor doesn't seem particularly disturbed. "So she's told you about that, has she?"

Ted doesn't understand how he can be so calm. "You're not denying it then?"

Trevor frowns. "No, I'm not denying it."

Ted's attention shifts to his mum. She doesn't seem surprised by the revelation either, which is what he was hoping.

But she does have a grave look on her face. Behind the counter, a freezer starts whirring.

"I've already apologized to your mum, but I'm happy to apologize again," Trevor goes on. "I'm afraid I haven't always been the best husband."

Hilary scoffs. "You can say that again."

"This was before you knew Denise, though," Trevor tells Ted.

"Yeah, she mentioned that," says Ted.

"Although I can't say her knocking about wi' you made things easy for me," adds Hilary. "And seeing her at t' wedding weren't great either. Which might explain why I got so bladdered."

"But we could see you two had become good mates," Trevor explains. "So we didn't want to say anything—and Denise didn't either. We kind of had an unspoken agreement to just pretend nothing had happened and to stay out of each other's way."

"Although I did have a brief conversation with her once," Hilary says. "She came up to me after your birthday one year and apologized. She said she weren't proud of what she'd done, which I suppose were quite decent of her."

"And I wasn't proud of it either," cuts in Trevor. "It wasn't my finest moment."

"It were more than a moment," Hilary corrects him. "And it weren't t' first time either."

Behind the counter, the freezer stops whirring.

"Is that true, Dad?" asks Ted.

Trevor joins his hands together. "Yeah, I'm afraid so."

Into Ted's head rushes the row he overheard when he was five. He holds up a hand. "Actually, I think I knew that."

Ted shares what he can remember of the row, and this time his parents do look upset.

"I'm sorry about that, love," bleats Hilary. "That must have been awful for you."

"To be honest, I didn't quite get it at the time," Ted admits. *And I was more bothered about finding out I was a mistake.* But he keeps that thought to himself.

Then, to his astonishment, his dad brings up the subject. "It's no excuse, but I struggled when me and your mum first got married. You've got to realize I was only young, and I had dreams. You know I've always loved my sailing, and I was looking into joining the navy. But then I met your mum and we fell in love. And she fell pregnant."

Hilary tuts. "*We* fell pregnant, Trevor. I didn't do it on my own."

"Yeah, well, anyway," rallies Trevor, "the point is, I had to put my dreams to one side and grow up. That's when I started working for the business."

Hilary frowns at Ted. "Sorry, love. This can't be very nice to hear."

"It's OK. I knew I wasn't wanted."

Wow, did I really just say that?

Trevor and Hilary both inhale sharply.

"That's not true!" protests Trevor. "You were always wanted! We just got the timing a bit wrong, that's all."

"Absolutely," vouches Hilary, "and I'm sure that's the case with a lot of people our age. It's not like young couples these days, planning the date so t' baby's born at the start of a school year, consulting apps to tell 'em when they're ovulating. It weren't like that in them days; it just happened when it happened and people got on with it. But that didn't mean you weren't wanted, love. Far from it."

"And I was happy, don't get me wrong," clarifies Trevor. "It's just that sometimes everything got on top of me, all the duty and expectation. Part of me couldn't help kicking back occasionally. Although I really regret that now."

Outside in the street, someone tips a load of bottles into a recycling bin.

Trevor picks up the menu from the center of the table and rotates it between his fingers. "Anyway, I was never serious about the other women. You know that, Hil."

I don't think Denise did.

"It was just my way of letting off steam," he goes on, "of getting it all out of my system."

Hilary gives something between a snort and a laugh. "Of getting your end away, more like."

Trevor puts down the menu. "I always loved you, Hilary. I loved all three of you. And I wouldn't have done anything to ruin what we had as a family."

"Well, you kind of did, Dad," Ted objects. "That's exactly what you did. The only reason you *didn't* ruin things was because Mum put up with it."

Hilary draws in her mouth. "Although God knows why."

Someone posts a leaflet through the door and the letterbox rattles.

"Why *did* you put up with it, Mum?" Ted asks. "Come on, you must have some idea."

Hilary massages her temples. "I suppose I didn't want anyone to think our marriage were less than perfect, especially my family—some of 'em liked nothing more than saying I'd got above myself and needed bringing down a peg or two. And let's not even start on your dad's side. All I'll say is, if his parents had realized owt were wrong, they would have been swinging from t' rooftops."

"Oh, Mum, that can't have been very nice for you."

"No, it weren't. Knowing your dad were unfaithful made me as miserable as sin, but I managed to get over it and put on a good show. I also wanted to do right by you kids. I wanted you to grow up in a stable home."

Ted glares at her. "But, Mum, you shouldn't have done that. Me and Jem would have coped."

She tilts her head. "Would you, though? I've heard you say Denise used to go for the wrong kind of bloke because she grew up with a dad who were always off gallivanting. I've heard you say more than once that she were damaged by it."

Ted feels a rumble of disquiet. *Shit, I didn't think of it like that.*

Hilary runs her finger along the edge of the table. "Any road, I did what I thought were the right thing as a mum. I kept my feelings buried. I turned a blind eye. And years later, when I found out your dad were carrying on wi' Denise, I didn't say owt as I knew it wouldn't last. I knew he'd never leave me."

She pauses.

"And, much as he do'n't deserve to hear this, I knew that deep down he were a good man."

Hilary sighs then looks away from them both.

"The other thing is," she goes on, "if I'm honest, I probably put up with your dad's shenanigans because deep down I were grateful."

Ted arches an eyebrow. "Grateful? What for?"

"For standing by me when I got caught wi' you." She looks at Ted. "They were different times, love, and lots of blokes would have done a runner. Especially blokes whose parents didn't approve, who already thought I were common as muck and dragging him down into t' gutter."

Ted can feel the burn of outrage. "But, Mum, you should never have been grateful. You had nothing to be grateful for."

Even as he says the words, he's reminded of the gratitude he felt he owed them not just for accepting him as he was but for bringing him into the world when he wasn't planned.

"Well, maybe I shouldn't, but I did," picks up Hilary. "And sometimes that were hard to live with. That might explain why every once in a while, I got carried away on t' booze."

From outside comes the sound of an engine backfiring. "But when I fell ill," she goes on, "when I got cancer, I realized I didn't want to put up with it anymore. Before I went in for my operation, I told your dad that if I came out of this, I wanted to wipe t' slate clean and start again—and I wouldn't put up with any more sneaking around behind my back. He had to pack in his cheating."

So that's what she was talking about when she finished chemo! That was the "important stuff" she mentioned. Ted feels a rush of pride in Hilary. "Good for you, Mum!"

She clasps her hands and raises them to her chin. "Yeah, well, by t' time I came out t' other end, I had a new respect for myself. I could see how much I contributed, not just to t' family but to t' business too. So I stood up for myself. I gave your dad an ultimatum."

"And I pulled myself together," Trevor says. "I felt ashamed of myself already, but seeing your mum suffering and being so strong made me feel *really* ashamed of myself. I just couldn't live with it. So I sorted myself out."

Ted feels a surge of annoyance at him. "Well, I'm not going to congratulate you, Dad. It shouldn't have taken Mum to come close to death to bring you to your senses."

Hilary lowers her hands. "Don't be too hard on him, love. You know I weren't always a saint myself."

Ted puts his hands over his eyes. "What? Don't tell me you had an affair too?"

I'm not sure I can hear it from both of them.

"No, well, not exactly . . . But I did get off with some barman when I were bladdered on your Auntie Brenda's hen weekend. Although I'd rather not go into detail, if you don't mind."

Ted removes his hands from his eyes. "I don't mind at all, Mum. I'm happy for you to stop there."

"Any road, I felt terrible about it," she expands. "I felt guilty as sin. So as soon as I got home, I told your dad."

"And I could hardly be angry with her," says Trevor, "not after the way I'd carried on."

Hilary looks at Ted beseechingly. "I hope *you're* not angry with me, love."

Ted can hardly believe what he's hearing. He's shocked, he's appalled, he's—weirdly—gripped, but his anger has faded. He's not sure he's even annoyed anymore. If anything, he's only annoyed at himself. Hearing his parents talk about their emotions, he's staggered to realize that it's only now—at the age of forty-three—that he's seeing them as fully rounded human beings. In the past, he just saw them as Mum and Dad, defined solely by the roles they played in his life. In his defense, this may have been down to the fact that he works for the business, so the family dynamic has always been impossible to escape. But now that he thinks about it, it seems obvious; of course his parents were feeling all kinds of complicated emotions— emotions that determined their behavior, emotions that shaped them as people. *Emotions that sometimes made them do bad things.*

This realization prompts another rush of relief—this time an immense, liberating relief. Because Ted now knows definitively that he no longer has to measure up to some unachievable idea of perfection that he saw his parents as projecting. Until today, he didn't realize just how much he's been trying to live up to this, trying to make up for falling short of it—for being gay, for being a mistake, for just not being good enough. *But now I don't have to because Mum and Dad aren't perfect either. They're human, just like me.*

"I'm sorry if all this is coming as a disappointment," offers Trevor. "I'm sorry if we've let you down."

Ted shifts on his seat, the leatherette squeaking. "You know what, you haven't let me down. I thought you had, but you haven't."

"So you don't hold it against us?" asks Hilary.

"Absolutely not," insists Ted. "Although there is one thing."

"Oh yeah, what's that?"

He takes a moment to compose himself. "I do wish you hadn't guilt-tripped me with all that talk about putting family first. With all that pressure to work for the business."

Trevor and Hilary share a look that suggests this is something they've already discussed.

"Yeah, well, maybe we did overdo that," admits Trevor.

"And we should probably apologize," adds Hilary.

Just when Ted thinks he can't be any more shocked, his mum and dad leave him dumbstruck. *Apologize? Is this really happening?*

"But you have to understand," says Hilary, "we only put pressure on you because we loved you. And we didn't want to lose you."

Ted narrows his eyes. "How do you mean?"

"When we first realized you were gay, we were worried that when you grew up we'd grow apart," she expands. "We were worried you'd get bored of us making ice cream in our quiet little seaside town, that you'd go off to Manchester or London, to all them fab bars and clubs you see on t' telly, full of gorgeous, trendy gays."

"Encouraging you to work for the family business was our way of trying to stop this," explains Trevor, "of keeping you close."

Ted can feel his eyes filling with tears. *So that's what it was all about. They weren't disappointed in me at all—they just loved me.*

"Mum, Dad," he murmurs, "I had no idea." A tear lands on the table and he wipes it away with his sleeve.

"Well, now you do, son."

Hilary reaches across the table and takes Ted's hand. "Although now that I think about it, it were a bit of a clumsy way of going about things."

Trevor nods. "But as you're finding out, we've made a lot of mistakes."

Ted draws in an unsteady breath and knuckles the tears away. "That's alright. We all have."

He gives his mum's hand a squeeze then releases it. For a moment, the three of them sit there smiling at each other.

Then—to his surprise—Ted feels the tiniest spark of excitement. Because all of a sudden, he can see a solution to his problem, the problem of how to balance family duty with his dream of being a drag queen.

He doesn't have to choose one or the other. *I'm absolutely right to put myself first and follow my dream—but I can also take the people I love along with me. I can do everything possible to keep them close.*

He slaps his hands on the table. "Mum, Dad, I'm sorry, but I'm not going to take over the business. And I know you don't want to hear that, with all the debt we're in, but I've got to put myself first."

The two of them nod, solemnly.

"That's OK, love," says Hilary.

"We understand," agrees Trevor.

"And while we're being completely honest with each other," Ted goes on, "I might as well tell you I don't even like ice cream."

Hilary looks at him as if his head has just turned into a pineapple. "You what, love?"

By now, Ted is so excited he's almost panting. "I just pretended I did to keep you happy. I didn't tell you because *I* didn't want to let *you* down."

Trevor begins kneading his wedding ring. "You didn't need to do that, son."

But Ted doesn't respond—because now he's started revealing his true feelings, he can't stop himself. "There's something else I need to tell you."

They look at him, eyes wide.

Come on, Ted, this is your moment.

"I'm going to be a drag queen," he announces. "Actually, I already *am* a drag queen."

Trevor and Hilary both blink, several times.

"I've been doing drag for a few months now," Ted steams on. "I love it and it's what I want to do forever."

"So that's what you've been up to," stammers Trevor. "Well, I can't say it comes as a big surprise."

"No," says Hilary, "the signs were always there. And I did try and find ways for you to enjoy your singing and dancing. I even tried to find ways for you to dress up. But I thought you'd grown out of that. I didn't realize you were just keeping it quiet."

"Yeah, well, I haven't grown out of it—and I'm not keeping it quiet anymore. I've got a show in a club in Manchester tomorrow night, and I'd really love you to come."

He's about to tell them that he's invited Denise but stops himself. *They've seen her with me loads of times, so they must have worked out some way to deal with it by now. Besides, I was that horrible to her I'm not even sure she's coming.*

Hilary clutches her neck. "But tomorrow we've got the meal with our Jem, love."

"Well, can't we just change our plans a bit?" Ted argues. "Can't you all come and see my show and we'll go out for a drink afterwards? I'd love you to be a part of it. So you can see this isn't something I'm doing on my own—and I'm not going to grow away from you."

They open their mouths to speak, but before they can answer, Ted gasps. "Shit, sorry, there's one other thing."

Trevor and Hilary stare at each other in disbelief. "One other thing?" mouths Hilary. "On top of all t' others?"

"Yeah. I'm not getting back with Giles—not now, not ever. Because I've met someone else. Someone I've fallen in love with. Someone I'm hoping will be a big part of my future."

That is, if he'll take me back . . .

CHAPTER 50

It's Saturday morning, and Oskar is on his way to Manchester to meet his dad. He's so scared, all his muscles are tense, and he's struggling to sit still.

He tries to take his mind off the meeting by opening the app that teaches him a new word every day. Today's word is "trepidatious," which he probably knew already—or at least he knew the noun, "trepidation." The definition offered is "apprehensive or nervous." Oskar wonders if this is strong enough to describe the way he's feeling. *No, "terrified" would probably be more accurate.*

After all this time, he's no idea how he and his dad will get on. *How will he react when I tell him I'm gay? What if he's annoyed that, after all the sacrifices he's made, his own gay son is still too frightened to enjoy the benefits?*

As the train rattles along, occasionally giving a little jerk to either side, Oskar imagines it coming off the tracks and crashing into the sidings. That's exactly what he feels has been happening to his life over the last few days; it's as if the train he's riding has derailed and is hurtling headfirst into a major collision. He tries to loosen his shoulders and wriggle away the fear.

But the funny thing is, as well as being scared, he's looking forward to the meeting—*really* looking forward to it. In fact, he's gripped by an excitement so intense, it's as if he's drunk ten coffees. He can't wait to see his dad again, to see his weather-beaten face, his fair hair, and his warm smile. His heart is beating so fiercely, he's worried the other people in the carriage can hear it.

Oskar tries to keep calm by looking around and observing the other passengers going about their business. Opposite him sits a young man flicking through a dating app on his phone; across the aisle are a middle-aged couple reading their books in contemptuous silence, while next to him perches a teenage girl attempting to apply a full face of makeup. *None of these people have any idea what's going on in my life. None of them have any idea what I'm about to do, or that this is the most significant day of my life for a long time—possibly ever.*

His phone vibrates, and he picks it up to see he's received a text message from Marina.

"Good luck, toots!" it reads. "If you've decided to go ahead with it, then it must be right. You must be ready. Trust in yourself xxx"

A warm feeling blooms in his chest. Just as he's about to read the text again, he receives another from Ted.

"If you're on your way to meet your dad, GOOD LUCK," it reads. "I won't distract you and I understand if you're still angry with me, but I'd love the chance to apologize. And if you change your mind and want to come and see the show, you'd be very welcome."

Oskar rests his head against the window. *What should I say?*

"But no pressure!" reads a second message. "You concentrate on the meeting with your dad. I hope it goes well xxx"

Oskar's gut twists with guilt. He wishes he hadn't been so hard on Ted and accused him of pushing him too far. *I told him he didn't care about anyone else's feelings. I called him a dick.*

He doesn't quite know how this happened, although he does remember being so angry it was as if he was possessed by some kind of demon. He also wonders if part of him was determined to destroy his newfound happiness, if part of him was trying to punish himself. That night was also the first time in weeks that the horrible voice that used to torment him had popped back into his head. *Just when I thought I'd got rid of it, it came back—telling me I was a pervert, just like my dad.*

Whatever his motivation, Oskar can't avoid the fact that he messed up. And he'd like to make amends with Ted. *Maybe I should go and see his show. Maybe I shouldn't say anything; just turn up and surprise him.*

Then again, he's worried that the two of them have said too much that can't be taken back, that they both got so worked up they've ruined what they had. *In any case, will I be in the right frame of mind to see the show after meeting my dad—or will I be a total mess?*

On the other hand, if I don't go, will Ted see that as a sign I really do *hate drag?*

Now that Oskar's had time to reflect on it, he's come to the conclusion that he doesn't hate drag—not really, despite what he said in their argument. When he and Ted were backstage in Queen of Clubs, he *did* feel uncomfortable; he can't deny that. But seeing the show helped him get over this, and afterwards he didn't feel half as bad—and he wasn't lying when he told Ted he loved it. The problem was, once he came away, he built up the discomfort in his head. His insecurities rushed in and turned it into something else. And by the time of their argument, he'd convinced himself that drag constituted a red line, something he'd never be able to accept. In the heat of his mental turmoil, he hurled this at Ted in order to hurt him, or to hurt himself—or both. But now his anger has faded, he's pretty sure he *could* accept Ted doing drag. All he'd need is time to adjust; being in a gay relationship is so new to him and, even though they both promised to take things slowly, they seem to have forgotten this and got carried away. *But do I have* time?

Just as he's considering how to reply to Ted's text, the train passes a sign saying WELCOME TO MANCHESTER PICCADILLY.

Shit, this is it.

Oskar closes his phone and, before he knows it, the train is drawing up alongside the platform. His mouth goes dry, and his heart rate rockets.

He stands up and waits for the train to stop, joining a queue behind the middle-aged couple. He tries to regulate his breathing, gulping in lungfuls of air and hoping this will slow his heart rate.

Can I really do this?

Yes, you can!

The doors open with a loud beep.

Cautiously, Oskar steps off the train. And there, standing just a few meters away, is his dad.

Dad. Oh, Dad.

Andrzej is dressed in a plain black T-shirt, multipocket cargo shorts, and functional—rather than fashionable—trainers. *It's him. It's really him!*

He gives Oskar a wave, and Oskar is delighted that he recognizes him. After so long, he wasn't sure he would.

Now I just want to see him up close. I just want to touch him.

Oskar moves slowly towards him, hyperaware of his actions, feeling as if he stands out from everyone else in the station, as if everyone is staring at him. But it's like he's forgotten to walk properly; his legs are stiff, and he thinks he's going to stumble or fall over. He tries to block out his surroundings and concentrate on putting one foot in front of the other.

Thankfully, his dad spots him, their eyes meet, and he too starts walking towards him. *I can't believe this is happening.*

When the two men are standing a few paces away from each other, they stop and just look at each other. They're so close, Oskar can see the grooves in Andrzej's skin and the light dusting of gray in his hair.

"Hello," Andrzej says to him in Polish.

"Hello, Dad," Oskar croaks.

Then Andrzej opens his arms, and Oskar steps into them. Straight away—with no warning—he gives himself over to full, body-racking sobs.

His dad hugs him tighter, and Oskar breathes him in. He's relieved to find he smells exactly the same as he used to; he smells of the sea. His sobs grow louder.

"I love you, Oskar," Andrzej whispers in his ear. "I've always loved you. No matter what."

"I love you too, Dad," Oskar splutters. "I never stopped loving you."

And in that moment, he knows he can no longer be disgusted by him—and he can no longer be disgusted by himself.

CHAPTER 51

Later that day, Ted arrives at Seraphina's. The main club area is a riot of kitsch, with ornate crystal chandeliers hanging from the ceiling, plush velvet drapes lining the walls, and tables and chairs upholstered in various animal prints covering the floor. Although the venue is one of the most popular in the Gay Village, today it's empty apart from Peg Legge and Pussy Squat—dressed in rehearsal clothes and heels—and a woman in her early fifties who introduces herself as the nightclub owner and director of the show, Seraphina Blush. Seraphina is wearing a zebra-print kaftan and some kind of elaborate headdress that draws on her African heritage. Although she's clearly a cisgender woman, at the same time she's wearing so much heavy makeup and such an extravagant wig—not to mention that camp, obviously invented name—that he doesn't doubt her identity as a drag queen. *Isn't she what they call a bio queen?*

But Ted doesn't have the headspace to answer this—he's too busy trying to focus on the show. Once he's greeted Peg and Pussy, he sits down and pulls a pair of heels out of his bag. "OK, I'm ready!" he announces.

"Right, let's get on with this sound check!" says Seraphina.

Ted, Peg, and Pussy totter up onto the stage. Ted shields his eyes from the glare of the spotlight and peers out at the auditorium.

"It's big, isn't it?" he rasps, suddenly wishing he'd brought a bottle of water.

"That's what they all say," jokes Peg.

"No, seriously," says Ted, his mouth getting drier. "It's much bigger than I thought."

"It's my first time here too," pipes Pussy, blowing down her T-shirt. "I'm so nervous, I'm sweating like a fat bird at a Gregg's counter."

"Well, I've played here loads of times, and I'm still shitting it," admits Peg. "I've been to the bog that many times I've got an arse like a chewed orange."

Seraphina claps her hands. "Alright, you girls will have plenty of time to get over your nerves later. What I need you to do now is get used to the dimensions of the stage and test out the mics."

While Peg and Pussy bombard Seraphina with technical questions about the lighting, all Ted can do is stand still and gaze out at the auditorium. He wonders who'll be sitting there tonight.

Will Mum and Dad turn up?

Will Jem come with Raj? And if she does, how will she feel watching her brother step into the spotlight?

His mind flits to Oskar; he wonders if he's been brave enough to go through with the meeting with his dad. He didn't reply to Ted's text, which worries Ted as he sent it a few hours ago. He's frightened to look at his phone in case he receives bad news or something that throws him off. He doesn't dare hope Oskar will turn up tonight. *That seems extremely unlikely.*

He stretches out his glutes and practices a few slut drops. But this only adds to his nerves. The problem is, tonight's about so much more than a show, even his first professional show, even in the most important drag venue in the north of England; it feels as though his entire future happiness is riding on it.

And what about Denise? Is she going to turn up?

He steps to one side to send her a quick text. "Sorry I've been quiet," he writes. "We've got loads to talk about. But I really hope you can make it tonight xxx"

Ted can't bear to wait for her answer, so he slips his phone back into his pocket.

He closes his eyes and pictures himself standing in the same spot as Gail Force. Another hook of fear rips into him.

Oh God, can I really go through with this? What if I'm walking headfirst into a massive disaster?

He decides not to think about who might be in the audience; he needs to concentrate on his performance. He tries to visualize himself nailing his set and being showered with applause—but he struggles.

He opens his eyes and switches off his phone.

There, that's better.

"Sorry I'm late!" yells a voice from the back of the hall. "I'm going to have to have a shave—it took me that long to get here, I've grown stubble."

Rushing towards them pulling a wheelie suitcase is a tall man with an Irish accent and the gravelly voice of a heavy smoker.

"And you are?" asks Seraphina.

"Fanny," says the man. "F—"

But before he can finish, Ted blurts out, "Fanny Spank!"

"Oh great, sorry," says Seraphina. "I didn't recognize you as a bloke."

Ted realizes he's been that preoccupied that he hasn't had time to check out the publicity material for tonight's show—and had no idea Fanny was on the bill. But there's no question it's her, even if she is out of drag.

She parks her case at the foot of the stage and looks Ted up and down. "Sorry, have we met?"

"Yeah, but it was nearly twenty years ago now—in Dublin,"

says Ted. "You won't remember me, but you put me in drag for the first time, backstage after your show."

"Yes!" A smile lights up Fanny's face. "What's your name again?"

"Ted."

"Ted, that's it! You were a little sweetheart—and a total natural, from what I remember. But you had a boyfriend who was a posh twat."

Ted grimaces. "Yeah, well, he's not my boyfriend anymore. I mean, he was actually my husband, but he's not now."

Fanny sits down and tugs some heels out of her suitcase. "Good to hear it. And if you're standing on that stage in a pair of spikes, do I take it you've fulfilled your destiny and become a drag queen?"

Ted smiles, bashfully. "Yeah, it took me a while—a *long* time—but I got there in the end."

"Well, better late than never."

Seraphina makes a big show of clearing her throat. "Ladies, can we continue with this little reunion later? We need to get on with the tech check."

"Sorry," says Ted. "Of course."

Fanny puts on her heels and joins the other queens on stage.

"I'm glad you made it," she whispers in Ted's ear. "I always knew you would."

An electric current shoots through Ted's stomach. And in that moment, he knows he *is* going on stage tonight. *And I'm not just going on—I'm going to slay!*

CHAPTER 52

It's ten o'clock, and Ted is in the middle of the show and in full flow as Gail Force. He's wearing a silver spandex corset with white lace gloves and thigh-high boots he's been breaking in for weeks. In a nod to his hometown, a pair of seashells are dangling from his ears, and there's a chain of them hanging around his neck. On his head is a synthetic wig that's exactly the same purple as Ainsworth's branding. He can't help thinking this is a subtle way of saying goodbye to his previous profession. *Although that's where the subtlety ends.*

He started his set with a blast of Britney, then introduced himself as probably the oldest drag queen to have ever made her professional debut on this stage. Now he's midway through his material about aging.

"I used to have a stomach like an ironing board," he says, frowning theatrically. "It's still there, but these days it's got a massive pile of ironing on top of it."

Every time he gets a laugh—which he's heartened to see is at the end of most lines—he feels a rush of confidence. *Wow, I really* am *slaying.*

"You know you're getting old when your idea of Happy Hour is having a nap," he jokes.

This is rewarded with a particularly big laugh from Stanley, who's sitting in the front row in another three-piece suit, his ebony walking stick propped up against his chair and his peacock-feathered fedora resting on the table. Sitting next to him is Alison, who's looking impossibly glamorous in a sheer scarlet dress with a V neckline, with long, false nails painted to match and wrapped around a blood-red cocktail that she lifts regularly to her rose-red lips. Both Alison and Stanley are grinning brightly and clearly enjoying the show.

"But that's not the worst thing about getting old," Ted storms on. "The other day someone told me a joke, and I laughed so hard the tears ran down my leg."

A loud hoot comes from a table at which Trevor, Hilary, Jemima, and a handsome man Ted assumes to be Raj are sitting. In fact, every time Ted has looked at them during the show, they've been laughing. At one point, he even thought he saw his mum wiping a tear from her eye. And Jemima is so keen to show her support that she sometimes breaks out into a cheer before he's even reached the punchline.

"Hey, have you heard the one about the drag queen with the saggy tits?" Ted asks. "It's a real knee slapper."

A loud whoop comes from a table at which Ted knows the only person sitting is Giles. He has no idea how Giles even found out he was doing drag, let alone this show. When Ted first spotted him, Giles's presence made him feel unnerved—and a little hesitant to perform the material about being abandoned by his husband. But then he realized that none of it was bitter or insulting. *And everything I say is true, so if it makes Giles reconsider his behavior, then all the better.*

"Talking about saggy tits," Ted chirps, "if there was a competition to see who had the saggiest, I'd beat everyone. In fact, I'd wipe the floor with them."

Giles gives another whoop. It's clear he wants to encourage Ted as he's making a big show of clapping and laughing as enthusiastically as possible. Suddenly, Ted is glad he's here. *Be-*

cause, like it or not, Giles has been a part of this journey, even if we did have to split up for me to get here—even if I did have to fight against his disapproval.

As he catches Giles's eye and sends him a smile, he wonders if it could have happened any other way. *Maybe I only got here because I had to fight his disapproval.*

Ted powers on. "You know, someone asked me the other day, 'Gail, what's that tattoo between your tits?' I said, 'Bitch, it's my belly button.'"

"Preach, sister!" shouts a voice Ted instantly knows belongs to Denise. He can only just make out her silhouette; she's sitting on the left-hand side of the auditorium towards the back—and is surrounded by so many people Ted can't tell if she's with anyone. But what's beyond doubt is the solidarity she's sending him. He feels almost winded with relief.

"You know, I hate looking in the mirror and seeing this old bag," he drawls. "Don't get me wrong, I do still feel like a fox sometimes. But then again, they have their tits on their stomachs too."

Although Ted makes sure he's directing his chat to all areas of the auditorium, he can't help arrowing a lot of it towards the far right-hand corner. Because there—hidden in the darkness but illuminated by the occasional flash of the house lights—is Oskar. And he's come with an older man who, from the little Ted has seen of him, must be his dad. When he initially spotted them, Ted was fired up by their presence. It made him want to push himself to give his best possible performance—and it still does. Although he knows from the script in his head that there isn't much of his performance left.

"Now I'm coming to the end of the show," he announces. "I want to leave you all with a little philosophical reflection. Life is like a toilet roll—the closer you get to the end, the faster it goes. So please, everyone, make the most of it!"

To the sound of raucous applause, cheering, and stomping

of feet, Ted rounds off his set with a performance of "Roar" by Katy Perry. He stalks around the stage, perfectly executing a routine made up of moves he's learnt in dance class, and belting out the lyrics—lyrics about being held back and cowed by a partner but finally breaking free to allow his authentic voice to roar for the first time.

By the second chorus, several people in the audience are singing along. By the final chorus, it feels like every single one of them is joining in. Then, much too quickly for Ted, the show is over.

It turns out it's over too quickly for the audience too.

"More!" they bellow.

"Encore!"

Ted is so overcome, his breath comes out in judders. His heart feels like it's leaping. And at the same time he thinks he might be about to cry.

He does his best to compose himself. He knows just what he has to do.

He signals to the technician to play the song he's reserved as an encore—something Stanley told him to do but he didn't for one second imagine he'd need. And pumping out of the sound system comes the introduction to Cher's "Believe."

Somehow, Ted finds the energy to give his strongest, most confident performance yet. He struts and shimmies up and down the stage as he channels all his emotions into the lyrics, asking the audience if they believe in life after love, wondering if he's strong enough to move on from a broken relationship, before announcing—quite resoundingly—that he is.

As he does, he thinks back to the man he used to be, the man whose only outlet for his passion was dancing around in secret to his mum's Cher videos. He thinks back to the man who was forced to suppress his dream by a husband and family who wanted something different from him. And he thinks back to the boy who first discovered that dream, who sat outside a bar in Spain gazing at a drag queen called Crystal Ball, desperately trying to catch a glimpse of his own future.

I'm doing this for you, he tells that boy. *I'm doing it for you, Ted.*

He storms through his dance break and one last burst of the chorus. Then the song thumps to a close.

This time, the show really is over.

CHAPTER 53

Once Ted has swapped praise with the other queens, he steps through the door leading from backstage into the auditorium. *OK, let's see how that future happiness is looking . . .*

Having witnessed the positive responses of most of the friends and family who came to see him, he's most eager to ascertain the only response he didn't witness: Oskar's. But he enters the auditorium at the front left, at the opposite end to Oskar, and it instantly becomes clear that he's going to struggle to reach him; standing directly in front of Ted, holding out his cane, is Stanley.

"Dolly, that was fantabulosa!" he trills.

"Hi," Ted splutters, "thanks, Stanley!"

"Honestly, they should prescribe your show on the NHS—it's much better than any of the medication they make me take. Honestly, it's made me feel young and ravishing again!"

Alison chuckles. "Well, don't go getting any ideas—I'm not taking you on a rampage around the Village. I promised I'd have you back by midnight." She turns to Ted. "Seriously, my love, that was brilliant. Well done!"

"Thanks, Alison. I'm so chuffed you enjoyed it."

Stanley brings his hand to his heart. "You really have done me proud, Ted. And not just me, but Alan too."

"That's lovely to hear," says Ted. "In a way it was Alan who got me up on stage. It was hearing his story that made me realize I couldn't back out."

Stanley's chin quivers. "Well, that makes me very happy. It means his life counted for something after all."

They come together for a hug.

"I promise I won't forget him," says Ted. "I won't forget what you told me."

Over Stanley's shoulder, Giles strays into view. *OK, I need to shift gears now . . .*

"If you'll excuse me . . ."

"Of course," says Stanley. "You go and bask in the adulation!"

To a cascade of congratulations, Ted picks his way through the audience and over to Giles's table. This time he knows exactly how to greet him: he gives him the hug of an old friend.

"That was amazing!" Giles gushes.

"Thanks. I was bricking it at first, but then I started to really enjoy myself."

"Yeah, you could see that. And you absolutely nailed it." Giles pauses and looks down at his feet. "I'm sorry I doubted you, Ted. I'm sorry I said you couldn't dance and you had a crap voice. I'm sorry I said you had no charisma."

Ted's so surprised, he can't help teetering back a little.

"Don't think I don't remember," Giles continues. "And don't think I don't know how selfish I was. Seeing you up there doing that Cher song really brought it all home."

Ted raises his forehead. "In that case, apology accepted."

But Giles hasn't finished. "Most of all, though, I'm sorry I stood in the way of your dream."

"You didn't stop me," Ted argues. "I stopped myself."

Giles pulls a face. "That's not quite how I remember it. And that's another thing, seeing Fanny Spank here brought back what happened in Dublin. I was out of order, Ted."

"Well, maybe we both played a part," concedes Ted. "But maybe this was how it was always meant to happen for me. Maybe I was always meant to hit my stride a bit later in life."

"Maybe you were always meant to be a second-act sensation," suggests Giles.

"Ooh, I like that!"

"Good, because there's plenty more where that came from. And plenty more encouragement. I'm hoping you'll let me make up for being so unsupportive in the past." Giles pauses and raises an eyebrow. "Have you had a think about what I said the other night?"

Shit, I wish we didn't have to do this now.

Ted drags one of his heels along the floor.

"Have you had a think about us getting back together?" presses Giles.

Ted selects his response carefully. "Yeah, and I'm sorry but it just doesn't feel right, Giles. I've changed too much. I'm a different person than the one you married. Well, not a different person exactly, but more me—if that makes sense. And part of me will always love you, but I'm sorry, I just don't want to go back to anything like the way things were."

Giles's face droops. "Oh. OK."

"But I do appreciate all the effort you've made," Ted insists. "And I really appreciate you coming tonight."

Giles bites his bottom lip. "That's alright, I get it. And I want you to know that whatever happens, I'll always support you. I'll always be cheering you on."

"I appreciate that. Thanks, Smiles."

They come together for another hug. But this time, Ted feels like he's hugging goodbye to his old self—for one final time.

Now I've got to find Oskar . . .

Once he's stepped away from Giles's table, Ted looks towards the far corner of the auditorium and catches a flash of him. *Thank God he hasn't left!*

But there are still several meters between them, and Ted is making little progress. Once again, he's steered off course—this time by his parents.

"Well done, love!" burbles Hilary. "That were fab!"

Ted wants to ask if she feels alright being in the same venue as Denise, but she seems as happy as he's ever seen her—and not remotely drunk. *That pretty much answers my question.*

His dad seems equally happy. "Yeah, that was top class," he bellows. "We're proud of you, son."

"*Dead* proud of you!" says Hilary.

Ted feels so touched he has to blink back the tears. His parents have said they're proud of him before—but that was never to the real him. *And this is.*

"And so am I!" Jemima leaps up from her seat and flings her arms around Ted. "I always knew you'd look good in drag, but I never expected you to be so *funny!*"

"Thanks, Jem."

"I might be asking to borrow those earrings."

Ted grins. "They're yours whenever you want them."

Jemima turns around and gestures to the man sitting next to her. "Raj loved it too. Here he is, darling; he's dying to meet you."

Raj steps forward and thrusts out a hand. "Yes, pleased to meet you, Gail—Ted—oh, I'm not sure what to call you."

Ted takes his hand in both of his. "That's OK, you can call me what you want—as long as you make my sister happy."

"Well, you've no worries on that front," Jemima interjects, her eyes twinkling. "And speaking of happy, I've never seen *you* looking so well. You're absolutely glowing, darling!"

"Thanks, Jem."

She puts her arm around him and guides him to one side. "Now I get why your heart's never been in the business. I totally get why you don't want to take over."

"So Mum and Dad told you about that, did they?" Ted gestures to his corset and thigh-high boots. "Well, yeah, this is why. I want to do drag full-time, Jem. And I've decided that after tonight, I'm going to."

Jemima folds her arms and grins. "Well, it's a good job I'm coming home then. It's a good job I'm finally going to chip in and do my bit."

"What do you mean?"

She widens her eyes. "Raj and I want to get more involved in Ainsworth's."

Once again, Ted is stunned. *Tonight's turning out to be full of surprises . . .*

Jemima lowers her voice. "Don't say anything to Mum and Dad yet, but I'm trying to persuade Raj to invest some of his money. I've got big plans for the business, darling. And the first thing I want to do is give that shop a monumental makeover."

Ted manages to recover from his shock enough to say, "Wow, that's ace, Jem! That's fantastic news!"

She raises an eyebrow and cocks her head. "I just thought, now you're suddenly so flamboyant and creative, I don't suppose you know any good interior designers, do you?"

Ted can't help breaking into a beam. "Funnily enough, I do."

"What are you two talking about?" booms Trevor, stepping in between them.

"Nothing to worry about, Dad," Jemima singsongs. "We're just talking shop."

"Well, you can stop that," Trevor says, wagging a finger. "This is Ted's night. And it's been a long time coming."

Oh my God, am I actually hearing this?

"Dead right!" agrees Hilary. "It's like your whole life has been leading up to this, love!"

"Yeah, we can see that now," says Trevor. "You were born to do this."

"Hear, hear," erupts Hilary. "So let's celebrate Ted and his fab new career. And let's celebrate Gail. Let's give her a proper welcome to t' family!"

Someone thrusts a drink into Ted's hand.

"To Gail Force!" proposes Trevor.

"To Gail Force!" everyone responds.

As they give a loud cheer, Ted feels overwhelmed by so many emotions, he's not sure he can identify them all. But he does know they're all positive. *And gratitude isn't one of them.*

But he still desperately wants to speak to Oskar.

Just as he's excusing himself with a promise to be back soon, he catches Denise's eye.

Shit, I need to speak to her too.

She's standing some distance away, waving him over.

But can I really do it now?

When she sends him a smile, Ted knows he can. *And not just that, but I want to.*

I want to speak to my friend.

CHAPTER 54

Denise watches Ted sashay towards her as Gail—and forgets all about the tension between them. *I just want to see my friend.*

"Honey, you were unreal!" she squeaks as soon as he's within earshot.

"Thanks. And thanks so much for coming."

When he comes to a stop in front of her, Ted's eyes flit onto Mick.

"Sorry," Denise gurgles. "This is Mick."

Mick stands up and the two men shake hands.

"Good to meet you," says Ted.

"You too, mate. And well done, you were incredible. I've never seen drag before, but my daughters love *RuPaul's Drag Race*. Next time you do a show, I'm going to see if they want to join us."

Wow, did I hear that right? Did he just say "us"? But Denise suppresses her excitement. *Right now I need to focus on Ted . . . I need to focus on repairing our friendship . . .*

"Thanks," Ted tells Mick. "I'll look forward to that."

There's a beat.

"Anyway, your glass is empty," Mick says to Denise. "Let me leave you to it and get us another."

384 / MATT CAIN

He's so sensitive; how does he know that's exactly what I want him to do?"

"What can I get you?" Mick asks Ted.

"Nothing for me, thanks," says Ted. "I'm alright for now."

Once Mick has left them alone, Ted slides into his seat. "He seems keen. Planning the next date already—and bringing his daughters along."

Denise sits opposite him. "I know, I can't get over it. We're only three dates in, but I really like him. And he seems like a decent bloke."

Actually, Denise *knows* Mick's a decent bloke. Last night they went out for dinner and she told him everything that had happened between her and Ted—about their row and the letters and her affair with his dad. *In all its gory detail.*

She was worried that awful word "psycho" might make a reappearance—but it didn't. In fact, Mick was very understanding and said he appreciated her honesty. After they shared a kiss, it was he who suggested accompanying her tonight, just in case she was nervous about seeing Ted. And she *was* nervous, as at that point Ted still hadn't replied to her text message—and she always feels uncomfortable around his mum and dad. *Well, uncomfortable and guilty . . .*

But, despite her worries, with Mick at her side, Denise hasn't felt uncomfortable or guilty at all. When she spotted Trevor and Hilary across the auditorium, she waved at them without feeling the slightest flicker of shame. And at no other point in the evening has she felt ashamed of a mistake she made twenty years ago. *How can I when I've learned so much from it?*

She certainly hasn't gone back to hating herself—and she doesn't think she ever will. In fact, with Mick beside her, she's managed to hold her head up high. She's managed to feel proud of herself. *And that's the first time a man has had that effect on me.*

"Well, if you think he's decent, I'm sure he is," says Ted. "Honestly, I'm dead happy for you."

Denise lays her hands on her knees and lets out a sigh. "Although I do still want to say I'm sorry, Teddy. I know I've said it before, but I can't say it enough. And when things have calmed down, I'd love us to get together one evening and talk everything through—so it doesn't come between us again."

Ted gives her a mischievous smirk. "As long as we can do it over a bottle of seccy."

Denise smirks back at him. "Just the one?"

"And as long as I can do it out of drag—I can hardly breathe in this corset!"

"I tell you what," says Denise, "give me another chance and *I'll* wear the corset!"

They both laugh.

"And please forget what I said the other day," adds Ted. "Of course I forgive you. I already *have* forgiven you. You might have made the odd mistake in life, but I know you well enough to be sure that isn't because you're a bad person."

Denise feels a flush of happiness. Suddenly, all the turmoil of the last few days feels like it happened a long time ago. "Thanks, Ted. Thanks so much."

"Besides, our friendship is too important for me to ever let it go," Ted continues. "Especially after everything you've done for me over the last few months. I wouldn't be here—I wouldn't have gone *on that stage*—if it weren't for you, Den."

"Teddy, you've no idea how happy that makes me."

Ted takes hold of her hand. "And while we're on the subject—and I can't believe I'm going to admit this—I might not have gone on that stage if it weren't for you sending me those letters. Or, come to think of it, shagging my dad. Isn't it funny how life works?"

Denise gives another chortle. "I'm not sure what to make of

that. I'm not sure what it says about fate or destiny or whatever you call it."

"Me neither," says Ted, "except that it can get very, very messy. And there's no point regretting things we did in the past because if it wasn't for them, we wouldn't be where we are in the present. And I've got to say, I'm pretty happy with where I am in the present."

Denise looks over at Mick, who's at the bar paying for their drinks. "Yeah, me too. Although something tells me it's not going to be a patch on where we're heading in the future."

She turns back to Ted, and they exchange a smile, a smile that says everything, a smile that expresses exactly how they feel about each other. Ted gives her hand a squeeze.

Well, who'd have thought it? Maybe you don't fuck everything up after all. Maybe you actually get some things right.

"That's not to say it'll always be easy," points out Ted. "And I imagine things will be tricky around my mum and dad. Well, for me at least, just till I get my head around it."

Denise nods. "That's alright, I totally understand."

"But if we both put the work in, I'm sure we'll get there."

Denise fills her lungs. Her whole body feels so much lighter. "Yeah, me too."

"Here we are!" says Mick, as he reappears holding two drinks. "Now, are you sure you don't want one?" he asks Ted.

"Yeah, thanks. If you don't mind, there's actually someone I've got to speak to. But I'll catch you guys later, I promise."

"Just make sure you do!" says Denise.

As soon as Ted's gone, Mick leans in and asks her, "How was that? Everything alright?"

A grin splits her face. "Yeah, everything's great, thanks. Or at least it's going to be."

"Good to hear it," he says. And he holds up his glass. "I think we should drink to that."

"Actually, I think we should drink to us," tweets Denise.

Mick looks surprised, but delighted. "Alright, to us!"

They bring their glasses together with a clink.

And, as she looks into Mick's eyes, for the first time Denise thinks that—finally—she might just be ready to start living up to her name.

CHAPTER 55

As Oskar sees Gail undulating towards their table, his heart gives a leap.

"This is it," he tells his dad. "Here she comes. Here's Ted."

A grin spreads over Oskar's face. Although Ted's in full drag, he doesn't feel the slightest bit uneasy.

"Well, that smile tells me everything I need to know," his dad comments.

They exchange a look of complicity, and happiness licks Oskar's insides. *I've had so much happiness in one day, I feel like I'm going to burst.*

After they met in the train station, he and his dad went for a drink in a nearby coffee shop. They had so many questions they each wanted to ask the other that neither of them knew where to start. But first, they updated each other on what had happened since they were separated. Oskar told Andrzej about his work as a painter and decorator, his move to the caravan site in St. Luke's, and his dream of becoming an interior designer. Andrzej told Oskar that he'd struggled to find employment in any kind of office or administrative role in the UK, so he worked first as a carpenter and is currently an Uber driver. While he admitted that the injustice of this sometimes rankles, he doesn't let it bother him too much as he's so much happier living here, where he's free to be himself.

They went back to Andrzej's flat—a modest one-bedroom place on the top floor of a Victorian conversion in Fallowfield, where he lives alone. He told Oskar that he's had a few boyfriends since coming to the UK but nothing serious or long-term. Instead, he's enjoyed exploring his sexuality and immersing himself in the gay community and queer culture. Oskar seized the moment and revealed that he too is gay—and Andrzej said he's always known; that it was one of the reasons he found it so hard to leave Poland: he couldn't bear to abandon his son to a fate that might be anything like the one he suffered. He said he'd searched for Oskar online on numerous occasions but with no success—and that's when Oskar confessed he's only recently come out and started to be open about who he is. When he outlined some of the torment he's suffered as a gay man, the mood turned somber.

"I'm sure you think I'm pathetic," said Oskar, "when you've had things so much harder than me, and here you are, living this happy gay life."

"Not at all. I've struggled too," Andrzej revealed. "It can take a long time to shake off the negative feelings we grow up with. It can take a long time to break free of the way we've been made to feel about ourselves."

Oskar was surprised to hear this but very moved. And he didn't think he'd ever felt closer to his dad.

"I think that's why I've never managed to settle down with anyone," Andrzej admitted. "No matter how openly I've lived, no matter how much I've embraced every aspect of gay culture, no matter how many Prides I've been to, I've never been able to completely escape the feeling that what I was doing was wrong—that *I* was wrong."

"Me neither," said Oskar. Then he remembered Ted's text.

He remembered that he still had a chance. And hope caught in his chest. "Or at least that's been my experience *so far*."

"The truth is, I've also missed being a dad," Andrzej cut in. "Ever since I left Poland, I've felt like something wasn't quite right, like I wasn't completely whole, and I couldn't really give myself to anybody like that. And while I'll always miss your sister, I really hope having you back in my life is going to make things better."

Oskar smiled. "You sound just like someone I know. Someone who told me the same thing about you."

"Who's that?"

Oskar told Andrzej about Ted—about how they met, how their relationship developed, and how they recently fell out and split up. Andrzej gave him a stern warning not to sabotage his chance of happiness, not to let love slip away. He insisted Oskar go and see Ted's show—and offered to accompany him.

And now here we are. And Ted was brilliant. And seeing Dad enjoy the show only made it better.

He steps forward to introduce the two men. "Ted, this is my dad."

"It's an honor to meet you," says Ted, with a bat of Gail's long, black eyelashes, the silver droplets on the ends sparkling. "Now do I call you Andrew or Andrzej?"

His dad thinks about this for a moment. "You can call me Andrzej."

Rather than shaking Ted's hand, he opens his arms and gives him a hug.

As he looks on, Oskar feels his heart swell. *That's my dad. My dad and my boyfriend.*

Or at least I hope he's still my boyfriend . . .

"Congratulations on a great show," Andrzej says, as he pulls back. Now he's switched to English, Oskar notices he has a strong accent—much stronger than his own.

"Thanks, but it was all over so quickly," chirps Ted. "I wish I could do it again now."

Andrzej folds his arms. "Well, I am sure they are inviting you back. I am coming here lots of times, but this is one of the best shows I am seeing."

Oskar notices his grammatical mistakes and wonders if he's had to teach himself English or if anyone helped him. It reminds him just how difficult things must have been for Andrzej, coming here on his own, without any time to set things up in advance, without any time to even learn the language. His heart heaves.

"Thanks," fizzes Ted. "Funnily enough, they've already asked me back. Seraphina grabbed me after the show and said she's going to email some dates."

"That's terrific news!" bursts out Oskar. "I'm so happy for you!"

Ted winches an eyebrow, presumably intrigued by Oskar's enthusiasm about his drag career. All of a sudden, the unresolved tension between them breaks through to the surface.

We need to talk . . .

We need to talk about what happened the other night . . .

"Yeah, I'm really pleased," Ted continues. Then he slips back into the voice of Gail. "Although next time I won't be wearing this corset—it's tighter than a virgin's snatch."

As he laughs, Oskar remembers what he said to Ted in his caravan. *"I don't like it when it's just me and you and you're dressed as a woman." "I don't like it when you're acting all camp and girlie." "Maybe I don't want to be forced into going out with a drag queen."* He wants Ted to know that he doesn't really feel like that. He wants to make up for how horrible he was.

"Well, it might be painful, but it looks great," he states, firmly. "And you look beautiful—absolutely beautiful."

Ted seems taken aback by the compliment. "Thanks. Thanks, Oskar."

Did his chin just tremble? Is he going to start crying?

"I'm very proud of you," Oskar adds.

"Really?"

"Yes, really."

Ted grabs a tissue and dabs his eyes. "Oskar, you're going to make my makeup run. If you carry on, I'll look a right mess."

"Sorry, but I wanted to say it. I needed to say it."

Ted gives his head a little shake. "Come on, not in here—I'm still on show." He grabs a breath. "Let's change the subject."

Oh no, please don't!

But it's too late. Ted's turning to his dad. "Andrzej, are you still doing lots of cycling?"

"Yes, I am still enjoying to go out on my bike."

On hearing Andrzej make more grammatical mistakes, Oskar thinks again of him arriving here with no money or connections, only for people to listen to him struggle with English and assume he's uneducated and unintelligent, only for them to disrespect him and decide he isn't good enough for their jobs. He feels overwhelmed with love.

"We've already made a plan to go out together next weekend," Oskar announces, brightly.

"Ace," Ted chirrups. "So Andrzej, does that mean you're coming to St. Luke's?"

"Yes. And I am looking forward."

"Me too," says Oskar. But the next thing he wants to say catches in his throat. He swallows. "I'll bring the radishes," he manages.

Andrzej grins at him. "Yes, please."

Oskar has to make a real effort not to give in to tears.

As if picking up on this, Andrzej chirps, "Maybe afterwards, the three of us can eat something together. If I am going to the seaside, I am loving fish and chips."

Ted's face lifts. "Yeah, I'd be well up for that. And you can see what I look like out of drag."

"Brilliant. So we do next weekend!"

Now I've got to get Ted on his own . . .

"Dad," Oskar cuts in, "do you mind if I take Ted outside for a minute? Sorry, there's something we need to discuss. I promise we won't be long."

"No, of course not," Andrzej says, giving him a reassuring nod. "Take as long as you need."

CHAPTER 56

Ted picks his way over the cobbles of Canal Street, holding

Ted picks his way over the cobbles of Canal Street, holding
onto Oskar's hand to steady himself. He comes to a halt in a
space by the wall that runs along the water. Oskar draws up
next to him.

Finally, I've got him on his own.

The two men don't say anything but look into each other's
eyes. All around them, rainbow flags flutter in the gentle summer breeze, lights of every color flare and flicker to the sound
of uplifting pop music, and chatter, laughter, and even the odd
shriek comes from the people congregating outside the bars,
clubs, and restaurants. *People just like us. Or people who love
and respect us.*

"I'm sorry," says Oskar. "I didn't mean what I said the other
night. It's no excuse, but I think I was frightened and feeling
fragile."

"No, *I'm* sorry," insists Ted. "I didn't mean to be so insensitive. I was angry and think I was probably scared too."

"Well, we're both sorry," says Oskar. "So let's try and
move on."

"Yeah, let's put it behind us." Ted mimes rolling up a ball in
his hands. "Let's wrap up all those negative feelings and chuck
them in the canal."

Oskar wipes his cheek. "I think a bit of water just splashed on my face."

Ted breaks into a smile. "I'd be careful, you never know what's in there."

They both chuckle. And, to the sound of a distant drumbeat, their eyes dance—dance together in a duet.

"I love you," says Ted. After holding back the words for months, he's struck by how good it feels to say them.

"I love you too," says Oskar.

Ted's stomach performs some kind of somersault. He knows Oskar has never said those words before—so he can imagine just how significant this moment is for him. His heart gives a little squeeze.

"So we're going to give this another go, then?" he asks.

"Yeah. I'd like to if you would."

Ted is about to smile but draws in his mouth. "But this time let's make sure we really do take things slowly."

"Agreed."

Ted hutches up his tights. "Unfortunately, that means I'll need to keep you away from my family tonight—if you don't mind."

"Not at all."

"I mean, they're champing at the bit to meet you. And they're all ace—I've learned just how ace over the last few days—but they can be a bit full-on. And my mum's emotional tonight, so if I introduce you, she'll only gush all over you."

"OK, understood."

Ted straightens out his corset. "I promise there'll be plenty of time for you to get to know them. But I think Lily's probably enough for you for now—and I know she'll be chuffed to see you again."

Oskar smiles. "'Chuffed.' That might have been the first word I learnt from you. Either that or 'old biddy.'"

Ted gives him a playful slap on the shoulder. "Hey, watch

who you're calling old! And I'll have you know that after all that applause tonight, I feel like I'm in the first flush of youth."

Oskar snickers. "You look like it too. What's the expression? You look like a young slip of a girl."

Ted can feel his smile entering his eyes. "Now that's more like it. And if you play your cards right, I'll be teaching you a lot more English from now on."

"I'll hold you to that," says Oskar. He pauses and swallows. "And I promise I won't back out of this again. I won't get scared and run away."

Ted takes hold of his hand. "Well, let's just make sure we keep working at it. We're bound to go through the odd blip every now and then, and you know what, there might be times when you do get scared and pull back. But if we're aware of what's going on—if we're aware of what's making you feel like that—and I make sure I'm as patient as I can be, then we'll get through them."

"Together."

"Together," repeats Ted.

A loud scream comes from a group of girls who lurch out of a bar and almost collide with a huddle of bearded men in lumberjack shirts. Despite the commotion, neither Ted nor Oskar turns to look.

"Now can I kiss you?" asks Oskar.

Ted crumples his face. "Nah, wait till I get all this makeup off. I only need to keep it on for a few more hours, then I promise I'm all yours."

"Alright."

"That's the reality of having a boyfriend who's a drag queen, I'm afraid."

"Don't be afraid." Oskar kisses him lightly on the forehead. "I can handle it."

Ted wraps his arms around him and, with the added height from his heels, rests his chin on top of his head. The two of them stand there in silence, their warmth emanating from one to the other, their breath softly stroking one another's skin, their heartbeats falling into rhythm. Ted imagines they must make an odd sight—him in drag, towering over Oskar—but nobody gives them a second glance.

I'm so glad we're here. I'm so glad we're doing this on Canal Street, among our people.

The chatter from everyone around them dims to a low hum, the colors from the lights shift out of focus, and the music recedes into the distance. Ted's love vibrates through him like an electric charge. And, whatever he may have thought before, he knows without any doubt that he's never been happier than he is right now.

All the effort he's put into following his dream, all the conviction he's had to summon, all the emotional upheaval and mental turmoil he's had to put himself through, all of it has paid off. And he's proud of himself for conquering his self-doubt and sticking to his vow of putting himself first.

He draws in a long, satisfied breath.

Then one other thought occurs to him . . .

Even though I'm dressed as Gail, I've never felt more myself. I've never felt more true *to myself.*

He pulls Oskar closer.

ACKNOWLEDGMENTS

First of all, I want to say a big thanks to you, my readers. Whether straight, cisgender or LGBTQ+, thanks for being open-minded enough to choose my book. And thanks to all those who've contacted me about previous books to let me know how much they've enjoyed or appreciated them. When I was writing this and times got tough, it was you who spurred me on to keep going!

Thanks to all the book bloggers—on both sides of the Atlantic—who've been supportive of my writing so far. Your cheerleading really makes a difference!

An equally big thank you goes to all the lovely—not to mention brilliant—authors who've supported my work. These include Rachel Joyce, Ruth Hogan, Adele Parks, Kate Mosse, Justin Myers, Laura Kay, SJ Watson, Alexandra Potter and Julietta Henderson. It's a great honor to have you all on side and fighting my corner.

Endless gratitude goes to my exceptional editors. I was lucky enough to have not one but three working on this book—Eleanor Dryden and Jennifer Doyle in the UK and the legendary John Scognamiglio in the US. Guys, you not only helped shape Ted's story but also drummed up the necessary support to give him the launch he deserves. And you put up with my regular blasts of enthusiasm, badgering and pressurizing!

Thanks to all the team at Kensington in the US, especially Lorraine Freeney, Jackie Dinas, cover designer Kris Noble, production editor Robin Cook, publicists Michelle Addo and Vida Engstrand, and the big boss Steve Zacharius.

Thanks to everyone who helped with the writing process, starting with my fab agent Sophie Lambert, who had the idea of setting *Becoming Ted* in a family-run ice cream business after visiting Morelli's in Broadstairs on the English coast. Thanks to friends like Rob Hastie and Fanny Blake, who might recognise a line of theirs in here. And thanks to everyone else I know but may have forgotten whose lines, ideas or jokes I borrowed!

Thanks to my cousin Rosie Robinson for helping me with Denise's chapter on the make-up counter—and for her general make-up advice, without which I'd have to rely on YouTube. And to another early reader, Diane Wareing, who was a great help with the details of life in a seaside town, told me there are no cliffs or lighthouses on the Lancashire coastline—and taught me the word Sandgrownun!

Thanks to my close circle of friends for keeping me going through the long, hard slog. These include (but aren't limited to) Amy Rynehart, Bianca Sainty, Laetitia Clapton, Chris Bollinghaus, Ste Softley, Ed Watson and our whole sisterly group.

An extra special thanks goes to my family, especially my mum Lynda, who read an early copy and had some great advice, as ever—and accompanied me on a research trip to Southport! And to my Nana Irene Clough, who has just hit the incredible age of 101. Nana, you'll always be my inspiration!

This is the first book I've written without my dad, who died while it was in the planning stages but before I typed the first word. It's no surprise that dads—and sons' relationships with their dads—feature so prominently. Although I think you could say the same of all my books, which may give you a hint as to just how important my dad has been in my life. I'm sad he'll never read this book but I went up to Bolton to write the final scene sitting at his desk, so at least I feel like he's been part of the creative process. And I like to think it would have been his favorite of my books so far, and he would have let me know in an email signed off in his usual way—with the initials PD, for Proud Dad.

I would have dedicated this book to my dad, but everything

I do—and always will do—is basically for him. And he and my mum have had two books dedicated to them already!

Likewise, I would have dedicated this book to my husband, Harry Glasstone, who supported me financially—and emotionally!—whilst writing it. Again, I've drawn huge inspiration from his experiences and the way he's turned his life around. But Harry had the last book dedicated to him! And again, everything I do is for him. So this book is as much his as it is mine, as they no doubt all will be from now on. I love you, babe.

In the end, I decided to dedicate it to my oldest nephew Lucan, who came into my life when I was 22. He's not a reader and I doubt that'll change but I like to think some of the themes would resonate with him. So Lucan, this one's for you!

It's also for all those gay men who—like my character Oskar—live in countries where they aren't free to be themselves. To all these men I send my love and solidarity. I believe in you and I'm rooting for you. Hang on in there! And if it's possible, please take from this a little hope. Things can—and will—get better.

BECOMING TED

ABOUT THIS GUIDE

The suggested questions are included to enhance your group's
reading of Matt Cain's *Becoming Ted*.

DISCUSSION QUESTIONS

1. How important to Becoming Ted is its setting in a quiet English seaside town?

2. Do you see any metaphorical value in Ted's dislike of ice cream?

3. How much do you think Ted's low self-esteem determines the course of his life?

4. Do you see a parallel between the kind of man Denise used to find attractive—and, in particular, Karl—and Ted's feelings for Giles?

5. Ted feels like a disappointment to his parents and is grateful for their love. Would you say this is a theme that can have resonance outside the LGBTQ+ community?

6. Oskar is scarred by his upbringing in a homophobic culture. Do you think we can sometimes forget how difficult it is for queer people living in less accepting countries?

7. Stanley provides a link to a very different time for gay men in the UK. Did you learn anything from the disclosure of his backstory?

8. What do you think of the use of drag in the book? Is it fundamental to Ted's self-discovery and journey towards self-fulfillment or could he have had any other dream?

9. In interviews, Matt Cain has said his original title for the book was *Ted First*, then it became *Ted Over Heels*, before his UK publisher suggested *Becoming Ted*; what do you think of these three titles and which do you think reflects the book best?

10. Matt Cain has also said he hopes the novel inspires people to let loose the full force of their unique spirit and sparkle as brightly as possible. Has it inspired you in any way?

**Please turn the page for some
fun facts from Matt Cain about
*Becoming Ted!***

1. The town of St. Luke's-on-Sea is entirely fictional but inspired by elements of several seaside towns I revisited while researching the book. British people might recognize the high street from Southport, the sand dunes and the mini golf course from St. Anne's-on-Sea, and the hippos and the statue of the prince from Eastbourne. These are all towns that have given me many happy memories, especially St. Anne's!

2. One of my favorite things when writing a book is to name characters after people who are special to me in real life. There are several in *Becoming Ted*, most notably Jemima—who's named after my goddaughter—and Ted's mum, Hilary. Her name comes from a family friend who was often around when I was growing up but died a few years ago. The fictional Hilary doesn't resemble her real-life namesake in the slightest and nor does her story, but it's my own little way of paying tribute.

3. Glasstone's department store is named after my husband Harry Glasstone! Harry's dad died several years before we met, but he used to be a buyer for the menswear department of a big store in South Africa, so I thought this would be a nice way of bringing him into the book and his son's life with me.

4. Nerja is a place that's very special to me as my aunt and uncle lived there for decades, so we'd often visit on extended family holidays. Choosing it as the setting for a key scene also meant that I wouldn't have to research or visit a new location but could describe it from memory. I actually went back to Nerja recently for the wedding of my cousin—the granddaughter of my aunt and uncle—and I found the place every bit as lovely as I remembered!

5. The fact that Ted doesn't like ice cream was inspired by my own childhood dislike of cake. When I was growing up, people just didn't understand the fact that a boy didn't like cake, especially when it came to birthdays. About fifteen years ago, I found out I had a gluten intolerance so

this may have had something to do with it; I probably understood on some level that gluten upsets my stomach. Now that I've discovered gluten-free cake, I'm fully on board again! But my memory of how people responded to my dislike of cake gave me an interesting metaphor to explore in the book.

6. Ainsworth's ice cream business and Ted's family surname comes from the village in between Bolton and Bury where my nana and granddad used to live. My granddad died in 1998, but my nana is still going strong and just turned 101. Unfortunately, though, she's recently had to move into a care home. But I have fond memories of both of the houses where she used to live in Ainsworth—and apparently I was conceived in the first one! So I couldn't think of a better surname for Ted!

7. When I was growing up, the football field was often the frontline for homophobic bullying, the place where the disapproval and outrage directed at me for failing to conform to traditional ideas of how a boy should behave were at their most intense. But the cricket field wasn't much better, and I have vivid memories of everyone laughing at me as I struggled to bowl overarm. It felt like a ritual humiliation! So I enjoyed exorcizing the unhappiness attached to those memories when I was writing this scene.

8. When I used to work directing documentaries for ITV—a network TV channel in the UK—I was once sent to Warsaw to film a ballet dancer called Irek Mukhamedov, who was collaborating with a ballet company over there. After we'd finished filming, the crew went out for a few drinks and some of us got carried away. I found myself wanting to strike out on my own and explore the gay scene, which in those days was very underground. The bar I visited is similar to the one Oskar describes from his memory—and the time I visited would have been around the same time as he was living in the Polish capital.

9. Queen of Clubs is loosely based on one of my favorite gay bars in London, The Glory in Haggerston. I love how relaxed and laid-back the atmosphere and staff are, how welcoming and unpretentious it is. I've never felt self-conscious or too old or unfashionable or underdressed when I've been in there. And I once judged a drag competition in The Glory, so I thought it would be fitting to work the place into *Becoming Ted*!

10. My dad used to love "pea wet" on his chips. I remember him sending me to the chippy once and telling me to ask for "plenty of wet," but I was too embarrassed. I'm more a fan of gravy, which is also a very northern thing. It's one of the first things people mention when I tell them I'm from Lancashire!

11 I studied French and Spanish through my teens and then at university, spending a year on the outskirts of Paris and then another year in the center of Madrid. Whilst living abroad, I remember keeping little vocab books and trying to learn a new word every day. I also remember being bewildered by all the slang and colloquialisms I'd hear. I drew on this when writing about Oskar's experience as a Pole living in the north of England.

12. Two of the biggest inspirations for *Becoming Ted* were the film *Shirley Valentine*, which I watched when it was first released, and the TV series *The Marvelous Mrs. Maisel*, which I discovered in the first national lockdown. They both depict downtrodden wives who break free from unhappy marriages to finally put themselves first and pursue their dreams. I thought it would be interesting to write a gay version of this and that was the spark that ignited *Becoming Ted*!

13. My mum had breast cancer more than ten years ago now, and it was an awful experience for all of us, but it feels like enough time has passed for me to be able to write

about it. I also didn't feel bad or exploitative asking my mum to confirm a few of the details of her treatment. One thing I do remember very clearly is the sense that Mum's cancer really brought the family together and that's what I was trying to draw on in these scenes; I wanted to show why Ted can feel guilty for stepping away from his family, why those bonds pull so tight.

14. I mentioned that I wanted to explore the theme of duty in *Becoming Ted*, and one of the reasons is I think lots of gay men feel a real sense of gratitude towards families who accepted them—not to mention a deep guilt for doing anything that could be interpreted as an act of disloyalty. Before writing the book, I rewatched the film *My Big Fat Greek Wedding*, and it really helped me get into that zone. Although the idea of setting the book in and around an ice-cream shop actually came from my agent, who'd visited Morelli's on a family visit to Broadstairs. But I'm afraid I've never been and had to do all my research online. Hopefully that will change soon!

15. I got married a few months after delivering the final manuscript of *Becoming Ted*. As we'd been due to get married the previous year but had to postpone because of Omicron, I'd spent months and months immersed in wedding planning and thinking about our big day. One thing I remember several people telling us was to make sure we created some time for ourselves in amongst the mad whirlwind of the day. Unfortunately, when our wedding finally arrived, it turned out to be so frenzied and frantic that Harry and I only grabbed the odd snatch of time together—but we did appreciate that. We had a brilliant day, and it was everything both of us wanted—and a whole lot more!

16. During the first and third national lockdowns, the only exercise I could do was walking around Hampstead Heath,

which is close to the flat where I was living in London. Just as I'd come to the end of my walk each morning, I'd pass a bench that's dedicated to the memory of a journalist and inscribed with the words, "If I don't do it, somebody else will." These words would ring in my head and inspire me as I started my day's work. I wanted to incorporate the message into *Becoming Ted* but decided to change the wording slightly. I wasn't interested in any kind of competition or worrying about someone else achieving your dreams; I was much more focused on the idea of self-fulfillment, getting the best out of *yourself*.

17. There was only one place I could set the ending for *Becoming Ted,* and that's on Manchester's Canal Street; the Gay Village played a huge part in my youth and was very much the setting for my own journey of self-discovery in the early 1990s. I have so many happy memories of the area and owe it so much. You might like to know that my next book is set almost entirely on or around Canal Street. It's my way of continuing to say thank you to the street that saved my life!

18. Music has played a huge part in my life and continues to inspire and energize me every day. I couldn't imagine writing about Ted and his journey of self-discovery without being spurred on by a strong soundtrack. My soundtrack for *Becoming Ted* was a series of sassy, message-driven, and uplifting songs, songs the reader can instantly call to mind. If you've enjoyed the book and want to keep its spirit alive, I'll leave you with this playlist I've created on Spotify: https://open.spotify.com/playlist/ 3tM3NG9H xq3hyxeLU6z6fR?si=CTB6Ee11QFmN6u4X8_5Xng &pt=2aedff88ce238bcd6fe0f07154e798a2

And thanks so much for reading!